Dear R

CW01659970

WATTLEBIRD BOOKS

On behalf of Geoff Davis and the team at Wattlebird Books, thank you for supporting PROVOCATION.

We invite you to join Geoff's Reading Group to keep up with Geoff's latest news. To join the free group, head to:
www.geoffdavisbooks.com/readinggroup

Members will receive exclusive content, behind-the-scenes glimpses, and updates on upcoming books.

If you'd like to contact Geoff directly, please email
geoff.davis.books@gmail.com
Thanks again for your support.

Warm regards,
Wattlebird Books

Books by Geoff Davis

The Jarrajarra Series

Book 1 – The Black Mist

Book 2 – Provocation

PROVOCATION

GEOFF DAVIS

WATTLEBIRD
BOOKS

Dedication

This book is dedicated to my family.

Helen, Jaqueline, Mathew, Anna, Jess, Josh, Alice, Glen, Loosh, Hollie, Javari, Eva, Bethie, Honey, Sunny, Augie, Bear, Maggie, Kit and Olive.

Part 1

Tuesday, March 7, 1991

Chris and Nan

Rusty's Gym, Reservoir, Victoria, Australia.

"I don't teach boxing. It's rubbish unless you walk around all day long with gloves and a boxing ring in your pocket. And a referee, I suppose."

Nan and I were listening to Mister Russell Collins, the proprietor of Rusty's Gym in Spring Street, Reservoir.

It appeared Rusty was not so keen on the boxing.

We had found him easy enough. Nan had looked him up in the Yellow Pages under martial arts. He was the only entry within walking distance of our home.

I was seven years old and had been living with Nan since Mum died and Dad vanished from my life. There was just the two of us, Nan and me, and we walked everywhere we could, mostly to save money but also, I think now, to infect me with the fitness bug.

On this particular day, I had come home from school wearing two bad shiners. Defeated yet again in defence of my tattered honour, or maybe it was in outrage at a perceived insult.

Who ever knew what set me off? Someone would say something, and away we would go. As usual, I had lost badly.

My right eye was cut and fully shut. My left eye was mostly closed. With a bit of a push and a lean to the right, I could see well enough. Enough to know, I wished I was somewhere else.

Nan had decided, as always, to solve the problem permanently.

"Well, as you can see, Mr. Collins, someone needs to teach this boy the art of self-defence," said Nan. "What exactly do you teach?"

"That is a very good question," he said to Nan.

"What's your name, mate?" He said to me. "You look familiar."

"Christopher Taylor, Sir."

He did a little shift of his head. A recognition, maybe?

Did he know me? Maybe he knew a lot of people with mincemeat faces. I was sure I didn't know him from a bar of soap.

I wasn't too happy with Nan at this point. I was getting beaten up enough at school, and I didn't need to be dragged here to cop more rough treatment, especially from some old bloke built like Superman with a face like bricks. This bloke scared the shit out of me.

I really wanted to go home and hide in my room.

Superman held out his hand to shake.

"My name is Russell Collins, but everyone calls me Rusty. OK?"

"OK," I answered.

"Can you see out of those hamburger eyes of yours?"

"A bit."

"How long you got?" Rusty was looking at me.

"Now?"

"Of course, now. When do you reckon? Yesterday?"

"We can stay as long as the lesson lasts," interrupted Nan.

"Lessons are done for today. We can make this a private. First one's a freebie."

Nan seemed delighted by the offer. A freebie? We both, normally, loved freebies; it was all we could afford. I wasn't too happy about this particular freebie, but Nan was as keen as ever.

"Well, thank you, Mr. Collins, sorry Rusty," she said, "that would be wonderful."

"Do you want to stay and watch, or do you want me to walk him home after?" Rusty was speaking to Nan.

"I'll stay if I may."

"Chairs over there," Rusty pointed to the chairs against the far wall. "You're welcome to stay, but gotta warn you, I swear a bit. Sometimes. Not always."

Nan retreated to the far wall and sat quietly. Above her head were shelves full of trophy belts, swords, and various weapons. On another shelf were photos of soldiers in scrubby uniforms, rifles over their shoulders, looking extremely dangerous.

Rusty looked at me and pointed to another wall covered in shelves full of equipment. Boxing gloves, headgear, shin pads and long painted sticks for hitting people.

God in heaven, what further violence was about to be perpetrated on me? Rusty's voice broke my terrified daydream.

"Righto Chris, go and grab me one of those long blue rubber sausages."

Under the wall of weapons, there was a barrel of thin, coloured, stick-like things. They were made of firm rubber, all about a meter long and a few inches thick. It was like a barrel full of long, brightly coloured, skinny arms.

I got a blue one and handed it to Rusty, who was now seated on a wooden chair in the middle of the gym floor.

He took the stick, weighed it in his hand, checked the balance, checked the weight, then looked at me and whacked me in the side of the head. It hurt.

"Didn't hurt, did it?" He asked.

"No," I lied. It did hurt, but not much and not for long.

"OK, one to me," he said. Then he hit me again.

"Two-nothing. You're losing, mate."

And so, it continued till we were nine-nothing. My ears were ringing on both sides. No matter what I tried, Rusty still managed to whack me on one side of the head or the other. He was killing me with a blue rubber sausage.

"I can see you're trying to dodge the thing," said Rusty.

"Yes," I said. Sounding feeble.

"Let's go for a block before a dodge, hey. Try this," he said and then, grabbing my hands, he showed me how to hold my clenched fists at my temples, chin tucked into my chest, my elbows tucked into my ribs, leaning slightly forward.

"OK," he said. "Keep that position. That's your guard."

He whacked me again, harder, but this time, the blow fell harmlessly on my bony wrists.

"Good stuff," he said. "Nine-one."

I'd scored, and I was elated.

He whacked my wrists again, harmlessly."

"Nine-two, good defence Chrisso. First to eleven wins."

"But you're already," I tried to say 'nine', but I'd dropped my guard an inch, and he whacked me on the ear again."

"Ten-two," he said with a cheater's smile. I got the message, and my guard shot back into place.

I made it to ten-nine. My guard was good. It felt natural, and Rusty seemed pleased with my attempts to not get hit.

"Did I mention fakes?" he asked and waived the rubber stick on my right side, floated it over my head to the left side, then swung it back to the right and whacked me in the ribs.

"Eleven-nine, didn't I say to keep your elbows tucked in? You looked like a bird flapping its wings there. Could drive a truck through the gap.

"I forgot," I said.

"Yeah, well, remember not to forget then. Eleven-nine, I win. You owe me ten."

"Ten?"

"Push-ups or sprints?"

"Push-ups."

"Push-ups it is. Go for it, Chrisso."

So, I struggled through my ten push-ups, and we did it all again and again until we had been going the best part of an hour, and I could barely move, hardly hold my hands in my guard position, totally exhausted, and I hadn't won a single round.

Somehow, I managed to lose by one almost every time. So many scores of eleven-ten, it should have been highly suspicious. I was too exhausted to suspect.

Along the way, I had done over two hundred increasingly pathetic push-ups.

After an hour, I was so exhausted the push-ups were taking longer than the punch-ups. I was so tired it hurt.

Eventually, Rusty stopped the one-sided competition and spoke.

"Feel that thing inside," said Rusty, "you can hardly get enough air. You can hardly move your arms and legs?"

"Yeah," I gasped.

"OK, that's called gassed. You are gassed, which means you've got no gas left in your tank. You're running on empty."

"Gassed?" I nodded.

"You just cannot go one more round, can you?"

"No," I said in the faintest, weakest whisper. Hoping against hope, we were finished for the day.

"That little voice is saying stop, fall over, lay down, rest. You cannot go on. Your body is telling you to quit, right?"

"Yeah," I gasped, nodding my approval of a good quit.

He whacked me firmly on my right side, which was a real cheat since my right eye was still mostly closed from my school beating at the hands of a ninth grader called Terry Morris. My guard was down while Rusty spoke.

Unfair, I thought.

"One-nothing," he said. "Never listen to that voice, Chris. You can always keep going. And never drop your guard when I've got the rubber stick."

I was still listening, and he whacked me again.

"Two-nil."

I got my guard up and concentrated. This time, when we got to ten-ten, I was ready for the fake. He waved the stick right, he waved it left, over my head, then back fast towards my right lower ribs. Somehow, miraculously, I caught it on my elbow. I had won eleven-ten. My first victory of the evening.

I held my hands aloft and cheered. I even heard a shout and some applause from the direction of Nan's chair. When Rusty and I both looked her way, she was quietly resuming her seat as though it had been someone else making the noise.

"OK," said Rusty, "what do I owe you?"

"Sprints," I said, still wondering what they were.

"You little shit," he said with a smile. He turned and sprinted the full length of the gym and then did ten push-ups, then sprinted back, another ten push-ups,

"That's one," he said, then he did the whole thing again, another nine times.

So that was sprints. I was glad I had chosen push-ups.

"Tomorrow, we play for sprints." He said. "Come straight after school, OK?"

"Yes, sir," I said. "Rusty."

"All done," he said to Nan, still sitting against the wall, looking pleased with what she'd seen. She rose from her chair and walked over.

"Rusty," said Nan, "I noticed your fees on the wall there. I don't think I can afford the Monday-Wednesday-Friday option. Maybe I could manage once a week?" Nan was negotiating a cheaper price. Haggling was a fact-of-life for the two of us.

Rusty was looking at me.

"So, this here is a Chris Taylor?"

"Yes," said Nan.

"Chris Taylor Junior?" He was looking at Nan now.

She didn't respond, but her stance shifted just an inch.

“I knew Chris and Emily,” he said. “I am guessing you would be Emily's Mum?”

“That is correct,” said Nan very carefully.

So, Rusty knew my absentee Dad and my dead Mum.

“No charge for Chris here, Mrs. Roland.”

Nan was speechless for one of the few times in her life, but not for long.

“Thank you, Rusty, thank you.” She fumbled for her words a bit. “Circumstances lead me to accept. I shall repay the favour somehow, I promise.”

It was time to go, so Nan said a few more words of appreciation, and we headed for the door. As we were leaving, Rusty was walking behind us, turning off the lights as we went. It must have been nearly 8.00 PM, bedtime for me.

“No more classes tonight?” Nan asked politely.

“Nope, tonight is my night off. I do private sessions all day on Tuesdays and Thursdays, then finish off with a two-hour workout just for me. You caught me at just the right time. I was heading home.” He said it with a smile.

“Oh, my goodness,” said Nan. “I am so sorry; we have intruded on your private time.” Nan stumbled for words again. Almost speechless twice in one night. It was a record.

“All good; it was fun,” said Rusty. “And, in answer to your first question, I don't teach boxing, Mrs. Roland. I teach Muay Thai. Not very well, but don't tell anyone that, especially anyone from Thailand.”

“Muay Thai?” said Nan. She had never heard of it, and neither had I.

“You could be good, Chrisso, a bit slow, but you can take a blow, and you listen,” he said to me. “Do the work, and you'll be alright.”

We were at the front door, ready to exit, beside a humble reception desk. Rusty reached up and took a picture from a shelf behind the desk.

He showed me a photograph of a football team from years ago.

“That's me, back row left, Reservoir High School Football team, 1967 before you were born. We were All-State High School champions that year.”

Nan looked politely. Neither of us was the slightest bit interested in football, but Rusty had been so polite.

"That's your dad standing next to me," he said.

Nan and I must have both flinched.

"Yes," said Rusty. "A long time ago, before we joined the army together."

He returned the picture of my father to its place behind the reception desk. He grabbed something else from behind his desk and handed it to me.

"Here's a book I want you to read. It explains a bit about Muay Thai, lots of pictures."

"Read it till you remember it, then give it back. It's a loan, not a gift."

I took the book, no mention I couldn't read all that well yet. But there were a lot of pictures. I was sure I could work it out.

Neither Nan nor I realised we had just passed the Rusty Collins interview.

We had shown up. I had lasted out the hour despite my face full of bruises and total exhaustion.

Nan had passed her part of the interview by sitting quietly in the corner and not interrupting or questioning Rusty's methods. Nan's brief cheering was acceptable.

Rusty did not take on anyone who showed up at his door. There was a process, and we passed.

I didn't know that then.

"Thank you," I said politely, for the book, and that was that. I was now a member of Rusty's crew. I didn't know it at the time, but it was a membership that lasted for life.

I had always wished I had a dad, like normal kids.

Rusty was not my real dad, but he turned out to be the next best thing.

Way better than the original, the evil bastard who had killed my mother.

Friday, January 8, 2002

Eleven years later

Virginia

Toorak, Melbourne, Australia.

Outside

"Thank God," she whispered as she turned into the driveway. Virginia "Ginny" Savage parked out front of a perfect two-story Toorak mansion. That house, almost a castle, had been her home for nearly twelve years, but not anymore.

She had hoped her soon-to-be ex-husband wouldn't be there, and from her view through the front gate, it appeared he wasn't. The house looked empty. That was good.

There had been one terrible meeting already this week with lawyers. She didn't want another, certainly not alone.

She had promised to call her dad if Phillip Savage was at the house. Phillip was intimidated by her dad, as most men were. But Phillip was six foot seven inches tall. For heaven's sake, he towered over her father. It made no difference. All men intimidated Phil, not just her rugged old dad, all men. Only the women of Phil's household got to see his special kind of selective courage.

But, it appeared the house was empty.

Good.

It was 4:00 PM. She could be in and out to collect her remaining property in a few minutes. It was a small tin box of photographs.

The photographs belonged to her father. Phil told her dad that he was interested in the Vietnam War. Her father had left his collection of war photos with Phil as a kindness. Then, naturally, Phil lost them the week after he borrowed them. Yet here they were, re-discovered after all this time.

Just another mind game.

She left her car in the drive and used the keypad on the side gate to enter the property.

She approached the house. There was no sound or sign of movement.

What if Phillip were hiding in there? What if the photographs were just a lure to get her back for one last round of abuse? He was always meanest when there was no one else around.

She was being paranoid. Even if her ex-husband was in there, she had already survived his worst.

She would keep the visit quick. Shorten the time window for any possible contact. Phillip and his family had been the bane of her existence, but not for much longer. No more Mrs Savage. She was already using her family name, Virginia Collins. She would make it legal on the day of the divorce, her old name and her new life.

Freedom from this horrible family she had married into.

This horrible, soulless house had been the epitome of everything wrong. An expensive wedding gift that turned into a chain. It was going to be sold.

Phillip had finally agreed to a sale. She always knew he would. Phillip was a one-on-one bully but, essentially, a weak man. He was being worn down by Virginia's lawyer as much as her own determination.

The last meeting had been two days ago.

The next day, yesterday, she had been to see a real estate agent. The agent had given her an estimated price. It was huge money, beyond her dreams. The agent also gave her a check-list of paperwork she would need to provide. Ownership documents, rate notices and such.

The list of documents was already done. Virginia had found copies of everything. She was ready to go. Ready to sell up and move on. Whatever had to be done, she would do.

The separation, the divorce, and the planned sale were a dark tunnel. Finally, she could see an end. She could feel it. She would have her auction and her share of the proceeds. Her own money. Freedom. So close.

This would be the last time she would ever have to visit this house of misery and pain.

In and out, quickly, then goodbye forever.

She hurried up the pathway to the front door, managed the lock, opened the door and stepped inside.

She was nervous, but she could manage that.

The house had a large, lavish entryway. Off to the right were the kitchen and dining room. On her left was a living space.

Something on her left caught her eye.

There was a green plastic tarpaulin laid out on the living room floor. Laying in the middle of the tarp was the box of photos Virginia had come to collect. Beside the box was a weird collection of items. A knife, gaffer tape, and some large, heavy-duty garbage bags.

What the hell?

Inside

I could hear Virginia before I saw her. I heard her use her key and then open the door. I heard her step inside, and then she stopped.

I was standing behind the partition wall on the kitchen side of the entry hall. In my right hand, I held a solid rubber mallet. I chose the mallet because I wanted her unconscious, not dead, not immediately.

Most importantly, I didn't want too much blood. Not at this stage.

She had stopped to look at my playful little diversion.

I leant forward to look around the corner of the partition wall. Oh my God, the ploy had worked perfectly. I almost laughed out loud, but that would ruin the next bit.

I was looking at her back as she wondered about the purpose of the tarpaulin on the floor.

She would find out soon enough the stupid, selfish bitch.

It was too easy. Virginia's lack of awareness proved she should never have married into the family. She was such an idiot. Yes, she had been beautiful once, no question. But where was all that after three children and twelve years of marriage? She had come to look and behave like a cow.

I could have easily allowed myself the joy of letting her see me, see my victory, see her stupidity. Maybe she would even acknowledge her wrongness and beg my forgiveness.

Who is to say I would not have granted it? I was always a forgiving person, never judgemental.

But there is only so much one person can forgive.

Anyway, I had too much self-discipline for mercy, self-discipline, something she would never understand. I had a plan, and there was no room for small personal victories. Her total disappearance from the face of the earth would be victory enough.

Discipline, strength of character. My father would be greatly pleased with me. I was doing the family a favour, given how much they all despised her.

In the instant she stopped to stare, wondering at the items on the floor, I stepped forward.

Perfect timing.

With her back turned to me, I swung the mallet in my right hand and struck her with a firm blow aimed at her right temple.

Bizarre, I had rehearsed the manoeuvre several times on a chopping board. Sadly, it seemed to have little effect. She took a step backward, half stumbling towards me. I detected a small line of blood flowing quickly from her ear down her neck.

Dammit, she was about to bleed on the Monsoon Forest Custom Rug. Eleven thousand dollars worth of floor covering. For God's sake, idiot woman.

I put my left hand on her shoulder and guided her. She stumbled but managed to follow my direction. I was quite strong. Brave in action, despite my prior nerves. I quickly had her in place at the centre of the tarp. Bleed all you like now, my dear.

Holding her steady in place with my left, I struck her again, much harder this time with my right. The mallet landed crisply on her right temple.

Much, much better.

She fell to the floor, instantly unconscious.

It was a worthy blow. I was quite impressed.

Possibly enough to kill her, possibly not. The next few moments would finalize that debate.

Much more straightforward like this. No arguments, no more discussion. No more back and forth about her rights. To hell with her rights. All I wanted from her right now was that she didn't ruin the expensive rug or carpet beneath her.

I centred her limp body on the tarp. It buckled and folded as I pulled her toward its centre. With a touch of finesse, I arranged her into something tidy. The tarp was now an impenetrable barrier between her bleeding head and the floor furnishings below.

Perfect.

Far too expensive to let this trollop bleed all over. How dare she believe she could sell this house as if it were hers to dispose of?

'To dispose of', Very appropriate words, I thought.

I used the grey builders' masking tape to bind her hands behind her. Then her feet, then finally, her mouth and nose.

She started to struggle now. Waking up.

I took the plastic bag from the items that had distracted her.

"Watch carefully, Virginia, and I will show you what the bag is for," I whispered. Just for her benefit. No harm in letting her know now.

"Yes, it's me, darling," I said.

Would she be surprised to know it was me? Maybe, maybe not.

Surely, she must have known it would come to this.

She would know it now.

Yes. Think about it now, you stupid woman.

I rolled her over face down, straddled her back and sat on her.

That didn't feel comfortable. I re-arranged myself, placing one knee in the middle of her back, pinning her to the ground like a captured animal. That felt so much better.

I was much more comfortable now. So much more control.

I slid the plastic bag over her head and wound the tape tightly around her throat, securing the bag. Then, a few more loops around the mouth and throat.

Oh yes, it was a different story now, wasn't it?

She had nothing to say for herself now.

I watched as Virginia struggled violently, helplessly, striving for her last breath.

Virginia Collins, she intended to call herself. Taking back her maiden name, her identity, she called it. What a pathetic joke.

"You want your last name back. Take it. A lot of good your father's name is doing you now."

Where was the father? The so-called war hero and martial artist, where was he now when she needed him?

She was delusional. She should never have been a part of this family, ever. The marriage was a mistake, and now that mistake has been corrected.

So much for 'till death do us part'.

So much for 'honour and obey'.

So much for 'selling the family home'.

"This is what property settlement looks like for you, Virginia," I laughed.

"Did you honestly think I would let you sell this house?"

The house that had belonged to my father.

The woman was an idiot.

I laughed, realising I was already thinking of her in the past tense.

I stood and watched her struggle silently against her death. It was better standing up. Her struggling about had made my knee ache. Small price to pay.

I ran my mind over the job list.

First and foremost, dispose of the body. That had already been arranged.

Tomorrow? Let this ridiculous real estate agent fellow know the house sale was off. Not happening

Then relax.

Stopping the sale would not be a problem. Selling the family home would not be in the children's interest. Not now.

What court in the land would deny them the security of the home they had lived in all their lives, under the care of their loving father?

The children would need their home and their father. God, they would need their father more than ever.

Especially now, their mother had just disappeared, leaving them behind without even the love and courtesy of goodbye.

The poor darlings.

They were practically orphans.

Part 2

Monday, May 16, 2022

Chris

Twenty years later

Coffee Lounge, Jarrajarra, Australia.

"Chris, I am sorry. Honestly, I am."

My administrative assistant, Barney Trail, had called my mobile from the front desk at Jarrajarra Police Station.

I knew that because I could see him clearly, through the police station window, from my seat outside of the Jarrajarra cafe, where I was drinking a flat white coffee in a large paper cup, soaking up the autumn sunshine.

Just enjoying myself.

"We have a request for police assistance approximately twenty minutes east along the river road," said Barney.

The river road ran alongside the Murray River. The Murray River in May, needing police assistance, usually meant duck hunters, but the season didn't start till May 26, nearly two weeks away.

"I am texting you the GPS of the location," said Barney. "Sorry, Chris."

My phone pinged as the GPS came through.

"Any other information you wish to share, Barn?"

"I believe the collective term 'Duck Hunters' may be relevant to the situation."

"Ah bloody hell," I said.

"Beyond that, from the nature of the call," continued Barney, "I am guessing there may be significant consumption of alcohol involved."

"Shit. Double shit."

"It appears a member of this hunting collective may have disappeared during the pursuit," said Barney.

"Pursuit of the ducks or pursuit of the alcohol?"

"The ducks."

"Disappearing out-of-season duck hunter?"

"Yes."

"Any word on the ducks, Barn?"

"None at this stage," said Barney.

"Sorry, Chris," he added gently one more time. He knew how I felt about drunks and duck hunters. Barney, as always, was ruining my day as gently as he possibly could. He was the gentlest, most caring man I had ever known.

"I will let you know how I go."

"Good luck," said Barney.

I walked across the street to my police truck. Fired it up, and away I went. In my mind, my only real duty here was to save as many ducks as I could. If duck hunters had to die, then so be it.

That was, possibly, a bit harsh, but even cops can dream.

Roadside, River Road, Jarrajarra Region.

My name is Chris Taylor, and I am the sole policeman in the tiny town of Jarrajarra in northeast Victoria. I cover a region containing less than one thousand people and covering over twenty thousand square miles. Dealing with people is my job. I see them all. All types in all seasons.

Every year, from May to June, duck hunting season, I see this mob of gun-toting idiots.

Untrained, incoherent and usually pissed to the gills.

"Can you just run that by me again, please?" I asked.

I was speaking to Ralph, mid-forties, dressed in expensive hunting gear. Until a moment ago, he had also been carrying a very expensive shotgun. I had taken the weapon away from him for various reasons. Mostly because he was drunk and in no fit state to stand, let alone shoot.

I am not sure he noticed he'd been disarmed.

Ralph also had a bag. The bag was open on the ground between us, and in his bag were five Blue-winged Shovelers. The Shoveler was a beautiful bird. It was also protected, meaning it could not be hunted. Ralph's hunting licence would have told him that if he had bothered to read it. If he even had one.

It might have been acceptable if the beautiful blue shovelers in his bag were alive, but sadly, they were stone dead. Shot to bits.

Barney's assessment had been correct. What we had here was the new season's first drunken duck hunter.

"Well, Officer, like I said," explained Ralph, "we just shot another two ducks. They fall in that little wetland area over there, right? Rocky, me mate, he goes over to collect."

The 'little wetland' he pointed at was, being picky, a swampy section in the middle of a soggy cow paddock. The paddock belonged to the Mellish clan. But hey, minor detail, given the breed of the ducks in his bag, what was a mere trespass on private property?

A Victorian duck hunting licence meant you were only allowed to shoot on Crown Land. Again, Ralph would have known that if he had read the thing.

But Ralph was not much of a reader.

I knew that because we were parked near a sign that said, "Private Property! Keep Out! Especially Fucking Duck Hunters".

I knew the sign. It was famous in the region. It had been written by a friend of mine, Wally Mellish, the owner of the local caravan park, also the owner of Ralph's alleged wetland.

Details.

Apart from his missing mate, Ralph was in a spot of financial bother.

I was guessing, no licence. There went eleven thousand dollars right there.

The five dead ducks in his bag would cost him five thousand dollars each. There goes another twenty-five thousand dollars, plus the mandatory loss and destruction of his very expensive weapon.

I guessed the shotgun I had taken from him would be worth around seven thousand dollars. Expensive day for Ralph and the boys.

But first things first. The missing mate.

"So Rocky is the duck collector?" I asked. "And you're the duck shooter?"

"Yeah, yeah. I shoot 'em. Rocky goes 'n gets 'em."

"Can I see your hunting licence? Thanks, Ralph."

"It's in the car somewhere, like I'm sayin', me mind is more on Rocky right now."

"Would your gun licence be there in the car as well?"

"Mate, mate," says Ralph. "Can we talk about the licences and shit later?"

I was willing to bet that Ralph's gun licence was out of date or non-existent. I couldn't remember the monetary fine, but possessing a gun without a licence could mean two years in prison. Bloody hell.

But, what's money and time to a wilderness man like Ralph?

One thing at a time. Let's see if we can find his mate.

"OK, go on and tell me about Rocky."

"Finally, yeah. So, Rocky's walking back, right? Boring as all shit, so I shout out to him to hold 'em up, let me get them in the video. Show some excitement, mate. Make a show of it for the internet."

"You were videoing him?"

"Yeah, yeah, on the mobile, for the Tik Tok, right? So, he holds them up, and I'm shooting the phone, not the gun."

"I understand."

"Rocky, he hams it up a bit. Screaming, 'woohoo ducks' sorta thing. Jumps up and down like a goose. Coulda been better, not sayin' he's your next Tony Bonner, not like a real actor, say. Anyway, Rocky is looking really happy. Then bang! He disappears, bang, gone like as he vanishes off the face of the planet."

"Disappears?"

"Yeah. Disappears, kapoof."

"And you took a video of all of this?"

"Yeah, yeah, like on the mobile."

"You have a video in your possession that you could show me rather than spend time explaining?"

"Yeah. I guess. Yeah."

We stood there looking at each other. A moment in time. Rocky has disappeared off the face of the earth, allegedly. Ralph has filmed it all, allegedly. Then Ralph called me to help solve their problem.

I wait as the penny refuses to drop on Ralph's brain.

"Listen," I say finally, "this may seem way out of leftfield, but I'm thinking."

"Yeah?"

"Would there be any possibility you could actually, sometime today, perhaps, show me the video?"

"Off me mobile?"

"That would be the one, yes."

"The one of Rocky disappearing?"

"Yes, that one."

“No worries. Of course, Officer, of course. Just have to ask me. No need for the attitude.”

So, Ralph, the hunter videographer, fiddles around inside his wellingtons and brings out a mobile. I can see a thought assembling in Ralph's mind and slowly working its way across his hapless, drunken face.

“Officer, I hope you won't get all aggro with me asking a question here?”

“Fire away, mate. The question, not the gun.”

Joke wasted. Too subtle.

“If this turns out something weird,” said Ralph, “like maybe UFO abductions or some other supernatural thing, it won't affect me selling price, will it? Like, if I have showed the video to you first.”

“Good question, Ralph,” I say admiringly, “I think if this turns out to be a UFO abduction, I am sure your returns will be unaffected by my viewing. I believe these digital films don't wear out with repeat viewing. Plus, thinking it through, police verification could even work to your financial advantage.”

“Great, great. Yeah. Zapruder time, yeah.”

Ralph positions his video to the viewing point.

“So, here ya go.”

He hands over the phone. I press play and watch.

The video image on the phone is incredibly stable, considering the cameraman was drunk. This is what I see.

A young bloke, presumably Rocky, is stumbling back from the Mellish dam, towards the camera, towards where I am standing now.

It is hard not to notice that Rocky is pissed to the gills, just like Ralph. Maybe worse. Bit of a stumble to the left. Bit of a stumble to the right.

Rocky is holding two ducks. More sad, dead little blue shovelers. Another ten grand on Ralph's debt to the State of Victoria.

Ralph calls out to Rocky.

Rocky stops, listening carefully, with a cocked ear, while Ralph shouts his stage directions. Mostly asking Rocky to give us some more joy.

Rocky behaves as directed, holds up the ducks and shouts an unconvincing 'woohoo', then waves his arms and the poor dead ducks. Jumps up and down. More a petulant protest at the cameraman than a celebration of the hunter's joy.

Very little theatrical enthusiasm from Rocky.

If I were Ralph, I'd be disappointed.

Then, at this point, Rocky, our hero, vanishes.

No tricks.

He is suddenly just gone. Out of sight, like magic.

Disappeared. just like that.

'Kapoof' to quote Ralph.

Totally, utterly, gone.

Two voices then call out, "What the fuck?" Or words to that effect.

Next, some other bloke from off-camera starts running toward the last known sighting of the vanished Rocky. He screams enthusiastically, "Rocky! Rocky! Rocky!"

This is way better cinematically. Real enthusiasm.

I do detect, from the style of his running, that this new bloke is drunk as well. Heaven's above. It is still morning, and I have three drunk duck hunters.

Nevertheless, Ralph, sensibly, with Tik Tok and posterity in mind, has continued filming.

The Abraham Zapruder of the Jarrajarra wetlands. Keep shooting, and count the bodies after.

The other bloke is running forward to Rocky's last known location. He trips, stumbles and falls. Then he rises again and heroically resumes running forward.

Forward. Forward.

"Rocky! Rocky! Rocky!"

It occurs to me they could be a comedy team, and I am the victim of some form of hidden camera stunt. But they can't be actors. No one can act that drunk.

"Who's this?" I ask, turning my body and the phone so Ralph can watch over my shoulder.

"Ah?" Ralphie looks closely at the video. It is as if there are many options, and only he can decide.

"Ah yeah, That's Bill?" Ralph nods at the image on the phone.

"Bill?"

"Yeah."

"OK. Where's Bill." I ask foolishly.

Then, as we watched on the phone, at the very moment Bill

reached the point where Rocky vanished, Ralph answered my pertinent question.

"Yeah, Like I forgot to say before, Bill's gone too."

As he spoke, 'Bill', in addition to Rocky, vanished from the video screen. Poof, into thin air.

Another one is gone, just like that.

Duck hunters.

"Right," I said as I pocketed Ralph's phone, "I will need this as evidence."

Ralph is suddenly angry. An angry, drunken duck hunter.

"I won't be a part of any cover-up, and if this is aliens, I'll need me phone footage," he shouts. Ralph then grabs for his phone.

I put him on the ground. He goes down easily; he is a hunter, a killer of birds, not a fighter.

I might have kneed him in the stomach, hard but not too hard. He stopped talking and started wheezing.

I also may have elbowed him in the nose. His nose is bleeding along with all the wheezing.

Some of these moves happen before I think about them. I could claim extensive military training, but my Nan always said it was just temper, and that was way before my army career.

If this bloke Ralph and his team are a candid camera-style comedy team, I am done for. 'In for a penny in for a pound,' my Nan would say. No turning back now.

I get out my handcuffs.

He starts to cry as I cuff him. Happy enough shooting a lovely family of blue-winged shovelers but sooks like a baby from a love tap in the tummy.

Bloody duck hunters.

"You are under arrest for assaulting an officer during an active investigation. If you speak again, I might have to shoot you."

As a sole cop in a massive area, there were times I could say any damn thing I pleased. This was such a time.

"Do you understand me?"

He nodded and groaned, wept and wheezed a bit more.

I took out my phone and called Barney.

"You sure can pick them, Barn," I said.

"Is there blood?" He asked.

"Bit of blood on the nose, a sore tummy, maybe."

"Cuffs?

"Yes, handcuffs are involved."

"Oh dear," said Barney. "Chris, you have to stop assaulting duck hunters every time you answer one of their calls for help."

Barney was the most honest person I had ever met. It wasn't the first time he had spoken to me sternly about my enthusiasm for arresting duck murderers.

"Chris, you know the tourists that come through here are a very important part of our local economy."

"Barney, mate, can you hold that thought? We have one intoxicated shooter and two missing members of the shooting fraternity. I need you to round up the troops, please?"

I was a sole cop, but I had a village behind me.

"Yes. OK. I am on the case," said Barney.

"Thank you."

"You're welcome," said the world's greatest police admin assistant.

"Dear Mother of God. Duck hunters," Barney sighed as he hung up on the call. I don't think I was supposed to hear that bit.

Before I hung up at my end, I spoke into the empty call.

This was for Ralph's benefit.

"Barn, can you tell Jack to bring the mind wipe and the rectal probe? Another two of these humans have fallen into the vortex portal."

"Thanks, Barney," I said. "Yes, I have him restrained."

I waited for a beat.

"No, I won't prep him till you get here with the probe."

Then I hung up on my end and looked at Ralph. He was sobering up fast.

Mellish Paddock, Jarrajarra Region.

"Another two metres," Jody Taggart was speaking via walkie-talkie. Her voice was coming in loud and clear on the fire truck's speakers.

It was a few hours later, and the Jarrajarra Emergency services were on the case of the missing hunters.

"Two metres," said Greg Farrell into his end of the two-way radio.

He then pressed a button that slowly released another two metres of steel rope from a winch mounted on the front bar of the Jarrajarra fire truck.

Jody, Jarrajarra's intrepid paramedic, was attached via a harness to the far end of the same winch line. Greg Farrell, our CFA captain, was at the other, controlling the winch, which secured Jody, just in case she also fell down the same mysterious hole that had swallowed our two missing duckers.

It had to be a hole.

We had hundreds of them: abandoned mines, dry water wells, flooded wells, drug laboratories, some abandoned, some still producing, especially on Mellish land.

We had holes to burn, but we had never had a spaceship. Not on my watch, at least.

The markings on the winch line told us Jody was already over one hundred metres from the roadside, hopefully near our missing duck hunters.

I was standing alongside Jack Farrell and Scotty Farrell, more Farrell family, both with a protective hand on the slowly extending line. If Jody should disappear like the duck hunters before her, and if the strength of the truck's winch could not retrieve her, these blokes would be the two men I would trust to drag her out.

They are an eccentric crew, the Jarrajarra emergency services.

Greg Farrell was the skipper of the local Country Fire Authority and filled in as boss of Emergency Services any time the emergency did not involve a fire.

Greg and his wife Norma were the casual, unchallenged leaders of most of the town's important activities, fire, netball, footy and fund-raising being their specialties.

Greg had arrived at the Mellish paddock with the truck and all its' ladders, ropes, pumps, and winches. He also had his nephew, Scotty.

Scotty Farrell was a teenage man-mountain capable of carrying both our missing duck hunters to the surface under one arm, should the need arise.

Jack Farrell was the town's paramedic, and Jody was his working partner. Jack was, incidentally, Greg's younger brother. Jack and Jody were the paramedic dream team. Jack, like all the Farrells, was as tough as old rope. He was also around my standard as a runner, on the plus side of very good, but like me, he was no Olympic athlete.

Jody Taggart was something else altogether. She was early twenties, a near Olympic standard triathlete, currently striving to meet the time requirements for selection in the national team. Her swim and run were world-class. Just her riding needed work.

Jody was on the dangerous end of the rope because, if someone had to be pulled out by hand, common sense dictated it should be the lightest member of the team.

"Another two metres," her voice came in over the speakers.

"Two more metres," said Greg as he pressed the button to unwind the mechanical end of the winch.

There was more to this rescue than mere missing hunters.

Love was in the air.

Normally, I would see Jack and Jody with their ambulance at any disappearance, car crash, or drowning.

I would also expect Greg and his fire truck, plus some capable assistant. The co-driver was usually a robust youngster from either of our football teams. Male or female, they were all in the CFA, and they all played footy. Rough, tough country kids, ready for anything.

Lately, the spare chair in the fire truck belonged exclusively to Scotty Farrell. Greg, Jack and I had reached the conclusion that our Scotty was smitten with our Jody. At this stage, he was, maybe, too young and inexperienced to find the words to ask her out. Plus, he was barely nineteen, and she was twenty-four. Was that important? Who knew?

Meanwhile, he just showed up whenever he could. Not a bad way to start a flirtation in my book.

As the cop in charge, I was giving instructions while doing as little as possible. Stepping frame by frame through the precious video of Rocky's vanishment and sending instructions, by proxy, to Jody.

"Maybe left a metre and then forward another two," I said to Greg.

"Left a metre and then forward two," said Greg into the two-way.

"Ready when you are," answered Jody.

"Roger," said Greg, pressing the button on the winch and letting out more metres.

Jody stepped carefully, sideways, then forward.

Greg, Jack, and Scotty were watching Jody. I was half watching Jody and half watching the video on Ralph's phone. The last time I checked Ralph, he was sound asleep in the prison seat in the back of my truck. Totally useless beyond the video he had provided.

Alcohol will do that, even in the most dangerous situation.

Jody shuffled, checked her footing and then shuffled some more. We watched and waited.

"Found it," shouted Jody, "it's a hole."

Then, like in a bad movie, we heard, "Whoops, Shit," and then Jody disappeared, just like the missing duck hunters.

"Shit," shouted someone at our end.

This was different to a bunch of strangers disappearing. This was one of our own. Kapoof! Gone!

The sense of urgency rose dramatically.

Greg hit the rewind button on the winch.

Scotty and Jack were pulling one hundred-plus metres of steel rope faster than the winch. Was that even possible?

Jody's voice boomed over the truck speakers, breaking the tension.

"Stop!" She said. "Hang on, hang on."

"You OK?" Shouted Greg, his voice displaying all our fears.

"All good, all good. No harm done. I was looking at the hole, and then the ground collapsed under me. I think the rain must have caused a cave-in."

"Keep talking, Jody," said Greg, "We all got a fright, mate. Just keep talking."

"Looks like a cave down below. Oh boy, this smells bad. A bit gassy. Greg, winch me up, please, and can someone bring me out a breathing mask? The small one."

"I got it," said lovestruck Scotty before the rest of us could think. Within half a second, he was sprinting along the line of the rope, carrying the small breathing mask, testing the oxygen bottle as he ran."

Never mind the danger, his true love called. Greg, Jack and I shared a look. At that moment, Scotty was beautiful, heroic and romantic, but you can't say that out loud when you've arrived in a fire truck, an ambulance and a police car.

"If anyone says anything sarcastic," I said, "I will tell Scotty."

"Not me," they said in unison.

"And the torch," said Jody over the speakers.

Scotty must have heard. Without a word, he pivoted, sprinted back to the truck, grabbed the big torch, and then turned again to sprint to Jody. It took less than a second, or so it seemed.

"OK," said Greg as he pressed reverse on the winch, drawing the line back toward us.

Slow and steady, in total control, Jody emerged from a hole in the ground. Not a spaceship, after all.

When she was standing safely on level ground, Greg turned off the winch.

"I am going to leave this thing on," said Jody, referring to her microphone. We watched as she stood there, clipping the microphone to her safety vest.

Scotty arrived next to Jody with the breather and the torch. He handed them to her. She looked up at him and gave him her beautiful smile. We could all see it from our vantage point about eighty metres away.

"Thanks, mate," she said to Scotty, and the three of us older blokes, listening to the speaker, just smiled.

"Oh, Jesus." Said Jack," I heard his young heart skip a beat from here."

"Young love, hey?" said Greg, "beautiful thing."

"I hope he can't hear us," I said.

"No," said Greg, holding up his microphone with the speaker switch clearly off. "I'm not that stupid."

"OK," said Jody through the speakers. "It is a hole in the ground, over some sort of cave, maybe an old mine. It's deep enough. I can't see the bottom."

"Could be another Mellish drug cave," said Greg.

"I thought the drug stuff was all finished," said Jack.

"So did I," I said.

I could see Jody fitting the breathing mask and testing the torch.

"OK, I am ready. Let me out slowly," she said.

Greg hit the winch button; Jody adjusted her footing and then stepped into the hole.

"Can you hear me?" asked Jody.

"Loud and clear," answered Greg.

"Jeez, it's deep. I don't like their chances if they fell in here."

Silence for a while. We could hear Jody's exaggerated breathing coming thru the mask. The occasional grunt as Jody struggled with the winch rope and the torch.

The winch just kept unwinding. "Twenty metres," said Greg to Jack and me.

"Keep it coming, slowly, slowly," came Jody's voice from the pit to the truck.

Then, a long period of silence as the winch continued to send her down.

"I found them," she said at last.

"How do they look?" From Greg.

Long pause, then a soft voice from Jody.

"They look dead to me."

There was a sigh or two from the team. Dead was never good. More silence from Jody, no doubt groping around in the dark. It would be true to say, at this point, none of us felt concerned for Jody. She was great at her job and had seen her fair share of corpses in her career. What she was doing now was part of her training.

"I am just about on the floor of this hole; can you slow it down." Greg slowed the descent. "I'm trying not to land on these blokes."

Silence.

"OK, I'm down."

Another long pause. Then eventually.

"How many are we looking for?"

Jody must have adjusted her microphone. It was now receiving.

"Two," said Greg.

"Two? You sure?"

I shrugged at Greg, nodding toward Ralph, asleep drunk in the back of my police truck. The unreliable Ralph had only mentioned two.

"Yeah, two, we think," said Greg. "Possibly, maybe. Who knows with this lot."

"I've got four here," said Jody.

"Four?" That was a shock.

"Looks like our two duck hunters and two older ones."

"Older ones?"

"Yeah, older corpses and the older ones are a lot deader than the duckers."

"Deader? What do you mean deader?"

"I mean, the earlier two are almost skeletons, and I reckon." She stopped talking at 'reckon'. Looking closer, maybe.

"I reckon," she said again and stopped. She was taking a closer look.

"Come on, Jody? What is it that you reckon?"

"I reckon yes, I reckon they have both been bashed in the head. Bashed dead in the head, then wrapped in a couple of tarps is what I reckon, Greg."

Oh, dear me. The search for our two missing duck hunters was now a murder mystery.

"Beam me up, Scotty," said Jody.

Was that a movie reference or just a small joke between Jody and her young admirer? Four dead bodies, and both Greg and Jack were smiling at lovestruck Scotty as they winched Jody back to the surface.

As she finally emerged from the hole in the ground, we three cynics, Greg, Jack and me, watched our young hero Scotty reach out and take Jody's hand, then lift her effortlessly out of the depths and onto the ground. I swear he lifted her all the way and higher, setting her gently upon the grass. He was so strong the winch line went slack.

It was all so romantic I was sure I heard violins.

But now, this was a murder scene, and it was time for a whole other process to begin.

* * *

"Four bodies," I said. "Two bashed to death by the looks of it."

"Goodness me," said Barney. "We need Carole and Glenda."

"Yes. As soon as we can get them."

Carole and Glenda Johnston were the Crime Services Unit from Seymour, who covered our region, great cops, sisters, and, most important, Barney's cousins.

"And we need to tell Sergeant Palmer."

"Yep, the Sarge, we need to do that," I was on a roll, confirming everything Barney said about correct police procedure.

Senior Sergeant Bruce Palmer of Wodonga Police Station was, officially, my boss. I was the Constable in charge of one of the few remaining one-man police stations in the State of Victoria.

I didn't report much to anyone unless I absolutely had to, and when I absolutely had to, 'Sarge' was the man. We were perfect for each other. The Sarge was ex-army, like me, and he hated paperwork and procedure as much as I did.

He was also the operational boss for this part of the State of Victoria in the Commonwealth of Australia. He worked out of the Wodonga Police Station. Wodonga, about an hour's drive down river from Jarrajarra, was a much bigger town. When I say bigger, that is relative. Wodonga's population is around 45,000. Not a lot, really, but nearly fifty times bigger than Jarrajarra, but still just a country town.

When I needed more police, the Sarge was usually my first call, though, to be honest, I meant Barney's first call.

"I will get Wodonga to send down young Constable Tim. He can do all the guarding of the scene stuff," said Barney. "Save your energy for criminal detection."

"That is a great idea," I said.

Young Constable Tim Silver was from Wodonga Police. Tim was just one of those straight-down-the-middle-up-country coppers. Big tough farm boy. Honest as the day was long and reliable as the sunrise. He could tend to be a bit hard-line, even angry, when dealing with miscreants, but give him a job, and you could trust him to do his best. Maybe not the sharpest tool in the shed, but if a police tape needed watching, young Tim would watch it till the plastic disintegrated. Which meant I wouldn't have to. Win for me.

Barney was looking after me.

"OK," said Barney. "I will make the calls."

"Great idea, thanks, Barn."

* * *

Constables Carole Johnston and Glenda Johnston from Seymour Police arrived early evening, the forensic dream team of rural Victoria. They were in high demand, but they always found the time to help our little town, police hierarchy permitting.

And here they were, back to Jarrajarra, in person and ready for action.

Jarrajarra had two particular advantages that kept these two amazing women coming back. First, they were Barney's cousins, and Barney was not afraid to play the family card. Second, we had all worked together in the year before the Covid pandemic to help solve one of the country's most infamous murders. We had all won police medals and every accolade you could dream of, short of a promotion or a raise.

Most importantly, when we weren't scared shitless, we had fun. It never felt like work.

They had arrived in their van with 'Victoria Police Crime Services' printed along the side. They had bounded onto the crime scene with their typical enthusiasm.

Then someone said cave.

“Shit-a-brick,” said Constable Carole, “No one mentioned caves.”

“It's more a hole than a cave,” I said, “Not really very wide. Think of it as a dry abandoned hole.”

“Jesus Christ, a freaking cave,” echoed her sister and co-forensic investigator, Constable Glenda.

“Alright,” I said, “OK, a freaking cave. Deep and scary, dark with dead bodies, only a rope between you and survival.”

“Bloody Hell,” said Carole.

“How deep?” asked Glenda.

“Only about thirty metres, straight down,” I said.

“Thirty fucking metres,” they both shouted in disbelieving unison.

“Jesus, Killer, what the fuck,” said Carole.

They had nicknamed me 'Killer' a few years ago after they were called in to examine some dead bodies I had caused. That was during a shootout deep in the Mitta Mitta ranges. All in self-defence, of course. But the girls liked 'Killer', and the nickname had stuck. Better than being called 'Dead', I supposed.

A question was slowly dawning. Were the two forensic heroes afraid of the dark?

“Would it help if I came down as well and Greg brought a lot of lights?” I asked.

“How many lights? Asked Glenda.

“A huge number, hundreds,” said Greg.

They thought about it a bit.

“That could work,” said Carole.

“Chris goes first,” said Glenda.

“I'm not climbing,” said Carole.

“We've got a winch and harnesses,” said Greg.

“First caves and now harness,” said Glenda. “What is this, horror porn?

Later, after a lot of mucking about with lights and harnesses and breathing masks, down we went.

I went first, and with Greg's help, we soon had the place lit up like a Christmas store.

It was something to see.

We were definitely in a cave, a very rocky cave. If bodies had been dumped here, there must have been a hole above us of some size. Perhaps the recent rain had softened the ground and widened the hole. Perhaps the weight of Rocky, the duck hunter, had caused more of the ground above to collapse. It was hard to tell.

The cave floor was mostly rock, with a thin layer of mud and water surrounding it. The point where the various bodies had landed was a large, ugly rock.

The two duck hunters were clearly dead from the fall. Splayed, broken, dead.

The other two were as dead as you could get.

Bashed in the head and dumped was my guess. They were dead before they were dropped in here, another guess.

Carole and Glenda would prove all of that or not. If there was anything down here that could lead to the killer, I was sure they would find it. Whatever 'it' might be.

Maybe the two bodies were all they would find to work with.

"I don't think we need these breathers," said Carole, and off came the oxygen masks. "It's not gas. It just stinks."

The masks were replaced with the standard cloth masks that covered the nose and mouth. The things we had all worn during the pandemic. The girls were already kitted out in the standard forensic anti-contamination gear, and so was I.

I was dressed to the nines in hazard overalls, gloves, and boot covers. My only real job here was to keep the lights on and stay out of their way.

* * *

By 11 PM, the two dead duck hunters had been hauled out and sent away. The bodies were in an ambulance on the way back to the mortuary in Wodonga. They had fallen about thirty metres into a cave, landed on the rock floor and died of their injuries.

"A simple 'open and drop case'," said Carole, with her usual dark humour.

"Drunk dropping," replied Glenda.

"If you drink and drop, you're a bloody idiot," I said, trying to add to the humour.

"Quiet please, Killer, professionals at work here," replied Carole.

Sometime during all this forensic recovery, Greg Farrell called down into the cave to tell me that Constable Tim had arrived from Wodonga.

"Tim's here," said Greg.

What to do with him was the question.

"Tell him to take Ralph back to Wodonga," I shouted back to Greg.

I hadn't realised that Constable Tim had not just arrived. He had risked life and limb to walk through the dangerously pot-holed paddock. Now, blissfully unaware of the danger he'd traversed, he was standing next to Greg, above ground, at the top of the hole, gazing down into the cave.

"Who's Ralph?" I heard Tim say. Casual as you please.

"Who's Ralph?" Greg shouted down the hole.

"Ralph is the drunk bloke asleep in the back seat of my truck," I said. "The last living ducker. If you look in the back section of my truck, you'll find Ralph's collection of dead birds and his very expensive, confiscated, and soon-to-be-crushed shotgun. Probably not licensed."

Tim had now moved to the edge of the hole. I could see him looking down, and he was now doing his own talking.

"So, charge him for the dead protected ducks, yeah?" said Tim.

"Yeah," I said.

"Plus, the unlicensed weapons? Yeah?" Tim was shouting now, just like Greg. I was only thirty metres away in an echo chamber.

"Yeah?" I shouted back. "Plus, I doubt he has a hunting licence, so have a go on that as well. Check all his licences."

"OK," shouted Constable Tim. "Got it."

"Can I take your truck?" asked Tim, always angling to swap his old bomb for mine. "Makes it easier if I just leave him in the back of yours, I reckon. All the evidence being where it is."

"No," I answered, "you are not swapping your way out of that shit heap you drive."

"You sure?"

"I am one thousand per cent positive."

With all that information, Tim disappeared into the night with our duckie, Ralph, and all the evidence we had against him. Ralph was now, well and truly, in the belly of the judicial system. I was sure it would be a few years and many thousands of dollars before he found his way out if he was lucky.

"Is he always that loud?" asked Glenda, referring to Tim.

"Was he loud?" I shouted across the two metres between us, "I didn't notice."

At the cave, it was just the five of us. Greg and Scotty Farrell were above the ground with Carole, Glenda and me down below. We had arrived as the rescue team. Now, we were the forensic team.

Carole and Glenda were back to chatting away with each other in their verbal shorthand.

"There's two tarpaulins," said Carole.

"Separately wrapped," said Glenda. "Both tarps ripped open when they landed? Maybe?"

"Or rats?" said Carole.

They worked around the bodies for a while. I could see that both had been wrapped in tarpaulins when dropped, but the tarps were torn open now."

"These tarpaulins were tied up in an old hessian rope," said Carole.

"Not the modern stuff," said Glenda, "not the nylon and polyester stuff."

"No, this is three-strand hemp by the look of it," said Carole. "Oh shit, it's been eaten, got petrified rat shit under the tarp here."

"Rats going for the meat, I reckon," I said. "Ate the rope, worked through the tarp to get to the meaty bits."

"The meaty bits?" said Carole.

"If anyone else mentions rats again, I'm leaving," said Glenda.

Silence for a few minutes.

"Same dentist," said Carole.

There was a long pause while Glenda checked the mouths of the two skeletons.

"This one has all composite resin," said Carole. "This one has composite in the front but amalgam in the back."

"Maybe re-did his original fillings to look better?"

"They look pretty good now."

They didn't take notes. Their conversation was recorded and would be transcribed later.

"Broken arm here on the younger one, maybe repeated breaks."

"This one is older."

"Could they be brothers, this one the bully, this one the victim?"

"Maybe the bully is the dad."

"Definitely related. Check out the chin."

"Slight twist to the right. Yeah, definitely."

"And the height. Both tall."

"Real tall."

I heard the soft metallic zing of a builder's tape measure.

"The older one is over two hundred centimetres," said Carole.

I heard the tape measure zing again. It sounded strange in the cave.

"This one is two hundred and ten. Jesus, he is nearly seven feet tall."

"Brothers?"

"Father and son, I reckon," said Carole.

"These facial breaks, nose, cheekbone. From the fall or before?"

"This one has landed on his back and cracked his pelvis at the rear. The older one has facial fractures, not from the fall, I'd guess."

"So beaten up before?"

"Before means what? The killer has given them a touch-up?"

"Torture 'em, then kill 'em, then dump 'em?"

"Maybe just test whacks with whatever weapon it was."

The two forensics just rambled on like this as time rolled on. Ad-hoc, random, but always on topic, all recorded and sampled for later investigation. They were a sensational team.

"Hey, Chris," Greg's voice from above. "Looks like one of your bosses is here."

"The Sarge?" I asked.

"No, the other one."

"OK, I am coming up," I replied.

This got me out of the hole, literally. I went upstairs.

Greg Farrell replaced me on downstairs duty, dressed in full police contamination gear, not usual practice at a crime scene to have a citizen involved, but here we were in the middle of nowhere and not a lot of staff options. Plus, Greg was the chief of the Emergency Service for the region, and Carole and Glenda liked him. There would be no complaints about Greg down the hole.

We had made a collective decision on Scotty's behalf. Scotty stayed upstairs, manning the winch and the generator for the lights. Maintaining the infrastructure. He may have been stronger than ten men, but he was still only a kid. When it came to checking out murder victims, we spared him the gore of four dead bodies and the pitch-dark humour of our forensic ladies.

When I was winched back to upper earth, I found Sergeant Will Walker waiting beside the fire truck.

The fire truck was about eighty metres into the paddock and closer to the killer hole. Close enough to make work easier but not so close as to follow us all into the hole.

Technically speaking, Sergeant Will Walker wasn't my boss. We both worked for the same man, Senior Sergeant Bruce Palmer. Walker was way up the ranks on me but had no hope of telling me what to do unless the Sarge agreed.

"Constable Taylor."

"Sergeant Walker."

Sergeant Will Walker was a good policeman, no question. If he wasn't, he would not have been on Sarge's team. Walker was extremely capable, tough as nails, fair and square and treated me well. He never played the hierarchical bullshit you often encountered on the job. But, for all his merits, Walker and I never jelled together like the Sarge and me. He was a straight arrow, no-nonsense, and did not have the greatest sense of humour. None whatsoever, to be honest.

We just didn't have the love.

Where was the Sarge, I wondered.

"Sarge is not coming." Walker read my mind as people often do. Apparently, I have no poker face. "It's late, he was tired, and I volunteered."

"I appreciate your help, Sergeant. Thanks for coming."

That sounded weird, as though he had shown up at a barbeque.

"What have we got?" he asked, and I filled him in with what I knew, no speculation.

"Two dead duck hunters, they are out of here, on the way to the morgue. Another living drunk duck hunter, off to the lock-up at Wodonga, unlicensed weapon, illegal birds, too pissed to stay awake."

"Plus, we have two dead bodies down this hole here. Murder victims. Heads caved in. Maybe related, maybe brothers, maybe father and son. We have the Seymour Crime Services down the hole now, still checking it all out."

"Constable, can I ask you, how tall are the two murder victims?"

"How tall? That's a strange lead question, Sergeant Walker."

"And the answer is?"

"Real tall, is the description Constable Johnston gave them both. Over 200 centimetres each."

"Carole and Glenda seem to think they may be father and son," I added.

Walker did a thing with his chin. He was having a think. He knew something I didn't know. His poker face was as transparent as mine. Don't die wondering, my Nan always said.

"You know something I don't know, Sergeant?"

"Maybe, maybe." He said. He took another long thinking pause.

"Chris, I have a strong feeling. I think I know who these blokes might be."

"I take it you don't mean the duck hunters, Sergeant."

"No, I am not talking about the duck hunters."

So, he might know them. Might? He sure didn't look so happy about it. He was still looking at me. Then he spoke.

"Chris, I think I might be able to help the girls identify these two victims."

"OK." I paused for more, but he had nothing to add.

"Anyway, we will see what we see," he said eventually.

I was not going to get any further information about the murder victims.

"I bought some coffee if you'd like some," he added by way of consolation.

We sat together in the front of Walker's police truck, sharing the coffee he had bought in his thermos. Very kind, I thought. But there was no further chat about the unidentified bodies in the cave and nothing more about what he might know or might not know.

We waited for another two hours till the call came from Carole.

"All done," she shouted from down below in a voice that would have woken the corpses if they had a bit more flesh left on their bones. "Beam me the fuck out of here, Scotty."

"And me the fuck, too," shouted Glenda.

Then Walker and I, with the Jarrajarra emergency team, slowly and carefully moved into action.

Greg and I worked down below in the cave. The ladies worked upstairs with Scotty on the winch.

First, we extracted the two separate sets of skeletal remains.

Carole and Glenda had arranged the rotted corpses of the two murder victims onto two separate stretchers. They were more concerned with keeping the remains of the victims separate than they were with keeping them in their normal human formation.

Above ground, Scotty Farrell waited at the winch till we were ready to hoist. We secured the first stretcher to the hoisting wire.

We called Scotty to apply a bit of pressure to raise the stretcher, lifting it just off the floor of the cave. He did that, and the two of us in the cave made sure it was all horizontal and set to go.

"OK, Scotty, slowly, mate, slowly," said Glenda.

"Don't you blokes drop my skeletons," shouted Carole.

"Helpful, Carole," shouted Greg Farrell in reply.

We had nothing to worry about with Scotty in charge of the heavy machinery. After a short while, both collections of murder victims were in the back of the Crime Services van, along with several bags of various items the girls had gathered.

As the various crew members packed up to say goodbye, I knocked up a next-to-useless fence of police tape around the hole in the ground that had led us all to the cave floor.

While remaining careful not to fall into the hole myself, I watched Sergeant Walker talking to Carole. He was handing her a folder.

As I was finishing my makeshift fence, Walker got back in his car and drove off, back to Wodonga, I presumed. The forensic ladies finished packing and stood by their van as I walked back to my truck.

Two remaining vehicles, sitting in a cow paddock, lit by a half-moon and the headlights of the Crime Services van. Strange times and weird places my police career has taken me.

"He's a cold fish, that Walker," said Carole.

"Cold but good," I said. "What was that stuff he handed you."

"Can't tell you. It is highly confidential," said Carole. "My eyes-only Constable, sorry."

"It's two names," said Glenda. "Well, one name for two bodies. He wants us to check the DNA to see if it is these blokes, both named Phillip Savage. Senior and Junior."

"Their DNA should be in the crime service database, he said."

"What happened to highly confidential?" I asked.

"We like to think of you as one of the girls," said Carole.

"If they have been dead for around ten years, they can't be on the database, can they?" asked Glenda.

"Doesn't Victorian law say suspect DNA cannot be retained without a court order," I offered my limited knowledge of the law. "Those orders only apply for twelve months at a time."

"He said to check the database," said Carole, "So, being a dutiful police person, I'll check. Far be it from me to ignore a Senior Sergeant's request."

"Chris is right," said Glenda, checking the law on her mobile Google like a conscientious cop should always do. "If it is still there, then someone must have been re-applying for retention every couple of years at least."

"Anyway," said Glenda, "we won't need DNA. This folder has dental records for both of them. So we can sort that out pretty quickly."

Glenda pulled a sheet out of the folder Walker had given her. It showed four sets of teeth. The teeth of two people, top and bottom.

Carole started flicking through photographs on her crime scene camera. "Here we go," she said.

They stood side by side, Glenda holding the sheet of paper beside the viewer on Carole's camera.

"Point your torch," Glenda said to me. So I pointed my torch at Glenda.

"At the paper, dickhead," she said.

They flicked through various pictures till they found something they liked.

"That gap on the left side bottom," said Glenda.

"Yeah," said Carole, as she flicked back and forth between pictures of bottom teeth. "Yeah," she said again with a confirmational tone of voice.

"Yeah, what?" I asked.

“Yeah, well, it is hard to say, Killer,” said Glenda, “we are looking at a front view of their teeth on the camera. But, on the paper sheet is a picture of their dental moulds, a sort of bird's eye view of the teeth and mouth layouts. Top and bottom.”

“So, it is bloody hard to match here, standing in a paddock, freezing my arse off,” said Carole. “We can't be positive until we make similar moulds from our corpses.”

“Very hard,” said Glenda. “Extremely hard.”

Neither had taken their eyes off the vision of teeth before them.

“Well, what about that gap on the left side bottom,” I said, as though I had found it myself.

“Yeah,” repeated Carole, as though I already knew what she was trying to say.

“I reckon they match,” said Glenda, squinting in the darkness.

“Well, not a court-ready opinion yet,” said Carole,” “and miles short of a DNA match.”

“But,” said Glenda, “it could be them. I'd reckon it definitely could be them.”

“Yep, definitely maybe,” said Carole, “Phillip Savage, Senior and Junior.”

“And Walker knows who they are,” said Glenda. “Incredible.”

“Bugger me,” I said.

What I didn't say is that I knew who they were myself. I had never met them while they were alive, and it was probably lucky for them that I hadn't.

But I had met them now, and their luck had run out.

“Home time, I reckon,” said Carole.

We shared exaggerated hugs and air kisses, a ritual that got louder and raunchier every time we performed our farewells.

We all drove out of the paddock. I was last to leave, so I locked the gate and read the sign again.

“Private Property! Keep Out! Especially Fucking Duck Hunters!”

If only Ralph, the Duck Hunter, had read the label.

Tuesday, May 24, 2022

Jarrajarra.

This morning was a treat. My partner Wendy came along on my regular 5.00 AM run. Starting the day with early exercise was a habit I picked up as a kid. For someone inclined to run, Jarrajarra was paradise. We ran out along the river road, through the caravan park, then onto a bush track that ran east, along the Murray River, toward the Eastern Ranges. It was perfect.

When we got to where we were going, we checked out the view, took a quick dip in the freezing river, climbed out, dried off and ran home.

"Bloody hell, that was great," said Wendy as we finished. "Just what I needed." Wendy was as addicted to exercise as I was. She'd been working such long hours lately she had been missing out.

By the time we made it home, we had run and swum for ninety minutes. We'd worked up a healthy sweat. We had time to share some love and affection and a shower before Wendy headed off to work at the Jarrajarra Bush Nursing Centre, where she was Chief Nurse and boss of all things medical.

"See you tonight if we're lucky, Soldier," she had said as she left, smiling. We had met in the Army. Wendy had been my nurse after I was wounded in Afghanistan. We had been together ever since, jobs permitting.

I was a cop, and she was the Chief Nurse and Administrator at the Jarrajarra Bush Nursing Centre.

Our nights together weren't always guaranteed. I was lucky to love someone who understood my weird hours. I was luckier still that she loved me back.

I was walking from my house to the station when my phone rang.

"You have to come and see this," said Barney.

"Is it about the dead bodies?" I asked. "Has the report come in about the murder victims?"

"Yes and no, it is about the duck hunters. No report about the other two."

"What is it?" I was puzzled.

"Just come and see," said Barney. "You are going to love it."

Jarrajarra Police Station.

"Ducks 4 – Humans 0".

So said the headline on the front page of the Jarrajarra Bugle, the town's new digital newspaper, published on the internet by Saxon Tyson-Howard, the town's leading and only publisher, a former graffiti vandal and leading layabout.

After tiring of graffiti, tagging and endless war games on his computer, Saxon had taken a small investment from his grandfather and turned it into Jarrajarra's very first newspaper. Strictly speaking, it wasn't a newspaper as no actual paper was involved; the Bugle was totally online.

It was a few minutes after 8:30 AM, and I was sipping coffee at the front desk, reading the Bugle over the shoulder of my police admin assistant, Barney Trail. We were at Barney's desk on Barney's computer, and he was hitting the buttons. My lack of speed on a keyboard was more than Barney could bear, so he always did the driving.

Tuesday was publication day for the weekly edition of the Bugle. So, this was our Tuesday morning ritual. Reading the town gossip, taking it all in with coffee and sometimes cakes, crime permitting.

The website masthead said 'The Jarrajarra Bugle' in a very elaborate, attractive script.

Saxon Tyson-Howard had always possessed a ton of creative talent, and within the last two years, he'd turned himself around, applying that talent to something almost worthwhile.

The Bugle was good, often very good, though it had a slight tendency to sensationalize the headings and could be eccentric in its choice of coverage.

The Bugle never had bylines because Saxon wrote almost everything. Everything except the sports reports. These were usually submitted by the mothers of the team's best players. This meant that the synchronized swimming club often got a double-page spread with photos, even though the club only had three members.

Meanwhile, the footy report often only had the scores. Everyone in town followed the footy team, but no one could be bothered writing an essay; usually, they had all seen the game.

Saxon argued that the choice of coverage was consumer-driven, one of the many corporate buzzwords that had crept into his speech since he'd handed in his tagging spray cans and taken up the pen that was mightier than the sword, or paint tin in Saxon's case.

Saxon's grandfather had told Saxon the secret of community newspapers; you had to photograph at least one member of every family at least once a fortnight, and you had to caption the photos with the names of everyone in the pictures. So Saxon could turn up at a netball match and not take a shot of the action, but he'd never miss any of the team line-ups.

A strange theory, but it worked. What with photos of nearly everyone in town every week, the little bits of gossip, plus Saxon's flair for layout, the Bugle was surviving. People kept coming back for more, including Barney and me.

It was a lovely small-town miracle. With the old Saxon, it couldn't possibly have lasted. With the new Saxon, the sky was the limit.

I called the Bugle front desk. Saxon answered immediately.

"Jarrajarra Bugle, Saxon speaking."

"Mate, you're facts are wrong."

"Wrong?"

"Yes. You said, 'Ducks 4 Humans 0'. In fact, it was 'Ducks 4 Humans 5', so much for being a smart-arse Saxon. You've used your newspaper to trivialise the death of five beautiful Blue-winged Shovelers, all of them shot illegally."

"Five? Can I quote you on that, Chris? Police verification drives engagement."

"No, you can't quote me. You know my rules on quoting me, on the record. You cannot quote me on any subject ever, not for any reason from now until infinity."

"That is a wholly negative thought structure, Chris."

"That's right. Anyway, it is irrelevant. I am calling your grandfather to get him to withdraw his funding and shut you down."

"I don't need his funding, Chris. We are profit-positive here."

Hearing him say 'we' did not feel good. He had recently acquired a new colleague, his first and only staff member.

"Well, I will call your grandad and get him to demand you pay back the seed money."

"Establishment debt has been refunded, Chris, with interest."

Shit.

"What's with all the business-speak?" I asked. "You're not some mogul, mate. You're a barely reformed graffiti spray painter. You'd still be in youth detention if I charged you for all your artwork."

"It's my calling, Chris. Modern journalism is important, and it has found me."

Saxon? A calling? Bugger me.

"Saxon," I said. "Listen, being a doctor, that's a calling. You're a reformed graffiti artist with a small-town website. That's a side hustle, mate. It's not a calling."

I ended the call before I was really angry. I had always tried to mentor Saxon, and now he'd gone legitimate. He used to be such fun when he was a vandal. Now, he was acting like another wannabe, Rupert Murdo-Zucker-Musk.

"Stuff him and his calling," I said loud enough for Barney to try and make it all better.

"You're only angry at Saxon because Joanne Farrell has gone to work with him," said Barney, the voice of eternal wisdom.

"Well, yeah." No point denying it.

"You'll be sorry if he tells Joanne you shouted," said Barney.

"I didn't shout," I shouted.

Joanne Farrell was our former part-time Police Administrative Assistant who had only recently gone to work for Saxon as his Director of Sales and Marketing, quite a title for a two-person business. The Bugle's advertising sales appeared to be booming, and, by all accounts, Joanne loved her new job. She would not be coming back to the boring old cop shop. Not ever.

My phone rang. It was Joanne.

"Chris, you have got to stop bullying Saxon."

"Bullying?"

"Yes, bullying. I know you think you are joking, but Saxon is very sensitive, and he thinks you are serious. He wants to report you to HR."

"You don't have any HR."

"Well, we do. That's me, but not our HR, Chris, your HR."

"Saxon is going to report me to the police?"

"Not yet. I managed to talk him out of it."

“Jo, I was only,” only what? Joking? How many bullies had I heard say that?

“OK,” I said, “no more bullying.”

“Promise?”

“Yes, I promise.”

“Hi, Jo,” shouted Barney.

“Hi, Barney,” she shouted back.

“Chris, Was that true about the five Blue Winged Shovelers?”

“Yes.”

“And they are ducks, right?”

“Yes, they're harmless little ducks. Protected species. Shot to death by vicious unlicensed hunters with unlicensed rifles.”

“OK, good colour. I like that description. Vicious, unlicensed.” She was typing as we spoke. “Right. Are you looking at the front page of the Bugle now?”

“Yes, 'Ducks 4 – Humans 0'.”

“OK,” said Joanne. “Hit refresh on that.”

I refreshed my screen, and there it was corrected.

“Ducks 4 – Humans 5”. Plus, there was a new 'colour' paragraph describing the poor dead shovelers.

“There you go,” she said. “See the power of the press and the police when we all work together. Do you see what we can achieve?”

“Aren't journalists supposed to ask if I am on the record?”

“I'm not a journalist, Chris, plus I didn't name you. I said police sources.”

“Well, mate, that's not exactly a huge cover in a one-cop shop.”

“That's true, I suppose. Anyway, gotta scoot. Bye, Chris. Bye, Barney.” she said.

“Bye Jo,” Barney and I harmonized as she hung up on the call.

Somehow Joanne's good-bye to Barney seemed friendlier than mine, or was I being over-sensitive, like Saxon?

“She's been tainted by Saxon,” I said to Barney.

Tuesday, June 7, 2022

Jarrajarra.

A couple of weeks had passed, and still no further news on the dead bodies we'd found under the duck hunters.

"Jarrajarra Police, Barney Trail speaking. How may I help you?" Barney always said his welcome and introduction faster than the human tongue was meant to travel.

He listened, and then he looked confused.

"Hello, is that you, Wally?" There was only one Wally in Jarrajarra, and our Wally was unique.

Barney handed me the phone, "I think he wants you."

I took the phone and listened. I heard the faintest of whispers. "Chrissy, Chrissy, come quick, mate."

"I am on my way, Wal. You're at the Park, right?"

"Hurry, Chris," he whimpered.

"Stay right there, Wal." I handed the phone to Barney.

"Keep him talking if you can," I said to Barney, "make sure he is at the Park. If he is somewhere else, better call me."

I sprinted for the door.

"Call Jack Farrell. Get the ambulance." I shouted back to Barney, and then I was gone.

Strange to get a call from Wally Mellish right at that moment. After my coffee and the co-reading of the Bugle with Barney, I had intended to visit the Jarrajarra Caravan Park for an official word with Wally regarding the dead duck hunters and the dangerous hole we found in his paddock down the road.

As well as owning bits of land about the place, Wally Mellish was the owner and concierge of the caravan park, Jarrajarra's number one tourist destination.

Wally was somewhere in his sixties, always dressed in a work shirt, shorts and steel-tipped work boots that always looked far too big for his skinny legs to lift.

He didn't lift his feet often, spending most of his time seated behind the reception desk in the front office, the ancient radio blaring either football or racing. If a race was on and Wally had a bet on the outcome, then a new arrival at the park would have to wait their turn till the horse race was decided.

For all his apparent indifference to conventional park management, Wally had created a small paradise here beside the Murray river. The place was a natural beauty with swimming in summer and fishing in winter.

Wally never tried to tame his flora and fauna. If trees and grass wanted to grow, he let them. If flowers appeared at random, then that's where they remained. If a snake or kangaroo wandered in or about your van, then so be it. The wildlife wandered where they pleased.

Wally was a man of nature, and he let nature take its course. The park was a small botanical wonder of natural bush wrapped around narrow winding gravel tracks to nicely separated camping spots. It was incredibly beautiful, and it was Wally's domain.

Jarrajarra Caravan Park.

Two minutes after I pulled out from the police station, I skidded into the caravan car park, cop lights flashing, siren wailing, and there he was, flat on his back, halfway out the reception area's front door. He'd collapsed on the exit, his body was out the door, and his legs were still inside. The open door was jammed around thigh level.

It was May, and it was cold, so Wal was wearing his vintage Kathmandu puffer jacket, his one concession to the weather. The jacket was covered in strips of gaffer tape, applied to cover the many rips and tears gathered over the years. The purpose of the tape was to retain the down within the jacket, to maintain what little puff was left in the puffer.

I hurried to his side and was pleased to find him still alive. Alive but groaning softly, clearly in a lot of pain. Wally's phone had fallen beside him. I could hear Barney trying to rouse some response from our friend.

"Wally, speak to me," said Barney through Wally's phone.

"It's OK, Barney," I spoke into the phone. "Ambulance is here."

As I closed the call on Barney, the ambulance from Jarrajarra Bush Nursing Centre screamed into the park. With a deft twist of the wheel by Jody Taggert, the driver, the ambulance was quickly parked with its rear doors only a metre or so from where I knelt beside Barney.

Jack Farrell and Jody were beside Wally in an instant.

Whatever they needed to do, they did quickly. Within two minutes, Wally was stretchered, put in the ambulance, and on his way back to the Nursing Centre. Naturally, I followed; Wally's misery gave me a valid excuse to visit my girlfriend during working hours.

Jarrajarra Bush Nursing Centre.

"Wally, mate, what's going on?" Nurse Practitioner Wendy Atcheson was leaning over Wally, still strapped to the ambulance stretcher, wheels extended.

"I am fucked, mate, totally and utterly fucked," he whimpered, barely audible.

"Let's see what we can find in there, Wally. This won't take long."

Wally was wheeled into the ultra-sound room. First, he was given a blood test, which he survived bravely, then the ultrasound, which was a process normally reserved for pregnant women, often to determine the gender of the unborn, and here was our Wally, not pregnant, no doubt at all considering his gender, possibly the first male customer of the pregnancy-checking machine, ready for his close-up.

So we all saw Wally's hairy belly as it was investigated sonically. I was still in the room. No one had kicked me out yet. I knew Wally wanted me there, and Wendy didn't object, so I stayed.

I was so confident I ventured to ask tenderly, "Can you tell if it is a boy or a girl." Wally laughed a tiny bit, and then he groaned a lot. Wendy's look told me to shut up, so I did.

* * *

Fifteen minutes later, Wally and I were waiting in a wardroom for the official verdict. He had been doped up on painkillers and looked battered but better.

I had already guessed that Wendy knew what she was looking for with the ultra-sound. When she walked into Wally's room, I could tell she had found his problem.

"OK, Wal," said Wendy, "The Doctor from Wodonga visits tomorrow. You need to see him to get the news officially, but if you want, I can tell you what's happening right now. OK?"

"Fuck the doctors, Wendy love. You can tell me." He sounded better, floating on the magic juice.

"OK, Wally, you have hit the double, mate. You've got gallstones, which are bad enough, but you also have Pancreatitis, and that, mate, is as serious as a heart attack."

"Fuck me, love. It's the most painful arsehole of a thing I have ever experienced in my life. Excuse me French."

"No problem," Wendy was a former army nurse. She had seen and heard a lot worse than Wally's way with words.

"So," Wendy continued. "First, the bad news, you are off the grog, mate, for life. Sorry."

"For fucking life? I can't believe it, no way."

Wally looked so miserable; he was like another person. His spark had deserted him in a moment.

"Wendy, mate, are there some pills I can take? I'd even consider an injection. Mate, you can fix this."

"Wally love, there is another name for pancreatitis. It is often called alcoholic's poisoning."

"Bullshit," said Wally. "Alcoholic poisoning? I hardly drink at all."

"That's not exactly true, Wal," I interjected. "You drink a lot, mate." Not that he was a bad drunk.

"Whose side are you on?" he said to me. "Trust you to turn against me in a crisis."

"Wally, listen," said Wendy quite firmly, "sudden attacks of pancreatitis are fatal in fifty per cent of cases. I know you understand the odds. I know you know what fifty per cent means."

"One in two," he answered with a pout.

"Yes, one in two, and you have just survived one. Your next one will be your last. So, mate, whether you drink alcohol or not, you are off it for life. Whether you choose to give it up or not, your next drink will be your last."

"Fuck me, hooray," said Wally in resigned despair.

"The other bad news is you will have to stay here for a few days while we get your inflammation down and your diet right."

"Stay here, holy Jesus Wendy, who will run the park?"

"Chris will work that out, Wal. Now, just so you know, when you see the doctor tomorrow, he is going to tell you that you need to have that gallbladder out. So, settle in and do what you're told, and in the fullness of time, all will be well."

Wendy said that in a tone I had seen in the army. She had made Staff Sergeants shrink and made Generals wither. Poor Wal would do as he was told, and eventually, he would be well. I had seen her miracles first-hand.

Then my phone rang. It was Barney. He knew where I was, but he was interrupting anyway; this could not be good.

"How's Wally?" asked Barney.

"He will be right," I said. "Pancreatitis and gallstones."

"Ouch," said Barney, "Alcoholic poisoning, off the grog."

Barney knew drinkers and their problems.

"I'm sorry, Chris," said Barney. "We have a real crime here. I have just received an email from Wodonga Station."

Barney read the email.

"Three escapees from Henderson Prison, possibly heading our way."

"Why our way?"

"One of the names is Jason Mellish."

"Oh," I said.

"Oh indeed," said Barney.

I had to think about the word Prison. "Henderson is not a prison anymore, is it?" I asked Barney. "I think it's a minimum-security Correctional Centre."

"I believe so," said Barney. "Let me check?" Barney searched the internet, found the answer and read aloud. "The Henderson Correctional Centre is a minimum-security prison in Henderson, Victoria, Australia. It was opened in January 2005 to replace the now-closed HM Prison Henderson."

"So, he didn't escape. He probably just walked out," I said.

"Maybe didn't come home to the Centre after his day job," offered Barney.

"He only had a few months to go. Why the hell would he escape with only a short time to serve?"

"It says here," Barney was back on the email, "the two other escapees were a fellow named Randall Thorburn and another Carl Agnew."

"Oh shit," I said, "I would say they are most definitely heading here, Barn."

"So, you know some of these people?"

"Oh yes, you could say that. I know Randall Thorburn. I shot his brother, remember? Don't know the other bloke."

"Oh my goodness," said Barney, "that Randall Thornburn."

This will be fun, I thought, like old times, Randy and Jason and some other like-minded maniac. I was pretty sure they would have a fourth person along for the revenge ride.

I had drifted into that nether world that people visit when they are on a mobile phone. I had forgotten where I was. Finally, my eyes returned to the real world, where I noticed Wendy and Wally both staring at me.

The volume on my phone was too high. They'd heard the lot.

"Oh Jason, Jason, Jason," said Wally. "Fuck me sideways."

Jason Mellish was Wally's wayward son. Though 'son' was a term used loosely in the extended Mellish clan. As I understood it, Jason was, in fact, the son of Wally's brother and Wally's wife. A behind-the-scenes bit of hanky-panky left Wally to raise Jason as his own. Wally's wife was Jason's Mum, but his real dad was his uncle. A bit of deep country parental spaghetti.

"Oh, Barney," I remembered, "could you organize someone to run the caravan park for a week? Wally is indisposed."

"Will do," said Barney, and we all knew it would be done.

Jarrajarra Town Hall, Conference Room.

"The three men walked out of the Henderson Correctional Centre at 11.00 PM last night."

The Sarge was speaking to a group of ten police, including myself, in the conference room of the Jarrajarra Town Hall.

It was a meeting, and I hated meetings. The Sarge only invited me when it was essential to my job. This meeting was about as essential as I could imagine, three bad men heading our way, so here I was, in attendance.

Bloody meetings.

The cops in the room were mostly from Wodonga Station, with a few extras roped in from further afield.

"We have three escapees," continued Sarge, speaking without notes, "two are doing their time for crimes of violence, and the third looks like a tag-along."

“So, gentlemen and ladies, we have three crooks on the loose. We not only have to do something, but we also have to be seen to be doing something.”

Ten cops was a good number for being seen. Maybe not so good for protecting the town of Jarrajarra from the two wild men we were anticipating. The town was a little dot in a region of around ten thousand square miles. More cops would be better, but police resources were always limited, even when the 'optics' required uniforms on the street.

Ten cops it was.

The Sarge had called the meeting here in Jarrajarra because he knew two of the escapees as well as I did. We were both certain they would be heading here.

“The escapees' names are Jason Mellish, Randall Thorburn and Carl Agnew,” continued the Sarge. “Mellish and Thorburn have a violent history in this region.”

Jason Mellish had been a serial pest in the Jarrajarra region since his birth about thirty annoying years ago. He was supposed to be in prison, serving time for a long list of charges. The top effort on that list was assault with a deadly weapon on the policeman sitting next to me, Constable Tim Silver.

Jason Mellish had stomped our own Constable Tim on the head with Jason's own size-twelve-steel-capped working boot and put Tim in hospital with a fracture of the skull.

Randall Thorburn was a member of a now-defunct bikie gang who, with several of his mates, had attempted to murder the Sarge and me at the Mitta Mitta car park back in 2018.

Randall was meant to be firing at the Sarge and me with a Russian model MK-47 machine gun. Fortunately for us, the usually reliable machine gun jammed at the relevant time. Equally fortunate for us, Randall did not have the skill or wit to unjam his weapon.

Both Mellish and Thorburn had ended up in jail, or so I thought, but here they were, recently resident in a regional correctional centre, barely a step below a country motel, now out and about on the loose, ready, it seemed, to fight another day.

Look out, Jarrajarra, here they come.

Then the news got even worse.

“Both Mellish and Thorburn,” continued the Sarge, “have received recent visits, at Henderson, from a woman named Jennifer McLain, a former associate of Thorburn and wife of the now deceased murderer AJ Davies. I am sure we all remember Davies from 2018."

AJ Davies was an ex-hit man for the New South Wales version of the mafia, a former police informer, rapist, drug trafficker and stand-over man. If it was evil and profitable, Davies was up for it. Davies had been murdered on my patch in 2018, and not long after that, Jen McLain had come to town in company with Randall and others to avenge his death.

Jennifer McLain was the wife of AJ Davies. Yes, Davies had a wife. It begged the question, 'what did she see in him'? Once you met Jen McLain, you realized it was like-loving-like.

Theirs was a love gone wrong, spectacularly wrong. The 2018 revenge ride had ended up on the Mitta Mitta trail south of Jarrajarra with a mess of dead bikies. In fact, by the end of that spectacularly bad day, there had been bodies everywhere, including local citizens and police, but mostly bikies, a few of whom I had killed.

The Sarge's voice continued as I reminisced.

"We have some CCTV footage that shows the three men walking out of the centre and through the car park towards some bush. Not long after, we have footage of a 2012 Toyota RAV, colour dark green, driven by the woman, McLain. This footage comes from a petrol station on the road east of Henderson, heading out of town, actually, heading in the direction of Jarrajarra."

"McLain was doing the driving, and she also did the petrol. From the garage camera, we can see three men in the car. We only get a clear shot of the man in the back passenger seat, driver side, and that is clearly Jason Mellish, not making any effort to disguise himself."

"Sergeant, wasn't this Mellish bloke the one who beat up Timmy and Chris over here?"

It was a smart-arse question from a smart-arse Senior Constable named Ralph Davey. My second Ralph in two days. Both dickheads. This Ralph couldn't fight his way out of a wet paper bag and spent most of his police career avoiding that necessity. Despite his lack of courage, nothing ever seemed to stop him from mouthing off at other people's expense.

One of his mates laughed a tiny bit, but it was strained. Personally, I wouldn't bother reacting to a dickhead like Davey. Sarge couldn't stand sarcasm and would shut him down soon enough. But, I should have remembered Constable Tim.

"You weren't there, Davey," said Tim, "Mellish king hit me from behind and then stomped on my head while I was down. He put me in hospital with a fractured skull, you prick. Come outside. I'll show you what he did."

Tim! No! No! Never react, mate. Never, I could hear my Nan's voice telling me as a kid, never show them they got to you, a wise word from the Queen of stoic resistance.

"Woohoo," said Davey, laughing louder, his eyes scouting the room, looking for eye contact with anyone who would support him. He was like a schoolyard bully, talking up a fight for someone else to finish. It was wasted. The faint laugh he had gathered at first had withered to nothing. Everyone liked Tim, and, as a group, the Wodonga cops were better than this. Davey was an outlier.

"That's enough, Senior Constable Davey," said Sarge over the top of the banter. "In fact, Senior Constable, I will put you in charge of vehicle inspections on the Jarrajarra South Road. You can check all vehicles passing there, in and out of Jarrajarra, for the presence of our absconders."

The room was silent. Davey had scored an own goal, it was a shit job on a minor road, and he would be out there, on his own, hours at a time between vehicles with next to nothing to do.

"Chris will show you the best point to set up. Take Constable Thompson with you," said Sarge to Davey.

There was an audible groan from the front row. A junior policewoman, Constable Joyce Thompson, was very new to the force. I didn't know her, but I gathered she was the Constable Thompson that the Sarge had just lumped with Davey.

Did Davey bully the recruits like he tried to bully everyone else? I made a note to drive by and check on the pair sometime later today. I would make sure Constable Thompson was alright on a long shift with Senior Constable Arsehole.

"The photos, Sarge?" suggested someone in the front row. The Sarge, like me, was a bit of a troglodyte with technical matters. He had a PowerPoint thing all set up that he had forgotten to show.

"Yes, yes, the photographs, indeed."

The Sarge fiddled with a hand-held device for a moment, and then a light came on, projecting onto the wall behind him. He stepped to the side to give us an unobstructed view of the light on the wall. It was a wall, not a cinema screen, but it would do.

Sadly, the light revealed nothing. Sarge had managed to turn on the projector they had bought from Wodonga, and that was about as much as he managed with the PowerPoint demo.

"Bloody thing," he said as he fiddled some more with the device in his hand. Eventually, three mug shots came into view, totally out of focus. One of the Wodonga coppers stepped forward and took control of the controller.

"Thank you, Gregory," said the Sarge, "thank you." I doubt the Sarge could have been more relieved if we had just arrested the escapees.

As the young cop fiddled and pointed with a sense of purpose, the headshots came into focus on the Town Hall wall.

"Right," said Sarge, "here we go."

We all sat and looked at two very rough heads, soaking them in. I knew those heads well. The third, Carl Agnew, looked rather non-descript, average.

"OK then, now the bloke on your left is Randall Thorburn, the chap in the middle is Carl Agnew, and on the right is Jason Mellish."

"Ugly buggers," chimed in Senior Constable Davey, as always, saying nothing as loudly as he could.

"Unfortunately, we don't have any photographs of the alleged female accomplice. Chris, have you got anything you can add here?" asked the Sarge.

"Well, Sarge," I responded, "With Mellish and Thorburn, what the photos don't show is how big they are. They were both gym junkies when I knew them, both on steroids and also on speed, both are around six foot three or bigger, and both of them are two-forty pounds plus, mostly muscle. They are big, and Mellish, in particular, is mean. So, be careful how you approach."

"Precisely," said Sarge, "be extremely careful how you approach. Remember, these two were in for aggravated assault, amongst other charges. Thorburn was doing eight years, and Mellish was on the back end of three, which begs the question, why didn't he wait a month and walk free."

"Sarge," I said, "If the woman involved is, in fact, Jen McLain, she could be involved with both men, ah, romantically."

"He's absconded for a three-way," said Davey, loud as usual.

"For once in his life," I responded, "Senior Constable Davey may be correct. Jen McLain is a very attractive woman, and lust may be one of the motivating factors in this instance."

That got a genuine laugh from the meeting, the Sarge included.

"For identification purposes," I continued, "McLain is around 180 centimetres, five foot ten say, she is a Maori, and she has a tattooed sleeve on her left arm, from shoulder to wrist. It is a Ta Moko, which only a real Maori can wear, as opposed to a Kirituhi, which anyone can wear. I think you will know when you see it. I would approach her like the others, with extreme care."

"Thank you, Chris," said the Sarge.

From there, we finished up with discussions of who would go where and who would do what. The Sarge was going to be resident, for a while, in Jarrajarra, so I would lose my office to the boss, and I'd be sharing the front desk with Barney.

We were heading for the door when the Sarge spoke one last time.

"Now, one last thing, you all know Chris, this is his town, and these are his people we are protecting, so I think it is in everyone's best interest to listen to Chris's opinion if and when he offers it. That includes you, Senior Constable Davey."

A nice little whack for Constable Arsehole to close the meeting.

The lockdown had begun.

The Jarrajarra region was way too large to go hunting for our escapees, presuming they were here. Thousands of square miles, mostly uninhabited, mostly bush, a lot of it impenetrable. There were a few small sections devoted to beef cattle and a couple of dairy farms, but a lot of mountains with a lot of thick ugly scrub. So many places to hide, hard to penetrate, and almost impossible to search.

The basic plan was to keep an eye on the roads and hope to catch our three bad guys and one bad girl in transit. We also had the use of a licensed drone operator, who had about as much chance of stumbling on them as the rest of us. But never say no to an offer of help.

Jarrajarra South Road.

At the end of the meeting, I had pointed Senior Constable Davey and Constable Joyce Thompson to a spot on the Jarrajarra South Road about ten kilometres out of town.

Late that night, approaching midnight, after I had driven by and checked out all the other road stops we had established, I drove out to Davey's location to check on the well-being of the rookie, Constable Thompson.

Of course, Davey hadn't set up where I told him to. That would be too easy. He had gone about five kilometres further south than the GPS point I gave him. His chosen position was beyond several side access roads permitting an escapee to drive in or out of Jarrajarra without passing him. That was not the plan at all.

Davey was probably too stupid to translate a GPS point into an actual position on a map. Alternatively, he was just too arrogant to listen to the advice of someone who might know a tad more than him about the town and its surrounding roads.

Fuckwit was the word that came to mind. I didn’t say it out loud. I’d promised Wendy I’d stop swearing.

I pulled up in my truck, about twenty metres behind the patrol car containing Davey and Thompson. They were facing away from the town, so a fugitive seeking to enter Jarrajarra would be heading toward them. That was about the only reasonable decision he had made.

They had also laid out traffic cones.

Luminous-plastic traffic cones, just as you would for a drunk testing setup, all cones guiding you towards a waiting officer who would, typically, offer the driver an opportunity to do a breath test, looking for signs of alcohol consumption.

The traffic cones were not such a brilliant idea. They might work for drunks, and, knowing Jason Mellish, he most likely would be drunk or souped up on something. I just didn't see it working for your desperate prison escapee, especially one like Jason, who was not known for recognizing other people's boundaries. It wouldn't matter to Jason how nicely those small plastic cones were aligned.

By the time I arrived, Davey and Thompson had been at their post for several hours. They were sitting in their police van, facing the empty road ahead of them. I was not surprised that the Jarrajarra South Road was empty. It went nowhere and came from nowhere. It just headed south through farmland and bush till it reached a corner of the

Victorian Alps, where it just stopped. To go anywhere important, you really needed to cut east or west away from this road.

I could imagine the two police officers were bored out of their minds.

Their flashing cop lights were about the only interesting thing on the empty road.

I switched off my vehicle and then turned on my own overhead lights to add some glitter to the flashing light show. I also turned on my bodycam, just to cover my arse in any argument with the fuckwit Davey.

The moment I had announced my arrival, Joyce Thompson emerged from the patrol car in front of me. She slammed the door, then shouted through the open window at Davey.

"You are a disgusting pig! You make me sick."

With that off her chest, Constable Thompson turned towards me and headed to my truck.

Interesting.

At that point, Davey emerged from the driver's side of his car. He had things he wished to say in response, in his usual loud voice.

"Can't you take a fucking joke? I thought you were a cop, not some sooky little teenage girl. Put your big girl pants on, for fuck's sake."

Constable Thompson kept walking in my direction, at which time Davey screamed his closing argument in her direction.

"You fucking princess."

One thing I'd learnt about big arguments in small country towns, you usually decide whose side you are on before you even know what they are arguing about.

I was with Constable Joyce Thompson in this one.

She jumped in my truck and slammed the door behind her.

"Pig of a man," she said, "I mean him, not you," in case I hadn't worked that out.

Now, if I were one of the fugitives on the run in the region, this would be a perfect time to try and bust the blockade on the Jarrajarra South Road. The blockade team seemed to have lost focus on the prison escapee capture process. I was pretty sure our three fugitives had not forgotten their side of things.

So, duty first.

"Constable Thompson," I said, "I am wondering how this is

helping the pursuit of our escapees. Did I miss a strategy session?"

She looked at me, suddenly embarrassed.

"Sorry, Chris," she said. She looked back at the car in front of us. Davey was still standing there like the complete idiot he was born to be.

"Sorry," she whispered again, followed by, "and call me Joyce, please."

"I'll go talk to Davey," I said. "You look out for our escapees. Can you do that, Joyce?"

"Yes," she said.

Before I went, my curiosity got the better of me. I had to ask. "What exactly did he say?"

"I can't even repeat it," she said. Angry.

"You should report him," I said, "give the Sarge a chance to get rid of him."

"Maybe I will," she said, and I hoped she would.

"And Joyce, a word of advice," I said, "as boring as it may be on a night like this, it is probably better to be outside of the vehicle in a roadblock. I don't see Jason Mellish pulling alongside and waiting for you to wind your window down to hand himself in. Just a thought."

Then, off I went to resume my friendly relations with our policeman of the moment, Senior Constable Davey.

As I exited my vehicle, Joyce came out on her side to assume a watching position on the road, like a proper cop on a traffic stop. On your feet, not your bum, was the way forward.

I was a few metres short of Davey's vehicle when I heard Joyce call from behind me.

"Incoming."

I turned to see what looked like a large truck coming from Jarrajarra, out of Jarrajarra, not into.

"Or outgoing, whatever," said Joyce, almost casually.

The truck was several hundred metres away from us, its full array of lights on high beam. Travelling fast.

Getting closer, but still travelling.

Not dipping the high beams.

Something about it was not right.

Could it be accelerating? Or was it an illusion? Maybe the dark and distance were playing tricks, maybe not.

I watched as it drew closer.

There is a point in your bog-standard police roadside stopper when you realize this one is not so standard.

You realize that the driver of the vehicle approaching you has no intention of stopping, not for you, not this time, not on this day.

Sound, speed, the vibe. Who knows what it is that gives you the message? When it's a car, it always gives you an adrenaline kick. When it's a truck as big as this one, that kick is like a mule.

"It's not stopping!" I shouted to my fellow police officers. "Get off the road! Now!"

I checked Joyce first. She was already moving around the front of my truck, getting off the road as ordered.

She jumped over the wide roadside drainage gully in a stride, landing safely on the grassy strip beyond the ditch.

She took a few more steps, getting herself fully out of harm's way.

"Go, girl," I thought,

I checked the truck. It was big and definitely aimed to go through us hard.

I checked the idiot Davey, and, of course, he hadn't moved, still on the road, on the driver's side of his car. He faced the oncoming truck, put his hand on his gun without drawing it, and then raised his other hand into the classic 'stop-I-am-a-policeman' salute.

Saluting a speeding truck, counting on the better judgement of someone like Jason Mellish. Jason's respect for the law matched my opinion of Constable Davey; it couldn't be worse,

The truck kept coming.

I looked at Davey. I took another fast look at the oncoming truck. Bloody hell, it was so big, a double trailer, maybe.

It was getting closer, louder and going faster.

"Get off the road," I shouted at Davey.

I ran to Davey, put myself on his inside and pushed him along the road for a few metres, then off the road.

He fell underneath me into the ditch, the idiot.

He whacked his head on the way down, heading face down toward the deep puddle at the base of the ditch. It was May, it was cold, and there had been weeks of rain. Davey landed with a splash. Big man, big mouth, big splash.

He lay there, not moving. I rolled him onto his side, his face clear of water,

I stood and looked back at the truck again.

Bigger, faster and closer still.

I had done enough for Davey and Joyce. Time to tend to my own safety.

I jumped over Davey and out of the ditch in my one-best stride. Davey was moving, groaning, like a pig in a trough of filth.

"Stay down," I shouted as loud as I could.

Another squint at the truck.

Was it my imagination? Did I really see the face of Jason Mellish peering at me from the passenger seat? It felt like one of those special Jason moments.

Closing fast.

Jason, me, a truck as a weapon, noise, violence.

Three people in the cabin.

Close enough now to verify it was Mellish, Thorburn and McLain. I couldn't see the other bloke, Agnew.

McLain driving. Jesus Christ.

Jen McLain was driving the double tandem monster.

For some reason, the interior light of the truck was on. Handy for me, but why?

Were they looking for something?

Mellish came up with a shotgun. Shit no.

He lifted the barrel toward his passenger-side window.

"Gun!" I shouted. "Get down, Joyce."

I could see her crouch further into the bush and shadows, out of my line of fire. Smart move.

I could see Jason laughing, happy and loaded. The shotgun barrel was out the window.

Sixty metres and closing.

It was too far for him to aim at me. With his barrel already out the window, he needed to be opposite me to shoot. Typical Jason, not quite functional but horrible in his intention.

I had my weapon out. I had no line of fire impediments. I put a shot out into the argument.

It was too far away for my skills, but it was a truck, and you have to try.

The bullet went through the truck windscreen, the correct line, but high.

I had been aiming at Jason.

Sorry, Wally.

I had hit the windscreen, not Jason.

The truck was still coming. Strong. Loud.

I fired again, twice. One sparked off the cabin roof. My second shot made another hole in the windscreen, but still, no hole in Jason. Damn.

I focused on Jason.

I might have been better off taking a shot at the driver, but I didn't. Call me a feminist.

It felt as though the truck was almost on top of our little encampment.

Thirty metres away.

This was my distance.

Me aiming at Jason.

Jason twisted and turned in his seat, trying to aim at me. Restricted by the truck window frame. Almost opposite our road stop.

Truck noise, dust flying, bloody hell, it was a double-decker cattle truck, huge, ugly and full of cattle.

I fired again.

At the same moment, the truck swerved.

My last shot left another hole in the windscreen. Exactly where I had aimed, but the truck had shifted left.

Damn it.

Still no bullet holes in Jason Mellish.

The truck horn blared.

I barely heard it. I had him now.

Dead centre.

Goodbye, Jason Mellish.

No court in the land will convict me for this.

Finger on the trigger. Ready, aim, damn.

The truck swerved again. McLain was driving it like a sports car. How?

This time, she moved her front left wheel onto the roadside gravel, stones, rocks and water flying everywhere.

She side-swiped the back of my own police truck, then right over it, then followed through into Davey's police van.

A double trailer, double-decker on each trailer.

Cattle? Shit, it was a cattle truck.

Bloody hell.

God knows how many cattle are on board. God knows the total weight of the thing.

It was no contest. My truck and Davey's van just evaporated in the collision. A violent rainbow of flying glass, roadside gravel and metal.

Large sections of the disintegrating vehicles flew sideways, mostly away from the truck.

The truck stampeding forward toward me, unchallenged.

Something hit me on my right side. Hard and heavy knocked the wind out of me. Hit me in the head, in the shoulder, on my side, everywhere at once and hard enough to lift me into the air.

I landed heavily on my arse, some metres further along from where I was struck.

The noise around me sounded like my head was in a metal bucket, like angry dogs screaming in a steel tunnel.

I struggle up to my knees, taking a breath, trying to work my way to my feet. I looked up.

The truck had stopped directly opposite me.

I felt I had missed something. What was it that hit me?

Where had I landed?

Whatever had hit me had not dislodged my gun. I still had it in my hand.

Yes, good, I still had my gun. In my left hand? That was strange.

There was no apprehending this animal. I was going to kill Jason Mellish and all his cohort if I could just stand up, just get to my feet.

Jason Mellish was right there, maybe five or six metres away. He had his shot.

The truck had stopped directly opposite me.

Jason looked me straight in the eye.

"Hello, Chrissy boy," he shouted above the sound of the truck engine, now idling. His voice and lips were in slow motion through the mayhem, through the foggy tin bucket that seemed to cloud my hearing.

I tried to raise my arm to a firing position. My right arm couldn't seem to get interested.

Why was I shooting left-handed?

It was slow going. I was covered in mud and shit from the soggy roadside, and whatever the hell had knocked me sideways.

Who's blood was that on my arm?

All I could see was the point of the shotgun barrel. Pointing directly at me. I was looking straight down the barrel centre.

Funny things come to mind in such strange times.

My Nan always loved that English crooner, 'Englebert Humperdinck', not my cup of tea personally, but Nan did love him. She had an old, long-playing record of his greatest hits, and I could tolerate it, for her sake, as it spun daily, ad infinitum, on our dinky little record player.

'Am I that easy to forget' had been the title of Nan's favourite amongst Engleburt's repertoire, closely followed by 'Please Release Me'.

Like poor old Engle, I had forgotten Senior Constable Ralph Davey. He was so easy to forget.

But suddenly, there he was, having emerged from his muddy ditch, standing now between me and the road.

Davey was standing between Jason and me, between me and the barrel of Jason's shotgun.

Davey wasn't looking at Jason Mellish. He was not looking at the truck. Instead, Senior Constable Ralph Davey was looking straight at me as though the truck and its passengers were no longer of any concern.

Looking at me.

Standing there, panicked, angry, hysterical. Between me and Jason and Jason's shotgun.

"Look at me!" shouted Davey, as if there was any possible way I couldn't look at him, standing right there in front of me, covered in his muddy ditch shit. His arms were raised in mucky anger.

"You fucking imbecile Taylor, you've ruined my fucking uniform!"

Did he really say that, or did I imagine it?

Did I say, "Get out of my way, you dumb bastard?" Maybe. I definitely thought it.

My slow-as-shit pistol had finally arrived at my line of fire on Jason, but this idiot, Davey, was now in the way.

Did Jason even see Davey? Covered, as he was, from his grovel in the ditch, painted head to toe with a week's worth of rain, mud and paddock run-off.

Just covered in shit, really.

There I was, up from my arse, on my knees, stunned by the flying debris of the destroyed police cars.

I was doing my best to discharge my weapon, but nothing worked between my brain and fingers.

Davey was still screaming at me.

"I had everything under control," he said. "You fucking idiot! Now, look!"

Jason fired his shotgun.

I have no doubt in my mind Jason was firing at me with the intention of killing me.

But, of course, he didn't hit me.

His shot went low. Most of it hit dead centre in the back of Davey's protective vest.

The upper circle of the pellet spread hit Davey above his vest and blew a two-inch hole through the base of his throat, right through the spine and out.

Oh, Dear.

I heard some of the shot-shadow hit the trees behind me. The few pellets that struck me had passed through Davey and were exhausted on arrival at my own vest.

Apart from the pellets, I was splattered in the bodily matter of my colleague.

My late ex-colleague.

I was alive and still an active shooter, struggling to engage but travelling on half-rat power. My ears were ringing.

But I was alive.

The 'alive' bit was the thing that annoyed the shit out of Jason Mellish.

"Fuck! Fuck! Hang on a bit, will you," I heard Jason shout. Was he asking me to wait, or was he talking to McLain, the driver? Who would ever know who he was asking?

The truck was stationary. Still, right there in front of me.

Jason had opened the truck door and swung himself to face me. He now had complete body freedom of movement and was cranking another round into his shotgun.

Davey, having pitched forward into the near wall of the ditch onto what was left of his face, was now out of my way.

I was ready and equipped to fire back at Jason. But, sadly, I was moving through a warm envelope of thick, hot soup. Willing but not able.

Jason lifted his ancient crank-loaded weapon to fire at me again.

I was moving like a slow, dripping treacle on a cold day. Just couldn't get the muscles twitching in time.

Fortunately for me, another player entered the arena.

Constable Joyce, God bless her, put a bullet into the truck door, another sparked off the side of the truck, and her third shot hit something fleshy, an audible squelch, a bloody spray and then a shout of "Fuck" from Jason.

Punches in bunches, that's the way. Well done, Joyce.

She kept firing. Perfect.

"Go, Joycey!"

Another loud scream from Jason, and he dropped his weapon. It hit the ground barrel up and fired itself back in the air, taking out part of the truck door and the wide side mirror. Forming another small rainbow of flying glass and destruction and noise.

Justin reached over with his right hand, slammed his door closed, and dived down, out of sight behind the truck door.

I think Joyce had hit the bastard. His left arm?

I finally managed to put a bullet toward his door, but God knows where that one went, maybe through the open window.

Constable Joyce kept firing, still behind the truck, passenger side, and out of my line.

Good shooting by Joyce.

I joined in again. Mentally, the fog had lifted partially.

My hands and fingers were working. At last!

Joyce was hitting the truck, but it was moving away.

I was struggling to see through the muck and gore. I wiped my face, clearing some of the mess around my eyes.

Red meaty gunk. Davey's spinal fluid?

I stood up. My legs were working.

The truck was moving away faster now.

Constable Joyce had moved up parallel to me. She was on the road; I was still on the grassy strip.

She was still firing at the moving truck.

God bless her.

I half-jumped, half-staggered over the ditch to stand beside her, not crossing our lines and not accidentally shooting each other.

She was a fighter and brave as hell.

We exhausted our ammunition into the rear of the fast-disappearing truck.

I heard no human screams, nothing telling us of a bullet strike on any escapees.

We did hear a plaintiff moo.

We had hit a cow.

There were so many in the back of the truck we might have hit a few.

We stood there and watched the cattle truck disappear into the night.

A final departing burst on the truck horn from our bragging enemies.

They had just killed a cop, a shithead but still, a cop.

Damn them.

Bloody Jason Mellish. He kept getting the better of me, mostly by accident. The last time we clashed, I ended unconscious, courtesy of Joanne Farrell, who had been trying to help me by knocking out Jase with a baseball bat. Unfortunately, on that occasion, my head got in the way of the swinging bat.

Now he had knocked me for six again with the flying remnants of a police car, and he wasn't even driving.

'Focus on what you are doing,' I thought to myself. I meant me, not Joyce. She was as focused as hell.

Joyce was on her hand-held calling in Code 9, the calling code for police on duty in urgent need of assistance. One of the few I remembered.

"Code nine, officer down," I heard her say through the weird fog surrounding my brain. She said other stuff. I heard other cops squawking back at her.

I took my mobile out of my pocket. It was still working. I called Barney, and he answered immediately.

"Barney," I said while looking at Joyce. "I am going to put Constable Joyce on. She will tell you everything. OK?"

"Chris, are you OK?" asked Barney.

I handed the phone to Joyce. "Tell Barney everything that just happened. He will know what to do and who to tell. I am just going to have a lie-down."

I really needed to rest my head.

She took the phone from my hand, probably surprised to be handed a private mobile phone when she already had a perfectly good walkie-talkie, but hey, my town, my rules. She started to recount the events of the last couple of minutes to Barney.

I looked at her for a moment. Not a scratch, no shakes, calm as can be. Some people are born for the job and never know until the job tells them they belong.

I patted her on the shoulder. She had just saved my life.

"Thanks, Joyce," it came out slurred. "You are a gun."

My head hurt like hell. My ears were still ringing. I might have groaned out loud.

I was sure I had not been shot. I was equally certain that something very weighty and fast from one of the smashed vehicles had hit me extremely hard.

I walked onto the grass, found a spot, wet but soft, and I lay down. I was not feeling good at all, struck by the remains of my own truck, was it?

"I need to lay down," I mentioned to myself, already lying down.

I was listening to Joyce file a good solid report to Barney, "Barney will know what to do." I mumbled, or maybe I just thought it. Then I passed out.

I dreamt of Englebert Humperdink again, and I realized, in my dream, that I had forgotten Senior Constable Whatshisname yet again.

"Dead as a doornail," I mumbled.

"They're on their way, Chris," I heard Joyce say through a cloud.

"Good old Barney," I whispered, "Barney will know what to do."

I heard the grass squelching beside me. Joyce was having a lie down as well.

Then I heard Constable Joyce retching, loud, strained heaving. Then came projectile vomiting into the grass somewhere nearby.

Splashing as it landed, then all again, on repeat.

"There, there, Joyce, you'll be right. Let it out, mate."

Did I say that, or did I just think it?

Jesus, my head hurt.

Senior Constable Davey's dead body was standing over me, looking down, with half a face. Hard to tell if he was smirking.

"You haven't heard the end of this, Taylor. I will be speaking to HR about you. My uniform is totally fucked because of you."

"Good to see you up and about," I whispered to Davey.

Or was it Saxon Tyson-Howard speaking to me? He was always going on about reporting me to HR.

Yes, it was Saxon, and he was smirking at me, reading me the headline on next week's Bugle.

"Ducks 4 - Crooks 1 – Cops zero."

It occurred to me about then I was semi-conscious and delusional.

And even in my delusion, my head was still giving me buggery.

I just needed sleep.

* * *

Time moves in a weird fashion when you've been bashed senseless. What is time anyway, when all you know is now? If Englebert was here, we could write a song about the passage of time. He could do the singing.

We would have a hit on our hands.

I had just had a hit all over.

I was lying on my back in the grass, an aching mess.

Then, I looked up at the work faces of Jack Farrell and Jody Taggart, and they were sliding me on a stretcher into the back of the Jarrajarra ambulance.

I love how the wheels folded up whenever I watched the stretcher fold itself into the back of the ambulance.

"Do it again," I said but got no response.

Typical Jack Farrell. Jack was never one for lots of roadside therapy, "Load them up and get them back to base as soon as possible, if possible," was Jack's philosophy.

I was in the "load-and-go" phase of the process.

Then, another jump in time.

I was in a hospital bed, looking into the beautiful face of my Wendy and some doctor I had never seen before. A busy night in the Jarrajarra Bush Nursing Centre.

I knew where I was, and that was good.

More importantly, I was in a ward and not the morgue. Plus, I was in my hometown facility, not the more serious Wodonga Emergency Department. All of this was good news.

I was also thinking again, in a straight line, in a regular flow, or so I thought. One thing, then another, then another. My thoughts flowed around me in a coherent sequence.

I was proud of my process.

Jarrajarra was real, Wendy was real, and here I was, so I must be real. My head still hurt like hell, but my brain was working again.

"Hello, Soldier," whispered Wendy, smiling at me. "You're banged up, my darling, bruised from top to bottom, but it looks like nothing broken, thank God." Her bottom lip and chin trembled a bit, but I was the only one who saw that, and she wouldn't care that I did.

Who the hell was that beside her? Doctor? Was it Saxon Tyson-Howard again? Surely not? One minute he is faking it as a journalist, now a doctor.

"Fortunately, your head took the brunt of the action," Wendy said, smiling, not crying, gently brushing my head with her hand. I was relieved. She was relieved.

"Sing along with me if you know the words," said Englebert Humperdink, standing behind a microphone in the corner of the wardroom.

"What's he doing?" I asked Wendy, concerned.

Engle didn't notice my interruption. He was wearing a dinner suit and a bowtie, standing behind his mic and looking off into the vague distance, just as he did on the cover of Nan's album.

He was singing something I had never heard before.

Watching him play 'LIVE' like this, with his movement and flair, and his dark, swarthy looks, he wasn't half bad, a deadset rooster. I had to admit. He was bloody good.

"I told you he was good," said Nan, angry at me but smiling at her Englebert.

I was happy Nan was there, to see her favourite singer and grandson, and for Nan to meet Wendy for the first time finally. It was lovely. I always knew they would be best friends if Nan hadn't died twenty years ago.

Perhaps my brain was not quite there yet.

I joined in the singing. Why not? I was among friends.

"I think we can safely give him some happy juice," said the unidentified doctor, and he must have because that is my last memory of the Jason Mellish homecoming event.

What a show.

Wednesday, June 8, 2022

Jarrajarra, Bush Nursing Centre.

"Well, Chris, you missed all the fun of the after-party. Cops everywhere, ambulance, fire truck, tow trucks, looked like half the town was out there."

Constable Joyce Thompson was visiting me in the Jarrajarra Bush Nursing Centre and bringing me up to speed.

She looked tired and not as happy as she was pretending.

"Did they break out the barbeque?" I asked.

"No," she looked puzzled, not knowing the great Jarrajarra barbeque tradition. "Could have, I suppose. There were a lot of locals. You are a very popular man around here."

"No, mate," I said, "they don't like me. They're just lazy. They don't want to train a new copper."

Constable Joyce liked my joke. It got a smirk.

I was off duty for a few days. Nurse Wendy Atcheson, my Wendy, had classified my various ailments as severe concussion, a dislocated right shoulder and a badly bruised right wrist. There were some ugly bruises on the right side of my face, there was my headache, and there was also some glorious deep-purple-black bruising to the right side of my body from my shoulder to my thigh, even the back of my right hand.

My right shoulder had also been dislocated, but Wendy had popped it back in, and the shoulder was as good as new, except for the bruises.

Bruises everywhere, from arsehole to breakfast, Wendy had said. There would be no swimming in the Murray River during my early morning run. That was fine. It was getting too cold anyway.

The bruises were all very dramatic and made me as stiff as a board down the right side. But here I was, with only one broken bone, and I could still run, though very slowly, which was a major blessing.

But bruises don't count in Wendy's estimate. Severe concussion was something real, and that was the official verdict.

I was lucky.

I was also still a bit foggy in the head, but clear enough to chat coherently. Englebert Humperdink had left the building, and Nan had gone with him. Maybe they had both gone back to God together. Was Engle still alive? I couldn't remember.

"I am sorry he is dead," said Joyce, "I honestly wish he wasn't, but he was a total dick. A complete bloody arsehole, he had absolutely zero redeeming features."

Joyce was talking about the late Constable Davey, not Humperdink.

"Joyce, I agree with you, but what I feel and what I will say in public are two different things. If anyone asks me about Davey, I will simply say I regret the loss of a fellow officer."

"Are you defending him?"

"No, no, Jeezus, no. He was a total dick, and he was stupid. He practically killed himself, the bloody idiot."

"Are you mansplaining?"

"No mate, shit, I don't even know what that means. For Chrissakes, I am not trying to change your mind or change your opinion, just warning you."

"Warning?"

"There's been a shooting, a cop killed, another one in a hospital, well actually a Bush Nursing Centre, but you get it. I bet you copped a ton of questions last night, and there will be more, I promise you."

"I did," she said.

"Yes, and you need to be honest with them and stay honest, but remember you acted perfectly. You should be proud of how you performed. Bloody hell, Joyce, you saved my life. I remember that bit clear as a bell."

"You saved my life, Chris. If you hadn't got me out of the car and onto my feet when you did, I'd be dead as well.

"Maybe, whatever, I just – in my opinion – I just don't think you need to be telling people what a dick he was. Somewhere in the force, he will have a friend, and someone will make a judgement on you."

"I can't believe Ralph Davey would have any friends anywhere, especially in the force."

"He must have Joyce. How else was he still a cop? Someone somewhere, probably higher up the chain, must be on his side. He probably has a list of complaints against him as long as your arm. Probably shifted out here, beyond the beyond, to move his problems onto someone else. Poor Sarge."

"So, more questions?" said Joyce. "Who will come around asking me more questions?"

"Most likely the Sarge. If you are lucky, it will be Sarge, and he might bring Sergeant Walker. He will have to. A cop has been killed, and there will be paperwork up to the roof."

"OK," she said tentatively.

"Did you answer honestly last night?" I asked her.

"I did."

"Then, just keep telling the truth. I will back you up. If it makes you feel better, then go ahead and even tell them what happened between you two before I got there. But just the facts of the matter, no opinions. Davey's dead. It makes no difference now what we both think of him."

She stopped to think about that.

I could see my advice was not helping. Who was I to advise her anyway? I still had a screaming headache. I had lost comrades in Afghanistan, some of them good mates and some not-so-good-mates. No point slagging them off when they were dead.

"Chris," she said. "I told Sarge last night what happened between Davey and me, and I will tell anyone who asks me. If Davey hadn't spent the whole night thinking with his dick, we might have been better prepared when the truck appeared. He might even be still alive."

"Fair enough. Absolutely. I will tell them what I saw as well, how upset you were, and how he was verbally abusing you. How totally inept his setup was. I will tell them exactly what I saw, what I remember. OK?"

"OK, thanks."

A moment's awkward silence.

Of course, we were not supposed to be conferring on our separate versions of the night's events until we had both been questioned, but here we were, conferring.

Colluding, they called it, and it was definitely not good form.

I hoped the truth would keep us safe from the higher-ups.

She was a good cop, but we also had a dead cop on our hands. Someone would end up in the shit. It should not be her.

The silence dragged on a bit then she said, "I thought you were dead as well."

"Me?"

"Oh God, yes, when the door flew off Davey's van, it just exploded forward, straight into you."

"Davey's door? I thought it was my truck door."

"No, your door, your whole truck, disintegrated. Davey's curbside door flew straight at you, and you just put your hand up like this."

She demonstrated a perfect right arm half guard, just the ticket against a left hook or a left kick toward the ribs. Meant to defend against a person, not a recommended defence against a flying police truck door.

I laughed, "That's years of ducking and diving at Rusty's Muay Thai gym in Melbourne. We used to practice it so hard we never had to think about it."

"Well, that's what you did."

"I honestly don't remember."

"Then they stopped, backed up the truck, then Mellish lined you up with the shotty."

"Hang on. Did they back up their truck? In the double tandem? Didn't they stop and just wind down the window?"

"No, they were going so fast. They travelled about fifty metres past you before they could stop. It was a big, loud, screeching stop. Smoking tyres, flying gravel, the whole catastrophe."

"They didn't jack-knife when they stopped?"

"No," she said. "Then, they backed up, and by the time they got back level with you, you were just kneeling up with your gun out. Which I would have told you not to do. I thought you were crazy brave."

"How long did that all take them? Going past, then backing up?"

"About a minute, maybe a bit more."

Holy hell, I thought I got knocked over and then got myself straight up. "I don't recall any of that. I must have been unconscious."

I thought I'd been knocked down, not knocked out.

"No," said Joyce, "I thought you were dead. You were down for a minute, at least. To be honest, I was hiding. I thought you were gone. Davey was in the ditch, useless as ever. I was on my own, so scared they would kill me," she said, "I was hoping they forgot about me, or maybe they hadn't even seen me."

"Maybe they hadn't," I said, "it was pretty dark. You were off the road by the time they arrived."

Was the word 'arrived' even appropriate for the way they ploughed their truck into our police cars? Exploded maybe?

"Then," Joyce continued, "after you got halfway back to your feet after they backed up level with you, Mellish was clearly going to shoot you."

Joyce started to cry. She let it just spill out.

"It took me so long to get my gun out," she said. "They took the first shot and killed Davey, then when Davey went down, and Mellish was lining you up again, you know, I was thinking, Jesus, Joyce, get yourself together. My hands were shaking so badly, and I was thinking 'do-something', 'do-something'. I was shaking so much I couldn't aim the gun."

"It's not like shooting at a gun range, is it?" I said softly, "But as scared as you were, you still acted. You did what you were trained to do, Joyce."

She really started crying now.

She put her hands over her face and had a real heavy sob.

"Joyce, you were frightened, but you still acted, and it was perfect. You saved my life."

"I suppose," she said, in a soft voice, but kept on crying.

What to do?

"I guess, being honest here, Davey was right about one thing," I said, "I had disrupted his sartorial elegance just a little."

She snorted, holding back a laugh, I thought.

"Don't laugh, Chris. It's not funny." Definitely fighting a laugh now.

"I know. It was tragic, and you won't get stains like that out with just an overnight soak, and who will pay for the holes in the shirt."

That got her.

We both started laughing. Davey was a ridiculous man, and he died an appropriately ridiculous death.

The more we tried not to laugh, the more we laughed. Eventually, I was laughing and crying too.

We'd almost controlled ourselves when a laughing tear fell from my face onto my pyjama T-shirt.

I looked at it intently. Then I hit her with my Davey impersonation.

"Look what you've done to me now, you idiot."

That got her again, another round of laughing tears.

"Please stop," she said, her arms around her ribs now.

After a bit, we both stopped laughing. Joyce cleaned her face from the box of tissues beside my bed, and then, after some more chat, she said goodbye.

The funniest things happen at the strangest times and are usually 'you-had-to-be-there' moments. In the last twenty-four hours, I think Joyce and I had become friends for life. The last thirty minutes had cemented it.

One good thing to come from a bad night.

* * *

I couldn't help thinking of Jennifer McLain, busting three blokes out of lockup, even a relaxed lockup like Henderson, and then stealing a cattle truck full of cattle.

And her driving? Bringing that whole truck and trailer to a screaming stop without tipping it, without jack-knifing it, in fifty metres, then reversing it, the double tandem, fifty metres in barely a minute.

Every time I met that woman, she surprised me. Every time I underestimated her, she made a fool of me. I couldn't let it happen again.

Fool me twice? Shame on me.

Fool me three times? I'd probably be dead.

* * *

I slept through lunch. When I awoke, Wally Mellish was there, seated beside my bed.

He had obviously heard about Jason and the events of last night.

"I am so sorry, Chris," said Wally. He still looked rather frail from his own stint in hospital. "You raise your kids as best you can, and then one turns out like this. I'm so fucking ashamed."

"Wally, mate, no one is blaming you," I said. "He's a grown man. Whatever happens is on him."

We let it go at that. It wasn't Wally who wrecked my truck and tried to shoot me.

Wally sat there quietly, reading his form guide. I fell asleep. I slept a couple of hours, resting in the loving care of the Jarrajarra Bush Nursing Centre. The second male in a week to take up residence with all the town's new mums.

* * *

When I woke up, Wally had gone. I turned on the TV to look for some news, hoping to find a report on our escapees. Eventually, I found a replay of a news conference on ABC Regional News. It was from earlier today; it was being held outside the Jarrajarra Police Station. There was some higher-up in a police uniform fronting the conference. The Sarge was standing behind him, looking dapper.

It would have been fun to hear Sarge talk to the camera, but the cop standing next to Sarge would have none of that. This new bloke was hogging every moment of his fleeting limelight.

The information strip at the bottom of the screen gave the police officer's name as Assistant Commissioner Jerrod Harrison.

Harrison was a soft-looking fellow. It didn't appear as though he would be heading up the hands-on section of the search himself, not on foot at least. He looked more your desk jockey type.

"There is nothing more serious on today's agenda for the Victoria Police than capturing the people responsible for this terrible murder of a serving officer," said Harrison, hogging the attention and strangling the language at the same time. He would have been far better off letting Sarge do the speaking. Give Sarge a camera and a question, and he was star material, a proven performer in past emergencies. But Harrison was not for turning.

"This is a heinous offence, disgusting to all of us. To apprehend these people, I have provided more officers on the ground here in the Jarrajarra region, and I have called in the Special Operations Group to assist in their capture. These criminals are a danger to every person in Victoria, and it is our intention to get them off the streets as soon as possible."

The last sentence totally confused me. Was he talking about the Special Operations team or the escapees?

Were the escapees really a danger to everyone in the state?

Last time I checked, there were at least six million people in Victoria. As evil as Jason Mellish may be, I did not believe he intended to kill everybody. Most likely, his intention was simply to kill me.

Harrison waffled on some more, and then he was asked about the murdered officer.

"Constable Ralph Davy was a highly respected member of the Wodonga police force. He had just moved to the area recently and has left behind a legacy of great work in the community and his loving parents and an older brother."

Please stop talking, I thought. Please.

He couldn't.

"Even though he'd only been in Wodonga a short time, I know he leaves behind many friends and colleagues among the police and community there."

That was bad enough, but then Assistant Commissioner Harrison put the icing on the Davey cake.

"From early reports, it appears Constable Davey was murdered while defending the lives of his fellow officers, one of whom was taken to the Jarrajarra Emergency Hospital in critical condition. I understand that particular officer, Constable Chris Taylor, has been removed from intensive care and is expected to survive. I don't think there is any doubt that Constable Davey saved the lives of two of his fellow officers at the scene of this horrendous event."

Wow.

I hope someone told Wendy the Jarrajarra Nursing Centre for expectant mothers had been promoted to a full-scale emergency hospital with an Intensive Care Unit. Maybe now, she'd get a raise.

Even more impressive, apparently, the dead-dickhead Davey had saved my life and Joyce's. There you have it, on national TV. What else had he done while grizzling about his dirty shirt? I assumed I would find out soon enough. Spin doctors like Harrison rarely quit while there was a camera about.

I turned off the telly and went back to sleep.

* * *

Two hours later, the man himself, Assistant Commissioner Harrison, with the Sarge in tow, appeared in my room. Surprise, surprise. I was a box, I guessed, and he would want to tick it.

"Here he is," said Harrison, hale and hearty as though we were old buddies. "So, how are you feeling, Constable Taylor? I hear you've been through the wars. Bugger me. You look like you've been painted purple. My God, I am glad to see you alive after all that. Good to be alive after staring death in the face. I bet it is. Well done."

Was I supposed to answer any part of that barrage? I felt like Lady Catherine De Bourgh from 'Pride and Prejudice'. I was not getting my share of the conversation.

Harrison didn't seem to care. He had the floor.

"Listen, Taylor, I know you've been through a bit with this Mellish fellow and his cohort, but I am keen to keep ahead of the story on Constable Davey. I know he was as dumb as dog shit, and you don't need to tell me anything on that topic. I am fully aware he was never one to volunteer for anything that might mess up his hair, and I expect he didn't perform all that well out there amidst the violence. I get all that. The thing is, his dad is an old school friend of mine, you see."

Bingo, there it was. The old school tie. I bet it wasn't Reservoir High.

"Anyway, long story short, it's hard enough for his parents, what with their son dead, murdered in such a horrible fashion. If this version of events I am hearing from the young female Constable, what's her name?"

"Constable Joyce Thompson," said Sarge.

"Thompson, yes, Thompson, she made some serious allegations out there at the scene last night. Allegations against Ralph Davey that, frankly, I find hard to believe. I'd hate this to turn into a he-said-she-said-hash-me-too gender war kind of thing when we are all up to our arse in the middle of a manhunt for police murderers."

He stopped for breath, maybe to let me absorb it all.

Manhunt? I was sure there was a very naughty woman out there as well, but Harrison interrupted my feminist line of thought with one of his own.

"How did she perform herself out there, I wonder? This Thompson woman, what do you make of her effort? Think she got herself in over her head out there, maybe?"

He was finally leaving gaps for me to speak.

"Take your time. I know your memory is probably a bit bashed about," he said.

I took my time, but I remembered well enough.

"She saved my life. I remember that much. She got her gun out and engaged the crooks, which is more than Davey managed. I am pretty sure she winged Mellish amid all the gunfire."

Joyce saved me, and we might have saved Davey as well, but the dumb prick was too stupid to listen. I don't think the Assistant Commissioner was ready for that thought. They would be words to end a career on.

"I'd give her a medal if I were you," I said.

"A medal? After the allegations she made, then she runs around hysterical, screaming rape in the middle of a well-organised road stop. I don't think so, Constable Taylor."

"She wasn't hysterical, Assistant Commissioner, angry maybe, and she didn't allege rape. Davey was shouting at her when I arrived. Whatever he did, he didn't deny it."

"He-said-she-said," said Harrison.

"He-said-she-said, and I am telling you," I replied. "And there's my bodycam, of course. Wherever that is after they dragged me here into the emergency room."

The good old bodycam. It had worked wonders for me over my time in the force.

"Where would it be now?" He asked, all innocent.

"Buggered if I can remember where it is, Assistant Commissioner."

Harrison went red. He looked like a balloon, ready to pop. I'm not sure how he expected me to respond. I was already purple. Better to deflate him nice and easy and keep my job.

You would have to be an idiot to tamper with the information on a Victorian Police body-worn camera or someone very high up the law enforcement food chain.

Harrison appeared to qualify on both counts.

But he didn't have the camera, and I did.

Thinking out loud, I laid out an idea.

"A medal for Joyce and a medal for Davey would get you where you wanted to go quicker," I said. "Mr and Mrs Davey Senior would have a good funeral for their son, with appropriate police honours for the fallen hero. Maybe his name ends up on an honour board at the old school."

Harrison had a tilt of the head, a thing he did when he actually heard what you said. I'd noticed it when he was actually listening to the reporter's questions during the news conference. He was thinking about my suggestion.

I was offering him a win-win. I always preferred win-wins. This was a good one, as good as this bloke Harrison was getting from me.

"Bodycams are a bitch, aren't they?" I added, just to help him over the line. "I'm sure you're aware, Sir. Your average old-school copper really doesn't appreciate how valuable they are at getting to the truth. But the courts love them. I just keep mine on all the time, and my admin assistant loads them up to a reserved location at the end of every day just to make sure the information is not lost."

The mention of uploads and secret locations was total bullshit, but I was counting on the fact our Assistant Commissioner was not a details man.

He seemed to get my hint.

"A medal, hey? For both of them?"

"Yeah, one each. Would be good," I said, "I know Joyce deserves one."

Wendy came in, lucky timing, or she had been listening at the door.

"Visiting time is not for another two hours, gentlemen, and this bloke hasn't even had his baby yet."

"We were just discussing," tried Harrison.

"Out," said Wendy. "The both of you."

They left. Sarge looked rather sheepish at Wendy and then shot daggers at me. Work that out.

Bugger them. You can't please everybody.

"Was that lucky timing?" I asked Wendy.

"No," she laughed, "I was listening. Well done, Soldier." She leaned over the bed and gave me a beautiful kiss. Then reached under the blanket in a very non-medical procedure. More of a monkey grip.

"Swellings gone down," she said.

I was trying to kiss back, but she was gone and back to work. A workday whirlwind.

I went back to sleep. I hadn't said anything too offensive to Harrison, I thought. They could sack me or not. I didn't care. If they did, they would regret it. I had the whole Constable-Ralph-Davey-farewell-tour on bodycam, and I knew Saxon Tyson-Howard, the fearless editor of the Jarrajarra Bugle.

Saxon loved his colour pieces.

* * *

I had been asleep, dreaming of the incident that put me here. I could see the truck directly opposite me the moment before Jason Mellish opened the passenger side door to get a better shot.

In my dream, I had a moment to see what I must have seen on the night. The truck was an old red Bedford monster, a red door with yellow cursive writing on it, a name of some sort that I hadn't time to read. Not when it happened and not when I dreamt of it.

Mellish fired his shotgun, and I woke with a fright.

It was just before 6.00 P.M.

I was still in the hospital; it was still daylight outside. My head was a lot clearer.

Jason Mellish, you murderous prick.

Where did you get that truck full of cattle?

Did Jason and his crew just see the truck on the road, full of cattle, and steal the thing? Hell of a thing to casually pick up along the way in the middle of a jailbreak.

Was it merely an opportunity, or was it part of a plan?

I could remember two things for certain; it was a red Bedford, and it was huge.

I did a quick search on my phone; the internet always knew more than me.

The escapees had been driving a tandem double-decker, two trailers, two decks per trailer. Apparently, you could fit twenty-eight cattle, an average weight of four hundred kilograms, on a single deck. A tandem double-decker had four decks, so that meant, possibly, one hundred and twelve cattle on the back of a truck.

What was a four hundred-kilo cow worth? Holy Jesus, over three thousand dollars. I couldn't believe the prices. My God, four times twenty-eight times three-thousand. That was over three hundred thousand dollars of moo-cow they'd nicked.

Three hundred thousand.

It had to be a plan.

Which suggested Jennifer McLain was doing the thinking. Jason Mellish was a steroid-damaged coke-head, not a planner. This was the McLain gang, not the Mellish gang.

The headache I had been carrying had eased, and my brain was working again. As well as it was able.

How did the two escapees and their team-mate on the outside do all that they did?

Gathering and loading cattle takes time. I knew Mellish had some idea of working with cattle. I had no idea if the other two shared a clue between them when it came to moving moo cows.

McLain was a Kiwi, and Thorburn was a steroid-pumped gym junkie pretending to be a tough bikie. I didn't see either of them as your farming type. I had no idea why they dragged this Carl Agnew along with them. What value did he add?

If it was me, I'd steal the truck and cattle from the same place. That raised all sorts of horrendous possibilities. Where was the owner of the truck now?

I found my phone in a side draw and called Barney. It was after work, but I knew he'd take my call.

"A red Bedford? With yellow writing?" asked Barney. "Let me think?" Barney made some thinking noises. I could hear people in the background.

"Where are you, Barn?"

"I am at the reception desk at the Caravan Park. There are a few of us here. We were working out a roster while Wally is in hospital, but it has sort of evolved into a barbeque, party type of thing."

"A few? Who?"

"Gosh, everybody. Say hello, everyone," said Barney.

"Hi, Chris," I heard from a throng.

"There is Greg," said Barney, "and Norma, Rob, Jack, Jody Taggart and Scott Farrell."

"I bet you that Jody and Scott are sitting next to each other."

"Yes, that is the case," said Barney discreetly.

"Carole and Glenda are here. They're actually staying over, in the park, while all this escapee stuff is going on, all of the other police are still on the stake-out, and Constable Tim is working the station with Sergeant Palmer."

"The Sarge had Constable Tim filling in for me. That was good.

"Joanne is here," continued Barney, "and so is Saxon Tyson-Howard."

"You are having a party without me, and you invited sooky bloody Saxon."

"Yes, they are running the Bugle from the caravan Park for a week, and Joanne is doing most of the park work as well."

Barney was as discreet as ever. I could see him, in my mind, smiling politely at the two members of the local press.

Damn, I loved those after-work parties that seemed to emerge fully grown into random places around town, and here I was, stuck in the hospital. My fear of missing out was worse than the concussion.

"Are Scotty and Jody holding hands, or you know, more?"

"Tentatively, yes, that is correct. We dropped the roster idea when Joanne volunteered to run the Park for the rest of the week. Really good local colour for the Bugle," she said.

No one spoke discreet code, as well as Barney.

"Now everyone has just settled in and having a really good time," said Barney, meaning that the Scotty-Jody romance was progressing nicely. "Very relaxed," he added.

The truck?

"So, let me ask everyone about this truck," said Barney, reading my mind as always. He must have moved the phone away to speak to the throng. It was muffled, but I could hear him clearly.

"Who owns a red Bedford truck around here with yellow writing on the side."

"That would be the Pendergasts," answered Rob Farrell. I hear him clearly. "Out past Towong, they are just before the turn-off to Mount Elliot. I go there to service it every year. It drags a fabulous old B-Double trailer, double-decker; it is old Ben's baby."

"They run cattle?" I asked Barney to ask Rob.

"Small herd breeders," said Rob to the relayed question, "they turnover maybe a hundred and twenty bullocks, good stock, but Ben and Irma Pendergast are mostly retired nowadays."

"Ask Rob," I said, "to come and pick me up if he doesn't mind. I need to check on them,"

Barney asked Rob.

"Of course," came the answer.

Time for my own escape.

Someone was having a baby in one of the Nursing Centre delivery rooms. You didn't need to be told there was a baby on the way. The sound of the mum carried down the hall.

I was shaky on my feet, but I was vertical. There was a nice clean uniform and a pair of boots in the locker beside my bed, but no gun or badges. Wendy would have locked them away in her safe before she washed and ironed my stuff.

I had to get past Wendy to get out of the Nursing Centre, but I could hear the birth down the hall coming to some sort of climax. Hopefully, it would be a happy fruition. Wendy would be fully occupied for a while.

I slunk down the hall to the entrance in my socks and put my boots on near the door. The reception area was empty. I was safe to sneak out unsighted.

A few seconds later, Rob Farrell pulled up in his twin cab four-wheel drive Toyota ute. It was a serious bush-basher.

Behind Rob was the Seymour Crime Services Unit van with Carole and Glenda on board, in uniform and ready for action. They gave me a thumbs-up as I headed to Rob's truck.

Pendergast Farm, Towong

"This is so wrong," I said to Rob as we pulled away from the hospital. Getting a lift to a possible crime scene from a civilian.

"Make a call. Cover your arse," said Rob. Knowing the problem and being ex-army like me, he knew the answer.

It was good thinking.

I called Sarge, and he answered. We did the hello and how you are feeling stuff.

"Sarge, anything new about the cattle truck?"

"No, nothing. I haven't got the manpower to go looking for missing cows. We still have the roadblocks in place. Assistant Commissioner Harrison has organized a busload of young rookies coming from Melbourne tomorrow morning. That gives me another twenty bodies to play around with. Enough to tighten up the roadblocks and maybe let me get some of the team out and about among the local farmers."

"OK," I said, looking for an angle to excuse what I was already doing.

"Davey's death has generated some cooperation, at least," said Sarge.

"That'd be a first for him," I said before I thought.

"Yes, well," said Sarge. "What can you say? His parents will be very sad, I imagine."

The Sarge was a good person, and he lived it every day in every way. Davey had always been a prick. Now, he was a dead prick, and Sergeant Palmer, who had nothing good to say, would say nothing at all.

"I could roll around some of the local farms with some of the local emergency guys if you like," I said, "see if we can spot any right cows in wrong paddocks. Maybe find some empty paddocks that should be full."

That was my pitch. I was just looking for the cattle.

"OK, if you feel up for it," he said. "Listen, son, these crooks will be lying low, but if you do see them, call it in and stand back. I don't want you to engage while you're not well. Wendy would have me for breakfast."

"I won't engage Sarge. I will just shoot them."

"Good lad, don't miss."

We ended the call.

"I think he knew I was arse covering," I said to Rob.

"Of course, he did. But hey, he is short-handed, right?"

"Are you still a paid-up member with the SES?" I asked.

"Paid up? Chris, the money they owe me on truck maintenance and bike hire, I could be captain of the whole thing if I wanted. If the current captain wasn't my brother."

"Which is why you never get paid."

"Exactly," said Rob.

Of course, he was paid up. What was I thinking?

"Have you got some weapons with you?" I asked.

Another silly question. He opened the lift-up thing between the two front seats, and there were two .40 calibre Smith and Wesson semi-automatic pistols. I checked both magazines. Both were full, 15 rounds each, and two spare mags beneath.

"I'll borrow one of these if you don't mind," I said.
"Go for it," said Rob. "Just don't lose this one to Crime Services. OK?"
"I'll do my best, but no promises."
We were ready to go.
I knew I was breaking police rules, with no badge, no gun, working with a civilian, but Rob was the best backup man I could hope for. I was heading to a place where my escapees might have been recently, and they could be there now for all I knew. Plus, they had tried to kill me once already, so stuff the rules.
Rob and I had practised this stuff forever. Army trained initially, and we kept at it because we loved it. The Jarrajarra rifle range was our second home when quiet days permitted.
With Rob-the-petrol-head driving, we were halfway to Towong by the time I had finished my phone call with the Sarge.
I could see in my side mirror that the girls, Carole and Glenda, were struggling to keep up in their van.
Rob was travelling hard on the not-so-smooth country road. I could feel my headache sneaking back to prominence. No time for that.

* * *

After twenty minutes, we pulled into the Pendergast farm. It was still light. The farmhouse was at the end of a five-hundred-metre track through some lovely old trees. The house was invisible from the road.
Rob stopped short of the house, leaving us plenty of tree cover.
I could just see the farmhouse front door through a break in the trees. It was open. If Mellish and his other two buddies were inside, with guns, this was not a good position.
"Can you back up a bit before the others get here?"
Rob backed up as Carole and Glenda entered the long driveway. They stopped behind us.
Protected by the trees, I had no intention of just walking up to an ambush.
Rob and I exited the ute. He opened the tool kit on the back of the ute and took out his Steyr Scout rifle.
The Steyr Scout is an Austrian bolt-action rifle used by some of

the US sniper teams in Afghanistan; it was Rob's now. On his last tour in Afghanistan, he'd traded weapons with a US marine quartermaster.

Rob had it chambered with .243 Winchester bullets in ten 10-round detachable box magazines. He had the rifle in one hand and half a dozen mags under his arm. There would be another full mag in the rifle.

It was a fantastic weapon, the best weapon within a hundred-mile radius of Jarrajarra, reliable and accurate. The last time I used it, I almost lost it permanently, into Crime Services custody. He pretended he hadn't forgiven me, but here it was again when we needed it.

He assumed a position behind a tree.

"When you're ready, Chris," he said. "Just keep to the left till you get to the front porch. If anyone starts shooting, I can cover you up to the porch. Then we'll see what happens."

Carole and Glenda were out of their cars and had moved up behind us.

"You know, Killer, we usually prefer getting here after the shooting," said Carole,

"Think of it as an early start," I said.

"I think we will take a tree, a wide one," said Glenda, and they skipped quickly to a huge gum on the other side of the road.

I looked over at them, and as I took out the weapon I'd borrowed from Rob, I gave them a sideways look with a friendly raise of the eyebrow.

"Oh yeah," whispered Carole, and they both took out their weapons. "Better ready than dead-y".

"If I get inside, give me five minutes," I said to Rob, "then," I paused.

"Then what?" he asked.

"Do something helpful," I suggested.

"Great field advice, Chris," Rob was focused on the front door of the Pendergast house.

Time to go.

It was my intention to get inside that door as quickly and as safely as possible. I hated these cold entries, sneaking up on something possibly deadly, most likely not.

But they only need to be deadly once.

So, you need to be cautious every time.

I ran, fast and low. All my aches, pains and bruises were throbbing away somewhere under the adrenaline.

Keeping myself behind the tree cover as much as possible, I sprinted hard to the end of my cover. Then, gun up, I made a crazy dash from the last tree to the left side of the porch.

Then, another sprint across the porch to the first window. My ribs and shoulders were aching as I ran. I'd go back to bed, except I was too far in to turn back.

I need not have bothered with all the dramatics.

Ben and Irma Pendergast were overjoyed to see me. Well, Irma was. Ben was unconscious.

They were sitting there, back-to-back, in the middle of the lounge room floor, bound head to foot with duct tape.

Irma had chewed through the tape around her mouth, and it hung in tatters from her chin.

"Oh Chris, thank God, oh God in heaven, Ben has collapsed. Help him, please." Irma was crying, worried for her husband. She didn't seem to notice her own predicament.

Using my pen knife, I was cutting the tape from the old couple as I called Barney on my mobile,

Barney answered immediately.

"Barney, can you get an ambulance to Pendergasts' place? Ben is unconscious and not responding. Straight away if you can, thanks."

"Right," Barney's 'Right' meant it as good as done.

"Then call Sarge, please, and tell him we've found the source of the cattle."

"OK."

Once I had finished with Barney, I had the rest of the tape off the Pendergasts in seconds.

The moment old Ben was released from the tape, he collapsed sideways. I just caught his head before he whacked it on the solid timber floor.

Irma fussed over him from one side, and I was on the other. She was struggling, taped up for however long it had been, but she was more worried about her husband than herself.

I did my best, but medical care was not my strong suit.

I worked through my basics.

He was alive, he was breathing, his airways were clear, he had a pulse, and with all that checked off, we were getting to the limit of my medical skills.

"How long have you been like this?"

"Since yesterday, after lunch, Jason Mellish and some horrible young fellow just arrived at the door," she was talking through tears.

"They tied me up and made Ben load all our bullocks into the Bedford, said they would hurt me if he didn't do what they told him. Mongrels, now look what they've done to Benny."

I made a mental note of the missing animals. They were bullocks, not cows. I would say bullocks from now on. I would sound country-smart, not city-dumb.

My phone made a 'message-from-Barney' noise. I checked, and it said,

"ETA Ambulance 15 minutes."

"Was there a woman with them?" I asked Irma.

"Maybe, but I didn't see her. Ben may have. They just appeared out of nowhere. I didn't see a car or anyone else except the two young men. They tied me up pretty quickly. Tied up? Taped up? Whatever. But they were the only two I saw. Didn't see or hear a car at any stage, just the sound of our old truck."

"When did Ben pass out?"

"Early this morning, he started moaning and groaning. He was in a lot of pain from the bindings. He wasn't speaking clearly, with the thing over his mouth, then about twenty minutes ago; he went quiet, just seemed to pass out. I can't remember exactly, Chris, oh God."

Irma was still crying.

"We were awake all night. He was so uncomfortable. He has terrible arthritis, and he needs a new hip. Oh, Ben love, please wake up, sweetheart."

She was holding his arm, stroking his face. Her tears were falling onto him as he lay there, still not responding.

Her mind was totally on her husband. I held off on my questions till we had him sorted.

I remembered my backup team, still probably counting the seconds to five minutes. Whoops. I called Rob's mobile.

"You can come in, mate. It's all clear, and I think Mrs. Pendergast will be happy to see you." I don't think Mister Pendergast knew we were there.

"What if we massage his legs and arms a bit to get his circulation going," I suggested. "Can't hurt."

"OK," she said and started rubbing his legs vigorously.

Something to keep her mind off Ben's potential demise till the ambos arrived.

After a moment, old Ben groaned loudly.

"There you go," I said, cup-half-full regarding Ben's resurrection.

Irma rubbed away determinedly on her husband's arms and legs until we heard the ambulance. First, it was off in the distance, and then it was screaming down the drive, then halting at the door.

Jack and Jody sprinted into the house. Were they ever less than fast? As they made the last steps toward old Ben on the floor, Ben pushed his wife's hand away and sat up.

"For God's sake, love, stop rubbing me. You'll give me carpet burns." He said to his wife. "Bloody hell."

He looked up, looked around at those of us here to save him, back from the dead, puzzled as you would be.

Jack and Jody were set back a beat. Where was the comatose invalid they had come to rescue? They were always quick and efficient, but this was extraordinary.

Jody was the first to recover from witnessing a miracle. She ushered Ben into a chair, knelt beside him, and, with her stethoscope, started checking things beyond my level of comprehension.

"How long were you asleep, Benny?" Jody asked.

"I wasn't asleep. I just shut my eyes for thirty seconds. Then I woke up." That's where Ben got stuck. "Then, umm, jeez, I can't remember."

"He has been unconscious for a good twenty minutes before Chris arrived," said Irma, "and it's been another twenty since then."

"Oh, rubbish," said Ben.

"How were you feeling just before your little nap?" asked Jody, probing away, avoiding argument.

"I was feeling bloody pins and needles everywhere, bloody tied up like a Christmas ham. Bloody Jason Mellish, thieving fool. I tell you."

Ben was slowing down as he spoke, exhausted, or something worse was happening, maybe.

Jody looked at her co-medic, Jack, "T.I.A.," she said.

Jack nodded.

"Benny, we will get you to Wodonga Hospital, mate. You've had a bit of a warning shot," she turned to Irma to finish the description.

"This is what we call a T.I.A., which stands for a transient ischemic attack. He has had what you might call a very mild stroke. The lack of circulation and the stress maybe brought it on, but we need to get him to Wodonga to make sure it doesn't turn into a full-on stroke."

"OK," said Irma, shaken but determined.

Jack was beside Ben, a glass of water and a handful of pills in his hand. "OK, Ben, we need to get these into you, mate. They are aspirin, a bit of blood thinner to make sure you keep pumping."

Jack was talking as he pumped water and pills into Ben. I doubt Ben could have avoided swallowing the pills if he tried.

"OK," said Jack as Jody appeared beside us with the stretcher. The stretcher legs were down, so the bed was at floor level.

"Just lay down, please, Ben," said Jack, assisting him to the floor. At the same time, Jack was nodding toward Rob and me with a sort of 'you-guys-get-his-legs' look on his face.

We got Ben's legs, Jack and Jody got his top end, and with a slip and a slide, Ben was on the stretcher, and the stretcher's legs were down and rolling.

Before you could count to five, Ben was in the back of the ambulance, and they were almost set to go.

"Load 'em up and get 'em back to base ASAP" was always Jack's approach.

"Wodonga hospital," said Jody to the group of us now standing on the porch facing the open back door of the ambulance. "Can someone drive you there, Irma? Pack some clothes for both of you, toothbrushes and all that stuff. He'll be there a few days, I think."

"OK," said Irma, sounding nervous.

"He is OK, Irma, it's all good," said Jody. Jody seemed very confident as she slammed the rear door of the ambulance.

In a cloud of dust, they were gone.

"I'll drive you, love," said Rob Farrell.

"Thank you," said Irma, suddenly looking very tired herself.

"We might check around here for a bit," said Carole. "Chris, mate, can you hang with us for a while?"

"Sure," Carole and Glenda were not your front-line coppers. They would not like being here at a crime scene without backup.

The three of us hung in at the Pendergast farm for two more hours while the forensic sisters photographed muddy footprints in the house, bagged the mud, and took more pictures outside the house. Some of the stuff they sampled and bagged, I couldn't imagine why they bothered. But they did.

If I had to hang around guarding the Crime Service sisters, I thought I might try and find something useful I could do for the Pendergasts. Something nice to balance up their universe.

There must be something positive we could do after all the negative of the last day, the home invasion, the cattle theft, the truck theft, and the painful indignity of being left duct taped - to what end? To keep them quiet? To be quiet and politely die if no one found them in time.

Bloody Jason Mellish.

I had a sneak around the little office at the back of the house. There was a desk loaded with bills. Used and unused envelopes, notebooks, and a small laptop computer under all that paperwork.

Above the desk were at least twenty framed photos of young kids in various activities around the Pendergast farm. The centrepiece in the photo collection was a framed 'Thank you Certificate' from Foster Care Victoria. It was a very glossy certificate in a nice frame. Looked grand. Thanking Ben and Irma for their loving service to the children of Victoria.

I turned my attention back to the desk.

I searched through the bills for any insurance notices.

I was good with insurance. Very creative.

Both their herd insurance and home insurance invoices looked like they'd arrived in the mail yesterday. The Pendergasts still received their invoices in snail mail, not a surprise, given their age.

Both insurance policies were with the same company, and both payments were due within the next seven days.

I turned on the laptop and waited till it came up asking for a password. I typed in the word 'password' and gained access immediately.

There was an icon for their bank, so I clicked on that. This one asked for a user and password, so I typed in 'user' and 'password', which took me straight into their bank accounts. I had to admit I was good at this cyber stuff. Better than the Pendergasts, at least.

I checked their accounts. They were not cash-rich but had enough to pay their bills.

I paid the insurance for the cattle and the insurance for the house. I also paid the electricity and phone bills, which were close to overdue. Then, I signed out of the bank website, powered down the laptop and put it away inside the top desk drawer.

Next, I went looking for more insurance forms in the tall metal cabinet beside the desk. There were hundreds of manila folders, all filed alphabetically. I found a thick wad of insurance documents under 'I' and searched through there till I found the renewal notices from the previous year for the herd and the house, all paid up, showing me the full details of the Insurance company and the Pendergasts' insurance contract numbers. I photographed those two papers and then put all the bits and pieces from the cabinet back where I had found them.

I sent the photos to Barney with a note.

> *"It would be good to get the insurance rolling for the Pendergasts, maybe first thing in the morning. They will be stuck in the Wodonga hospital for the next little while. Cash could come in handy."*

A minute later, Barney texted back.

> *"Great idea, will do it first thing. Hope you're feeling better."*

I had a thought and went back to the filing cabinets to look for more farm-relevant folders. Under 'F', I found a folder labelled FENCING. I looked through that and found half a dozen invoices from Jason Mellish, all hand-written, grubby in fact, the last invoice dated about a year before Jason had gone to jail if you called Henderson Centre a jail.

From what I could see, Jason Mellish had worked for the Pendergasts at bloody generous rates. Then, the work stopped. I wondered why?

I used my phone to photograph the last two Mellish invoices. Maybe useful, maybe not.

Not long after that, Carole and Glenda signalled they were finished, and they drove me back to Jarrajarra. I asked them to drop me home. I was done with the hospital.

Wendy's push bike was at the back door. I was tired from my evening back at work and crept quietly to our bed.

Wendy was asleep. I recognized her breathing pattern. She was exhausted and out for the count.

Any wonder?

She was CEO, chief nurse, mid-wife, short-staffed, under-funded, no regular doctor and on the tail-end of a pandemic.

The government promised more hospitals, but she needed more staff to cover the beds she already had. Her job had become impossible, but she kept trying anyway.

My horrible concussion headache was back, but sleeping next to Wendy would fix anything.

It was good to be home. In my own bed, sleeping next to my beautiful, exhausted girlfriend.

Thursday, June 9, 2022

Jarrajarra, Chris's Kitchen.

"So, Chris, do you know this bloke?" asked Sergeant Palmer, showing me a photo of a very old friend.

It was morning. I was sitting at the kitchen table in my house. I was still officially off-duty, so the Sarge had left the station and come to me, and Sergeant Will Walker had come with him.

It was the second of my 'few' official days off. I was resting at Wendy's insistence. Wendy's plan was to keep me away from cop meetings like this. She worried I would be sucked back into police work while still injured. By staying home, hopefully, I could rest my damaged goods for a day or two.

That had been the plan. But here we were.

A concussion is a funny thing. I heard Sarge's question, but I forgot to answer.

"Chris? Hello," he prodded.

"Yes, yes, I do, Sarge. I know, Rusty, yes. Haven't seen him in a long time. But yeah, I know him. I know him very well, in fact." My concussion was speaking in triplicates.

Concentrate.

I was at the head of my kitchen table. The Sarge was sitting on one side of the table, and his right-hand man, Sergeant Will Walker, was sitting on the other.

We were looking at a photo of Russell "Rusty" Collins, my original Muay Thai trainer, coach, substitute father figure, and the best male role model I ever had as a kid. Maybe the only one.

Carole and Glenda, our Seymour-based Crime Services team, had come back to Walker with a preliminary report on the bodies from the hole, the pair we found under the dead duck hunters. The two that had been bashed in the head, those ones.

According to the report, their names were Phillip Savage Senior and Phillip Savage Junior.

Two Phillip Savages.

The bodies in the hole were a dental match to the dental information Walker had provided Crime Services the other night. The teeth aligned.

"Perfect match," according to Walker, reading from a paper he was holding. "We still have to wait for the DNA, but the girls have no doubt about the teeth."

Carole and Glenda were a gun team. They were still in Jarrajarra last night after the Mellish fiasco, yet they'd found the time to answer Walker's weird request.

I knew Rusty Collins. I also knew these other names, Savage Senior and Savage Junior. Fortunately for those two, we had never met. I'd have put them down the Mellish Paddock hole myself.

"I've called in Homicide from Melbourne on these two," said Sarge. "We might be teaming up again with your old friend Detective Jordan.

I could barely contain my enthusiasm.

"Try to contain your enthusiasm, Chris," said the Sarge, looking at me and reading my mind as usual.

"So why are we here at my table on my day off," I asked. They both outranked me, but I could say what I wanted. I was off duty and recently concussed. One could argue I was not myself.

Sarge would argue I was perfectly myself, rude and insubordinate to authority.

"Did you know about his daughter's murder?" asked Sergeant Walker.

"Not at first. I was away in the army. Then, after the coroner's inquest, it didn't take long for word to get around amongst the crew, even the ones overseas, like me. So yeah, I knew about Virginia and Phillip Savage, but all that was after I had joined the army."

"OK," said Walker, "Let me fill you both in, get us all on the same page."

So, Sergeant Walker told Sarge and me the story.

"Russell Collins' daughter, Virginia, disappeared in 2002. Her married name was Virginia Savage. It was widely assumed she had been murdered by her husband, Phillip Savage Junior."

Walker looked grim as he discussed Rusty's daughter, a woman I had known.

"There had been a brief history of domestic violence in Virginia's marriage. I had been called to their house from the local station where I was working. A few complaints, and then it stopped."

So, Sergeant Walker knew her as well.

"I didn't like this Savage fellow at all," said Will, "he was a six-foot-eight-inch, long drink of water, but that's just my opinion. He was a bully with women, but he would go to pieces when police arrived."

"We couldn't get her to lay charges. I think she was scared that people would find out he was an abuser. Maybe she was worried about the stigma. She worried her father might get angry and do something to Phillip."

I interrupted Walker at one point.

"You know Virginia didn't live with Rusty growing up."

"Yes, I knew that," said Walker. "Collins was married to the mother, Raelene Collins nee Pegler, very briefly. I believe it was a shotgun marriage. She was from a strict Catholic home, Russel Collins was in the army, they met between one of his several tours of Vietnam, enlisted man, not a conscript."

"Anyway, Catholic boys and girls being what they were, Russell and Raelene got themselves together without the benefit of contraception and surprise, surprise, they find themselves pregnant."

"Well, we've all been there," said Sarge.

That caused a slight shock for Walker and me. We both gave the Sarge a slightly surprised sideways glance.

"Carry on, Sergeant Walker," said Sarge, giving us nothing further.

"Yes, well, then the two young lovers get themselves married to avoid all the stuff that was so important to people back then, around 1970, child out of wedlock, scandal, disgrace. What would the priest say? What would God think, and what have you."

"They would have married in the side aisle of the church, I assume," said Sarge.

"Yes, probably, that was the go for that kind of wedding back then. So Russell and Raelene marry, and he goes back to Vietnam. He comes back a year later, and they divorce."

Hell of a summary, but pretty much what I remembered of the story as it was told to me many years after the fact.

"Divorce? My word," said Sarge, "did you know with Prime Minister Gough Whitlam, elected in 1972, Australia became the first country in the world, the entire world, to have no-fault divorce? Fancy that. Great man, Gough. Best Prime Minister ever."

"Debatable," said Walker.

“Way before my time,” I chimed in. “But I hear good things,” I nodded at Sarge, taking his side as always.

“Sorry,” said Sarge. “Irrelevant. Go on, Will.”

“Anyhow,” said Walker, “yes, Virginia’s parents get divorced without much hassle.”

“But Rusty and Virginia were still close,” I said, “he loved his daughter. I remember that.”

“Yes, so I believe,” said Walker. “No question there.”

We all stopped for a moment to think. Walker seemed almost wistful. After a moment, he resumed the story.

“Anyway, Virginia disappears. A subsequent coronial inquest recommends Phillip Savage be investigated further, but no charges ever eventuate.”

“If the husband, Savage, had murdered his wife, he did a good job disposing of the body. She has never been found.”

“At the coronial inquest, Savage Junior claimed Virginia had run off and left him, joined a religious cult or some other bullshit. He claims there was a written message she had left behind. He claimed he subsequently lost it. It allegedly said, ‘Don’t look for me. I am not coming back.’ All totally unverifiable nonsense.”

“Anyway, we believed he had murdered her, and so did the coroner.”

“The Prosecutor at the time, a rather spineless fellow, I think, also an old school chum of Savage Senior, couldn’t decide if Savage Junior was telling the truth. According to the Prosecutor, we had no bodily remains and no evidence of foul play.”

“So, no charges,” I said.

“Exactly, for whatever reason,” he continued, “the murder charges never happened. From what I recall, the Homicide higher-ups never really invested. They seemed happy to believe the religious-cult-runaway rubbish.”

“So, Savage never gets to court?” asked Sarge.

“No. Never inside a cell, not even for one night. The family is filthy rich, money no object, so Phillip Savage Junior never faces a jury.”

“Then, in 2010, Savage Senior and Junior disappeared.”

“Yes. And in my opinion,” said Walker, “Russell Collins got sick of waiting and did them both. Alone or assisted by others? I don’t know."

"When was this photo taken?" I asked Walker, holding up the photo of Rusty we had all been looking at.

"That was taken in 2010," said Walker. "We bought him in to see if he had done the vigilante thing on the husband and the father-in-law, and we just couldn't crack him. Kept him in for forty-eight hours."

"Back in the day, we could keep them that long," added Sarge.

"Yes," answered Walker, "and it didn't faze Collins, not one bit. A very hard man, I must say, no bluster, just hard."

"You were involved in the murder investigation?" I asked. Was this personal?

"I wasn't really involved. It was a Homicide job, not mine. But, yes, it was all run out of my station, St Kilda. And yes, I suppose I made myself a part of it all. As much as I could. I knew Virginia from my visits to the house on personal protection calls, and I got to watch the interrogation of Collins."

"But you were more involved than that?" I said, guessing.

"No, not really," said Will. "Virginia was a beautiful woman but out of my league. I liked her and cared enough to feel guilty when she disappeared. Could I have done more to help her? I wish I had."

Walker did one of those little look-away twitches.

Maybe he cared more than he liked to admit.

"Virginia was actually in the final stages of obtaining a divorce," said Will. "She was beautiful, inside and out, I thought. Maybe I had a chance with her. I don't know. Probably would have asked her if I had the chance later."

"But she disappears," I said, "so you don't get a chance, and it sounds like your Homicide team played dead?"

"Didn't bring their A-game to the case?" added Sarge.

Walker was staring into space before he spoke. Thinking hard, seeing it all in his memory.

"No, and even though it was way above my pay grade, it felt wrong."

That stopped the conversation for a moment. Every day, something new among the Wodonga Regional Force.

"Love from afar. Corruption from above," said Sarge.

"Not quite love," said Will, "maybe some corruption."

"You old blokes are getting a bit nostalgic. Would you like a tune?" I nodded toward my guitar, leaning against the side wall of the kitchen cupboard. I bought it online, with ten YouTube lessons, a year ago. I was still only ten minutes into lesson one.

"I could go another coffee, son," said Sarge.

"I wouldn't say no," said Will. "For the coffee. Hold the serenade."

Three coffees. I obliged. Chance to think.

I never knew about Rusty's interview or coronial inquests, and I didn't know much about the state of Virginia's marriage.

I knew Virginia Collins from my days at Rusty's gym. We were gym buddies for sure, great friends in that section of my life. She was great fun to train with, but she was fifteen years older than me. By the time I was ready for the army, Virginia was losing interest in martial arts.

As for Will, I had never met him before working at Jarrajarra.

Strange connections.

"Let me guess, when you had Rusty in interrogation, at some stage, he bought in a lawyer named Richard Martin, and that was as far as the interrogation went?"

"How did you know that?" asked Sergeant Palmer.

"I didn't know it, Sarge. I guessed it. Richard was one of the Muay Thai crew. If Rusty needed a solicitor, he would have called Richard. We all did. He was our go-to legal man."

"What was your mate, Rusty, running down there? Some sort of teenage suburban crime syndicate?" asked Sarge.

"No," I said, "it was totally the opposite. Rusty led a lot of kids out of trouble, not into it. He had a big team of really dedicated students. You didn't get to be part of his mob unless you were heavily into the hard work and discipline."

No one could criticize Rusty to me, not even the Sarge.

"The Muay Thai crew were a tribe," I explained, "and there were builders, plumbers, electricians, accountants, students, you name it. Maybe a few who bent the rules outside the gym."

"We had one lawyer, Richard Martin. If you ever needed professional help, you asked one of the team, and you usually got the help you needed. At mates' rates."

"Mates' rates on a double murder?" asked Walker.

"I meant mates' rates on the professional help. If it was a lawyer you needed, Rick Martin was the man. As for a partner-in-crime? If Rusty Collins decided to send off these two blokes, I promise you, he would not have needed help. Not from anyone."

I sat there looking at these photos of my old mentor. Where was I when he needed me?

Virginia disappeared in 2002. I was in the army, prime military meat. I would have been in training, resting, or rotating to Afghanistan.

The Savage men, Junior and Senior, disappeared a few years later, in 2010.

In 2010, I was still in the army, supposedly a highly trained warrior with the mighty SASR. But I was not so mighty that year. I was emerging from two long years in rehab after getting blown up in Afghanistan in 2008.

In 2010, I was working my way back to strength and fitness, bit by bit, one day at a time, building a base, just as Rusty had taught me when I was a kid.

The Rusty Collins credo.

You plan, and you prepare with discipline. Never leave the preparation to the last minute. Start early and work hard. When the time comes to execute, you are READY! Rusty's words of wisdom, I could still hear him.

Sergeant Walker's voice broke my trance.

"Eventually, later in 2010, after the Savages both disappear, after we interviewed him, Collins sells off his boxing gym, and he goes off the radar as well."

"It wasn't a boxing gym," I said. "It was Muay Thai. Big difference."

They both looked at me, puzzled, oblivious to the many variations of head bashing and how important those differences were to their exponents.

"If you say so," said Walker.

"OK, so Collins has gone as well?" asked Sarge.

"Yes. Not sighted since the interview."

The Sarge breathed a sigh of disappointment,

"So now," said Sarge, "we have Virginia Collins still missing, presumed murdered by Savage, the son. Then, a few years after that, we have these two Savage fellows, the father and son, go to God themselves, presumed murdered by Chris's friend and mentor, Rusty Collins, in revenge for the death of his daughter."

Walker was nodding at Sarge's summary.

"Then Collins goes missing after we interview him."

"That's about it," said Will.

"And here we are now," said Sarge, "years later, the two Savages turn up down that hole under some random drunken duck-hunters. And Collins, their likely murderer, is still gone. We don't know where."

"Yes," said Walker.

"Holy mother of God," said Sarge. "What a mess."

We all stopped for another moment of contemplation.

It occurred to me this was a good meeting. Usually, I hated meetings, where it is deemed necessary for someone to be talking all the time. All the bloody time.

Someone should make that a meeting rule. Stop talking and allow some thinking time.

Something Dirk Gently, fiction's greatest detective, may have said, "Thinking. It should be compulsory." I didn't throw Dirk's fictional theories into the mix. Sarge was bordering on information overload already.

"So now," said Sarge, interrupting my own thinking, "we have the Savages' bodies or what's left of them. This may give us another crack at nailing down Collins for their murder."

"If we could find him," said Walker, "and if we can collect anything incriminating from the bodies."

"Or if he is even alive," added Sarge. Then he looked at me.

"What do you think, Chris? I know how loyal you are to your mates, but could your man Collins have done all this? Two murders? Dump the bodies down a hole? Gone the full vigilante?"

What could I say? The Sarge, who is like a father, asks me if my first substitute father is a double murderer. They say the truth will set you free. I could give Sarge part of the truth.

"Yes, Sarge. Rusty could have done it alright, absolutely."

What I didn't say was if Rusty had murdered these two men, the men who took his daughter, there is no way on this earth I would assist with his arrest.

I looked at the photo of Rusty from 2010. He looked like a very hard man, which he was. What the mugshot didn't show was how soft he could be. Soft as custard with the kids he took on board. How important he was to all of us.

Four people, Virginia, the Savages, and the man himself, Russell Collins, my Superman, gone. Two dead, two missing.

Where were Rusty and Virginia?

The meeting had completely devolved into silence. It was a lovely room for it. To sit back and contemplate, sunny, warm, and with coffee on the table.

It occurred to me, in our relative comfort, that we hadn't even discussed the situation that had landed me in the hospital the other night.

"Any news on our escapees?" I asked.

"Nothing," said Walker.

"Vanished," said Sarge.

"Anyone seen the Bedford truck?"

"Nope, that's missing too," said Sarge.

"Along with the cows," said Will Walker.

"Bullocks," I said, "not cows, bullocks. Bullocks are way more profitable than cows." I was adding a bit of internet knowledge to go along with the gender specifics of the stolen cattle, which I had gathered from Irma Pendergast.

"Right," said Walker. "Bullocks." I could tell he was impressed by the way he faked complete indifference.

So, we had a Bedford truck, about 100 bullocks, three escapees, and Rusty Collins to look out for.

My caseload was looking more and more like a junior Aussie rules football match.

Loose men everywhere, and no one can find the ball.

Rob Farrell's garage.

I got bored sitting at home, so I donned my police uniform, walked back to the hospital to collect my gun and badge from Wendy's safe, stole a kiss from the Head Nurse, and then floated on air over to Rob Farrell's garage to return his gun and borrow a car.

"It's not a library here, mate," said Rob. "You don't return a gun and then take a car and just mark it down on a card with a return date."

"You don't? Oh!"

"No."

"What about coffee?"

"Oh bloody hell," said Rob and went off to make us both coffees on his whiz-bang machine.

After two rounds of beautiful coffee, sitting in the lunchtime sun out the back of Rob's garage, I drove Rob's borrowed car over to visit the Pendergasts at Wodonga Hospital.

Wodonga Hospital.

Old Ben was still in a bed under a stroke-watch-prevention thing, whatever it was called, and Irma was right there beside him, still fussing over him.

"How's it going, folks?" I asked.

"Bloody horrible," said Ben.

"Very good, thank you, Chris," said Irma, "Don't mind Ben. He gets cranky in hospitals."

"No love, the hospital is good. Bloody good," said Ben. "I'm cranky as hell at that bloody Jason Mellish. That's who I'm cranky with."

Jason Mellish. Just the man I came to discuss.

"Ben, you had Jason working with you a while back, but then you let him go. What was all that about?"

"Well, this sounds bloody ridiculous in retrospect. It makes me look a fool, and in normal circumstances, I wouldn't say."

"But?"

"But he stole a cow."

"Not a bullock?"

"No, a cow. A cow that was due to give birth to a baby that would become a bullock."

"How did he sneak that one past you?"

It was hard to imagine how a cattle thief could get his stolen cow past the Pendergasts' house. From my brief view of the place, all their paddocks led to the house paddock. And the house paddock was the only way out onto Towong Road.

"Very easily," said Ben, "you see, I had him doing fencing and general work about the place. He was a bloody hard worker, but, I don't know, it was never quite right. I'd ask him to mow the lawn, and I'd come back to check, and the lawn would be half mowed, and he'd be giving the mower a service, or he'd be heading off to town to get a spark plug."

Ben was wandering off track, but I had plenty of time, so I let him go.

"Everything with Jason was always just six inches to a yard short of what I asked him to do and always halfway down some path that Jason thought he should do as opposed to what I asked for. And no bloody thing was ever fully finished."

"OK," I prompted, waiting for the point.

"Anyway, the last paid job Jason did for us was to fence the back paddock, and for once, he did a good job, except, as well as a fence, he put a gate down the back into the forest, a gate to nowhere, put a padlock and everything on it. It was just supposed to be a bloody fence. To separate our place and the Mount Elliot National Park there. Now, it's a fence and a gate. I never asked for a gate. Why would I want a gate?"

"OK," I felt we were almost there.

"Anyway, I got the invoice. It has the extra charge for a gate I never asked for, plus the charges for a padlock and chain I never needed. Jason's invoices were always a bone of contention, but this was ridiculous."

"He charged you for the gate you didn't ask for?"

"Exactly, he told me, and I mean he, the bloody hired worker, told me, the stupid bloody idiot that hired him to work on my own farm, he told me I would need the gate to get back my cattle if they ever escaped into the national park back there. Which should have warned me about his intentions since if they had escaped into the forest, the cattle that is, there was no way you could herd them back in through that stupid bloody gate, what with where he put it."

"He put it in the wrong spot?"

"Yes. You can only push cattle from the farm side. You would use the cross fence. You can't push cattle from the other direction, from the forest. There is no guide fence. You'd need a dozen trained cattle dogs, for Christ's sake, or my old girl Roo, but she died ten years back."

"Ben," said Irma sharply, "focus, please."

"Sorry, love, she was a good dog, old Roo. She could have managed. Anyway, sometime after all that, I am out there counting all my lovely ladies, as you do."

"You mean your cows?"

"Yes, counting all the girls and their nice new babies and, bugger me, Thelma, who was due to drop any day, is missing. Gone. Hooroo, see you later."

"Jason stole Thelma?"

"My bloody oath he did. I go down there to see if I could find Thelma, see if she had wandered off into the bush down there, my bush, not the park bush. Thelma was always a bit solitary, especially late-term. She liked to do her business uninterrupted, so to speak. She had a bad experience with a veterinarian that time."

"Ben," said Irma. "Don't wander off, love."

"OK, OK. Well, bugger me, Thel wasn't there. But here's the thing, there are her hoof-prints, walking straight out my new bloody unwanted gate, and not jumping it, mind you, WALKING out of it! And here is the gate, all padlocked, nice and tidy, and there on the other side of the fence is your big bloody horrible Beaurepaire tyre tracks, belonging to that ridiculous giant four-wheel drive, with the trailer, that hoon-thing Jason drives, or used to drive, before he went to jail for bashing you up."

"That's not why he went to jail, Ben, but never mind," I said.

"Sorry, Chris, I just get angry thinking about that fellow. You try to do the right thing and help out a young bloke from the region, what with him being a bastard. You know about all that nonsense, I presume. Anyway, this is where it gets you. Should have just hired his brother Justin. Irma warned me Jason was no good, too much like his real dad."

"Ben, you are telling me you knew Thelma's hoof prints by sight, and you were able to track them to the gate."

"Yes, of course." Old Ben answered as if I was an idiot.

"And you could tell these were Jason Mellish's tyre tracks on the other side of the gate."

"Yes, Chris, of course," Ben was making it apparent by his tone that I was certainly an idiot, not knowing the obvious.

"Jason drove on Beaurepaires. Can you believe that? My God, you wouldn't buy anything but Goodyears around here."

"Goodyears are the best tyres?"

"No," shouted Ben. "No, mate, it's not the tyres. It is the dealer."

"Ben, you are shouting," said Irma, "calm down, you're being rude. You know Chris is a city lad."

"City-stupid," said Ben. "No offence, mate,"

"None taken," I said

"Anyway, with your tyres, you have to go to Wodonga for the Beaurepaire bloke. But here's the thing. Garry Forrester, the Goodyear guy in Jarrajarra, will come to your door. No charge. He'll do it all on the farm. It is the dealer that makes the difference. The convenience is the ticket."

"OK, I get it." I actually think I did get it. "So, to sum it all up, Jason Mellish stole Thelma. You are absolutely certain of it, no question in your mind, so, after that, you sack Jason."

"Well, not exactly sack him, more like I just voted with my feet, as they say, we walked away from him. The next time I needed fencing, I hired young Scotty Farrell. Oh, my goodness, what a difference, like night and day. A fabulous job he did. Should have got him years before."

"Probably wasn't old enough, first time we hired Jason," said Irma.

"That boy was born old," said Ben.

"Such a wonderful young man," said Irma in admiration, "Tell me, how is he going with that lovely young lass who drives the ambulance?"

"Jody?" I asked.

"Yes," said Irma. Now Irma was drifting off-topic. Ben's mental meanderings were contagious.

"Sorry, Irma, I have no idea," I said, "Ben, do you think Jason may have been planning to steal more of your cattle, like on a slow drip system? Every time he wants more free meat, steal some from you?"

"No question, he's probably too stupid to realize how closely I check my girls and boys. I'm sure he meant to come back for more."

"Which he did two days ago," I said rather indelicately.

"Yes, I suppose," said Ben. "But, you see, it was not just cattle. I have an old shed down the back. I put stuff in there, like old fence posts and wire, that I might be able to use again. Any firewood that I cut down at that end of the property, I stack it in there to dry out for a year or so. All good stuff, all second-hand, but ready to go again if you need it. Anyway, I went down there a while back, and the whole bloody lot is gone. We both know who took it, in and out the back door, mate."

"Ben, have you ever mentioned this to anyone, not just the thefts but the gate?"

"No, Chris, why would I? Makes me look like a bloody idiot for hiring a Mellish."

It occurred to me that the Sarge had the region full of cops watching roads, trying to catch the escapees on their way from one place to another. Hoping to intercept them. But what if they weren't moving? Could we catch them at their hideout? They would not be the first Aussie bandits to evade police with a clever choice of hidey-hole.

I was thinking of Ned Kelly and Power's Point.

Friday, June 10, 2022

Jarrajarra.

I had spent much of the previous night taking phone calls from the out-of-town cops who'd joined the escapee hunt. Some were slightly confused, some were bewildered, and some were just totally lost.

If it wasn't the geography that confused them, it was the funny ways of the locals.

I had about twenty calls at home. I was trying to have a sick day, but no one else was respecting my brush with death. Where was the concern for my well-being?

It seemed easier on everyone if I returned to the job and sat on the phone.

It is hard taking sickies in a one-cop town, even when you have ten regulars and about twenty rookies on hand to help hunt for escapees. Everyone with a telephone wants to gouge the local copper for local information.

Even worse, for my psychological well-being, my days off in the sick bed had ended my latest running streak. I had been up to one-hundred-and-ninety-three consecutive days, frustratingly close to my first two hundred. Now, I was back to zero.

This morning, my head still ached, and my right shoulder hurt like hell. I decided to fight my running compulsion and take another day off from morning exercise. Wendy was happy with that. She desperately needed more sleep. The town needed a permanent doctor and at least two extra nurses. Till that happened, she just soldiered on alone.

People would have to stop getting sick and give up having babies. My beautiful girlfriend was exhausted.

I was showered and heading out the door when Wendy struggled out of bed to give me a goodbye cuddle. She was vertical but still half asleep.

"Did you go for a run yet," she asked in a sleepy mumble.

"No, we both decided on a sleep-in, remember."

"Oh yeah." She was rubbing her face, trying to wake herself up.

"Sweetheart," I said, "you should go back to bed. You look stuffed."

"No, gotta get to work," she said, punctuated with a long, loud yawn. I had no chance of changing her work intentions.

"Hey, listen, soldier," she added, "maybe you should run at lunchtime or shoot some bullets at the tin targets with Rob."

"OK. Why?"

"I know you. You need exercise, or else you will get cranky and start shooting some of these rookie cops for asking stupid questions or not saluting, and I will end up with even more patients than I can handle."

"Rookies don't salute constables, and what if I just shoot them in the leg, like on TV, just a flesh wound, and ship them to Wodonga?"

"Love, Wodonga Hospital is even more under the pump than we are. Just get out and run, please, or go to the rifle range. You will be miserable all day if you don't."

She moved in, and we had a long hug. Somewhere during all of that, she woke up.

"What are we going to do about your job?" I asked, worried.

"I don't know, Chris," she answered, "it is beyond my pay grade that question." She was exhausted before her day had begun.

"OK, work time," she said.

I got a kiss goodbye, and off we went in our separate directions.

Jarrajarra Police Station.

I arrived at the station at 9.00 am. An hour later than normal. Maybe it was a protest at being dragged back when I didn't want to work at all.

Normally, I loved my job; something different every day, never boring. Today, I was flat.

Barney was talking on the phone. He looked at me and gave me the raised eyebrow treatment.

"Can I call you back, Irma," he spoke into the phone, "Something just came up," he paused, "OK, Bye."

I guessed Barney was talking to Irma Pendergast, sorting out the insurance claim for her damaged house and lost cattle. Not that it was our responsibility to manage her affairs. But that was the way it was in Jarrajarra. When you were down, others stepped up on your behalf.

"Chris, my God, what are you doing here? You look like you've been bashed up by a gorilla."

"I thought I was on the improve."

"The right side of your face is purple with bruises, oh my goodness. Sergeant Palmer is still using your office. Oh dear, look at you. Just sit down here, and I'll get you a coffee."

"Thanks, Barn, you're a gem." Barney gave up his magnificent office chair, with wheels and arms and a nice lean-back-relax feature that I loved. Usually, at the front desk, I sat on one of the hundred-year-old wooden things we kept as spares. Greater love hath no man that he give up his comfy roll-a-chair for another.

Barney had purchased it himself since the police-provided furniture was such crap.

I eased myself into the lovely chair. To be honest, I felt OK. Way better than I looked. Just tired. My black eye and facial bruises were all working their way out of my existence, but if Barney intended to make me a coffee, who was I to fight?

I might have let out an audible groan of pleasure as I sank into the chair.

"No need for the dramatics," said Barney, "I told you I would make the coffee." You could never play Barney. Truth and honour were on his side, always.

Two minutes later, Barney returned with a beautiful cup of coffee latte. I could see the foam edging over the top of the cup.

The Police Station phone rang.

"Ah shit," I said.

Barney reached over the desk and placed my coffee in front of me. As he reached for the phone, he mouthed the words, "You're not supposed to be here."

"Jarrajarra Police Station, Barney Trail speaking, how may I help you."

He paused to listen, then spoke.

"Doctor Newton," said Barney into his phone. "I've already sent Constable Tim down to assist you. Does it really require a second officer?"

My heart sank.

"I will see if Chris is available. We are extremely busy at the moment."

Doctor Newton was in his eighties and was battling Alzheimer's disease. He was a former General Practioner who'd been the town doctor for forty years or more. His working career had ended long before I came to town. Now, he was retired, a widower, and living in Jarrajarra to be near his daughter, Mrs Janine Faraday, a teacher at Jarrajarra Primary.

As his dementia progressed, many things in Jarrajarra bothered him, and whenever he was upset and couldn't find his daughter, he would ring Barney. Typically, that ended with me visiting Doctor Newton to try and calm him down.

It was getting more complicated with each visit. Doc's concerns were getting worse, and his poor daughter was reaching the stage where she would have to send him off to a care facility.

Barney brought me up to speed on the latest phone call.

"Apparently, Doctor Newton has taken a hostage, and Constable Tim wants to release the hostage and arrest Doctor Newton. Why, I can't imagine. Anyway, Doctor Newton is outraged at Tim's suggestion that he be arrested and has locked himself and the hostage inside the outside toilet at the back of his home and won't come out till you come."

"Me, specifically me?"

"Yes, you, Constable Chris Taylor, in person. He needs you personally to arrest both the hostage and Constable Tim and put them both before a judge. Doctor Newton is confident you will know what specific charges to bring. He also added that you should not worry about him as he has a gun, and you know he knows how to use it."

Barney finished the task description with a sigh.

"OK," I said and called Constable Tim on his mobile. I put him on speaker so Barney could hear.

Tim answered,

"Mate," I said, "this gun Doctor Newton has. Is it an old 303 with a broken strap? An old World War 1 thing."

"Yes," said Tim, "that sounds about right."

"Did it have a painted yellow magazine inserted?"

"Yes," said Tim. "Very yellow."

"OK, don't get nervous, mate. The magazine is welded shut and empty. No bullets. The rifle has no firing mechanism. Doesn't work unless you were to hit something with it. That might hurt a bit, but it wouldn't kill you, I don't think."

I had decommissioned Doctor Newton's rifle when we first met. He may not have noticed, or he did notice, and then he forgot.

"I don't think he has room to swing it in there, Chris. It's basically an outside shithouse. I'd break down the door, except it is so small I'd probably push Doc and the hostage down the long drop."

With anyone else, that would have been a little cop-joke between colleagues. But this was Tim. No jokes on duty.

"OK, so why doesn't he like you?"

"He doesn't like me because he said I was a police imposter. Said he'll only come out for a real policeman, namely you."

"Fair enough, can't argue with that."

"Ha-ha," said Tim, with no humour at all.

"Oh mate," I said before hanging up on the call, "who is the hostage?"

"Dazzle, Darren Everett, the drone operator. Supposed to be searching for the escapees."

"Dazzle?"

"Yes," said Tim, "he was out with his drone scouring the backyards around town, looking for the crooks when Doctor Newton took umbrage at the invasion of his privacy and made a citizen's arrest. I had it all sorted when Dazzle got lippy with Doctor Newton, who pulled out the 303. When I tried to take the gun off him, it all went south. I was too gentle because of his age. Now, here we are. They are both locked in the outside dunny."

"Why's Dazzle droning the houses in town?" I asked.

"Between you and me, I don't think he is game-ready for the wilderness. I think he is a bit scared to get out in the bush. Scared, he might find himself a bad guy with a gun."

"OK, I get it." I said, "I will be there in five minutes."

"Ten," shouted Barney to Tim before I ended the call.

"Finish your coffee, Chris," said Barney, so I did.

And, while I enjoyed myself with the coffee in the comfy chair, Barney returned the call to Mrs. Pendergast. He held up the form he had been working on. At the top of the page, it said – HERD INSURANCE, CLAIM FORM.

I whispered to Barney, "Barn, whatever number of cattle they say they lost, add ten,"

"Add ten?" asked Barney.

"But don't go over one hundred and ten. The Bedford can't fit more than that."

I'd checked the internet and found that Bedford B-double-road trains with double-decker trailers had a maximum carrying capacity of one hundred and ten. This was the recommended maximum number of eight-hundred-pound bullocks that these monster road trains could fit and carry with that particular configuration.

The Pendergasts should not claim more stolen cattle than would fit in the Bedford. Insurance companies loved information like that. Facts, they called them.

Barney looked at me, exasperated.

"Hello Irma, Barney again. Could you hold on one second, please?"

Barney held the phone against his chest and whispered to me quite forcefully.

"Chris, I am not getting involved in one of your little insurance exaggerations. I've told you before there are no degrees of honesty."

"OK, OK," I said, holding my hands up in surrender.

Barney resumed his call.

"Hi Irma, back again. Sorry. I'm good, thanks. What say we finish off this insurance claim for the stolen cattle."

"Oh Barney, thank you, you are a godsend," I heard Irma say via Barney's phone.

I listened to Barney, and when he got to the important number Irma didn't know, she had to ask Ben. She didn't know about the bullocks; that was Ben's job.

Irma returned to the call with Ben's cattle count.

"One hundred and ten, apparently." I heard Irma say to Barney.

I finished my coffee and headed off to rescue Constable Tim and Dazzle, the hostage, from the clutches of Doctor Newton.

As I left the station, Barney took back his comfy chair.

Doctor Newton's place, Jarrajarra.

"Doctor Newton, it is Chris Taylor here. Could you come out, please?"

"Chris? How do I know it is you?"

"I am standing right here, Doctor Newton; you can check me out."

A grizzled old eye appeared at the knot hole in the centre of the wooden door to the ancient backyard toilet. It looked me over with a strong hint of suspicion.

"You're not Chris. Your face is all purple."

"It's me, Doctor Newton. I had a collision with a car door. My face is bruised. Check out my other side."

I offered my left profile to the knot hole in the door, which was duly inspected. I felt like Englebert Humperdink on the cover of that album. Handsome side view, eyes to the horizon.

"If you're Chris, show me our secret handshake."

"I can't see your hand, Doctor Newton; you're inside the toilet."

The door opened two inches, and Doctor Newton extended his right hand. He had a closed fist, except for his extended index finger. I made a similar pointy-fingered fist with my own right hand. I then touched the tip of my finger to that of Doctor Newton. Very gently.

This was our secret handshake.

We had formulated this one just for ourselves during the height of the pandemic. Doc claimed there was less contact with just the single fingertips, and he was right. So, we did away with the government-recommended fist bump and tippy-touched our pointed fingers.

Secret men's business. Just the ticket for handling old blokes who aren't quite as sharp as they used to be. There was a growing number of men, like Doctor Newton, around the region, losing their way in various stages of dementia, bringing nothing but sorrow and hard work for their wives and children.

After our special shake, he slammed the dunny door.

"OK," he said. Had a bit more of a think, "It could be you."

"What say, as a gesture of compromise, you release the hostages?" I suggested.

He thought about that for a moment.

"I've only got the one," he said, "a chunky little bloke."

"OK, I'll take him."

The door opened, and Dazzle, the drone operator, stepped out.

"Freedom," said Dazzle, a bit irritated, not quite joining in the fun.

"How about we let the gun go free as well," I asked the toilet door.

The door opened, and the gun was handed out. I handed that to Constable Tim.

"What about you, Doctor Newton? Do you want to come out? Or

are you alright in there? Would you like a cup of tea, maybe?"

"I might stay here for a bit, Chris. A cup of tea would be wonderful, thanks if you don't mind. Feeling a bit confused here. I was looking for Janine when that idiot started buzzing me with his sky thing."

"Well, don't worry about him. I'll cuff him and put him in the van. You just rest in there for a minute while I go inside and make the tea for you. I'll see if I can find Janine."

"Thank you," he said through the closed door, "and make one for yourself, and those other young chaps can have some too. There are a few Scotch Fingers left in the tin in the cupboard. I'll have one of those myself if you don't mind."

"Have you got any Tim Tams," asked Constable Tim.

"I think so," said Doctor Newton, "but leave some for Janine. They're her favourite."

So, with the hostage crisis sorted and our catering planned, Tim, Dazzle and I retreated to the kitchen to make the tea.

While the kettle boiled, I called Doc's daughter Janine at the local primary school to let her know the situation. She organized her way out of class and promised to be here soon.

By the time Janine arrived at her dad's place, the four of us, Doctor Newton, Tim, Dazzle, and I, were taking tea and biscuits on the porch. All the previous shenanigans had been forgotten.

"Doctor Newton," I said, "while I was inside your house, making the tea, I noticed some old trophies and photos in the living room. You were a bit of a bike rider?"

"Yeah," he said, "I was pretty good back then during the sixties and seventies. I loved it."

"He was better than pretty good, Chris," said Janine. He made the Australian team for the Olympic games in 1964."

"Tokyo?" I asked, impressed.

"That's the one," he said. "It was the only time I made the team, unfortunately. I was a better rider in 1968 and 1972 but couldn't get a guernsey. Bloody good riders around back then. A long time ago now. I'd improved, but my opposition had improved some more."

"Amazing," I said, "you must be proud."

"Yeah," said Doctor Newton. "Great thing to represent your country. I can remember the opening ceremony like it was yesterday."

He took a sip of his tea and a bite of his chocolate biscuit.

"Trouble is I can't bloody remember yesterday," he said without a hint of sadness or self-pity.

"Have you ever done any coaching?"I asked.

"Bloody oath," said Doctor Newton. "I loved coaching the local kids. Never much talent among them around here, but I loved their enthusiasm."

"We've got a triathlete here in town," I said, "could probably do with some expert assistance."

"Would love to," he said, "send him down. I'll give him some tips."

"It's a she," I said.

"Makes no difference to me," he said. "As long as she's not afraid of hard work."

"She's not afraid of anything," I said.

I called Jody Taggart, and it took barely half a minute to convince her to walk down the street from the Ambulance Station to Doctor Newton's house and join the tea party.

I had her at 'scotch finger' but closed the deal with the chance to meet a real live Olympic bike rider.

Through all of this back and forth, Constable Tim was looking at me with a little fleck of chocolate on his chin and what I thought maybe a new-found respect for my diplomatic handling of the whole delicate matter. It was either respect or total bewilderment. He didn't say.

Tim was an excellent backup, strong as an ox, as reliable as the day was long. He was assigned here from Wodonga station whenever we had a crisis. Or whenever Sarge thought I could use some extra hands. He was a great cop but had absolutely no sense of fun. And not a huge understanding of the human race.

"Win-win, Timmy," I said, pointing at his chin.

He cleared the chocolate crumbs successfully but didn't have a clue what I was talking about.

When we left, Doctor Newton and Jody Taggert remained at the table with a fresh pot of tea, talking about bikes and riding.

Jarrajarra Police Station.

"So, Dazzle, what's the go here?" I asked.

The three of us were back at the police station, sitting at the small table in the station kitchen.

"I thought you'd be out and about in the region," I said. "You could be droning the bush area for evidence of our escapees, not flying about town taking random shots of backyards about the place. It feels a bit suss."

"Well, that's a bit harsh," said Dazzle. Aggrieved.

"It's not harsh. It's bloody ridiculous," said Tim, gliding into the role of the bad cop to my good one, "why aren't you out in the bush, Darren. You're just annoying people flying that thing over their houses. It's not right. You could have set Doctor Newton over the edge. It's borderline harassment."

"I'm chasing criminals here, Constable, for the good of the community at the invitation of your boss, Sergeant Palmer."

Dazzle was past aggrieved, progressing to indignant.

"I heard you volunteered," said Tim to Daz. "You're not even getting paid. Sarge didn't call you. You called him. You offered your services."

Dazzle's anger throttle went up just a bit.

"Yes, I did volunteer," he said. "When you're on the leading edge of scientific investigative technology, sometimes you have to push your best foot forward. I was hoping I could demonstrate to the police the benefits of the science here in a case like this. It's not like you lot are kicking any goals on your own."

Good point.

Old Daz was sounding borderline eloquent. He was a podgy little bloke. Chunky and with clothes that didn't quite fit. I noticed when he was rescued from his hostage situation his T-shirt was three sizes too small. It was a muscle shirt without the body to match. His tattered old board shorts were at half height, barely staying in place, under his muffin belly, showing a very generous hint of bum cleavage.

I don't think he dressed for vanity. More like he chose his clothing from whatever was available. Most of that was years old.

"So, how have you been, Daz?" I asked, trying to distract him from an argument with Tim.

"You two know each other?" asked Tim

"Yeah, of course," said the Dazzler. "We've worked together

before, mate."

"Daz was Angela Adam's camera guy on the Folliero case," I said to Tim, "He did all the camera work when they interviewed the Sarge and those other homicide detectives outside the town hall."

Angela Adams was the biggest name in television crime reporting in the country. She had been to town and sprinkled her stardust all over us when the drug baron and murderer Michelle Folliero brought his mayhem to Jarrajarra three years ago.

Dazzle, Darren Everett, sitting in front of us, was Angela Adams' local camera guy. Not that she was local all that often. To claim that he and I 'worked together' was a long stretch of the bow. He never pointed his camera at me. I was in the daily news a bit at the time, and I did win a medal, two in fact, but I never saw Dazzle when it was down and dirty. I had only ever glimpsed his bum crack from behind while I was looking at the incredibly beautiful Angela Adams talking into a microphone in front of Daz's camera.

But, to give him credit, he was good with his camera work. He had always managed to make our little town shine.

"So why did you give up the camera gig?" I asked.

"I didn't give it up. I still work for TV when something is happening around here. If any news happens within a hundred miles of Wodonga, I'm the man. Car accidents, floods, all that stuff. Like with Angela trying to find Folliero, they hire me. I've got all my own gear and my own bike. I can get anywhere in an hour."

"Don't they have their own camera people?"

"Permanent staff, Chris, it's too expensive," he said. "The TV stations hardly have any permanent camera staff. Budget restraint is the go these days. They just hire blokes like me on an as-needed basis. I work for all the channels. It's a good gig. Self-employed. Always on the go. It's the gig economy. Side hustles are the go, baby."

"So, do you really know Angela Adams?" asked Constable Tim, getting down to the important stuff, namely what was the famous TV star like in person and if there was any possibility, in this universe, she could fall in love with Tim.

"Of course, I know her, Tim. I did the murder trials down here, all the cop trials in Wodonga after Folliero went down. We work together all the time. We are drinking buddies, Angie and me."

Daz's tilt of the head and the look away as he spoke suggested to me that this friendship with Angela Adams was a touch exaggerated.

"What's she like off camera," asked Tim, getting to the real nub of the interrogation.

"Great girl, great girl. Always there for the after party. You'd love her, mate."

Well, that's a given, I thought.

"So how come you're doing this stuff?" I asked Daz, pointing at the drone kit at his feet on the floor.

Tim gave me a side-eye that suggested I was wandering off-topic.

"It's not just another camera, Chris," answered Daz, "it's a very special kind of camera. It goes three-dimensional while the old cameras only go two, another quiver in my arrow, so to speak."

I'm not sure that the quiver-arrow alliteration was quite what he was looking for, but Tim and I both got his drift.

"Another income stream," I suggested.

"Exactly, mate," said Dazzle. "Plus, I thought this would be a chance to win another customer, another income source, namely the police."

"Well, you're off to a flyer," added Tim. "Nearly got yourself shot by an aged pensioner."

"Yes," said Dazzle, "very nearly, so yeah, are we laying charges against that old bastard, or what?"

"No," I said firmly. "We will leave Doctor Newton in peace, and I'd prefer you not to talk about him in that tone. He is a lovely old bloke. Just dealing with some personal problems."

"And locals out-rank outside drone operators anyway," added Tim. I would have laughed, but Tim never joked.

"Sorry," Daz said.

I had an idea, "what say the three of us go for a drive and see how good you are with this stuff? Get the old band back together," I winked at Daz, charmingly, I thought.

I remember Daz was very good with a normal old camera. Maybe, with his new thing, he could solve a problem for me.

Constable Tim looked at me rather dubiously.

"Trust me, mate," I said. "I've got a plan."

I gave Tim the keys to my truck. I was still feeling battered and bruised. Stiff as a board.

Pendergast Farm, Towong

Half an hour later, we parked at the front gate to the Pendergast Farm while Daz unpacked his drone kit, and Constable Tim wandered about having his first look at the scene of the recent crimes. I called Irma Pendergast.

"How's it going, Irma?" I asked.

"Bloody horrible," said Ben. Irma obviously had me on speaker.

"Very good, thank you, Chris," said Irma, "I must say we are so thankful for everything you and Barney have done for us with the insurance. I was sick with worry, but the insurance assessor has already been in touch."

"All part of the service, Mrs P," which was a fib. "You know what Barney's like. He loves to help."

"Oh, Chris, you've got to learn to take a compliment. We can't thank both of you enough. We know it wasn't just Barney."

"Irma, I am putting you on speaker here. This is going to be a team effort.

"OK," she said.

"Can you hear me, Ben?"

"Yes," he said. That was the shortest sentence he had said in the last three days.

"First, can I ask you if that gate that Jason Mellish put in is still in place?"

"Yes, still there," said Ben, "I paid for the bloody thing, pointless taking it away, changed the locks, though."

"Good," I said, keeping it short.

"Haven't touched the bloody thing since before Jason bashed up you and Constable Tim and went to jail."

"Jason never bashed us up!" I said. Even I was getting tired of this rumour.

"He king hit me, Ben, if you don't mind," said Tim. Constable Tim was now standing right there beside me, listening to everything.

"Yes, well," said Ben, "whatever he did to render you blokes unconscious that time. Whatever happened is none of my business, nothing to be ashamed of. I'd have used my boxing if I'd been there, but that's just me."

"Ben, mate, can you just slow down a bit," I intervened. Ben was getting worked up. "I don't want you having another stroke, mate, and I've got a job to do here."

"We are listening, Chris," said Irma sternly.

By this stage, Dazzle had joined Constable Tim and I. He was standing beside us with his drone ready to fly. I gave Daz a sort of raised eyebrow thing, with a thumbs up and mouthed the word "Ready?"

He thumbed up in response.

"So, Ben, I am standing at the top of your drive. I am looking toward the house. I can see Mount Elliot off there in the distance."

"OK," said Ben.

"Where is this gate?"

"Oh jeez, now you've set me a challenge," he said, "how to explain the location of the gate to a city boy. Bloody hell."

"Could we show you?"

"What?" grunted Ben.

"Can you direct the image to a phone?" I asked Daz. I knew it was possible, having checked on the internet.

"Yes," said Daz.

Within five minutes of faffing about, sending phone numbers back and forth, sending hyperlinks to websites, and getting Irma to manage Ben through the whole mobile-phone-television-internet thing, we FINALLY had Ben and Irma, looking at the real-time-drone-supplied vision of their farm.

From the sky above, it was a splendid vision. The Pendergast farm was truly beautiful.

"My goodness," said Irma after we were finally all connected. "Isn't technology wonderful?"

"We are working with a true professional here, Irma," I said, smarming a smile at Dazzle. He soaked it up as though glowing praise was his daily due.

Starting there, keeping Ben to one-word directions, after a few minutes of left-right-further-back-back-back-too-much-go-forward, we were all looking, via our separate phones, at the infamous Mellish gate.

There it was, and there on the other side of the gate, the track by which Jason Mellish had gained access to the lands of Ben and Irma Pendergast and, once there, stolen Ben's beloved Thelma, not to mention her unborn child. Possibly a bullock.

But that was a few years ago now. Never reported and long forgotten.

What we could see today, via the drone camera, was the much-discussed 'Mellish gate'. It was now open, and the lock and chain lay useless on the ground beside the gate post.

"Ben," I asked, "was the gate locked up last time you checked?"

"Yes, it was. Locked and rusted over, should have known bloody Jason would buy the cheapest rubbish he could lay his hand on, but yes, locked tight."

"Not anymore," said Daz, trying to sound clever.

Constable Tim shot Daz a look that, to the sensitive eye, indicated something along the lines of 'Shut the fuck up'.

So, this was how Jason and his sidekicks managed to appear from nowhere.

On closer view, Dazzle's drone revealed that the track to the back gate was rough and muddy and not a formed thing. It was a path of deep tyre gouges, broken bushes, and flattened grass, not made by machine but bulldozed into submission by the hard-driving of an all-terrain vehicle, simply getting where it wanted to go. The sort of monster vehicle preferred by Jason Mellish.

The interesting thing about the rough-muddy track was it didn't just come from the nearest 'conventional' backroad to Ben's back paddock and stop there. It went into the bush beyond.

From the Mellish gate, it appeared from the drone vision that the track made a right-hand turn into the bushes toward Mount Elliot itself.

"Follow that track," I said to Daz.

"I am already beyond one kilometre," said Daz with a pout. "The drone is physically outside my line of sight. You realise this is now a completely illegal flight. I could lose my flying licence for this."

"Don't be a diva Dazzle," said Tim, angry, "just fly the bloody thing and see where it goes."

I gave Tim a side-eye toward the phone. He'd forgotten the shared line we had going with the Pendergasts.

"Oh whoops, sorry, Irma," said Tim, "excuse me French."

"That's perfectly alright, Timothy," said Irma, "this is exciting."

"Well, you've all been warned," said Daz, and so he flew, illegally but quite expertly, his camera work perfection, following the trail, above the trees, toward the distant hills and bush, never losing focus or our trail.

"Are we recording this, Daz," I asked in a very friendly tone. Keep the diva happy.

"Yes," said Daz, still in a huff. "Of course, I am recording this. That's the point, isn't it?"

He followed the track, up and up and up, closer and closer to the peak of Mount Elliot, till eventually, we reached its end. Daz zoomed in, without prompting, toward something we would have never found, not on foot, not in a hundred years.

A small clearing. In the middle of the tiny clearing was a tent. A camo-coloured tent, almost invisible without the tight zoom and the steady focus of our petulant drone operator. The tent was clean, and it was new, fit for purpose.

"Bugger me," said Ben via his phone.

"It's a hideout," said Tim, sounding impressed.

"Can you turn the point-of-view around so it looks back toward the valley," I asked very politely.

"POV rotating," said Daz, giving us a bit of technical flourish.

Mount Elliot was on one side of the Towong Plain, and on the other side was the Mitta Mitta Ranges. The Pendergast farm was almost dead centre within the four-kilometre valley.

Daz manipulated the drone controls, and the eye of the drone turned away from the tent at ground level, up toward the tip of Mount Elliot, which was mostly hidden by the surrounding bush, then around toward the farm, toward the Mitta Mitta. The steep slope meant the bush on the downside of the track just fell away out of camera view.

There was the farm, in perfect focus, and there, further beyond that, was the Mitta Mitta ranges. The view was spectacular, as far as the eye could see.

"Oh my god," said Irma, "Jason has made his own Powers Point."

"His what?" asked Tim.

"Powers Point," said Irma, "Ned Kelly's high ground. He hid out there for nearly two years, around 1878. He could rob a bank, then head back there to his eagle's nest and watch the police searching for him. He could see them while they were preparing to search. And he could watch them as they rode about in circles, and he could watch them despair, give up, and go home. Jason Mellish was probably watching us just a few hours after he escaped from prison."

"Till he stole your cattle," I said.

I knew about Powers Point. It was so effective that Ned Kelly had actually inherited it, like a secret gift from his bush-ranging mentor, Harry Powers.

"OK, Ben, great work, Irma. Thank you both for your help today," I said, trying to close them out politely. "It is all police work from here. I would appreciate it if you made it a point not to discuss what we have done today with anyone."

"No, we won't, absolutely not," said Irma.

"I'll do my best," said Ben. I wasn't sure what that meant in the context.

"You just focus on your health, Ben, OK," added Tim. What with it being a meeting of sorts, everyone felt the need to say something at the end.

"Pay attention to what Chris said," continued Tim, "this could be an advantage for us. These escapees don't know what we know, so let's keep it that way. Alright, Ben?"

"Yes, Tim, I understand," said Ben.

"OK. Great. Bye," said Tim, and ended the call.

"I was just going to add a few points," said Daz.

"I know," said Tim. Rather pointed.

"Great work, Daz," I said, and I meant it. Hopefully, that would keep him happy.

He just nodded in a meek response. I'd keep quiet myself if a big boof like Tim shut me down like that. Why poke a bear?

"Stuff the drone, great police work, Chris, I reckon," said Tim, smiling at me. Daz would need to arrange a date with Angela Adams if he ever wanted to get out of Constable Tim's bad books.

The whole hideout thing was too smart for Jason Mellish. This had to be the planning of Jennifer McLain or this Carl Angwin fellow. Who the hell was this bloke, Carl Angwin?

"Do you imagine Jason Mellish planning a Ned Kelly type of lookout like this?" I asked Tim.

"Dunno mate," he said, "it would make two things Mellish and Kelly have in common."

"Two?" I asked.

"Yeah, two, Kelly was a cop killing shithead as well as a cattle thief," said Tim, expressing, in his own brutal vernacular, the official police version of our national hero.

I was thinking to myself, I didn't quite agree with Tim when my phone rang. It was Barney.

"Chris, are you out at the Pendergast farm with Darren Everett?"

"Yes, I am."

"There has been a complaint from the Mount Elliot Hangliding and Paragliding Club. Apparently, someone is illegally flying a drone out there. Just below their launch space."

"OK, umm, well, just tell them I will get out there and put a stop to that nonsense immediately."

"Will do," said Barney and hung up.

Teamwork.

I figured I had a little bit more time before the Hangliders and Paragliders took up arms against us, so I asked Daz, ever so politely, given his sensitive nature, to zoom in a bit closer and check there was no one in residence in the mystery tent.

Who knows? We could have been lucky enough to find someone at home. But not today. There was no criminal inside the camouflaged residence.

After that, Daz summoned his flying beagle back to base. Then we packed up and headed home to Jarrajarra.

Jarrajarra, Chris's Kitchen.

"How are you feeling, Son?" It was the Sarge on my mobile.

"I'm alright, fit for purpose," I answered. The headache from my concussion was retreating, "I reckon I'm up for anything short of a fistfight or a marathon. What is happening?"

"Are you up for a drive? Me driving?" asked Sarge.

"Always."

"Where are you now?"

"At home."

"See you out front in two minutes."

After the trip to the Pendergast Farm, Constable Tim dropped me home. Back in my kitchen with my laptop, I had spent some time looking up what I could find about Carl Agnew on the various criminal databases I had access to.

I struck gold early on the CDA Database. CDA stood for Court Data Australia. All Australian courts publish the cases they handle. They do it daily. All those cases find themselves on the CDA Database, where they can be searched by people like me, whether you're a cop or not. It is an excellent way to get a discreet heads-up on whether someone you know is a crook. The CDA might not tell you all you want about their personal or criminal history or even their sentences, but it will tell you quickly if and when they were in court and why.

I didn't have to search hard to find Carl Angwin. He was a crook, alright. Been charged with cattle theft in 2017.

Presumably, it was bad enough, and he was guilty enough to end up in jail.

I checked the Victorian Police LEAP system and found out Angwin had been found guilty of theft under section 74 of the Crimes Act 1958 and sentenced to seven years.

He must have stolen more than a few bullocks to get that whack. Seven suggested he was a bad enough crook for a custodial sentence. Then later he is clean enough for a holiday resort-style prison such as Henderson. I couldn't find any offences involving violence. That would have worked in his favour with Corrections Victoria.

So, there was the connection. Angwin must have buddied up with Thorburn and Mellish somewhere in the system, and from there, they decided to team up. Merging their muscle with Angwin's knowledge, they all escape to steal some bullock.

Why the hell not?

Maybe Angwin was my criminal mastermind. Maybe Jennifer McLain was not the brains of the operation after all.

Hard to tell without more information.

Two minutes after Sarge had called, I was in the passenger seat of a police car. Sarge was driving, and we were heading southeast.

"We found the Bedford cattle truck," said Sarge.

"And the bullocks?"

"All gone."

"And our three escapees."

"Two escapees," he corrected me. "We have regained Angwin."

"Yes, I see." I said, "I guess 'regained' is as good a word as any for a prison escapee no longer at large but not heading back to jail in the foreseeable future."

"I thought so," said Sarge.

"I had considered that he might be the brains of the whole Mellish cattle theft extravaganza. I guess that idea has been shot to pieces."

"It might have been his idea, Chris. I'm not sure about your use of the word brains, though. What with the headshot and all."

We drove on in silence. I resisted the temptation to make a joke about scatterbrains, which I knew the Sarge was expecting.

We were heading to a place called 'Upotipotpon', which the Sarge pronounced as 'You-Potty-Pot-Pot'. Don't ask me how he got there. I checked, and Google agreed with Sarge.

You-Potty-Pot-Pot was a tiny town with a strange name, which, according to Sarge, derived from an Aboriginal expression 'pootong-pootong', meaning "plenty of grass". I hope Ben and Irma's bullocks fared better than Carl Angwin.

Upotipotpon was a three-hour drive. As always, when the Sarge was driving, I went to sleep.

We were both ex-army, so 'sleep-when-you-can' was the applicable code of behaviour.

On the road to Upotipotpon

"Chris, we're about an hour out of our destination," said Sarge, waking me up. "There's a dinner basket on the back seat. Vilma prepared it. More for you than me, I think."

He was smiling when he said it.

Vilma was Sarge's wife, a lovely woman. Amongst all of Sarge's team, I was probably her pet policeman. Saving his life in a shoot-out on the Mitta Mitta trail will do that.

I opened the basket and found a thermos of steaming black coffee, perfect. I poured a cup for both of us. While sipping my coffee, I checked the pile of individually wrapped sandwiches. Chicken breast and caramelized onion for me, ham and salad for the Sarge.

What a pity we were heading for work.

"Save some for the trip home, son," said Sarge.

"There's enough here to feed half the force," I replied.

"Let's not be silly," he said as we tucked in. "Vilma only caters for the select few. You and me in this case."

We settled in to enjoy our coffee and sandwiches, a lovely way to wake up.

"You know, Sarge, no pun intended, I was wondering if Agnew was the brains of this cattle enterprise. That was before today's news."

"He may well have been just that. The cattle thing may have been his idea, a relatively easy steal, then plenty of easy money if you know where to sell them."

"Then," I said, "if they'd completed their transactions and had their cash in hand, Angwin may have been 'no longer relevant' to the partnership."

"Exactly, Chris, pretty ruthless decision-making, I'd say."

"According to Google, the cattle would have been worth, maybe, over four hundred thousand dollars at a legitimate market. More if the buyer were a butcher, able to cut them up and distribute them as meat product."

"Oh, my goodness," said Sarge, "you tend not to think of that when you look at those magnificent cattle roaming around their paddocks."

"Enough to turn you vegetarian," I offered.

"Let's not go overboard."

We thought about all that for a moment. Was the buyer another cattle haulier or a butcher?

"OK," said Sarge, "take this all back a step. You're selling to another crook, who has to dispose of this herd legally. I am told these types of people often demand an eighty per cent discount for cash. What's that leave your thief?"

"Eighty thousand dollars," I said, being the numbers man of the team.

"Split three ways now, not four."

"Means you get Twenty-seven thousand plus instead of twenty," I said.

"Which is not a lot of money to go and murder someone with a shot to the back of the head."

"Maybe. Or maybe they were getting on each other's nerves," I offered, "they've been on the run for four days."

"So, it is either an argument gone wrong," said Sarge.

"For which I would nominate Mellish as the shooter. You can

upset Jason by breathing."

"Or," Sarge continued," it is an extremely ruthless decision taken to increase their individual share of the cattle money and streamline the whole escape and hiding process."

"If it's just ruthless, I'd nominate McLain every time."

"Hide the sandwiches, Chris. We're here."

Cop car flashing lights ahead indicated we had arrived at our destination.

I stashed Vilma Palmer's magnificent travel feast back into the basket and hid it in the back seat under a tarp.

Some secrets you just don't share.

Upotipotpon, Northeast Victoria.

"That's what's left of Carl Angwin," said Detective Sergeant Peter Jordan.

He was pointing at the corpse of Carl Angwin, lying on the ground, face down, just outside the passenger door, a bit toward the back of the vehicle, as though he had been shot from behind after climbing down out of the cab.

He was speaking to Sarge and me. We were standing about two metres away from the passenger side door of the Pendergast's old Red Bedford. Detective Pete was standing beside us. We were all giving the dead body a wide berth, as you do.

Underneath Angwin's body was a large pool of blood.

Sarge and I were the last to arrive at the location of the Bedford truck and the dead body that was lying beside it.

Behind the Bedford, there were the tyre tracks of another large double tandem and a mass of flattened grass. Someone had backed up a similar size vehicle. Presumably, the cattle had been transferred from the seller to the buyer.

We were standing in an otherwise empty paddock inside the forensic perimeter established by the Crime Services team from Melbourne. The perimeter was marked with yellow tape, which protected a large area from the entry gate to the truck and a healthy distance beyond.

We were allowed into the inner sanctum by virtue of being with Detective Pete, who was the lead homicide detective on the murder of

Constable Ralph Davey.

To step past the perimeter, we all had to wear the full protective-anti-contamination catastrophe, the body suit, the head covering, gloves for our hands and covering for our shoes. All that stuff, we looked very scientific, crime-scene-pure, non-toxic, and white as white could be.

Technically, we were looking at one of Constable Davey's murderers. If he was still alive, Angwin might argue he had never fired a gun, but he was dead, and he was part of it all. As far as the cops were concerned, he was as guilty as hell.

Detective Pete had one of his crooks. There were three to go. Life might not be a scoreboard, but I'd never mention that to Pete Jordan. He'd mark you minus one for weakness.

The Crime Services team had stepped back for a moment while Pete showed us through what was, officially, his crime scene.

The Sarge and Detective Pete were looking at Angwin. I was looking at the truck. Eventually, Detective Pete noticed.

"Would you like to take a look inside, Chris?" he asked.

"Do you mind?" I asked.

"Go for it," said Detective Pete.

I jumped inside, and Sarge and Pete looked in through the driver's door to avoid the bloody puddle on the passenger side.

"You can see here," I said, "behind the driving cabin, there is a narrow sleep cabin. The way it is set up, you can either use it as a bench seat for extra passengers. Or, alternatively, you can use it as a bed, wide enough for two in a tight squeeze."

I moved into the sleeping cabin. There was a doorway behind the middle front seat. The driver's seat and passenger seats had walls behind them.

There were no windows on either side of the sleeping cabin.

"If you sit in the back like this," I continued, "you can only see out the front windscreen. Plus, it is a mattress on a bench, not really a seat. Not a very comfortable place to ride."

"So, whoever sat back there was, was most likely, the low man on the totem pole," said Sarge. We were both still wondering who was in charge on the crook's side of all this mayhem.

I tried, sitting on the very same uncomfortable bench myself. Shit, it was firm. You'd have to fight to make me sit here.

I had moved into the sleeping cabin for a reason, several reasons, in fact.

First, I looked for a gun cabinet, and there it was, an unlocked-lockable rifle cabinet right there on the floor, behind the driver wall, on the sleep cabin side. The cabinet was open, and there was also a small pool of blood on the floor nearby, next to the cabin door.

The gun itself was gone from the truck; it was now in police custody. Collected by Carole and Glenda after Jason Mellish had dropped it during his shootout with Constable Joyce and me.

Next, I looked for a bullet hole in the back wall, and I couldn't find one.

Finally, I looked around for light switches. There were two standard switches close together on the inside of the sleeping cabin, not the driver-side, but the inside-the-sleep-cabin-side.

"Light switches are inside the sleeping cabin," I said.

I flicked them both, and lights went on, illuminating both the front seat area and the sleep cabin area.

"There you go," I said, "learning all the time."

"Learning what?" asked Detective Pete.

I had seen what I wanted to see from within, so I climbed out of the cabin and out of the truck.

I joined my colleagues to explain.

"The interior light was on when they rammed us. It came on just before Mellish lifted the shotgun to the window. Lighting the cabin seemed a very strange action at the time because it allowed me to see what they were doing."

"So, what did you see?"

"Well, I believe I saw Mellish ask Angwin to find the shotgun and pass it to him. Mellish knew the truck and knew the shotty was in the cabin section. He probably put it there himself when they stole the cattle." I said.

"But Angwin can't see it. So, he finds the light switches and flicks them on. Probably doesn't realize he has also flicked on the front cabin."

"That gave me something to see," I added. "Then Angwin passes the shotgun to Mellish. All I see is Mellish lifting the gun from beneath and behind, then he pushes the barrel out the window, and we start shooting at each other. We both miss mostly, at first."

"OK," says the Sarge, wondering where this is going.

"After the first few rounds, I am vaguely aware of Thorburn diving for cover in the back. I don't see Thorburn after that, and I am certain I never see Angwin at all. Never saw him. This makes sense. He is the low man on the team, so they shove him in the back bench, in the cabin, out of sight. I am guessing, but maybe Thorburn dived on top of him to get out of the way of the gunfire. Wouldn't be the first time he had stage fright."

I had arrested Thorburn a few years before after a shoot-out on the Mitta Mitta Trail south of Jarrajarra. He had frozen then, and I reckon he had frozen again.

"Anyway, I remember I put a couple of shots through the windscreen," I said as I led the Sarge and Detective Pete around to the front of the Bedford.

There were bullet holes in the windscreen. Mine, most likely.

"So here are my first few misses. I am hitting high here." You could see my high-hits, and you could also see where the bullets had ripped into the roof of the cabin above the passenger seat.

"Didn't miss by much," said Pete.

"A miss is as good as a mile," I replied, quoting my Nan, not my army instructors.

"This one here, right in the middle of the windscreen. With this one, I had Mellish, dead centre. He was maybe thirty metres and closing. I had him."

"OK," said Sarge.

"But then, as I fire my weapon, McLain swerves left to hit our cars, and my bullet goes where I was aiming, but it is now right of Mellish, through the middle of the window and straight through the door to the back seat cabin."

"So, you are sure McLain was driving?" asked Detective Pete.

"Absolutely, she was driving, no question at all," I said.

"The thing is," I continued, "I think I might have hit Thorburn with that last shot."

There was blood on the floor of the cabin, but no splatter on the back wall, no bullet hole that I could see, nothing.

"I think I hit him," I said, "and the bullet may still be sloshing around inside him along with all the steroids and huge muscles."

"Wow," said Detective Pete, "So they'd need to find a doctor, or."

"Or," continued Sarge, "whoever shot Angwin in the back of the head, maybe shot Thorburn?"

"But where is he now?" asked Pete.

We all went back to thinking. It was a good meeting. The thinking was permitted.

"Could Thorburn be dead as well?" I asked, "and they stuffed his body in the truck somewhere?"

"So, that takes Mellish and McLain from a four-way split of the proceeds to a two-way?" asked Sarge.

"Maybe you already killed Thorburn in the shoot-out, and you gave the other two the idea of reducing the shareholders," added Detective Pete, with a raise of the eyebrows. I think he was joking.

"One way to find out," said Sarge, pulling on his gloves.

Gloved up and still, suited up like snowmen, the three of us examined every nook and cranny around the truck, including the huge welded toolboxes and all of the under-body compartments that weren't immediately obvious.

There was nothing.

There was a bench seat in the sleeping cabin.

" Is this a lift-up?" asked Detective Pete.

"I didn't notice," I said.

"Could be?" said Sarge. "You're the youngest, Chris," he added, nodding toward the truck.

"And only a Constable," chimed in Pete.

I climbed in and took a fresh look. No handholds on the bench lid that I could see, but it did extend an inch beyond the base.

I put both hands under the lip of the bench and lifted.

The first thing I see is blankets. I carefully lifted the blankets.

"Oh dear," I said. "Hello, Randall."

There he was, gym junkie, man-mountain, would-be bad guy, but so ill-equipped for a life of physical violence, Randall Thorburn.

All that money he must have spent on gym membership and steroids. To end up like this.

Another dead escapee. Make that two down on Detective Pete's scoreboard. Two to go.

I let the blanket down carefully and climbed out of the truck to leave the detailed examination of Randell Thorburn's corpse to the professionals. As I climbed down from the truck, I could see the eyes of the forensics team lit with expectation.

"One last thing before the team moves in," I said.

"What?" asked Pete.

"The inside passenger door."

I go to the passenger side, avoiding the body and the puddle of blood. Before anyone can say stop, I open the door.

There, on the inside of the door itself, is a splash of blood just under the window.

"There you go, Constable Joyce hit Jason Mellish in the arm, I saw it hit, and he dropped the shotgun. Her bullet goes through him, I guess, and on through the open window."

"How do you know the window was open?" asked Pete.

"Because he opened it before he started firing the shotgun at me," I said, "then, after I got knocked over by the flying car parts, Mellish opened the whole door, intending to finish me off, but he accidentally killed Constable Davey. Then Constable Joyce started firing before he could have another go at me, saving my life."

"All very interesting," said Detective Pete.

"Pretty interesting for me, Pete," I said. "Looking down the barrel of a shotgun, with a head like mush, can barely move my gun to save myself. And mighty bloody interesting for Constable Joyce, with Assistant Commissioner whatshisname Harrison questioning me about her performance."

"OK, I hear you," said Detective Pete Jordan, making one of those non-committal, yeah-yeah shrugs he made when he wanted to avoid saying anything impolitic.

I had worked with him before, and he was an honest cop, hard-working and a great investigator. But Pete was a born politician. He wouldn't argue with his higher-ups on Constable Joyce Thompson's behalf.

He wasn't really interested in either Joyce or me. All Detective Pete wanted right now, today, was to be the man who nailed the cop killer.

"So," said the Sarge, dragging us back to escapees, "we have Mellish and McLain out there, still at large, Mellish apparently wounded."

"I think so," I said. "That makes him more dangerous than ever."

"Well, Chris, you were there when the guns were blazing, so let's take it that Mellish is wounded. Where does that put the two of them now?"

We all went back to silent thinking.

"I might know," I said. "I have a theory."

On the road home from Upotipotpon

After I told Pete and Sarge about our discovery of a potential hide-out at Mount Elliot, just down from the Hang-gliding centre, the three of us de-camped from the Upotipotpon crime scene back to Jarrajarra Police Station.

We were heading home to plot a capture or a wild goose chase.

The Sarge and I had successfully kept our secret food stash away from the hoi polloi at the crime scene. We shared the leftovers in Vilma Palmer's picnic basket amongst ourselves. It was a delicious drive back to Jarrajarra.

About an hour out from home, I called Constable Tim.

"Tim, mate, can you roust up Darren Everett, our drone operator, and get him back to the station within the hour. Barney knows where to find him."

"Ah, shit, no! No! Why me? Can't it wait till you get back? He loves you. He is a prima donna. All he wants to do with me is argue, and he doesn't bloody know Angela Adams, and that's a fact."

I had Tim on speaker. Maybe I should have mentioned that to him before we started.

"Tim," said Sarge in that ex-army officer voice they spend years training you to use. "Get Everett to the station by the time we return. Make sure he brings all his gear. Understood?"

"Understood, Sarge," said Tim.

Jarrajarra Police Station.

"I can't promise perfection," said the Daz to Detective Sergeant Pete. "Drone work is an inexact science. The art of visual discovery and observation is still a largely unrecognized craft."

Here we were in the police station kitchen, close to midnight, buzzing on coffee, listening to the words of wisdom from our crime-fighting drone master.

"Some people would tell you that I am primarily an artist," said the

Daz, "Not true. First, I consider myself primarily a craftsman, then a technician, and only then am I an artist."

"Fascinating, fascinating," said Detective Pete, as though he was sincerely fascinated.

'Once you can fake sincerity, you are halfway to world control,' said every bullshit artist I ever met. Detective Sergeant Pete Jordan was way beyond halfway.

"It is not enough just to get the bird to the target," said Daz.

"The bird?" asked Assistant Commissioner Harrison. He was still hanging around, much to my surprise and disappointment.

"The drone," said Detective Pete, as proof-positive of his fascination with the new science.

"Location is only half the challenge," continued Daz. "Once you are situated, you then need to shoot."

"Shoot?" asked Harrison. "You can fire a weapon at the target from the bird?"

"No AC, not with this particular bird," said Detective Pete, the new disciple of the dronic arts. "He means 'shoot' as in shoot the camera, like get the vision and the sound."

"Oh shoot," nodded AC Harrison.

"The vision is the true test," droned on Dazzle. "Essentials are orientation, focus, colour and pixel depth, bitrate being the term we use in the industry. Any civilian can get a drone operator's licence, gentlemen, but there is a reason the major television news networks and now the Victorian Police come to me. You need vision and sound that stand up in the courts. You need evidence."

"Precisely," said Detective Pete, with enough enthusiasm to carry us all over-the-line to believer-ship.

"So, tell me," Asked AC Harrison, sounding more impatient than fascinated and clearly having no idea of Dazzle's name. "Can you get this thing in the air so we can all have a nice close look at this alleged hide-out?"

"Yes, I can," answered Daz, with the eyes-closed resignation of a Michelangelo being asked to back up and cut us a second statue of David by lunchtime. "But," he continued, "I may need just a tad more patience and understanding than I received in our earlier collaboration." He side-eyed Constable Tim as he spoke.

"Of course," said Pete, "Cooperation at all levels is the go.

Constable Tim will remain here with AC Harrison at Police Command Jarrajarra, while Constable Taylor and I will accompany you personally to the location of this target."

Constable Tim did not exactly do a fist pump at the news that he was off the drone team, but his smug side-eye at me and a faintly raised eyebrow told me he was a happy man.

Tim hadn't spent much time with AC Harrison. I was sure he'd be begging to get back as a second-string Daz-whisperer before the night was over.

"Then there is the question of payment," added Daz, ever the hustler. "I am a contractor, gentlemen, and I am already thousands of dollars out of pocket on this project."

"Don't tie yourself in a knot about money, Mr. Aaaaaah Everett, just send your invoices to me," said AC Harrison with his usual bluster. It was not what I would call a commitment to pay, but it seemed to satisfy the Dazzler.

"Senior Sergeant Palmer," said AC Harrison, "Do we need the SOG for this?"

"Constable Taylor believes they could be there," said Sarge. "You've seen the vision from this morning, AC. It certainly looks like the tent was set up recently to be re-used. I think it would be the safest option to bring in the SOG. My team has already been involved in one unplanned shootout with these characters. Let's not risk another."

The real leader in the room had spoken. What a guy.

"Done," said Harrison, who then called the head of the Special Operations Group who had established their camp in the cricket club rooms. What with it being the footy season, the football rooms were out of bounds.

Soon enough, we were on our way.

I was hoping we found Mellish and McLain at Mount Elliot. I had a few reasons. Justice, revenge, the safety of the community, all of that. Most importantly, I didn't want to look like an idiot.

If this was all a wild goose chase, I would be the one to own it.

If we found them, I had no doubt AC Harrison and Detective Pete would fight it out between themselves for the greater share of the glory. There'd be little room for second place and none for third.

Saturday, June 11, 2022

Mount Elliot, Towong

We set up our base at the launching point used by the Hang-gliding club at Mount Elliot. It was little more than a clear space, scraped clear and mowed smooth, on the top of a bush-covered mountain. Perfect for running like a crazy human kite and launching yourself into the sky above.

We were above and east of the Pendergasts' farm and what I hoped was the McLain-Mellish hideout. It was either that or some tent somebody had planted randomly out here in the high mountain bush just to annoy me.

We had rolled in very quietly. Sarge, Me, Pete, Daz and some very serious SOG operators.

I had shared the map point with everyone in our convoy. Sarge and me in one car, the Dazzle and Detective Pete in another, and the SOG all together in two of their pseudo-tanks.

The SOG vehicles were noisy, but it was a public place, and we had come in from the opposite direction to Mellish's improvised track. I was pretty sure Mellish wouldn't hear us. If he was actually there.

Please be there, Jase.

This whole prison escapee thing was feeling like one humiliation laid upon another.

On arrival, it was apparent that Detective Pete's fascination with the art and craft of drone science was wearing thin. I wasn't sure he could hold it together for another hour. Dazzle would have to perform if he hoped to retain the police as clients.

We were all in place. On Pete's signal, half of the SOG team headed down the hill toward the tent location. The team was almost perfectly silent and looked suitably deadly as they moved out. I would not like to be on the other end of their intentions.

The other half of the SOG team, from tank-two, stayed with us at the Hang-gliders club.

The bush below was reasonably thick, not impenetrable. It had that Aussie high-country flavour. Enough canopy to look impenetrable from above, but at ground level, more scrub than trees and enough space that you didn't need a machete to hack through. I am sure some local cattle had been given free feed there over the years. Government land was considered fair game for struggling graziers so long as you weren't caught.

If it was me heading to the tent, and I was not so banged up and bruised, I expected I could get there comfortably, in stealth mode, within half an hour.

Forty minutes later, the call came through on Sarge's comms. The SOG team were in position. One hundred metres east and above the location of the tent.

Ready and way more than able.

Daz was in his element, a whole team of hard cops waiting on his call. It was the light, apparently. It had to be just so, meaning we all had to wait.

We waited on the light.

Daz always surprised me by being so good at what he did. Among all the bullshit and petulance, he was good with a camera. He had pride and real curiosity in his job; I gave him that.

It was approaching 4.45 AM. Still dark to my eye. Daz had been fiddling with his gear. He wandered over to me.

"Chris," he whispered, "I think I am ready to go, but I am a bit scared."

"You'll be right, mate. You've got an army looking after you," I said.

Humility? Admitting his fears? Where the hell did this come from?

"I am not scared of getting shot at," said Daz, "I just don't want to let you down, mate."

Oh, dear! Had someone traded the old Daz for a new one? Worried about me?

"You were the only one who believed in me," he said. "I don't want you to end up in the shit because of me."

"Daz, I do believe in your ability, and that is all we need from you. Trust me. I have been in the shit before without any help from anyone. You just do your thing. You are very good at what you do. Bloody Hell, mate, who is the Angela-Adams-go-to-man in the Jarrajarra region?"

He was getting there. A mention of Angela Adams always pumped his tyres.

I grabbed his hands in mine and faced him, man to man.

"You are Dazzling Darren Everett. Unequalled in the droney arts. Daz, mate, you've got this," I said, looking down at his artisan's hands in fake-sincere awe of the talent therein.

I let go of his hands and patted his shoulder, reassuring-like.

"Thanks, Chris," he whispered, then he turned to the waiting cops. "OK. Let's go, boys," he shouted, about three decibels too loud for any stealth operation I'd ever been on.

Oh well. I tried.

"Keep it down, fuck head," said one of the SOG guys in a hard whisper that probably un-did all my morale boosting.

"It is not too dark, is it?" I asked Daz, trying to keep him focused and calm.

He held up a light metre.

"No," he said confidently, "we are good to go. If they are there, we will see them. This is a very light-sensitive machine."

We had done the same hyper-techno-hook-ups we had done earlier with the Pendergasts. Sending web-links-emails-clicks-and-more-clicks back and forth till finally, we all stood back, weapons ready, watching the vision from the drone on our tablets and phones.

Irma Pendergast was right. This was bloody exciting.

I watched on Sarge's tablet as the drone rose above us. There we were, lit up like Christmas. Surprisingly bright. Looking up to check the drone, I couldn't see it in the dark sky above.

Looking back to the tablet screen, there we were, like daytime.

"Fascinating," said Detective Pete, looking over Sarge's other shoulder. I think he meant it.

Sarge, Pete and I stood a short step back from Dazzle on his controller, keeping the others at bay. Sarge would be the only one telling Daz what to do. For now, Sarge was happy to let Daz fly solo.

We all watched as the vision from the drone gave us the Mitta Mitta in the distance, down a fraction to focus on the Pendergast farmhouse. Daz was skillfully giving the audience a view of his intended direction.

Context, I thought.

"Good visual context," whispered the Sarge. "Evidence," he said, light praise at the right time.

Then the drone changed its point of view, so we were again looking at our collection of cars and cops, and then it started to move, at speed, over the bush between us and the hide-out.

I had butterflies in my stomach. This wasn't like the gunfight the other night, with action or reaction. This was sitting an exam and then having to wait in the principal's office for the results.

This particular drone could travel up to 80 kilometres per hour. I checked on the internet after noting the make and model on our first go-round this morning.

We were there, above the tent, in barely a minute.

There was a very faint light coming from the tent. Somebody was home.

Beside the tent, there was a motorbike. Transport.

In a moment, Jason Mellish emerged from the tent in perfect focus. He looked up. He had heard the drone.

"Can he see you in this light?" asked Sarge.

"I am not sure, I doubt it," said Daz.

"Hold your position, Darren," commanded Sarge.

Mellish was wearing jeans and a T-Shirt and in bare feet.

He pointed toward the drone.

He had a pistol in his hand.

He fired. He missed.

"He can't see you," said Sarge, "Hold it there."

Sarge spoke into his comms to the SOG team. "Move!" He shouted. "Suspect armed and shooting."

"Roger that," came back to the Sarge.

The comms line stayed open. We could hear the SOG moving toward the tent location. Then silence.

On the tablet, we could see Mellish. He stopped firing and moved back inside the tent.

After a moment, he came out, boots on now. Jennifer McLain was behind him. Was Mellish holding hands with McLain or dragging her by the wrist? It was hard to tell.

Hand in hand or dragging, Mellish looked up toward the drone and fired again.

Missed again.

"Keep it there, Darren," said Sarge, "you're doing well."

Mellish dragged McLain to the motorbike. Was it a drag? They didn't look friendly to each other.

Mellish tucked the pistol into his belt, around about his right hip.

Then, he started the bike, and then, with his left hand on the steering, he reached out his right hand and beckoned toward McLain.

It was then I noticed Jason's right arm was bandaged around the wrist. Joyce Thompson had hit him, fair and square, in the shoot-out. 'Well done, Joycey,' I thought.

I then saw something else. Something I don't think I will ever forget.

After Jason called Jennifer McLain to mount the motorbike behind him, she stepped to the side of the bike.

She was standing behind him. At first, I thought she was going to take the passenger position.

She stopped.

Jason Mellish looked over his shoulder briefly and said something to her.

We couldn't hear what he said or if she replied.

Then McLain took the pistol that Mellish had stuffed in his belt. She had it in her hand before Mellish reacted.

He had both his hands on the handlebars of his bike.

Did he realise that McLain had the gun?

Mellish was looking forward. Was he waiting for her to mount the passenger seat of the bike?

She raised the pistol.

Mellish started to turn as if finally aware she had wandered off script.

McLain stepped toward the back of the bike, remaining out of Mellish's vision.

They both seemed to freeze for a moment.

Then, she shot him.

As best as I could tell from our bird's-eye view, she shot him point blank in the back of his head. The bullet emerged from the other side of his skull, somewhere between his ear and his eye, in a vivid red spray of blood, bone and brain matter.

Mellish fell forward on the bike, and then the bike fell sideways, away from McLain.

Jason fell awkwardly, his left leg caught under the body of the bike. He landed twisted, face down, as though his last dying thought was to protect his injured right arm. That could not have been possible. He would have died the instant after she pulled the trigger.

Jason's face was buried in the ground, the back of his head toward the sky, toward the drone. No question he was dead. The entry hole in the back of his skull was in clear, perfect focus. Well done, Dazzle.

The blood puddle was quickly spreading like a halo on the ground around Jason's head.

McLain put her arm out to the side and, quite theatrically, dropped her weapon.

She stepped away from the mess she had made, knelt on the ground and put her hands behind her head in the arrest-me-officer position.

She looked up at the drone and just stared.

"Oh my God, she murdered him right there," said Daz. Daz was crying, shaken, his first death on camera.

"Suspect has surrendered," said Sarge into his comms. "I repeat, the suspect has surrendered. The suspect is NOT resisting."

My boss, Senior Sergeant Bruce Palmer, I loved him. He was a perfect man and a perfect cop. I'd have told the SOG lads to kill the mongrels. If Mellish was dead already, I'd have killed him again, but that's me.

Barely seconds passed after Sarge's call to the SOG, and they were there, moving in fast. McLain was face down, cuffed and in custody within a second.

On the tablet, Sarge, Pete and I watched silently, impressed, as the SOG lads cleaned house.

"Well-done, well-done, lads," came a voice from the universe somewhere. "Wonderful effort."

It took me a moment to realize it was AC Harrison, speaking through the comm lines from Jarrajarra, safe in the office, sitting on his arse in Barney's comfy chair, I bet. Taking ownership of the show now. Now, it was a hit on Broadway.

A hand gripped my shoulder. It was Detective Pete. He was shaking his head, happy, it seemed.

"Goodness me, Constable Chris Taylor, you never cease to amaze me. Bloody, great police work, mate. Bloody amazing."

There was no acting. He meant it.

"Mate, come and work for me," Pete continued. "You are a born investigator. You are wasted out here in the jungle."

"I heard that," said Sarge, busy helping Daz unwind and pack up.

"Don't try that again, Jordan," concluded Sarge, and he wasn't joking either.

"Chris, son," Sarge continued, "give us a hand over here, will you?"

I moved over to help.

"Sarge, let's get this wrapped up and inform Wally Mellish as soon as possible," I said. "This will be out and about very soon."

"Yes," said Sarge. "Good idea. Not looking forward to that."

"I'll do it," I said.

"Yes, of course, best coming from you, I think."

Jarrajarra Caravan Park.

"So, you caught him already?"

"Yes, Wal," I said.

Wally greeted us at the front door of the small cabin he called home behind the caravan park reception office. He was awake when we called, getting ready for breakfast by the look of it.

His tiny cabin was old, the furniture was 1950s modern, but it was all immaculate. The place was neat as a pin. Perfect for a one-person show like Wally Mellish.

Wally looked tired, like a man just out of the hospital, facing his own mortality and off the grog for life if he wanted to have a life.

Wally scanned our faces for a moment, then turned to lead us inside.

"Come in," he said, "I'll make you some coffee."

Sarge and I followed him into his tiny kitchen. We took a seat each at his ancient Formica dining table. We had reached the cabin's maximum seating capacity. There was only one chair left for Wally.

While the kettle boiled, he pulled instant coffee and three cups from one of his cupboards.

He turned to look at us for a moment, still face scanning. I wasn't sure whether to just blurt it out or wait for the coffee.

Blurt first, coffee later. I went early with the bad news.

"It didn't go too well, Wally," I said.

"I can tell by the look on your face it didn't go well," he said. "How bad was it?"

I was ready to speak, but Wally beat me to it, saved me the agony, really.

"He's dead, isn't he?"

"Yes," I said.

The kettle clicked. It had boiled. Wally turned back to his bench and made the three grim cups of black coffee, no extras. Something to do with his hands in a terrible moment.

Time to think.

He carried the three coffees to the table and sat down in the remaining chair.

He looked at me more sober and serious than I had ever seen.

"Just tell me it wasn't you who shot him, Chris."

"It wasn't me, Wal," I said, "it was one of his colleagues."

Strange word to use, colleagues, in such a death or gory enterprise.

Wally wasn't crying, but tears were running down his face.

"This is not some stitch-up like those pricks from Melbourne tried on Ricky Chalmers," said Wally, referring to a couple of corrupt Melbourne cops who'd spread their evil in Jarrajarra three years ago.

"No, Wal, it's not a stitch-up, just a simple straight-forward horrible murder."

"It is all there on video, Mister Mellish," added Sarge. Very gentle. "I am sure we could arrange for you to see the video if you wanted to."

"No thanks, I don't want to see it. Chris's word is good enough for me."

We sat in silence for five or maybe 10 minutes. I don't know. Wally was looking at me mostly. Reading my mind like everyone else in Jarrajarra.

"Stop worrying, Chris," he said, "I'm not looking for an excuse to hit the grog."

"Are you sure, mate?"

"I am fucking positive," he said sadly, "there is nothing on God's earth that would tempt me to face that pain again, not even this."

We finished our coffee.

I was looking for an out. We were busy. The Sarge had a lot to do. I had been going for twenty-four hours. I was buggered.

I didn't care about Jason Mellish. I only cared about his dad, Wally, not his sperm donor, the crazy uncle. I cared about his real dad, Wally. The bloke who did his best raising his wild bastard son.

What could I do for Wally? I had nothing for him. No words. No help.

"Shit coffee, I reckon," said Wal.

"Truly shit," I answered, "unbelievably shit."

"Go on fuck off, back to work," said Wal, not angry or bitter, just being himself. "I'll be OK."

"You sure?"

"I'll call Sue and get her to visit with the kids."

Sue was officially Wally's niece. Unofficially, Sue was Wally's daughter. That is how the previous generation of Mellish men rolled. Not so much #Me-Too as '#Me-First'.

Sue would be as much comfort as Wally would find today. Sarge and I stood up to leave.

"Give me a hug, you big boof," Wally said to me.

He leaned in, we hugged, and Wally let out one loud, uncontrolled sob, then more quiet tears, and then we broke it off, and he led us out the door.

By the time we were in the police truck, Wally was back inside his cabin, and the door was closed.

We headed off toward our police rendezvous at Jarrajarra Station.

"Who is this woman he is calling? Sue?" asked Sarge.

"Sue Mellish, allegedly, legally his niece, BUT, according to the twisted genetic back-story of family legend, she is actually Wally's revenge daughter."

"Revenge daughter?" Sarge was not up to speed.

"The story is," I said, "after Wally's brother had a night of non-consensual sexual relations with Wally's wife, thus spawning our Jason. Wally had neither the muscle power nor the will to strike back physically at his brother."

"OK," said Sarge.

"He took his revenge the Wally-way by seducing his sister-in-law, and over many nights of consensual relations, they spawned their own child, Wally's niece-revenge-daughter, the truly wonderful Sue Mellish. A genuine diamond in the rough."

"My word," said Sarge. "That is complicated. I don't know how you manage to keep up."

"Me neither," I said, "the first time someone told me the story, they made it sound funny, but it's not funny, is it?"

"No," said Sarge, "it's horrific."

Family secrets, life-long hatreds. Wally was barely sixty years old, yet he looked a hundred. Now, most of the members of the two families are dead from grog or drugs or violence."

"There is always a price to pay, Chris," said the Sarge, reading my mind once again.

I was sad for Wally but not for Jason. Jason had set his path as a kid. He was a bad-tempered bully with a lifetime of bad choices behind him, then he had taken up with Jennifer McLain, and that was the worst choice of all.

When we shared a vehicle, Sarge always drove. Suited me.

Still stiff and bruised from my accident and tired, I actually fell asleep on the two-minute drive from the caravan park to town.

When I woke up, the Sarge had stopped outside my house.

"Take the day off, son," he said. "Get some real sleep."

"What about McLain?"

"She will wait," he said. "She's not going anywhere."

I looked at him, trying to think of an objection.

"I don't want to see you tomorrow morning till 10.00 A.M. at the earliest," said Sarge.

It was too good an offer to refuse.

"And turn your phone off," he shouted from the car as I walked to my door. "If I need you, I'll find you."

Sunday, June 12, 2022

Jarrajarra

Six in the morning, it was heaven.

Wendy and I were up early and ran down to the river, then along the river trail to a private spot, where we jumped in and splashed about for the better part of twenty seconds. Even managed to get our hair wet.

It was painfully cold. Twenty seconds was way too long.

We dried off using the single small towel I carried in my running backpack, then sprinted home as fast as we could.

I couldn't keep up with Wendy. What with my injuries, or so I claimed.

But, on the road home from the river, the sun was rising, my bruises were clearing, and my legs were moving again. Sufficient to call it 'running'.

Wendy had called in a support nurse from Wodonga. She was determined to spend what remained of Saturday with me.

My treat. We had slept for most of the afternoon. Then, a peaceful night, both exhausted from our jobs. Now, on Sunday morning, life was simply magic.

It was the best morning I'd had since Jason Mellish and Jennifer McLain had tried to kill me twice, once with a truck and the second time with a shotgun. Today, I was alive, and Jason wasn't. I was free, and McLain was behind bars.

It felt great.

Part of being a cop is the secret stress that something you are involved in might kickback on your loved ones. I knew Jason, in particular, was stupid enough to hurt anyone, especially if he thought that would hurt me. He would have no qualms about hurting Wendy, and now he was dead.

Good riddance to him.

Great result, I thought, and made a note to check on Wally.

After our run, Wendy and I had hot showers, a kiss and a cuddle, and breakfast, and by 7.30 AM Sunday morning, she was off to work. Our little twenty-four-hour holiday was over.

I took my time, then ambled into the station at the assigned time,

10.00 AM and not a minute before.

Refreshed. Happy. Looking forward to sending McLain away forever.

Jarrajarra Police Station.

"Oh, Chris, you look so happy."

"I am Barney, I am."

His sigh told me this happiness might be fleeting.

"You are not going to believe this," said Barney. "Pull up a chair."

We didn't have a fancy interrogation room as you see on television. No big two-way mirrors in one room.

Always looks great on TV, the darkened room, the light from the interview room shining through the two-way mirror.

Not in Jarrajarra.

We had an interview room. If you'd call it a room, more a grown-up closet, with a small table, a couple of chairs on each side, and a door you could lock from the outside.

When Joanne Farrell still worked for us, before she ran off to the world of internet journalism with the aspiring media mogul Saxon Tyson-Howard, she had found us the money to set up a camera system so we could watch an interrogation as it happened.

Usually, it was just Barney watching if he wanted to. More often than not, he didn't bother. Pretty boring just watching me interview some drunk driver I had brought in. Typically, I would be trying to explain to the drunk why he couldn't drive himself home because he was pissed, and he couldn't catch a taxi because we didn't have them in Jarrajarra. Didn't have trains either, but why share all the good news at once?

Barney was watching now, and he wasn't bored. I pulled up the old wooden chair. As I sat down beside Barney, he handed me a pair of headphones so I could listen to the action I could see on his PC screen.

Our tiny interview closet was full.

On the cop side, I could see Detective Pete Jordan and, beside him, our Sarge, Sergeant Bruce Palmer. On the bad guys' side of the table sat Jennifer McLain and Jarrajarra's very own Eddie Doolan, our Main Street solicitor. We may have been a small country town, but our local lawyer was as good as you would find anywhere.

Seeing Eddie on the other team just felt bad. Wrong in every way. Eddie Doolan was one of the home team. Nevertheless, McLain was in good hands, better than she deserved, but how Eddie would ever help her out of the charges she was facing was beyond me.

Detective Pete was speaking.

"You are saying that your client did not drive the Red Bedford Truck with the trailer full of cattle at any time? Ever?"

"That is correct, Detective," said Eddie, calm as always, "my client did not drive the truck. Not at the time of the collision with the police vehicle, nor at any time while she was being held hostage by these escapees."

My heart sank at the word 'hostage'.

"Jennifer," said Detective Pete, "We have an eyewitness who has declared that you were driving the truck, and you chose to ram the police vehicles that were parked beside the road. You were the driver, and you did this deliberately."

McLain looked at Eddie Doolan. He nodded. I assume that meant it was OK to answer.

"I don't have a truck driver's licence," said McLain, "and I don't know how to drive a truck, especially one as big as that, with a dual trailer. Like I told you before, I couldn't have driven the truck if I wanted to. They had me in the sleeping cabin from the time they picked up the truck, with the cattle, till they got to the point where they delivered the cattle to the blokes at Upottyfuckwhat or whatever it's called."

Detective Pete had not mentioned my body cam. Smart move. I was sure McLain was the driver. When I stopped shooting and jumped out of the way, the truck was less than twenty metres away. I could see her clearly. I was sure the bodycam would have caught her. Pete was letting her tell a lie.

I had seen Pete's work before. He was excellent. He would lead McLain over and over her story and over it again. He was under no obligation to tell her what he knew. He didn't even have to tell the truth if a lie suited his purpose. But, if she lied, and it came up in court, she was gone.

"So," said Pete, "who was driving the truck?"

"Angwin."

"Angwin?" asked Pete, with a hint of disbelief. "He drove the truck the whole time, including the encounter with the police?"

"Yes," she said, "he was the only one who drove the truck. I am pretty sure he was the only one who knew how. Maybe Jason did, but he didn't volunteer anytime I saw."

"Tell me, Jennifer, where did this cattle stealing plan come from?" asked Pete.

"The whole thing was Angwin's idea. Randall said they worked it out when they met in Henderson. They both had a few more years, and Angwin wanted out. They both wanted out. Angwin said he knew a bloke would pay two hundred grand or more in cash for the right cattle. Cash enough to disappear for a bit."

"So why was Mellish there? He was due for release in a month or so."

"I don't know. You are asking me to work out the mind of a fucking juiced-up junky. I don't know why someone like Jason Mellish does what he does. Does anybody?"

"I have no idea how they worked out the who and what of their brilliant plan. It didn't turn out so well for them, though, did it? I just know what Randall told me. Jason, apparently, finagled his way in. Said he could get the cattle easily. Knew just where and how. Angwin was the bloke who knew the cattle business, or so he said, and he was the truck guy. Driven them all his life according to him."

"So, Jennifer, if they kidnapped you, how do you know all this planning information."

She stopped for a moment, thinking. Perhaps she realised Detective Pete had set a trap. He had broken her thread, but only for a moment.

"Randall told me."

"When?"

"The night in the tent, the first night we were there up on the mountain before they got the cattle. Randall and I slept in the tent. The other two slept outside in swags."

"You slept the night with Randall Thorburn," said Pete, "even though you say you were a hostage?"

"Yes, I was dragged into all this because of him. I thought he was my boyfriend. I was hoping whatever connection I had with him would keep me safe. I didn't realise he was just another user."

She paused for a moment.

"Randall and I were supposed to be having a party. I told you before. He was going to sneak out of Henderson for the night. We were going to have a party in a motel somewhere nearby, and then before morning, he would sneak back into Henderson. That was what I was expecting. The next minute, I am on the run with three blokes. One of them, Angwin, a vicious little shit, and Jason, I am sure you all know, a certified maniac."

"For the first few hours, I hoped Randall would keep me safe. I was trying to pretend I wasn't scared to death by the other two. I tried to talk Randall into ditching them and getting away, but he wouldn't. Said it would be an easy seventy grand."

"How did he arrive at seventy thousand? There were four of you."

"You are not listening. There were three of them. They were going to split over two hundred between them. I was just Randall's woman. I wasn't part of the plan. I was just the dumb fucking taxi woman."

"Why didn't you just leave when they all went to sleep?"

"Asleep in the tent?" She almost shouted. "What the fuck was I going to do? Just walk off into the bush in the middle of nowhere? If Angwin or Jason didn't kill me, I'd probably starve. At the very best, I'd cop a beating. It might be hard for you big, tough cops to imagine, but I was alone in the bush with three armed men. They had drunk all the grog, did all the speed and the dope. I was scared fucking shitless."

"Can we just step back a bit," asked Pete, "How did you come to be in the tent on Mount Elliot? Where did the tent actually come from?"

"We drove all the way to Jarrajarra the first night. It took about four hours. Jason collected guns and the tent from a farm he said belonged to him and his brother. I'd never been there before. It had an underground thing he and his brother built. They used to grow drugs once, had guns, ammo, camping gear, a ton of stuff, all of it mostly rubbish except the camping stuff and the guns."

"Why didn't you stay there? In the underground thing you mention."

She pulled a face, a grimace.

"It was beyond disgusting."

She paused, thinking, maybe getting ready to tell a long-complicated lie.

"Jason said it was too far from the cattle, plus I think he was scared his brother might find them. They were not on good terms, apparently. If Jason was scared of anyone, it would be Justin, his brother."

"So, you stopped at this farm of Jason's, collected the camping gear and guns from a sort of cave, then headed to Mount Elliot, set up the tent, then went to bed, you and Randall inside the tent, Angwin and Mellish outside in swags?"

"Yes."

"What time did you get to bed after all this?"

"Was still dark. It would have been just after 5.00 AM."

"You made good time to do all that in that short time, five hours since walking out of Henderson."

"What can I say," she shrugged. I could tell by her body movement that the next sentence would be true. "We were in a hurry."

She said 'we'. Barney looked at me. He'd noticed as well.

Pete said, "Eddie, Jennifer, we will take a short break. If you would like coffee, that can be organized."

They sorted out a coffee order for Eddie and McLain.

Detective Pete then said the usual interview-suspended spiel you usually say for the benefit of the person reviewing the tapes later. The date, the time and the people present, all that stuff.

He then turned off the recorder in the room, then turned toward the camera in the corner ceiling and reached up and turned it off.

A moment later, Sarge and Detective Pete emerged from the interview closet and locked the door behind them.

"Well done, Pete," said Sarge softly, not wanting the other team in the closet to hear us.

They walked over to Barney and me at the reception desk.

"She said 'we'," said Pete with raised eyebrows and a smile.

"And denies she drove the truck," said Sarge.

"Is that bodycam footage anywhere we could check it?" Sarge asked Barney.

"Just give me a second," said Barney, fiddling with the keyboard on his PC.

"What do you think, Chris?" asked Pete while Barney set up the bodycam vision, which I hadn't seen as yet.

"I think it is all bullshit," I answered. "I reckon she had the guns, the camp, the tent, all set up before she picked them up."

"She would have had the grog and the drugs and the guns in the car," said Pete, but they were never going to a motel."

"I agree," said Sarge

"Me too," said Pete.

"Ready," said Barney, and the four of us crowded around Barney's desktop computer screen to watch the action.

"Barney, can you get us to the point just before she crashes into the police cars?" asked Sarge.

Barney fiddled, and the vision on the screen raced through all the nonsense with Constable Davey, past the point where Joyce called the incoming truck.

From there, he let it run at normal speed.

Sarge and Pete were sharing headphones, one ear and one earpiece each, listening to the action.

"I can't get over Davey," said Pete, as we watched Davey standing there like a statue, as though the sight of his uniform would stop the approaching beast. "What the fuck does he think he is doing?

It was my bodycam, so we could see my point of view as I ran at him and then scrambled him into the ditch.

It was hyper-shaky as I jumped over the ditch and then turned to face the truck. The light in the cabin was already on.

Barney had the video running in very slow motion.

As I turned to face the oncoming truck, I could see Mellish bringing the shotgun up and out the window. I could see Jennifer McLain driving the truck. The vision was very shaky, and she was still a fair distance away from the camera, but I had no doubt it was her.

The vision steadied.

I started firing. You could see my hands, the recoil, and the camera shake. I had a two-handed grip, so my left arm kept covering the camera's view, and each shot shook the bodycam and the resultant vision. There were only glimpses of the driver's cabin.

Then, the moment I realised I better get out of the way. I dropped my arms, and you could see the truck. It had already started the swerve toward the police vehicles.

There they were, Mellish and McLain. I could admit it was not exactly portrait photography standard, but there they were, clear as day. Clear as cabin light.

"Stop there. Thank you, Barney," said Sarge. "Just go back and forth over that bit, can you please?"

Barney stopped on the relevant frames, then looped it back and forth just a few frames, and then eventually, without being asked, he stopped on the best frame.

There she was. Jennifer McLain in the pixelated flesh.

Barney zoomed in for a closer view.

"That's her," said Pete.

Sarge and Barney just stared at the frozen screenshot of McLain trying to run me down and Mellish trying to shoot me with a shotgun the very moment I thought I was done for.

The Sarge and Barney just stared, silent, till the Sarge broke the ice.

"That cap she is wearing," said Sarge, "it says H.C.C. It is an outside work cap for Henderson Correction Centre."

More silence.

"She looks very masculine," said Barney, which was true.

"They will say it is Angwin," said Sarge, not angry, just disappointed. "We can see it is not, but what we see doesn't matter."

I stared at the screen.

"Fuck, fuck, fuck," whispered Detective Pete.

It was her, but it was clearly not clear enough.

"I guess you just had to be there," I said, knowing already our expert would argue it was McLain, and theirs would argue it was not.

I had seen her in action, in motion, through my own eyes, not through the lens of a camera with all its' focal limitations, with my arms jerking in and out of frame, covering the vision. It was McLain in the driver's seat. I knew it. But as Sarge indicated, I wasn't on the jury.

"It is not perfect, but we will argue it," said Sarge.

"Can you let it roll," Pete asked Barney, "I want to see the crash again. This is fucking spectacular."

We watched as McLain exploded into the parked police cars, first mine, then Davey's, just disintegrating. Then, at the moment before I turned, the door of Davey's police car burst out of its' frame and flew towards me like a bullet from a gun. Not spinning, just flying flat through space. Like a flying car door, really.

I turned an instant before it hit me.

Bang.

Ouch. I could feel it all over again.

"Holy fuck Chris," said Detective Pete Jordan laughing. "That is amazing. Chris, I can't believe you're not dead."

* * *

It was after 11.00 A.M. Sarge and Pete were back in the interview room, and Barney and I watched via the camera on Barney's PC.

They did all the resumption rigmarole, nominating who was in the room, the time of day and all of that. Then they got straight back down to question time.

"Jennifer," said Detective Pete, "Please run me through exactly what happened the night the three men escaped from Henderson."

She didn't betray any tired looks or any hint of being intimidated. She showed nothing that suggested she was sick of telling her story. Eddie Doolan had schooled her well.

Jennifer McLain was ready for another go-round.

"I was waiting outside Henderson, on the dirt track just past the proper car park."

"Why did you choose that spot? Why not park in the car park if you were there for legal reasons?"

"I parked there because Randall had told me to. I guess because it was dark there, and I wouldn't be seen, and it wasn't really legal, was it?"

"When did Randall Thorburn instruct you to park there?"

"He gave me the time and date of my last visit, a month before. He told me not to visit him in prison again till that date, the Monday."

"And you didn't visit him in prison on the day of the escape."

"No. he told me to wait there. From 9:00 PM onwards, after dark. He told me to bring some speed, some Jim Beam and some dope."

"Amphetamines, alcohol and marijuana?"

"Yes."

"You were going to have a party?"

"Yes."

"You knew this party would involve him leaving Henderson?"

"Yes, but that was on him. He was a grown man. I just turned up in the car, thinking we would have some fun."

"You didn't see this as assisting three men in an escape from custody."

"No, I was meeting Randall. He had found a way to sneak out and then sneak back into Henderson without being seen. The plan, he told me, was to go to a motel, have a night together, and then he was going to get back before daylight. That's what I thought was going to happen."

"Just a one-night party. No harm done."

"That's what I thought."

"But it didn't go like that?" Detective Pete prompted.

"No, when Randall arrived, he had Jason and this Carl Angwin fellow. Randall just said, 'Change of plan, sweetie,' and told me to head off down the road."

"So, you weren't hostage at this stage."

"I was definitely a hostage, and I was frightened. Angwin was a pig. Jason has always been very intimidating. I was scared of them. They said drive, I drove."

"Weren't you and Jason boyfriend-girlfriend at one stage?"

"No, never," she said forcefully. "I was with his brother Justin, very briefly, when I first moved to Jarrajarra. Jason might have wanted to be my boyfriend, but that was his big idea, not mine."

"Weren't you two an item when you moved to the caravan park?"

"No, I left Justin when Randall moved in there. I joined Randall, and Jason followed and hung around with the crew of fellows I was with. In the caravan park there. He hung around, free country, but I wasn't with him."

"Never?"

"No, I told you, never. I don't know if you ever met Jason, Detective. He was a horrible man. He was violent, angry, a drunk and a junkie. I reckon he got worse, more violent, more fucking crazy every day I was around him."

I hadn't seen Jason in the three years since he went to prison, but she pretty much summed up the man I knew.

"When Randall got shot by you blokes," she continued, "by the cops at the road stop, Jason didn't give a shit, just stuffed him in the lift-up thing in the sleeping cabin of the truck, like he was nothing, just forgot about him. Randall was dead, and Jason was screaming and carrying on about his sore arm. He was so angry I was scared he was going to kill me."

"So, to be clear here, both men, Randall and Jason, were shot in the encounter with the police?"

"Yes, Randall was shot in the chest and seemed to die straight away." She was close to tears again but managed to keep going. "Jason was shot in the lower arm, about here," she indicated a point on her right wrist. "To be honest, it didn't look much, but the way he carried on, you would have thought his arm had been chopped off."

"What happened after the encounter with the police?"

"Angwin drove down some back roads, Jason knew. Got themselves off the main roads. I was crying, Randall was dead, Jason had just killed a cop, I was very upset, Jason and Angwin were both shouting at each other, shouting at me. Angwin was screaming he didn't sign up for any cop killing. Jason was screaming his usual angry bullshit back at Angwin."

"I was in the back with Randall lying on top of me. He hardly had a mark on him, hardly any blood, but he was dead. He had a wound near his heart, I guess, here."

She indicated a spot that was very definitely the heart area. That would do it. I hit the heart. The heart stops beating. Not much blood to show for death by bullet.

The Sarge and I had killed Randall's older brother in the Mitta Mitta car park a few years back. Now I had finished off the younger brother. I hoped he was the last of them. If there were any left, I would not be their favourite policeman.

Jen McLain continued.

"If I made a noise, they both just screamed at me, shut up bitch, all that. After a couple of hours, they stopped on some dirt road. I don't know where. They stuffed Randall in the lift-up thing, and Angwin says, 'What about her?' I was sure they were going to kill me, but Jason said, just tie her up, so they used the tape on me that they got at the farm where they picked up the cattle. Taped me up, stuffed me in the sleeping cabin."

"Tell me about the disposal of the cattle," said Pete.

"I don't know anything. I heard them using my mobile phone maps to find the 'Upotty' place, the paddock, or town, or whatever it was. I heard our truck and another truck backing up. I heard the cattle leaving the back of our truck. I didn't see anything."

"Where did the motorbike come from?"

"It must have come in the other truck. I don't really know."

"Tell me exactly what you heard after you reached this place. Upotipotpon?" Even Detective Pete struggled with the name.

McLain closed her eyes to remember or make it all up. Jesus, she was starting to convince me.

"They stopped, turned the engine off, then, a while after that, I heard the other truck. It stops right near us. I hear three motorbikes start up, one at a time, the first two I hear driven down a ramp to somewhere beside our truck. I guess they were in the back of the other blokes' truck. Then someone starts up a third bike, and I hear Jason say, we only need two bikes, which makes me think they are definitely going to kill me or just give me over with the cattle. I don't know."

She stopped, more thinking time.

"Anyway, they do all the shifting around, getting the trucks lined up back-to-back, then run the cattle out of our truck to theirs. There was a lot of mucking about doing that. It took a long while."

"Then they have a huge argument about money. Jason and Angwin had been too stupid to get their money before they handed over the cattle, fuckwits. But the other guys go on about cop killing and all that. They had heard on the news and all that shit. Apparently, the two hundred thousand was suddenly more like fifty thousand, take it or leave it."

"They take it?" asked Detective Pete.

"Yes, they take it. There is more argument, the other guys drive off, Angwin says something to Jason, then I hear a shot, and I presume that is when Jason shot Angwin."

"Jason shot Angwin?"

"Yes. I guess so. There was no one else there."

"Not you?"

"No! I told you I had been tied up in the back with that fucking builders' tape, trussed up like a mummy since after the thing with the cops just out of Jarrajarra. How the fuck would I shoot him? I didn't have a fucking gun. When are you going to get it in your head? I am the victim here, not the fucking cattle thief, the murderer, Jesus Christ."

She stopped at the end of the outburst.

If this was just a rehearsal for a jury, I think we were already fucked. I almost believed the whole thing, yet I had seen her myself. She killed my truck and tried to kill me at the same time.

"What happened then?"

Then, dammit, our station phone rang, and Barney answered in his usual brisk fashion.

"It's for you he whispered, Sergeant Will Walker."

"Put it through to the office. Thanks, Barn."

Fuck, why now? What did he think we ran here? A Police Station.

I retreated to my office, leaving Barney to watch the McLain-Jordan show in peace.

I didn't know what Walker wanted, but I was sure it would not be as much fun as watching the interview on Barney's computer.

* * *

"Chris, well done on sorting out the escapees," said Sergeant Will Walker at the other end of the line.

"Thank you, Sergeant Walker, Team effort," I replied.

"Chris, I've been holding back on the Savage murders. I knew you had your hands full, but now that's all out of the way, I thought you'd be keen to help me find your old kickboxing trainer."

"Muay Thai, Sergeant, big difference."

"Yes, yes, I'm sure." He wasn't sure, and he didn't care.

Walker would never get it, but there was one bit I needed to spell out very clearly and very soon.

"Don't wish to offend you here, Sergeant Walker, or upset your plans," I said. "But I feel I need to make it very clear; I will not go hunting Rusty Collins just so anyone in the police force can bring him back to face murder charges."

Walker went silent.

When in doubt, double down.

"Just so we are clear, Sergeant, I would quit the force before I will do anything that lands Rusty in prison."

There, I thought to myself, best to get that out of the way. I debated whether a fuck you and fuck your investigation would fit in here, but Walker was such a decent bloke. Maybe hold back on the vocabulary and the emphasis.

"Well," he resumed slowly, "It is a bit early to discuss murder charges, Chris. I thought you might want to help me find the man so we can talk to him."

"Talk to him?"

"Yes," Walker spoke, then stopped, uncomfortable with what he wanted to say, was my guess. "Look, Chris, I understand it is all ancient history now for most people. But not for me, and I will bet, not for your mate Rusty. If we could find him to speak to him, it might even answer a few questions. For him as much as me."

I was anticipating he would tell me I was a Constable, and he was a Sergeant, and I would do as I was fucking told. It wasn't going that way at all, nothing like it.

"I believe," he was struggling for the right words, "I feel guilty I didn't do more while she was alive. Having met her, I am sure she is dead. It may be way too late, but it would mean a lot to me, and I am sure it would mean a lot to Rusty if we could find her body and we could give her a proper burial. Maybe if we all worked together, we could do that."

He took a big breath and stopped talking. Walker wasn't the type of bloke to ask twice. He'd said his piece.

My turn.

What to say?

"OK," I said, "I'll help as best I can." I knew I would qualify my help if Rusty found himself in trouble with the law.

"Have you had anything back from Carole and Glenda?" I asked.

"Not yet," he said. "I am just going with the dental match at the moment. They said the DNA will take a few weeks maybe and that they were also looking at other possible causes of death."

"So, what are you doing first?" I asked.

"Well, Rusty shut his Muay Thai gym in 2010," said Walker.

Thank God he had finally said the words Muay Thai. It physically grated every time he called Rusty's passion by its' wrong name. It was disrespectful.

"I actually found an old website from the late 1990s. It looks pretty ancient by today's standards, but I tracked down a couple of names on there. I called them, and I have to tell you they weren't too excited about helping me find your Mister Collins. No one was quite so explicit as you."

It was a little joke, so I laughed politely. The hard-core members of Rusty's crew were from all walks of life. At their core, despite their differences, they were a universally rugged bunch. I doubt anyone would push them anywhere they didn't want to go. They were all good friends of mine. Friends for life.

"I was hoping you might call some of these people and see if you have more luck with them."

"I can try," I said. In fact, I would most definitely try. It would be wonderful to speak to them again, the ones I was close to, the ones I sparred with, the few who had kicked my arse as a kid when I needed it.

"I will send you the link to the website," Walker continued. "There is a picture of you there, taken in early 1996. You're collecting a little medal. You must have won a fight, maybe. You look like a scrawny teenager."

I was. I would have been barely twelve years old and in the early blemishes of late pre-puberty. If I won a medal, it was most likely the hardest trier Rusty handed out weekly. I had made 'hardest-trier' my own for want of better skills.

"I will also send you these phone numbers I collected," he said, "you might find some more. They were all so unhelpful I gave up calling them till I could speak to you."

"Yeah, let me handle the first contact. I will let you know how it goes."

"Thank you, Chris," said Walker, sounding like he meant it.

We ended the call, and I hurried back to Barney to resume perving on the interrogation.

"What's happened?" I asked.

"Same, same," said Barney with a pained sigh. "Our Jennifer, she's the victim. She was kidnapped, never a part of any decision, never a cop killer, trussed up like a turkey in the back seat of the truck, tricked into the whole thing, and, Christopher, I hate to tell you this, but if she performs this well in front of a judge, I doubt you'll even get her to trial."

"Fuck," I said. It was depressing.

My phone dinged. I checked and saw it was a message from Sergeant Will Walker, the link to Rusty's old website.

"Chris," said Barney, "you might have to find when and where she obtained that camping gear."

"I can't help tomorrow Barn."
"Why not?"
"I am organizing a reunion."

Monday June 13, 2022

Jarrajarra

I woke early, and by 5.00 A.M., I was pounding the clappers out of my heavy bag hanging there on my back porch. It must have been all the talk and thinking about the old Muay Thai crew.

No matter what the bag threw at me, I slipped perfectly, side, in, out. I was un-hittable by bag. No matter where it ran, I was after it, landing with crisp precision every time. Elbows, knees, push-kicks, sidekicks, occasional fists, then more elbows.

I had been fighting this bag for six years, or thereabouts since I moved to Jarrajarra. I had never lost a single fight. Then again, after twelve-three-minute rounds, I was in danger of going down from exhaustion.

Wendy appeared as I was flailing through the last sixty seconds of my final round.

"Go, Chrissy," she said, "don't show it your fatigue."

I finished with a lame head kick. This was meant to impress my girlfriend. Sadly, it came in about knee-high, one-half custard power.

"Did I wake you?" I asked, concerned. Wendy had arrived home and collapsed around 4.00 AM.

"No, mate, it wasn't you. It was the house. It was shaking from floor to ceiling spontaneously. Don't know why."

I felt guilty. The old heavy bag was almost too heavy for the ancient back porch of our home. When the bag started swinging, for whatever reason, the house rattled with it.

"Want to go for a run?" I asked. A clever distraction.

"Why not," she said.

We ran out to the river, and she started slow and sleepy; at the river, we had our morning swim, and by the time we were back in town, Wendy was sprinting and wide awake.

It was another great day to be alive. I was still feeling the glow of escaping the Red Bedford truck driven by the crazy woman Jennifer McLain and her now-dead mates.

Jarrajarra Police Station.

Constable Tim was still with us in Jarrajarra. The rest of the escapee hunters had gone home to Wodonga. They had taken the one surviving member, Jen McLain, back with them. She was in the cells in the Wodonga Police Station for the next little while, and Constable Tim was here with us, occupying the front desk with Barney.

Constable Tim, in exchange for Jen McLain. We had the better end of that deal by far.

Best of all, I had my office back. I also had an email from Will Walker, telling me Tim was with us while I followed up on the Rusty Collins Alumni. He suggested I should follow the names wherever they should lead.

A very strange open-ended instruction from a higher-up.

I started working through the list of names and phone numbers that Walker had sent me and whoever else I could think of, prompted by the faces on the ancient website.

By lunchtime, I had managed to nail down two old friends who were happy to meet up. I settled for that and decided to take a wander around town.

Before I left, I unlocked the gun safe and took out some extra magazines. I wore the standard police issue .40 calibre Smith and Wesson semi-automatic pistol. It had a magazine capacity of fifteen cartridges. The best part of being a copper in a one-man station is my expenditure on ammunition is not too tightly controlled. I can make extra purchases, and no one bothers me if I tend to shoot a lot of the office budget while practising at the range.

Lunch at Rob Farrell's garage, and then we drove out of town to the rifle range. We had the whole range to ourselves, as usual, and I spent a good part of the afternoon pistol-shooting with my left hand.

"I couldn't believe how shit you are left-handed unless I'd seen it myself," said Rob.

Hurtful. True, but next time, I'd be better.

Tuesday, June 14, 2022

Coffee & Cakes Bakery, Glen Iris, Melbourne.

"Well, look at you, all grown up and handsome," said Tina Harris, a woman who had clobbered me with her lethal left foot head kick more times than I could count.

"Apart from the shiner," she added, "forget to duck?"

"Too slow," I said.

"Nothing changes," She laughed. "You never had any acceleration."

She was smiling and friendly as she always was when she wasn't deadly serious and sparring.

She looked wonderful, mid-fifties, fit as a trout, with just a few scars that told of her Muay Thai fighting life. I must have looked too hard at the scar tissue around her eyes and forehead.

"Yes, I still run five days a week, take Muay Thai class four times a week, spar twice a week, and never eat a thing. It all makes me look punchy, I know."

"You look wonderful," I said, and I meant it.

"Would be nice to have some heavy-duty sparring again," she said, looking at me. "All my students are way too respectful, even the good ones."

"I can understand that," I said. "You don't want to belt your teacher. There's the respect thing and the likelihood they will belt you back only harder.

"Bullshit reason, in my humble opinion."

Tina had always been direct, inside and outside the gym.

We took another long, happy look at each other. I was thinking how good it was to see her again.

'Female friends, it's a poor man who doesn't have any,' my Nan always said.

"Have a gander at you, a fucking cop," said Tina. "Jesus Bloody Christ Almighty." Fortunately, she was smiling as she said it, and she had shown up for coffee, all of which led me to believe she was as happy to be here as I was.

"Friend first, cop second," I said.

"Good," said Tina and took a sip of her coffee, a nice little trick, maybe, to avoid saying anything.

"You read about the bodies in the cave?" I asked, deciding that 'cave' was the best description for the weird hole-in-the-ground that had housed the dead Savages, father and son, for the last ten years.

"Amazing," she answered. "What weird karma that you were the one to find them."

"Well, Tina, I didn't find them so much as stumble on them while looking for a couple of drunken duck hunters. They dropped in their hole, so to speak. But you're right. It was weird. Not so sure it was karma."

"The two men who murdered Rusty's daughter, discovered by Rusty's best friend's son. If that is not karma, Chrisso, what is it?" she asked.

She still called me Chrisso, my gym name. You get labelled in a Muay Thai gym, and it sticks for life.

"Well, there is an interesting thought," I said. "You say two murderers. Why is that?"

"Why? Money! Inherited money. It makes people really fucking weird. Phillip Junior, what a piss-weak rich-boy-bitch he was. Wouldn't, couldn't, shouldn't get a real job because who knows how many people he'd fuck up, plus he'd get tired by lunchtime, the great big sook. He simply had to work for his dad. There was absolutely no alternative on this planet for such a soft little cock."

"What did he do working for his Dad?" I asked.

"Fucked if I know," said Tina. "Phil Senior was a big-wig doctor, and the mother-in-law was born rich. Filthy rich. Apparently, the oldies had a lot of investments, and Phillip fuck-head Junior was somehow the caretaker of all that. Always sounded like he did bugger-all to me."

Tina had always been the loudest and funniest of the Muay Thai crew, the top-most dog in a team of top dogs.

"The dad was a doctor?" I asked as I wrote it down. Seemed important.

"Yes. Doctor Phillip fucking Savage Senior. Of all the people in the world to have as a parent. What a self-satisfied sanctimonious arsehole bastard he was, topped only in arseholery by that soul-shrivelled razor-lipped bitch-from-hell, Missus misery guts herself, the mother-in-law, whatever her fucking name was, Mrs. Savage, I suppose."

"So, reading between the lines here, you didn't like the Savage family much?"

She laughed at that. "Miserable miserly purse string puppeteers. No, mate, I didn't like them, not at all, not one little teeny tiny bit. Virginia was my best friend from school, Reservoir High, the same as you. We got into Muay Thai together. I got serious, and she lost interest. But we were still friends for life. So, yes, I knew the Savages through her, and I fucking hated the lot of them."

"How did you meet them?" I asked.

"I met them with Ginny. She was going out with Phillip Junior. Got me stuffed why. He was such a prick. Anyway, she was intimidated by her parents-in-law. They were so rich, so upper-class, so up-your-arse, so utterly up themselves. Every time she had to meet them, she managed to drag me along as protection. She knew they wouldn't bother me."

That made me laugh. Nothing, and nobody, ever intimidated Tina.

"Chrisso, if Fuckhead Junior killed Virginia, and that is a teensy-tiny-microcosmic, non-existent 'if', then you could bet your last dollar Fuckhead Senior knew about it. Before, during and after. So yeah, I call them both murderers based on absolutely zero evidence. Nothing that you might have used in a court."

"Do you have anything at all that I could use?"

"Is gut feel considered court-worthy by the cops?"

"Not in my experience," I said.

She paused for a moment.

"I know for a fact," she said, "Virginia was lured back to their old home, the one she'd shared with Junior Fuckhead. She was out of there, never going back. Her only plan for that place was to sell it and collect her half."

"He didn't want to sell the marital home?" I asked.

"No," she said. "But he had to, didn't he? It was a wedding gift. Anyway, after a lot of sooking and grizzling, Phillip had finally agreed to sell at their last meeting."

"If she had already left him, why go back to the house?"

"Someone had found some old photos of hers, and Ginny wanted them back."

"Her dad's photos?"

"Yeah," said Tina, "some old photos from Rusty's time in Vietnam and other family stuff."

"How do you know this?"

"She asked me to go with her to the house the night she disappeared," Tina's tough shell softened. "But I couldn't. I was running consecutive classes at the gym that night. Not exactly something you can get a fill-in for. I asked her to wait, and we would go late."

"Why didn't she wait?"

"I don't know. When I first said I couldn't go, Virginia said she was being silly. She'd been separated for six months. Deep down, I think she was convinced she was safe."

Tina's bottom lip quivered. "I told her to call me when she got to the house, but she never did, and then she was gone."

"Did you tell this to the police?"

"I did. Some fucking homicide thug found me at the gym and asked me what I knew. I told him. Then he asks me if Ginny might have joined the fucking Harry Krishnas or whatever the religious nuthouse of the day was back then."

She shook her head in disappointment.

"He was pushing the idea that Virginia would leave her children and join a cult overnight. The guy was a fuckwit or corrupt or both, but yes, I told your precious policeman."

"Do you remember his name?"

"No, just a big thug. He thought his size would intimidate the people at Rusty's gym, dickhead. Not a very impressive character. I remember he was Homicide, and he said it was his case."

"OK," I said.

"He literally just made the one visit. No follow-up. Never returned phone calls when I checked what was happening. I swear they didn't try."

"And you can't recall his name?"

"No, sorry."

"It's OK," I said.

"No, it is not OK, never OK, the whole thing sucks and, as much as I love you, you not-so-little-anymore-bugger, make sure you don't ever, for one minute, suggest to me it was Rusty topping those two fuck heads."

"Tina, if I have one job left as a cop, it is to make sure Rusty doesn't go to jail for killing those two. If it means helping him stay missing, then that's what I will do. Simple as that."

My Nan used to say never trust a man who tells you to trust him. Tina was giving me that look. Words don't count. It wasn't worth the breath to say anymore. I'd just have to prove it by my actions.

She was listening.

"First," I continued, "I want to know if Rusty is alive. If he is, I want to see him for my own selfish sake and to check he is OK. Then, I want to use whatever the police force can provide me to help find Virginia. Dead or alive."

Tina was still thinking. Listening.

I could tell she had something she wanted to tell me.

"Is he alive?" I asked.

She gave a downward flick with her eyes, then looked back at me.

"If he is alive, I am sure he will find you if he wants to."

"So he is alive," I laughed.

"I didn't say that," she said.

"You are such a terrible liar, Tina." I was still smiling. "You practically screamed it out loud."

Moment of silence between us. It was so good to see her.

"Give us a hug, you big goose," she said.

We hugged it out, shared a tear, and promised to stay in touch forever. As you always do when you catch up after twenty years with someone who felt like family way back when.

Office of Richard Martin, Solicitor, Reservoir, Melbourne.

"If I were you, Chrisso, I'd be looking at the mother-in-law?"

"Penelope Anne Savage?" I asked.

"She is back to Penelope Anne Fenwick these days," he said.

I was in the office of Richard Martin, Solicitor, the second of the two alumni from Rusty Collins' Muay Thai gym I had found alive and readily locatable. We had fought thousands of rounds in the gym against each other. He was older than me, but with all those organized fisticuffs between us, we had emerged friends for life, as you do.

This was before the army, before the police, back when I was just another Housing Commission kid learning a bit about self-defence and discipline at Rusty's gym.

Back then, Richard was a fighter by night and by day, a rookie lawyer answering calls for help from his Muay Thai mates whenever they found trouble. Rich or poor, it didn't matter. With Richard, you always got the best that money could buy, even if you were short on ready cash.

After a warm welcome, he had plenty to say about his friend, Virginia Collins and the family she had married into.

"Rich, miserable, entitled scum, Mrs. Savage Senior and her brother, the solicitor, Albert Fenwick, Master of Laws. Pompous arsehole. What a prick."

"So, mate, you didn't like them much?" I asked.

"No," said Rick, "not at all. Wouldn't blame Ginny for running off and joining a cult to escape that lot. The trouble with that cult bullshit is she would never have left her children behind, and the kids would never have wanted to stay with their Dad either."

"You know the children?"

"Yes, absolutely, know them well, still see them now and then, pair of twenty-first-century hippies, great kids, though not kids anymore. Both into their twenties now."

"Let me guess," I said, "You manage their affairs, help them out when they need legal advice."

He laughed. "It's all very informal, but yes." He looked at me, "Nothing changes, hey mate?"

"How did you get to know the Savage mother-in-law and her crew?" I asked.

"The Fenwicks," said Rick. "Penelope Anne Fenwick. You heard of her?"

"No, not before this," I said. "Just to give you a starting point."

He laughed, "I wouldn't expect you to, from your end of the social spectrum, housing commission rubbish that you were. No offence, mate."

"None, taken."

Rick Martin was like Tina, my other old Muay Thai buddy. Happy by default, open, robust, funny. How did I allow myself to lose touch with such great people?

"Where do I start," he said. "Late nineteenth century, 1880, thereabouts, the Fenwick family started out selling sly grog under the banner of cough serum, youth elixir, that sort of bullshit. Lots of sugar, more sugar, and forty per cent alcohol. What do they say about all great fortunes starting with a crime?"

He shook his head, "Anyway, sometime between the wars, 1920 or thereabouts, they go legitimate and start selling real headache powders. They were already rich from the grog. The honest dollar makes them even richer. Around the 1930s, along came Penelope Anne and, some years or so after that, her arsehole brother, Albert. They are the third generation. I'd like to say they follow the grand old tradition of sitting fat while their inherited fortune withers on the vine. Unfortunately, it doesn't seem to wither, not at all. Just gets bigger."

"But isn't the brother, Albert, a lawyer?" I asked. "A Master of Laws. How is that sitting on your arse?"

"Master of 'Take-my-money-and give-me-a-degree'. Holy Jesus, I forgot how naïve you are? Albert James Fenwick, a Master of Laws, as you correctly point out. He went to a real University, got a couple of degrees, and probably bought a wing of the library with his granddaddy's money in exchange for the pieces of paper saying he was a master of whatever bullshit-fill-in-the-space he wanted."

"You don't respect his skillset?" I asked

"Well? What does it mean when it is only paper? Look at you. You were in the army, yeah? Stumbled into the SASR and, apparently, even won some medals. They were probably meant for someone else, right? But out there in the real world, shit. I'll bet you still don't know how to salute properly. Please prove me wrong."

I gave him the middle finger, and we both laughed. I had come to Melbourne to investigate a crime, but here I was, swept up in nostalgic meetings with old friends.

Focus.

"Chrisso, believe me, these are not good people, and Albert, the Master of Laws, is a shit lawyer. Survives on the family fortune. Please, God, may it one day crumble to the ground."

I was getting the picture.

"Tina probably told you all this at coffee this morning, right?" He tilted his head in question mode.

"You spoke to Tina already?" I asked

"Of course I did. We speak every day, mate. She called me after you split this morning."

"OK," I said, "that is one seriously fast grapevine."

"Here is what Tina didn't tell you," said Rick. "The Fenwick side of the Savage family. Them and me, we had a little war after Virginia's death."

War? I let him talk.

"Old mate, Master of Laws, fought the house sale. It was originally the Fenwick family home where Penelope Anne and her brother grew up. It was Fenwick heritage, Fenwick bought and paid for. It had never been a Savage property, and, get this, Penelope Anne and Savage Senior were still living there when Virginia and Junior got married."

"Whoa, back up a moment," I said. "The senior Savages were living there, but they gave it to the junior Savages as a wedding gift?"

"Yes," said Rick.

"So what then," I asked, "they all moved in together, one big happy family?"

"No, mate," he answered. "They didn't move in together, and believe me, none of that crew was ever happy, especially Penny Anne and fuck-head Master of Laws."

"Go on," I said, intrigued.

"Penny Anne Fenwick would probably tell you that Phillip Savage Senior had taken advantage of her depression and loyalty, whatever, to hustle her into a transaction against her will and for his own financial benefit. Significant benefit."

"Depression and loyalty?" I asked.

"Yes," said Rick, "depression and loyalty, neither of which our Penelope Anne ever experienced, in my humble opinion."

"I've got that bit," I said. "Penny Anne is a horrible person."

"Exactly? Alright, you are showing faint glimmers of comprehension. Good work. So, Penelope Anne, the mad bitch mother-in-law, was, according to Fenwick's family lore, lost in a brain fog of personal grief over the loss of a child somewhere in her past. Sorry in advance, but I don't know the details of the lost child."

"OK," I said, "Lost child, got it."

"Anyways," said Rick, "Phil Senior nags, or bullies, or cajoles Penny Anne into gifting the property to the newlyweds, Virginia and Junior."

"Wedding present?" I asked.

Rick rolled his eyes at my naivety. Did it with enough flourish that I couldn't possibly miss.

"Oh, Chrisso, mate. It wasn't a gift. It was a massive transfer of wealth. It was all about money."

"OK, a very expensive gift then?"

"No, mate, it was money," he said, "what else but money? Holy Mary, Mother of God, should I get a whiteboard and write this down for you, old son?"

"Phil Senior," continued Rick. "He swaps the old Fenwick family home, which just happens to be on an acre in the most expensive street in Melbourne, and one hundred per cent in his wife's name, into his son's name."

"It is still a gift," I argued.

"Then, he buys a massive mansion, two acres this time, further up the road, on the top of the hill in Saint George's Road Toorak, and this freaking mega-mansion now has his name on half the title. Are you getting a picture here, Constable Clueless?"

"All for the money?" I added. Showing I was listening.

"Yes! Halleluiah! Money in the form of land, mate," he answered. "Huge money. Good old Phil had swapped out of a zero share of about a million bucks worth of 1990 property. He moves into a half share of something worth three, even four million of 1990 money, with no cash out of his pocket. Zero."

"He had upgraded?"

"Significantly upgraded. Today, Phil Senior's new house would be worth, guessing, thirty million all up. Maybe more.

"Quite the deal," I said.

"If you live to spend it," said Rick. "Which, you have now shown us, Constable Clouseau, he didn't."

"No," said Rick, "and it is worse, the 'marital-gift-home', which Penny Anne, probably, never wanted to hand over, is also worth, maybe, fifteen to twenty mill at today's prices."

"So, if they'd lived, Savage Senior would have extracted half of the big house from the Fenwick fortune. Junior would have come away with half of the little house."

"Senior and Junior would have been looking at upwards of thirty million dollars of Fenwick money."

"Goodness," I said.

"No goodness involved, Chrisso, pure unadulterated greed. Marry for money and suck the life out of the lemon."

"Who are you talking about now, Phillip Senior or Virginia?"

"I am talking about Phil Senior, mate," said Rick. "Our Ginny had her faults, but she was on our team, Chrisso. I would deny till the death that she married for anything but love."

"How do you know all this," I asked.

"I was Virginia's lawyer, you twat. Through the separation, heading toward the divorce and, ultimately, we were going to force the sale of the gifted house," he said.

"Force?" I asked.

"Absolutely, we weren't there by the time of Virginia's disappearance, but I was going to make it happen."

"How?"

"I have my ways," he said.

"Rusty?"

"Well," he said, "Phil Junior was shit scared of Rusty, you can trust me on that, but we hadn't reached the physical intimidation point of negotiation. We had several meetings. I might have spoken sternly. I really believed he was weakening on selling the house."

"Weakening?"

"Going mentally floppy, yes."

"Then Virginia disappeared."

"Yes," said Rick. "Honestly, Phil Junior had conceded the divorce. But the house sale, oh boy. It started out all no, no, no, no, no! But at the end, with a few months of the single life under his belt, I reckon he was set to roll over."

"So, the no, no, no was tilting toward a maybe yes.?"

"Yes, definitely a maybe yes. But then Virginia disappeared, and, according to old mate Albert James, Master of Laws, the kids needed the stability of their home and their father's presence. Consequently, there was no reason to sell. Plus, Virginia had gone to a mad religious cult somewhere in the wilderness, so who would benefit from the selling of the home? Blah, blah, blah."

"So, they managed to stop the sale?" I asked.

"Yes, but," said Rick with a smile. "I still made the fuckers pay."

"How?"

"When she was planning her departure from Phil-the-dill-junior, she came to me and gave me total power of attorney over all of her affairs. She also rewrote her will, leaving everything she owned to her kids, and she made me their trustee. The plan for the divorce was rock solid, mate. So was her clear intention to sell the house."

"OK," I said.

"Around 2009, with my help, the kids petition the Family Law Court to move in with Virginia's mother, the grandmother who actually loves them and cares about them."

"The Savages and Fenwicks fight this?"

"Chrisso, mate, the Savages and Fenwicks didn't give a shit. Couldn't care less. Which I had anticipated."

"OK, then what."

"The kids move in with their Nan, and suddenly, there is a lot of contact with their Granddad, Rusty. So the kids are happy."

"And then?"

"And then, as soon as that is all cleared, I petition the Supreme Court to have Virginia officially declared dead. Now, given that seven years have elapsed, and no religious Messiah has fessed up to having her physical person held hypnotically within their realm, that goes through without a hitch. In the eyes of the court, by early 2010, Virginia is officially dead."

"Everyone knows that by then, surely," I said. "What does that achieve?"

"It enables me to force the sale of the house, which was Virginia's intention and which, by the terms of Virginia's will, means half the proceeds will go to the kids."

"What happened in the court?"

"Well, as I had hoped, it never went to court."

"Phillip Junior settled?" I guessed.

"Exactly. Took a while for it to happen. Lots of argy-bargy, angry words you could say. Eventually, he folded, mate. Offered to settle for half the then-current value of the house."

"How much?"

"Chris, mate, you're a cop. Didn't you ever learn anything about client-lawyer privilege? Did they ever discuss confidentiality in cop school? Were the words too big, or were you away that day bashing up pensioners?"

"No, no, pensioner bash-up was Tuesdays, big-words was Friday, I do big-words good. Let me put this a different way."

"OK, go ahead," he said.

"So," I said, stretching the word a bit. "How much money did the kids get?"

"Since you asked so politely, they won a grand total of four million dollars." He paused for effect, then added, "Each."

He stopped for a moment, sad.

"Anyway," he said, "I hit the Fenwicks where it hurt, in their pockets, or I tried to. Probably could've got more. Even that was a tiny drop from a big bucket."

"Where is the kids' money now?" I asked.

"Sitting in the kids' bank account, mate. They've hardly touched it, hardly a penny."

"Then the two Phillip Savages disappear as well?" I asked.

"Yes. Around 2010, Phillip Savage Senior and his useless dickhead son, Phil the Dill, disappear and are never heard from again till my good old Muay Thai mate, namely you, finds them sleeping permanently down a deep dark hole under a couple of sloppy-footed duck hunters. Our hero, the local cop from up-country-whatchamacallit."

"It was destiny," I said.

"Kismet," said Rick.

"Tell me about the police who were involved after the disappearances."

"The cops," said Rick. "Lot of good they did. When Virginia disappeared, everyone, including your colleagues, assumed it was Phil Junior."

"Did you agree?"

"Not so much. Rusty was sure he didn't do it. Junior would be too scared of the consequences."

"The consequences being Rusty."

"Yes. With Virginia, the investigating police kept pushing the bullshit idea Ginny'd join the cult. God spare me."

"And when the Savages disappeared?"

"Well," said Rick. "Naturally, everyone believed Rusty had offed those two, especially with the timing. Virginia is declared dead. The kids get a settlement from the Savages. Goodbye, Phil and Phil."

"Rusty looked guilty."

"He looked as guilty as hell, except he told me he didn't do it. And you know our guy as well as anyone."

"If he had done it," I answered, "he wouldn't say anything."

"Exactly," said Rick. "He wouldn't lie."

"The cops tried him on and got nowhere. And, of course, they had no evidence. Same shit, different missing bodies. No corpses, no court cases."

"Do you remember the police officers names?"

"The head homicide honcho was a bloke named Hughes. I see you put him in the shitpile a couple of years ago. Well done, Chrisso."

"Went to jail and died of a heart attack on day one," I said.

"Karma," said Rick.

"His off-sider, I can't remember the surname but Hughes kept calling him Kenny, was almost patronising. Big ugly thug. Thought he was tough, never got the chance to find out. Kenny was just the lap dog."

We went silent.

"You following all this, Constable," said Rick. "You need me to write it all down in big letters."

Friendship. Over twenty years, but it was still there, still solid. The rhythm, the rhyme, the dialogue, the seamless insults, it was all unchanged.

"I'll do my best to remember," I said.

"So, Constable Taylor, there you have it. Now tell me, why doesn't your lot get off their collective arses and find Virginia?"

His last question was not a joke.

Out and about in Melbourne.

After leaving the office of my old Muay Thai mate, I called Detective Sergeant Peter Jordan for an update on our shared murder mystery.

"Glory be to Jesus," said Detective Pete. "You've accepted my offer to come and chase killers in Melbourne. Great news. Give me five minutes, and I will get you a cheap suit, a shit car and a desk in homicide. You are gonna love it here, Chris."

"I've never seen you in a shit suit," I said.

"I'm the boss," he answered in a heartbeat.

Which was why I would never work for Homicide, that and the fact I loved where I lived and who I lived with.

A pause.

"My powers of deduction tell me you are not accepting my job offer," said Detective Pete.

"No, it would all be too hierarchical for me, I think, moving closer to the mothership. Bosses, bullies and bullshit."

"I don't see you being bullied for long, Chris."

"Not so far," I said.

Could have bantered like this all day. I had called him, so it was up to me to get on with it.

"Virginia Savage, nee Collins, could you share her murder investigation files with me."

"Of course," he said. "You in Melbourne?"

"Yes."

He thought about it for a moment.

"Can you meet me at that coffee lounge at 8.00 AM tomorrow?"

"I can do that," I said.

I knew the place, just around the corner from Victorian Police Headquarters in St. Kilda Road, Melbourne. We had met there before, during a previous case.

He was a strange bloke, Detective Pete Jordan. We had reached a point of trust. Pete trusted me to never interfere with his natural love for promotion, glory and media approval. I trusted him to tell me things when it suited his innate love of promotion, glory and media approval.

Somehow, it worked.

Life is just a trade, my Nan would have said.

My next call was to my beautiful girlfriend, Wendy.

I wanted to let her know I would not be home till tomorrow. Turned out she wouldn't be there either. She was two hours into delivering a new Jarrajarra baby. She guessed she'd still be there in the morning.

I was good to go, or more accurately, good to stay.

I opted for a motel near Police Headquarters on St Kilda Road. There was a supermarket on the corner, so I went semi-Jack-Reacher. I bought myself toothpaste, a toothbrush, and a razor. I also invested in new undies, T-shirts and socks. I didn't throw away my cop gear. Unlike Jack, I hadn't retired yet. I'd need my uniform and gun in the morning.

Most importantly, I had my running gear in the truck. After dumping my new personals in the motel room, I changed and then took off for a run. I headed past the Shrine of Remembrance, then along the famous 'Tan', a four-kilometre, dedicated running track around Melbourne's Royal Botanic Gardens. Halfway around the Tan, I took a turn and found myself on an eastbound trail along the Yarra River.

I followed the Yarra till I reached the southernmost end of St Georges Road, Toorak. This was one of the most exclusive, most expensive locations in Melbourne.

Old money.

Whoever wrote the theory of trickle-down economics had never lived here. On a street like this, you got your money and then kept it. Fuck anyone who'd try to trickle it from you.

Simple.

I had started running with no real intention beyond exercise, finding myself here, where Virginia had lived, my intentions had changed. I called Richard Martin's mobile.

"I charge double for after-hours, especially for thugs like you, Chrisso."

"What's the address of those two houses we discussed, in St Georges Road? And don't call me a thug."

"OK," he said and gave me the addresses.

"I am at the river end. So, which one is which?" I asked.

"Going up the hill," he said, "away from the river. The numbers go down, and the prices go up, generally speaking. So, the higher number is nearer the river. So that one is Virginia's original house, the one she was half-gifted and planned to sell. The lower number is up the hill, the castle. Now the home of the evil stepmother."

"Stepmother?" I asked.

"Yes," said Rick, "did I forget that bit? Penelope Anne Savage, nee Fenwick, is not the mother of Phillip Savage Junior. She is the stepmother. In my opinion, she probably hated her stepson as much as she hated her daughter-in-law. She is a good hater, Penelope."

"Penelope was wife number two?" I said. "What happened to wife number one?"

"Buggered if I know," said Richard. "Knowing Phil Senior, I wouldn't be surprised if he dropped her down your cave with the duck hunters after he met the fabulously wealthy Penny Anne."

"No, mate," I said. "The timeline doesn't fit. You're out by around forty years."

"Well, you're the cop. You work it out."

We ended the call, and I resumed running, looking for the house that was once the home of Virginia Savage, nee Collins.

I found the place. It had a high wall around it that looked 'keep-out-solid'.

"What matter brick barriers to a knight?" Did Cervantes say that in Don Quixote, or was it the bloke who wrote the songs in Man of La Mancha, or was it my Nan? Buggered if I knew. I think it was the song, and he was singing about wounds, not barriers, but hey, the thought was there.

I was the avenging knight for Virginia Collins, and a barrier was before me.

On the roadside of the house, there was a perfectly manicured nature strip. In the centre of the strip, there were several artfully shaped oak trees. I dragged myself up the tree nearest the wall. I climbed to a point high enough for me to see over. There was not a lot on view.

A very expensive house, old, landscaped, beautifully fashioned, and large. The lights were off. Nobody was home.

I had no sense that this was where my friend Virginia had ever lived. No sense of her existence here.

Virginia and me. It was a long-gone period of my life. She was fourteen years older than me but always friendly and tonnes of fun in the gym. She didn't enjoy training. Whenever it was time to do pads or even spar, you could rely on Virginia to joke around and make you smile rather than work up a sweat.

She was a real person. There on the edge of my highly focused martial arts world. Then, one day, she was not there.

She had lost interest in learning how to punch people and dropped out of gym life. A couple of years later, she was married. Bagged a rich guy was the word. She had disappeared from the commission homes forever to a better, wealthier world.

Different circle of friends, different priorities.

Gone to better things, and then, a few years later, gone for good.

I can remember her in the gym, usually laughing at one of Tina's jokes. Alive, happy, real.

What had happened?

Where in the universe had she landed?

I was pondering all this when a passing car reminded me I was also up a tree, in jogging clothes, in the richest suburb of the city.

A white four-door BMW passed below me. It was May, and my chosen tree was shedding leaves. I was in my running gear with very little foliage left to hide me. A young girl looked up at me from the front passenger seat of the car.

Eye contact.

I smiled and waved. She smiled and waved back as the car moved past.

It wasn't even that dark. If the local cops came by, I could be arrested for looking over a private fence in my running gear. Invasion of privacy, intent to commit a burglary, climbing a tree without a permit or inappropriate clothing for local standards.

Time for me to move along to my next target.

I ran for another forty minutes, doing a lap of the area, basically waiting for it to get dark.

The second address. The current home of Penelope Anne Savage, nee Fenwick. The evil stepmother, mother-in-law from hell. The house was exactly as described to me, a fucking castle.

It was surrounded by a tall brick wall, and immediately inside the wall was an even taller, perfectly trimmed cypress hedge.

In for a penny in for a pound, I found a spot of cover along the wall behind the manicured oak trees on the nature strip. I was out of range of the nearest streetlight. I used a jump, a grab, a chin-up, and finally a leg up to scale the brick wall and then slide down the other side between the wall and the hedge.

The hedge was as scratchy as hell on my bare legs and on my arse where the hedge hoiked up my running shorts.

More important than any minor discomfort, I was in the castle grounds.

I was so far over the procedural lines drawn in every police manual I had read I suddenly had an attack of conscience. The conscience that strikes when you worry about getting caught. But hey, I was away from home and out of uniform. I could be naughty.

I was sure Penelope Anne could afford security. What would it be? Sensors, cameras? Probably both.

Oh dear, what if she had dogs? Big dogs?

What the hell? I crawled at ground level, staying beneath the hedge. Found a spot where I could see the house. More like a castle as it appeared to me.

I could see a couple of CCTV cameras.

There were people at home. Lights, activity, someone in a maid's uniform passed an open window.

From what little I knew, Penny Anne had outlived everybody in her immediate family other than her brother.

I could see servants moving back and forth past the windows.

I had no telepathic insight that there was a murderer living here. None of Rick Martin's certainties could be proven by anything I could see from crawling along the ground twenty years after Virginia's death.

What I could see was money. Money enough for a home as big as a hospital, for after-hours staff, for garage doors wide enough for a dozen cars. Money for hedges and lawns trimmed to perfection.

Ninety years old, single, with enough money to hire someone to give an acre of perfect lawn a haircut better than my own.

Know your enemy. This one was rich beyond any purpose I could imagine.

The car park was interesting.

Beside the highfalutin garage, there was a separate, uncovered parking area, gravelled, clean, and almost as manicured as the lawn before me. There were several cars parked there, most of them in the make and model range that suggested they belonged to staff. Not the sort of vehicles that would carry Penny Anne.

But there was one, a large cut above the rest, a gleaming Mercedes S450. New by the look of it, over two hundred thousand dollars' worth of motor vehicle. No wonder the driver had parked it a body length from the adjacent Corolla.

Why wasn't it in the garage? If it was mine, I'd park it in the bedroom.

The Mercedes was parked at the end of the line and well apart from the rest. The placement suggested it was the last to arrive.

A visitor?

A rich friend, maybe? According to Tina Harris and Richard Martin, Penny Anne had no friends. Totally unlovable despite her wealth.

The cameras I could see were fixed. I was sure they couldn't see me here under the hedge. No doubt they would see me if I went for the house to get a closer look. But what would I do once I got there? Demand a confession? Find the murder weapon? Ask the people inside to wait till I get a legal warrant.

It was all a lot of fun, snooping about in the dark, but not very productive. Felt more like a private detective than a real policeman.

Time to go.

Then the front door opened, and a large, overweight man in an expensive suit emerged. Behind him followed an old woman, a very old woman, but tall, slim, erect, moving easily, and very elegant.

They were lit from within the open door and by the entrance lights above. I guessed this was Penny Anne waving off her brother, the Master of Laws.

By their movements, she was saying goodbye. They were a pretty cold pair. No hugs or smooches. Wendy and I exchanged more love and affection when one of us went to make a cuppa. That was usually me, given the relentless urgency of my caffeine addiction.

I was close enough to hear them clearly.

"Tell this policeman I am not seeing anyone," said Penny Anne. "They're all dead, and good riddance. What difference does it make after all these years? Who cares?"

"Well, my dear," answered the bloke, "this new policeman has decided he cares."

"The policeman can care and suspect whatever he wants," she said. "Can he prove anything?"

"Well, my dear, now that two of them have been found, I'm worried it won't be very long before the others appear. Who knows what evidence the police will discover."

"We paid a lot of money," said Penelope Anne. "They were all supposed to vanish. How did this happen now?"

"I read they were searching for missing duck hunters," said the bloke I suspected was her lawyer-brother.

"Don't be ridiculous, Albert."

Albert? So, it was the brother.

"Someone told them where to look," continued Penelope Anne Fenwick with some certainty. "We both know it can only be one person. It has to be Carruthers. He is probably looking for more money.

"Always more," said Albert.

"You need to do something about him before this goes any further," said the old woman.

"Well, first, I will have to find him, my dear," said Albert. "We don't have our other greedy policeman friend to help us anymore."

"I don't care how you do it, Albert. Just get it done."

"I will, dear. I will."

"And sooner rather than later."

With that said, she turned and went inside, closing the door after her without any further comment.

What a totally unloving, cold-blooded brother and sister.

And what an interesting choice of words from Albert, "Now that two of them have been found," he'd said. He was worried it won't be long before others appeared.

There are more bodies. More? Are the extra bodies close to the ones I had stumbled on, or are they further afield?

And who the hell was Carruthers?

It was definitely time to get out of there.

Albert, the Master of Laws, was heading to his magnificent car, making to leave.

I moved very quietly, intending to get back over the wall. I must have triggered something. An alarm screamed from the wall of the house. Frightened the shit out of me for a moment.

I took a quick look back through the trees to the car park. The lawyer-brother had stopped at his car at the sound of the alarm. He was looking in my direction. The front door re-opened. Penny Anne came out for a look as well.

Whoops. This was exciting.

I backed deeper under the hedge into the darkness.

With a jump and a self-hoist, I was quickly over the brick wall the way I came. More scratches on my backside. Nothing serious. I landed in the streetside shadows of a large oak tree. I did a quick wipe of my muddy knees and brushed off the dirt on my front.

Good to go.

I ran. I headed away from the driveway gate, up the hill, then left down a side street, then another couple of lefties, till I was heading back down St Georges Road toward the Yarra River.

Before I got there, just a few minutes after I left the castle, I saw a private security vehicle speeding up the hill, blue light flashing, no doubt towards the rescue of Penny Anne's security and comfort.

Prompt response in the top end of town. I doubt the cops would be there as quickly if they bothered to come at all for a burglar alarm.

Too late for them, I was gone. I was laughing as I made my way back to the track beside the Yarra River. I was heading back to the tan and the motel.

After a few minutes running along the riverside, thinking about the new name I had acquired, I stopped and called the number I had for Tina Harris, my first interview from earlier in the day. Tina, my old Muay Thai tormentor and Virginia's best friend.

"Chrisso," she answered immediately.

"How'd you know it was me?" I asked.

"I've got you on my contact list already," she said, "you're not escaping me again, young man. We have many rounds still to fight, and I want to see if you have improved without me belting you around."

We had a laugh and then down to business.

"Tina, that police officer you said came around in the days after Virginia disappeared. Was his name Ken Carruthers?"

"Yes," she said. "That's it. That is definitely it, Carruthers. Ken Carruthers, that was it, Ken, Ken, yeah, definitely Ken. They called him Kenny. I remember he didn't look like any Ken doll I had seen. Big ugly shithead."

"Tell me again why he visited you?"

"He claimed he was searching for Virginia, working on the assumption she had run off to join a hippy religious cult, that newspaper bullshit. Pushing the Savage family line to anyone who'd listen, trying to come on heavy if you suggested Ginny had been murdered by Phil Junior, the slimy little turd."

Only an Amazon like my mate Tina would call Phillip Savage Junior, a man who was nearly two metres tall, little and slimy.

"Carruthers was a pig," she said. "But yeah, Carruthers, that's his name, nasty prick if you ask me. You found him?"

"Not yet, mate," I said. "But I will."

By the time we ended the call, we were back to old times. Talking and laughing about weird friends and crazy fights. Tina was happy to be back in the hunt for her missing friend with a real policeman to help her. God help Virginia's murderer if she found them before me.

This had been a weird, sneaky kind of day.

I was painting a picture. I could never show that picture in a court of law, but I would use it.

I sometimes wondered if I had joined the wrong team. So many rules for policemen. Going ninja on a suspect was easier in Jarrajarra, where there were no other cops.

In Melbourne, there were thousands of other cops, security companies and technology to burn. I doubt my lawless approach to enforcing the law would last too long in the big city.

But I was moving forward on this one. And so far, I was still free and clear.

"Now that two of them have been found," Albert Fenwick had said.

"Two of them," his exact words. Clear as a bell, like he knew there were more.

Also, he had said, "We may be suspects at last," as though he had been expecting it sooner.

I had probed my enemy's perimeter. I had nothing to warrant an arrest, but I came away primed for the next encounter with these murderers. Don Quixote would be proud.

What matters bum scratches to a knight?

Thank God there were no dogs.

Wednesday, June 15, 2022

Cafe, Off St. Kilda Road, Melbourne.

"Constable Taylor. Do you want the ordinary bad news, or do you want the very bad news?" asked Detective Pete.

We were sitting in the same little cafeteria we had used three years ago, just around the corner from Police Headquarters. It was not as busy as last time.

The place had new owners, a touch of paint and smaller tables. Also, less noise and no customers.

Post-pandemic struggle, maybe, or bad coffee. I'd soon find out.

We were in a cute little private booth against the wall, lovely fake red leather, still waiting for our coffee after ten minutes.

When Pete mentioned bad news, I had a tweak of conscience. Had my illegal entry into the sanctum of Penelope Fenwick been detected? I kept a tight poker face.

"May as well give me the ordinary bad news first," I said.

"This place has gone to shit," said Pete. "Coffee is terrible. Service is worse."

"And the very bad news."

"The name of the investigating officer is on the first page here."

He pushed a folder toward me. The name on the folder tab was Virginia. I opened the folder to the first page, and there on the top, in the little rectangular box reserved for the name of the investigating police officer, was the name 'Hughes'.

Where to start?

Detective Senior Sergeant Robert Anderson Hughes was the name back in 2002 when he was investigating the death of Virginia Collins. By 2018, he was Superintendent Hughes and a massive thorn in my side until all his corrupt schemes unwound around Jarrajarra.

Then, in early 2020, after all the various judgements against him were finalized, he was inmate Hughes for almost a day.

Delivered to the prison door in a police wagon in the morning. Out the back door in an ambulance that night. Dead.

Heart attack.

Shit himself to death, most likely. Spending the better part of what's left of your life among various criminals you had put away or betrayed could not be much to look forward to.

"This is our Hughes?" I asked, pointing at the name.

"The very same, late and unlamented."

The folder in my hand was about two inches thick. Thick enough to appear like work was done. But, compared to most investigation documentation I had been involved with, it looked skinny.

Inconsequential, especially for the disappearance of a respectable Melbourne mother of two. Barney had run up thicker notebooks on traffic offences.

"So, what will this little book tell me?" I asked.

"Well," said Pete, "it tells me Hughes was pushing the idea that Virginia had run off."

"Virginia did not run away," I said, "certainly not from her kids. Her best friend and her lawyer agree with me."

"That would be Tina Harris and Rick Martin," said Pete, reaching over and flicking through the pages before me. After a moment of upside-down flicking, he landed on the interview with Tina.

I read it. It didn't take long. There was hardly anything there.

"Well, Tina was either lying then or lying today," I said.

"Why?"

"It doesn't mention that Virginia called Tina the day she disappeared. It doesn't mention that Tina feels Virginia was lured to the former marital home and probably killed there."

"No, it doesn't. You spoke to this woman?"

"Yes, I did. I spoke to my good friend Tina. You can call her by her correct name if you like."

I bristled at Detective Pete calling my friend 'this woman'.

He laughed.

"You definitely wouldn't last in Homicide, Chris. The higher uppers would have you out the door in a week. You are the most anti-authoritarian, non-hierarchical cop I have ever met. How on earth did you survive in the army?"

"I very nearly didn't. I almost died."

"So I hear," he said.

"On the night she disappeared, Virginia called Tina," I said, "to get Tina to accompany her to the family home as a safety measure. Tina has thirty years of Muay Thai and twenty in BJJ. On hell of a bodyguard."

"BJJ? Brazilian Ju Jitsu?"

"Very good," I said, "you have come along in leaps and bounds, Detective Sergeant."

"This lovely woman, Tina, would run defence for Virginia if they met any rude and nasty Savages."

"Exactly," I confirmed. "But Tina couldn't go. She was running classes that night?"

"Classes?' He asked. "In how to kill people with your bare hands and stuff like that."

"Yes, stuff like that. Stuff at which she is very good."

"Why did Virginia go there at all?" asked Pete.

"To retrieve her family photos. Photos that were important to her. These photos had allegedly been lost, and then suddenly they were found."

"A perfect lure."

"Yes," I said.

"But why would Phillip Savage Junior wait? What was it, close to six months after the separation, to lure her back to their home to kill her?" asked Pete.

"Good question," I said.

"It doesn't make sense," he continued, "especially back then, do it on the day of the separation, claim 'Provocation', spend six months at a happy farm, and you're free."

Provocation was a defence used in the years after the Second World War. It lasted on the books till around 2005. A husband who had bashed or strangled his wife to death could claim he'd been 'Provoked'. Maybe not the intent of the law, but that was how it was used.

Sadly, claims of 'Provocation' worked for many years until one too many high-profile cases led to community outrage. That led, in turn, to the removal of 'Provocation' from the legal defence armoury.

The final provocation belonged to the community.

"Sounds like you've thought about it," I said. "Murder by Provocation."

"Not me. I am happily divorced, mate," said Pete. "Plus, my ex is a good woman, and I was a shit husband. I can't blame her for the breakup. However, she did cut up my Melbourne Cricket Club tie in one argument. I could have done her for that. You'd struggle to find a judge in this town who wouldn't let me off with a warning."

He made eye contact for a laugh he felt he deserved. I was a refugee from the Reservoir Housing Commission. He was barking up the wrong tree with jokes about his MCC membership.

He raised a disappointed eyebrow.

"Wouldn't expect a housing-commission-cretin like you to understand the deep and meaningful relations formed by your betters during their private school educations."

I laughed at that. "My betters. That's funny. I just discovered another reason I don't like you," I said.

"Another? Something other than my colleague-crushing lust for limelight and promotion."

"Yes."

"OK, lay it on me."

"You went to Scotch College."

It was Pete's turn to laugh out loud. I had struck home. I had picked the old-school lilt in his accent.

"I did go to Scotch, but on a scholarship. My parents couldn't afford a school like that," he said, almost defensively.

"Yeah, but you still went."

"Yes," he said, smiling. "You got me, I went, and it is worse than you imagine, mate. Much worse."

"How could it possibly be worse?" I asked.

"I was captain of the rowing," he said, "and my cox and my number six are now both judges."

I had to laugh. I was warming to the selfish prick yet again. It was becoming conceivable that I might eventually get to like him in another hundred years of working cases with him.

It was possible.

"So," I said. "To sum it all up, Virginia never got to sell her house while she was alive."

"No, she didn't, and that is another thing," he said, "this business about selling the house." He did his upside-down flicking of my pages again. Found the one he wanted and tapped it."

I read where Pete had tapped the page.

"This sale dragged on for years," he said. "The Savage family fought it, denied Virginia was dead and not entitled to walk away from the shared ownership of the asset."

"Ultimately, after a few years, the coroner declares Virginia is dead," I said, "and then, not long after, there is a property settlement based on the then-value of the house. The money goes to Virginia's kids. Who, by then, are living with Virginia's mother. This is all forced through by her lawyer, no help from the Savages."

"That lawyer would be your other punchy mate, Richard Martin, Solicitor?" said Detective Pete. "You know he is a crim lawyer, has all sorts of baddies on his books."

"So?"

"Just making sure you know who you're dealing with," said Pete.

"I know Rick very well, and I can tell you why he has so many clients."

"You're going to tell me he is good."

"He is outstanding," I said. "I'd use him myself, but I never break the law."

That made Pete laugh. I didn't think he'd want, or need, to know about my late-night spying on the Fenwicks.

"I spoke to Rick Martin yesterday," I said. "He thinks the mother-in-law is our murderer."

"Penelope Anne Savage, nee Fenwick," said Pete. "Ninety-years-not-out, or thereabouts, going strong. All marbles still rolling in the same direction."

What did Tina say about the mother? A soul-shrivelled razor-lipped bitch-from-hell. Something like that.

"Has Penny Anne been informed about the bodies yet?" I asked.

"No, not personally," said Pete. I guess she has read about the discovery in the papers."

"It has been a week, and you haven't spoken to her personally?" I was surprised. The nearest of kin was usually the first visit and the first suspect.

"Yes, well, not so easy when you are dealing with this level of wealth, young Christopher. You don't just rock up to the door in your Jarrajarra police truck. Correct channels are the words we are dealing with here, channels."

"OK, who is this channel-obstructing person?" I asked.

"You can come and meet him if you want. I am meeting him in his office in thirty minutes."

I had guessed the obstruction would be the Fenwick brother, the

Master of Laws, the man in the expensive Mercedes, the man in the Toorak castle car park.

"I'd love to meet him," I said, all innocent.

"Great," said Pete, "you can read this on the way." He passed me another Manila folder. "Your mate Rick could be on to something."

He had passed me a printed report from Carole and Glenda, the Crime Services team.

"Your girlfriends have done it again," he said. "They sent this through this morning."

I opened the folder. The first page had some strikingly clear photographs of some truly ugly toenails. I think they were toenails. Hard to tell, given there was only bone below.

Our coffee arrived as we were making to leave. Pete put ten dollars on the table and ignored his cup. I took a quick sip out of mine. It was half full, barely warm and diabolically bad. Toenail bad.

Out and about in Melbourne with Pete.

While Detective Pete drove us to visit Penelope Anne's lawyer, I read the forensic report.

Carole and Glenda were worried about the state of the three surviving toenails they had discovered. Two large from the corpse of Phillip Senior and one large from Phillip the Younger.

According to our forensic wizards, the toenails had somehow survived their entombment in much the same state they had started it, apart from the usual mould and grit of a decade down a hole. The toenails were horrible and had been horrible when the two Savage boys breathed their last.

Indicative of gradual ingestion of Thallium, according to Carole.

To put it another way, according to Glenda, the two dead Savage men had been chowing down, repeatedly, on a derivative of good old-fashioned rat poison.

Taken in small, steady doses, of course.

"Fucking hell," I said.

"You just got to the good bit, I am thinking," said Detective Pete.

"Thallium?" I asked, bewildered.

"Rat poison," said Pete.

"Served in your mains or your entrée, do you reckon?"

"Dessert for sure, with the ice cream and fried banana."

We had a think while Pete dawdled through the crowded Melbourne traffic.

"I don't see my old coach, Rusty, as your sneaky slow-drip revenge-style rat poisoner?" I said.

"No," he answered. "Me neither."

"So, if Rusty is not the killer?" I ventured.

"Is he another one of the victims?" ventured Pete.

Oh gosh, the thought of it nearly made me cry.

Maybe Detective Pete was sympathetic enough to sense the sadness that swept over me.

"Let's not get ahead of ourselves, Constable Taylor." Detective Sergeant Pete Jordan went formal on me as we parked outside the lawyer's office.

"Two Phillip Savages and one Rusty Collins," said Pete as we parked. "Two dead and two missing. Let's you and I sort them out, one at a time."

Office of Fenwick, Fenwick and Carstairs, Solicitors, Melbourne.

"Mister Fenwick will be with you in a moment, gentlemen. He asked if you would wait in the boardroom."

The very elegant secretary turned without waiting for a response and led the way from the very elegant reception area to the plush boardroom.

The corporate heart of the Fenwick family.

It all looked lovely and soft. Extremely soft.

"Let me guess, the family law firm, Penelope Fenwick's brother, nephew and niece?" I said.

"Nailed it," answered Detective Pete Jordan, with a cynical raise of the eyebrow. "How did you work that out?"

"You need glasses," I said, nodding to the three law degrees of the partners, hanging framed on the boardroom wall.

"Assuming they all graduated around age twenty-five," I said, "then that has the senior partner around seventy and the other two somewhere forty to fifty, so I am guessing brother, nephew, niece. You can see from the degree. The niece was a Fenwick when she graduated then, I am guessing, she married a bloke named Carstairs later."

"Let me see," said Pete, taking out a pair of glasses, putting them on and reading the three documents. "Very clever young apprentice," he observed.

"A closed shop," he whispered, "just family, only Fenwicks get a guernsey, no other partners. All Melbourne University educated, no second-rate institutions for your Fenwicks."

"So big family money from previous generations," I said, "then you breed three lawyers to be what?" I asked.

"Financial custodians?" Pete offered.

"Maybe they were too thick to be in the family business."

"We'll soon find out."

We sat.

We waited.

If it was a power trip from the lawyer, it was wasted on Detective Pete. It was Pete's show, and he would wait all day if necessary. It is hard to shift a man with a plan.

We waited some more.

Finally, some action.

"Gentlemen, gentlemen, terribly sorry, extremely busy today. Please accept my apologies."

It was the Fenwick Elder. The same man I'd viewed only last night from my secret hideout underneath the darkened hedge.

He didn't look at all sorry and, by the look of him, he hadn't been busy in a long time.

There was a word for him that I couldn't find. Ruined? Dissipated? Degenerate? All of them worked, but none were quite enough. Years of self-indulgence were written on his bedraggled face.

He had a sort of manchild mullet of thick white hair swept back in a rock star mane that he obviously loved.

Dissolute was the word I was looking for. Self-satisfied, self-indulged. Physically repulsive but dressed and coiffed like a million dollars.

His hair was ridiculous, pure white, so thick it had to be a wig, except it wasn't. All clearly his and brushed back, teased and puffed till it stood in a styled pompadour that sat on his head like a carefully tousled castle of powdered snow. He had a Superman-style forelock that had to be waxed into place and fashioned to appear casual.

It was the most arrogant head of hair I'd ever seen in my life. Handsome, but more suitable for a wealthy madam somewhere around the 1950s.

This was the brother of Mrs. Penelope Savage.

He reached over the table to limply shake both our hands.

He shook by rank, Pete copped a wet-fish-shake first, then Fenwick soft-balled an even limper version for me, the uniformed plod.

"Albert Fenwick, Master of Laws," he said as he barely tickled my hand with his fingers.

His jowls fascinated me almost as much as the hair. They were sort of squeezed into his collar and tie but still hung over the edge, like a teenage muffin belly under his chin.

The jowls wobbled as he spoke. They had a life of their own. I was in danger of being hypnotised.

"So, gentlemen, how may I be of assistance?"

"Your client, Mrs. Penelope Savage," said Pete. "I want to speak with her."

"Why?" asked Fenwick.

He knew why.

"Victoria Police have discovered the bodies of her missing husband and stepson," said Pete.

"Yes, of course," said Fenwick. "We have read the newspapers and seen the terrible news, quite terrible."

He wobbled his head in fake sorrow.

"My client will not need a consolation visit from the police. She knows her husband and stepson are dead."

"Does she know these men were murdered?" asked Pete.

He feigned deep shock. He made sudden eye contact with Pete and smoothed his tie flat against his ample belly. It was amongst the most overt tells I had ever seen.

"Murdered? Oh my God."

What a bullshitter.

"This is not a consolation visit, Mr. Fenwick. We have some questions we wish to clear with your sister?" said Pete.

Fenwick was taken aback by the use of the word 'sister'. He'd been referring to Penny Anne as his client.

"Pardon," said Fenwick.

"Your sister," Pete repeated, "Mrs. Savage is your sister. We have some questions we wish to ask her."

"And some for you as well," I added.

"Yes, yes, of course, questions," said Fenwick.

I sensed Pete was a bit surprised that I'd joined the conversation. Not to worry, he'd survive the shock. I wasn't so sure about the Master of Laws. I threw a few more words his way.

"Now that two of the bodies have been found, we are wondering how long before the others turn up," I said, putting his own words from last night right back at him.

The ancient lawyer's face went blank, but his right hand went crazy. He stared at me, saying nothing but stroking his tie flat against his massive belly with some vigour.

Detective Pete said nothing.

I said nothing.

Eventually, Pete reached into his coat pocket and retrieved a folded paper. He smoothed it flat, then slid it over to Fenwick's side of the table.

Fenwick was looking confused. His lizard-lawyer brain was telling him not to acknowledge the document, but he couldn't help himself.

"Mr. Albert James Fenwick," said Detective Pete very formally. "This document I have just given you is a request for your client, Mrs. Penelope Anne Savage, to attend Saint Kilda Road Police Station at the date and time shown in the document for a video record-of-interview."

Fenwick was looking down at the document, "Friday, June 24, 2.00 PM," he said, speaking to himself more than us.

Perhaps with all his wealth, it had never occurred to him that a policeman might tell him what to do. Perhaps my recitation of his exact words from my ninja stunt last night had frightened him.

Who knew?

"That is correct," said Pete, confirming the date and time.

"This interview," continued Pete, "is one component of a police investigation into an alleged murder. I am taking this opportunity to warn your client that she would be well advised to have an attorney present."

Fenwick was in a daze. Finally, he lifted his eyes from the

paperwork and stared at Pete for a moment. Then, he stopped with the obsessive flattening of his tie, looked down again, and picked up the paper in front of him.

"I am sorry, how terribly rude," he said. "I'm sure you gentlemen would appreciate refreshments. Coffee? Yes?"

With that, he stood up and left, taking the police paper with him.

We waited.

We did a lot of waiting in this bloke's boardroom.

After another five minutes, the very-elegant secretary returned with two cups of coffee served in two cardboard cups to go.

The smell of the coffee was beautiful, rich and strong.

"Mr. Fenwick asked me to tell you that he has been called away," she said. "He regrets he will not be able to provide you with any more time today."

She smiled so elegantly.

The pompous old prick had done a runner.

"Thank you," said Pete, standing to leave.

I reached for the coffee just for a little sip. I just about had it to my lips when Pete spoke.

"Smell good?" asked Pete.

"Fantastic," I said.

"I am told the rats can't get enough of the stuff. Apparently, it tastes so damn good they just keep eating till they drop."

My jaw must have hit the floor.

"Come on," he said, "I will buy you a mug of the good stuff. I know a place where we can watch them make it."

Back on the road, in Melbourne, with Pete.

"More bodies? What the fuck was that about?" Asked Pete.

We were back in the car, driving to get some real coffee,

"Well," I said, "speaking theoretically, I may have accidentally overheard a conversation during the course of my evening jog around Toorak last night."

"You, the country hick, jogging around Toorak these days?" said Pete.

"Yes, when my busy schedule allows, it is so lovely, and you meet a better class of people."

"Any particular people you theoretically overheard on this jaunt?"

"Well, it could have been our mate Albert, Master of Laws and his sister-client, Penelope.

"Theoretically?" he asked.

"Yes," I said, "and quite accidentally."

"Oh Jesus," said Pete. "Better lay it out for me."

And so, I did.

I came clean about my adventures beyond the high brick walls of the Toorak mansion. I explained my eavesdropping under the hedge while the Fenwicks discussed their situation. I also mentioned the key phrases I had heard.

At the end of my revelations, Pete just shook his head.

"Chris," he said after a very long pause. "Mate, we don't work this way in the big city homicide. You are with the big boys now. You are not dishing out bush vengeance on the local pissheads."

"I find the pissheads pretty much the same everywhere I go," I said. "I'd say your mate Albert is typical."

"Chris, Chris, Chris, we are the big boys, the grown-ups. Here in the real world, we have processes in place to ensure the bad guys go to jail and stay there."

"So you're one of the big boys, are you?" I don't know why, but the notion Melbourne cops were better than me simply because they were based in Melbourne irritated me.

"Mate," he said. Very patient. "You are puffing your chest at me over the wrong words. Don't be getting pissed off at 'big boys'. Just wrap your tiny bush brain around the notion of 'process'."

We went silent while I lost the attitude. He was right, of course, all the more reason I'd never work in Melbourne.

"So. Tell me, what's this process thing I hear all you grown-ups raving about?" I asked.

He laughed.

"You sure you weren't seen?"

"Sure?" I said. "Not absolutely, no. Am I sure what I heard? One hundred per cent."

I could tell he was not really surprised nor outraged by my off-the-books adventure. His glory-hungry cop nose was smelling opportunity.

"The Fenwicks think these dead duck hunters are just a smokescreen for an informant, this Carruthers bloke?"

"Fake news, to hide who is talking," I said.

"Holy Mother of God," said Pete. "And this Carruthers is the only one they suspect? Coming forward now for money or maybe a plea bargain now we've found the bodies?"

"Yes, and yes," I answered. "Carruthers and money. Apparently, he can never get enough."

"We should offer a reward," said Pete. Looking at me with an evil grin. "A fake reward, with plenty of publicity attached, asking for information related to the discovery of the two Savages, father and son, and the murder of the missing mother, Virginia Savage, nee Collins."

"That would worry our Fenwicks," I said.

"Mate," said Pete, "I think it will totally fuck their minds. Might even smoke out this Carruthers."

"Who do we know that could organise instant publicity and public attention."

"Who, indeed?" Said Pete, smiling.

Publicity and promotion, Pete's backyard.

"Murder and mayhem, God, I love it," Detective Sergeant Pete Jordan was having more fun than a kid at Christmas.

He stopped smiling long enough to make a serious point.

"So, let's be straight on one thing. You never told me any of this, the Carruthers bloke, more bodies, none of it, not a breath of it. OK?"

"Never a word has passed my lips," I said.

"And you never climbed a brick fence in Toorak without a warrant, and you never will again."

"Toorak? Never heard of the place," I said, "but climbing walls, Pete, that could be a thing. I could get to like it."

"Well, if you do it again, make sure you don't get caught," he said, sounding more like my kind of policeman.

We drove on in silence. I was thinking about how to go about finding the mysterious Ken Carruthers.

"The shit has now officially hit the fan, young apprentice," he said. "You might as well head back to the bush for a while. I have some running around to do with the DPP and some journalists I know. Might see if I can scratch up some reward for information."

The DPP Pete referred to is the Director of Public Prosecutions. Typically, they were responsible for kicking off and then conducting serious criminal prosecutions in Victoria.

I guessed that Pete, being Pete, had not consulted anyone higher up before going after a prestigious Melbourne lawyer and his mega-wealthy sister.

"Are the DPP aware you are looking at Fenwick as a suspect?"

Technically, the DPP should already be aware since initiating significant prosecutions on behalf of the community is their job.

"No, Chris. Not yet."

"Good process there, Detective Sergeant," I said. "My old coach Rusty Collins, he had a phrase for blokes like you."

"Oh yeah, lay it on me."

"He would call you a flat-stick-cowboy."

Pete laughed out loud.

"I believe your mate Rusty would like me," he said. "What did I read on that website of his? It is easier to apologize than to ask for permission."

"No," I answered. "Rusty never said that. He would say, 'Do it once, do it right, and practice like hell before you do it at all'."

"Then don't you worry, my young apprentice," he said. "I have been practising for scumbags like the Fenwicks all my life."

We drove in silence for a bit. A thought occurred to me.

"What the fuck is going on with Albert Fenwick's hair?"

We laughed at the memory of it for a good minute.

"Is it wrong to laugh at a person's appearance?" I asked.

"Appearance? Yes," said Pete, "but pompous self-deluding vanity? Definitely acceptable material."

More laughter.

"I'd have to say," he continued, "that is the purest epitome of lipstick on a pig I have ever seen."

We didn't like the Master of Laws. It would make our day to prove he was guilty of something.

* * *

Pete dropped me back at my truck, still parked outside my motel. I started the truck, ready to head home.

Barney had texted me. It was long and detailed.

Lawyers acting on behalf of Jennifer McLain had made an urgent bail application in the Wodonga Magistrates Court. The hearing was scheduled for tomorrow, and I was required to attend.

Bail? For an accused cop killer? It did not seem likely.

Just when the Virginia Savage case was getting interesting, Jennifer McLain surfaced again on my next day's agenda. I thought I had her packed away, safely secured for her date with justice.

How wrong could I possibly be?

Thursday, June 16, 2022

Wodonga Magistrates Court, Cafe.

There is chaos and calamity, then there is catastrophe, then there is the bail application for the cop-killer Jennifer McLain. You could call that a chaotic, catastrophic clusterfuck.

I was sitting at a large table in the Wodonga Court cafe.

Mid-morning. People in motion. The Magistrate's courtroom had emptied, and a thirsty herd was pouring into the cafe for their caffeine fix.

As a potential witness, I was not supposed to hear what everyone else said till it was my turn in the witness barrell. So while the police crew, including Dazzling Darren Bennet, drone wizard and the first witness, had gone into the courtroom, I'd waited here sipping coffee. Not all police work was unpleasant, but when you had a good moment like this, you usually had to pay later.

The arriving police were not happy.

"You're not sitting here with Chris and me," said Sarge to Assistant Commissioner Jerrod Harrison and a young police prosecutor named Rowlands. "Go somewhere else, the pair of you."

"I'll sit where I please," said Harrison.

"Good for you," said Sarge. "Anywhere but here."

Harrison and Rowlands had followed Sarge into the cafe with the intention of finishing yet another of the arguments that followed Harrison everywhere. Harrison's bright purple, blood-pressured face was more ready to explode than ever. His tame prosecutor, Rowands, just looked embarrassed. Arguments between senior officers were best avoided by us lesser lights. They usually happened behind closed doors and could stay there as far as I was concerned.

Harrison had dragged Rowlands five hours up the road from Melbourne to do everything Harrison told him to do. Apparently, the Police Prosecutors working out of Wodonga Station were not compliant enough for Assistant Commissioner Jerrod Harrison. His loss.

Sarge gave me a smile. He'd faced down the Tailban in his army time. An argument with an Assistant Commissioner was not the stuff to bother about.

"Fifteen-minute break," said Sarge. "Another coffee?"
"Yes, please," I said.
"Where's Daz?" I asked, almost an afterthought.
"Darren," said Sarge. "Our expert witness?"
"That's the one," I added, feeling something coming my way.
"Our boy is in the cells below us."
"The cells?" I was shocked. "Inside? With the doors locked?"
"I would presume," said Sarge.
A moment's bewildered silence.
"I'll get the coffee," he said and walked off.
"What did he do this time," I asked when Sarge returned.
"Sorry, Chris, I can't even talk about it."
"Not even a hint."
"I think this is the most embarrassing day I have ever spent in a courtroom in my career."
"Because of Dazzle?"
"Well, he certainly didn't help."
The Sarge closed his eyes and laughed to himself,
"My God, what a comedy show," he said, then looked at me. "Sad day for justice, son."
We sipped our coffee. No point asking Sarge the same question twice.
We finished our coffee as the clock on the fifteen-minute break ticked away.
"Well, son," said Sarge, eventually, "you're up next. I'm pretty sure we've lost already, but if you can avoid incarceration, we will count it as a win."

Wodonga Magistrates Court, Courtroom.

"So, Constable Taylor, let's run through this video, so graciously provided by the prosecution team, and perhaps you would be kind enough to show the court exactly when you decided it was Miss McLain driving the Bedford truck."
"Yes, happy to," I said.
It was my turn in the barrel. My sole purpose today was to keep the cop killer in the clink.
But here I was, facing Australia's greatest Barrister, Jeremy Oakley,

with all his eloquence and theatrics. I was doomed.

Jennifer McLain had done very well for herself and hired Jarrajarra's solicitor, Eddie Doolan, a wonderful man who was as good as any lawyer in the country. His ability belied his humble location in Main Street Jarrajarra, population nine hundred or thereabouts.

Eddie had briefed his go-to Barrister, Jeremy Oakley QC.

Oakley was a star of the big show in Melbourne, normally appearing in the big cases, on the front pages of newspapers and front and centre on the nightly news. But when Eddie Doolan called, Oakley came. Why? Because they were mates.

"Mr Doolan, if you please," said Oakley.

Oakley nodded to Eddie Doolan, and Doolan started the video at a point where the truck first came into view of my bodycam. From memory, it was after I had hustled Senior Constable Ralph Davey into the safety of the muddy ditch beside the road. This was just before I started shooting at the truck, trying to kill Jason Bloody Mellish.

The camera was perched high, close to my left shoulder and gave a jerky view of all the violent activity. You could see my shooting action, and it was hard not to notice that I kept missing.

Bloody hell.

There they all were, on the screen, back in action with the truck bearing down on me, and in those frantic moments, right there was a perfect picture of the woman in question.

"Right there, Mr. Oakley," I said, and the video stopped as I spoke.

Jennifer McLain wearing a man's cap, and, yes, she had big shoulders, and yes, she looked very comfortable behind the wheel of the Bedford, towing a double-decker tandem trailer containing a few hundred tons of expensive cattle. But it was her, no question.

"You are claiming that is Jennifer McLain," said Oakley. Dubious.

"Yes," I answered confidently, not conceding even the slightest doubt.

Oakley gave another subtle nod to Eddie Doolan, and the screen changed to a split view.

On the left side of the screen was a still frame of Jennifer McLain driving the truck, but enlarged so it was mostly her and not much truck. On the right side was a mug shot of her now-dead accomplice, Carl Agnew, the escapee's cattle expert.

"Do you know who that is on the right of the picture, Constable

Taylor?" asked Oakley.

"Yes, that's Carl Agnew."

"Surely," said Oakley, "when you look at these photographs, side by side, you can see it is the same Carl Agnew who is driving."

"No," I said, matching Oakley's confidence, "there's no question in my mind that the picture on the left shows Jennifer McLain driving the truck. No doubt whatsoever. The bloke on the right is just another one of her victims if you ask me."

"Your Honour," asked Oakley of the magistrate. Both of them seemed to be raising eyebrows in unison.

"Constable Taylor," said the magistrate. "Please restrict your answers to yes or no. We have enough of your team downstairs already."

"Sorry, Your Honour," I said.

"So, you're absolutely certain, Constable, it is Jennifer McLain behind the wheel?" asked Oakley.

"Yes," I said.

"You remember it clearly?"

"Yes, I do."

"I wonder, Constable Taylor, with your perfect memory, do you recall this other part of the evening?" Oakley nodded at Eddie Doolan, and a still frame of almost perfect solid black came up on the screen. A tiny bit of light filtered onto the screen from the right.

"Ummm," I said, "this could be later when I was lying in the ditch after Miss McLain tried to run me down."

"Your Honour?" Oakley raised his eyebrow again.

"Constable Taylor," said the beak.

"Sorry, Your Honour, sorry," I said, saving us both from his full just-yes-or-no soliloquy.

"Try to behave," said the Magistrate, insisting on the last word but in a kindly way.

"No," said Oakley, "this would be an inside wall of the emergency room of the Jarrajarra Bush Nursing Centre. I presume they have removed your vest and camera but forgot to turn the camera off."

"OK," I said.

"So, do you remember this bit, Constable?" asked Oakley.

"Yes," I said, "I remember it very well."

"As well as the previous video where you identified Ms McLain as the driver of the Bedford?"

"Yes," I said, starting to worry.

"With this wonderful memory of yours, Constable, would you say that you know the identity of the Nurse who is treating you?"

"Absolutely," I said. "The nurse is my partner, Nurse Practitioner Wendy Atcheson."

"Correct. It is indeed Nurse Atcheson, " said Oakley. "You know, Constable Taylor, I am amazed, with this unquestionable memory of yours, in your statement given on the night, you didn't mention your karaoke session from this particular visit to the hospital. Oakley held up a copy of my statement and looked at me as though I were a fish he had just hooked on a perfectly baited line.

"Karaoke?" I asked helplessly.

"You don't recall, Constable?"

"No."

"No memory of any love songs to your sweetheart, perhaps?"

He was smiling as he spoke, having fun.

"No," I said. "None at all."

"Let's have a listen, shall we?" Oakley nodded one more time to Eddie Doolan, and I guessed my goose was cooked. The black, empty video started to play. You couldn't see anything, but you could hear plenty.

Wendy was laughing out loud.

"Chris," she said, "Shut up, you idiot, this is serious."

She was telling me to shut up, but she kept laughing. There was a mixed signal right there.

Funny thing, concussion, I had forgotten the next bit, but here and now in the Wodonga Magistrates Court, it all came rushing back.

I wasn't shutting up, not one bit. I was singing very loud, a labourious country and western love ballad.

"Don't forget to remember the time we had together.
When we promised us forever
that we wouldn't part till never.
But then, the change of weather,
And I went and joined the army,
To go and kill the evil Nazis
off in Europe."

Oh, dear.

How to explain this particular music to the sceptics in the Wodonga Magistrates Court.

I could hardly mention that I was singing to my Nan, who had been standing behind Wendy as she tended my wounds. Couldn't mention Nan, not since she'd died twenty years ago and had never been sighted at the Jarrajarra Nursing Centre.

I couldn't mention that standing there with Nan on that evening had been Englebert Humperdink, who had been singing along with me, wearing his signature dinner suit and looking just like he did in his prime way back in 1972 before I was born, in fact. He'd seemed quite encouraging as I chased the higher notes.

I didn't want to mention that the lyric came from a love letter from my grandfather to my Nan, sent from somewhere in Western Europe in 1945, during the climax of World War Two.

Nan loved those letters, and I could always get a smile out of her by singing them in my best country voice, something between Slim Whitman and Engleburt, her two favourites.

My grandad's lyrics had a way about them, short on pentameter, long on heartfelt love, and they rhymed nearly all the way till they didn't. It was as if his capacity for rhyme wilted as his poems progressed.

The video kept playing, and I kept singing.

> *"But one day, I will come home to you,*
> *and heaven knows just what I'll do,*
> *but I know that in my boots, I will be true,*
> *to you,*
> *F-o-r-e-v-v-v-v-v-e-e-e-e-r-r-r-r-r."*

"Objection," called out my Prosecutor Rowlands at last, as though he'd just remembered why he was here and whose team I was on.

"Yes, indeed, thank you," said the magistrate, Mr. Holland. He had to bang his gavel a few times as the courtroom took a minute to stop laughing.

At me!

The video stopped and the court turned its attention to Police

Prosecutor Rowlands, the next-to-useless talking head for our team. He seemed to have lost the thread on the point he wanted to raise.

"You have an objection to the defence's line of questioning, Mister Rowlands?" asked the magistrate. "We would dearly love to hear it."

"Yes, Your Honour, yes, of course," said Rowlands. "What is the point of showing this video? Making a fool of Constable Taylor like this?"

Me? A fool? According to my own prosecutor.

Great team-mate, this bloke.

"Can I object to that, Your Honour," I asked, miffed.

"No, Constable," said Magistrate Holland, "you're the witness. You can't object to your own prosecutor."

"Your Honour," interrupted Jeremy Oakley, the golden one, "no one is suggesting Constable Taylor is a fool, heavens no. I am simply pointing out that in light of the injuries Constable Taylor suffered on the evening in question, injuries that are still evident today, nine days later, his memory of the events may be fractured. His recall may be incorrect, not wholly accurate."

"Hard to imagine anyone forgetting a song like that, objection denied," said the beak. "But, point made, let's move on. Thank you, Mister Oakley. Quite a tune there, Constable."

"Yes, Your Honour," said Oakley. "Let's have a look at the real villain here."

Oakley nodded at Eddie Doolan again, and another video came up on the screen. This time, the show was in slow motion, incredibly slow motion. Oakley wanted us to see it frame by dawdling frame.

Centre screen was Jason Mellish, shotgun barrel out the truck window, pointing directly at me.

It was the moment before a very muddy and ridiculous Senior Constable Ralph Davey emerged from his muddy ditch beside the road, arising like a sludge-covered phoenix between me and the business end of Jason Mellish's shotgun.

"Do you remember this moment here, Constable?" asked Oakley.

"Yes, this is just a few seconds before Jason Mellish murders Senior Constable Davey," I said.

"Before Constable Davey intervened to save your life?"

"Yes," I said, doing my best not to reveal my true thoughts on Constable Davey.

"Indeed," said Oakley. "This would be a few moments before Senior Constable Davey died heroically defending you from the escapee Mellish," said Oakley, looking at me in such a way that I knew that Oakley knew that Davey's death was not so heroic at all. Nothing like it.

"Yes," I said.

"Constable Taylor, do you see the face there at the left side of the screen, sneaking a peak from the driver's seat around the shotgun held by the escapee Mellish?"

"Yes," I said, "that is Jennifer McLain, encouraging Jason Mellish to shoot me."

"You're sure of that, are you?"

"Yes," I was sure.

I remembered what came next, and it was not the heroic death our Assistant Commissioner Jerrod Harrison had been painting for public consumption.

Next up on the big screen would be Constable Davey's mud-caked diatribe, angry at me for getting his uniform all wet and dirty. Screaming at me because I'd pushed the idiot into a ditch to try and save his life. Not a performance for which you typically received a bravery award, post-mortem or otherwise.

"Objection," said our prosecutor, Rowlands.

The video paused, with the top of Davey's head arriving, just barely, on the screen.

Everyone looked at Rowlands, who appeared to have nothing to say beyond his objection.

Silence.

Neither Rowlands nor his ventriloquist, beetroot-faced Harrison, wanted to see what came next. There would be no medal for dead Constable Davey if the court saw that little cameo.

"You objected, Mr. Rowlands?" prompted the magistrate, Mr Holland.

"One moment, please, Your Honour," said Rowlands.

Rowlands turned to confer with Harrison. Harrison spoke, and Rowlands listened. Eventually, after a thorough verbal bashing, Rowlands turned to face the magistrate.

"Your Honour," said the prosecutor, "at this point, we withdraw our objection to Ms McLain's bail application."

Bloody Hell.

After that bombshell, the rest of the hearing was just minor detail.

Jennifer McLain had tried to murder me with a stolen truck. She had executed Jason Mellish, her former boyfriend, with a gunshot to the back of his head, and now, after a bit of paperwork and a promise to behave, she would be free to leave.

Wodonga Magistrates Court, Front steps.

"You are an idiot," said Sarge to Assistant Commissioner Jerrod Harrison.

"I am wondering if you need a visit to the PSC," said Harrison.

"Don't wonder a moment longer," said Sarge. "I've already reported you."

PSC was cop-speak for the Professional Standards Command. The PSC handled all integrity and insubordination issues. We were outside the court, in public, and the two senior cops were going at it. Definitely PSC-worthy.

"I beg your pardon," said Harrison. Flustered, his threats and bluster wasted on Sarge.

"Beg all you like, you won't be getting any pardons from me." Sarge was always ice-cold in a verbal stoush. Always able to speak the pointed truth perfectly.

"What are you doing here anyway?" Sarge continued. "You've never been involved in a murder case or a manhunt in your life. I understand you were a traffic cop, for heaven's sake. Why inflict your pompous arse on my team?"

"Someone had to take over," said Harrison. "You and your so-called team had managed to get my nephew killed by those escapees that you couldn't find."

"Your nephew! Your fucking nephew?" I don't know what shocked me more. Sarge's angry shout or his use of the F-word.

"Yes, my nephew, you knew Constable Davey was my nephew. Don't act surprised now."

"You told us he was a friend of a friend, you lying dog."

Oh, dear me. We were in extremely dark territory now. Words may never hurt you, but they can sure get you sacked, particularly inside the Victoria Police. Sarge and Harrison had crossed a line, and one of them would be looking for a new job soon.

Harrison blustered his way through a few more threats to Sarge's job and a couple more how-dare-you's. He was all piss and wind, the very worst of the inner-city desk cops.

"You can explain to our peers your conflict of interest," said Sarge. "Touting thoroughly undeserved bravery medals for your thoroughly useless nephew, may he rest in peace. How do you think the PSC will view the video you shut down in the courtroom? You're finished, Harrison. It will be worth my job to get a stain like you out of the uniform."

Sarge had spoken. Bring it on, the theme of the day.

"Come on, Chris, we are done here," said Sarge, and away we went.

We headed back toward Wodonga Station, where I'd left my truck.

"How do you think you'll go at a PSC hearing?" I asked.

"I don't know, son," said Sarge. "Fifty-fifty. If I play it right, it won't get to a hearing. Anyway, we've faced worse, hey?"

He laughed. I laughed. We had indeed faced a lot worse.

We were halfway to the station when I realized we were a man down.

"Shit," I said. "Dazzle will die if we leave him behind."

"Go," said Sarge. "I'll phone the magistrate. You gave him a good laugh. He's probably softened by now. Try singing the next verse of that song."

Road from Wodonga to Jarrajarra.

"What the hell did you do?" I asked.

"Mate, I just can't talk about it," said Daz, "sorry. Fucking Magistrate."

Homeward bound. Darren, freshly released from incarceration, was beside me in the passenger seat of my police truck. Not in the back, as the Magistrate would have preferred.

"Give me a hint, Darren."

"Nope."

We drove in silence for a bit. I'd get it out of him.

"It's OK, mate. Win some, lose some. Swings and slides. Couldn't have been as bad as my performance."

"No," he agreed, "probably not. The court cops were pissing themselves. Said you looked a total idiot."

My own humiliation seemed to cheer him up. 'One man's misfortune, another's triumph,' my Nan might have said.

My phone rang. Detective Pete.

"Chris Taylor, crime-solver, how are you?"

"Not great," I said. "Driving back to Jarrajarra with Darren Everett, camera guy with me. You remember Daz? We are on speaker."

"Yeah, Dazzle, just the man we need. Why the sads?"

"Just had our bums kicked by Jeremy Oakley QC in the McLain bail hearing. We lost."

"You lost?" said Pete.

Long pause.

"Mate, Oakley is good, but I can't believe you lost a bail app to a cop-killer? Holy shit."

Long pause.

"Anyway," said Pete, "What I need from hillbilly country is to put on a little bit of a show. Monday at Jarrajarra, I need you and your troops. Might even have Daz's girlfriend, Miss Angela Adams, along for the ride."

"Why me, and why Jarrajarra?"

"Well," sighed Pete, never keen on justification. "Your 'bodies-in-the-hole' is as much your case as mine, and I want to plant a seed," said Pete. "A giant seed in the mind of the enemy."

"And you win yourself some meaningful publicity in the process," I said.

"Meaningful publicity?" he laughed. "Is there any other kind? See you Monday." He ended the call before I could say no.

Daz and I drove in silence for another twenty minutes.

At least Daz had stopped crying. He was a hard man to console since it was never his fault.

Eventually, he spoke. Stream of consciousness, victim babble mostly.

"I'll show those ignorant bastards," he said. "Know bugger all about the capability of modern video, idiots."

I was getting a flavour of how Daz ended up downstairs in the cells.

"I tried to tell them, wouldn't listen. Put me in the Gulag, made me a Mandela, a prisoner of the system. They fucked me over, Chris. Fucked me over."

"I'd still be there if it wasn't for you. Locked up like a rat in a cage."

The prison experience had not sat well with Dazzle. Relatively short and comfortable in comparison to his new hero, Nelson Mandela. It seemed to have fired Daz to new levels of what? I wasn't sure. Resolve? Anger? Ego? Self-obsession? Martyrdom?

Did he have any more capacities in any of these directions?

"I saw what she did, the murderer. I'll prove to the world what she is, don't you worry."

OK, 'resolve' it was to be.

I am not sure the whole world was that interested in Daz or me or the goings on at our little country corner, but if he could use his video skills to put Jenifer McLain back in jail, I would be grateful.

One thing occurred to me.

"Darren, mate, why did you hand over my singing bit to the defence. There was no vision on it. You didn't have to cough it up."

"No vision? Oh, mate, really. Do I have to explain to you as well. Poor vision is still vision. It was a video, Chris. It's not my fault if it only showed a blank wall. God, you're sounding like that fuckwit Magistrate. You may not be aware, Chris, but as a quasi-officer of the court, I was obligated to provide the defence with all available evidentiary material."

Daz was using big words, none of them quite where they needed to be.

"Quasi-officer of the court?"

"I am an expert witness, Chris. My duty to the process of the law overrides all my personal feelings and even my friendships. In this case, you."

Our Dazzle, now a man on a mission. It was a ninety-minute drive from Wodonga to Jarrajarra. It felt a lot longer.

Friday, June 17, 2022

Murray River, Jarrajarra.

"Get in, you great wimp," Wendy was floating on her back in the freezing water of the Murray River in June. Two weeks to winter, and she was showing off her superior endurance.

"Give me a moment," I said, shivering on the bank, getting my mind right for the ice-cold water.

"You great wussy," she laughed before diving under.

It was early morning, and we had run north from our home in Jarrajarra to the caravan park, then along the river trail to our secret swimming spot, where a little indent in the banks allowed us to swim without having to deal with the stronger currents mid-stream.

It was our own private swimming pool. Clean, clear water, almost perfect, except it was as cold as buggery.

Paradise for a woman like my beautiful Wendy, who had never expressed pain or fear as far as I could recall. Certainly not fear of the cold.

Which was all OK for her, not so flash for me.

"Get in now, Corporal Taylor, you great big sook," she said in her Navy Officer's voice.

What can you do? I got in and screamed like a baby, which only made her laugh some more.

I lasted five minutes in the water, by which time I was shivering so hard I couldn't speak, and I had totally forgotten about my humiliation at the hands of Jennifer McLain's Barrister in the Wodonga Magistrates Court.

Thankfully, the run home warmed me up. I was warm enough for fifteen minutes on the heavy bag in my back yard. While Wendy prepared herself for work, I punched and elbowed the bag to a points victory. After all these years, the heavy bag still hadn't laid a glove on me. I was still a tiny sluggish and stiff from my run-in with the escapees, but I was moving again. The whacks were landing where I aimed.

Wendy emerged from the house and gave me a kiss and a cuddle goodbye.

"I might have the weekend off," she said. "You want to go camping?"

"Sounds great," I answered. "Where?"
"Anywhere really, but in the tent mostly."
"That sounds even better."
She rode off, on her push bike, toward the Nursing Centre. I watched her go, still smiling. About fifty metres down the road, she did a wide, graceful doughnut in the empty Main Street. As she completed the circle, she looked at me and gave me her perfect smile and best impersonation of the royal wave.
She knew without looking that I'd be watching her.
How could I not love her?

Jarrajarra Cafe.

It was around 10.00 A.M., and I was shouting coffee for Barney and myself. The beauty of having Constable Tim available to us was that, when things were quiet, we could escape the Station and enjoy the comforts of the Main Street cafeteria.
Tim was back at the main desk, collecting the yellow Post-it notes for any minor infractions that were called in, and if something urgent arose, he knew where to find me.
Seated in the sunshine, getting a fix of caffeine.
I should have been in work heaven, but something had ruined my view.
"Barney, any idea who owns the Harley parked outside Eddie Doolan's."
Barney looked toward Eddie's legal office and checked out the bike. It was a Harley-Davidson Fat Boy, probably from 2013 or thereabouts.
"Can't say that I do," he answered. "Is it bothering you?"
"It has two new panniers on it," I said, "someone intends to travel."
"Are you thinking it's Jennifer McLain ready to skip bail?" asked Barney, reading my mind as always.
I took out my mobile and called Wodonga Police Station. After waiting a while, my call was taken by one of the admin assistants.
"Constable Chris Taylor from Jarrajarra speaking. Can I speak to Sergeant Will Walker, please?"
That took another moment or two.

While waiting for Will to come on the line, the owner of the bike emerged from the lawyers' office. Whoever it was, they were wearing full leather and a helmet.

"That could definitely be her," said Barney.

"Chris," came the voice of Will Walker on my mobile.

I put the phone on speaker loud enough for Barney to hear.

"Will, quick favour, do you know the details of Jennifer McLain's bail reporting?" I asked.

"I do indeed," he said. "9.00 A.M., Monday, Wednesday and Friday. She's already been in this morning. I saw her myself."

"Do you remember what she was wearing?"

"She was in her leathers, said she was riding over to Jarrajarra to see her Solicitor, Eddie Doolan, then finding herself a motel room there."

"Here? Can she do that? Stay here in Jarrajarra?"

"Legally? Yes, she's on bail, Chris. She is allowed to consult her lawyer, and reasonable travel to do so is permitted, and she can stay where she pleases as long as she reports in when required."

Bugger.

"I have to say," said Sergeant Will Walker, "that newbie prosecutor Rowlands was not very active in opposition to her bail conditions."

Shit.

While I was talking to Walker, I was staring at McLain, less than fifty metres down the road. She was slowly putting on her gloves, and, as far as I could tell, through the dark window of her helmet, she was staring straight back at me.

"Let me guess," said Walker, "she is there now, and you are getting annoyed?"

"You're absolutely correct on that, Sergeant Walker," I answered.

"Chris, if she is not breaking the law, just let it go."

"She is not breaking the law yet, but she is definitely planning to skip bail."

"What makes you think that?"

"Large, new Panniers on a ten-year-old Harley-Davidson Fat Boy, that's what makes me think she is leaving soon."

He thought about it for a moment.

"Could be," he said. "Well, Chris, the good thing is if she runs, it is a solid admission of guilt, and even your singing efforts won't get her off a second time."

He laughed at his own joke.

Everyone's a music critic.

We ended our call. I was still watching Mclain, and she was still watching us. She was seated on the bike now, ready to depart, and it was obvious, even with the helmet, she had focused her attention on me.

She lifted her hand, pointed her finger at me, and carefully sighted her aim as though her index finger was the barrel of a gun. She held that pose for a few moments and then fired an imaginary bullet in my direction.

Well, that seemed a statement of intent right there, not quite enough for me to draw my own gun and fire back, but close.

She kicked her bike into gear and then turned away from Barney and me to head north toward the motel, or she could be skipping bail at this very moment.

"Well, that was chilling," said Barney.

"Barney," I asked, "do you think she planned this whole thing?"

"What?" Barney answered. "Do I think she organized the prison escape, taking the Pendergast family hostage, the cattle theft, the road train, murdering Constable Davey and then Jason Mellish, then the bail application?"

"Yeah."

"Chris, it all sounds a bit coincidental, a bit too flukey to be planned, doesn't it? And why? All that, just to get back at you?"

"Yes," I said, "Exactly. Maybe our Jen's made me the point man for the death of all her various boyfriends."

"I think you're being a bit paranoid, Christopher."

"I may be paranoid, Barn. That doesn't mean the bastards aren't out to get me."

"That would be one of your Nan's sayings, I assume," said Barney.

"Yes," I said. He really was a mind-reader.

"Chris, I don't think McLain could have planned it all. Maybe the escape was her way of recruiting some troops to help her in a task of her own."

"Like killing me?"

"Maybe," said Barney, "or, possibly, punishing you or someone else who she blames for her problems. Or maybe she planned it for some reason we can't imagine."

"Not yet," I said.

He didn't look convinced.

"Or," he continued, "most likely of all, she just recruited a team for the cattle theft, for money, and everything after that, she just made up as she went along. Maybe she is just an extreme opportunist."

"Riding off on a trail bike," I said, "hanging onto Jason Mellish with a SOG team on your bum, she might have thought shooting Jason and then surrendering was the best way to stay alive."

"So, now she is out on bail. Jason is just an inconvenient dead memory. Her agenda for today? She wants the money from the cattle theft. Plus, she'd like to bump me off as a bonus if she gets a chance."

"Yes, on retrieving the money," said Barney. "But I say no on the other. I don't really think she would risk trying to kill you. Another dead police officer on her hands? She would have the whole of Victoria Police chasing her."

We sat with our coffees and had a silent team thinking session.

"The panniers looked empty," I said.

"Yes," said Barney. "So she is not leaving just yet. Probably needs time to retrieve the money."

"A Friday would be the best day to skip," I said.

"I agree," said Barn. "So, if the money is around here, she would collect it on a Friday, then she has her regular Friday check-in at Wodonga, leaving nearly three days to disappear."

"To where?" I asked.

"From what we've seen," said Barney, "she likes to have a team around her."

Which raised the question, who would team up with a woman like Jennifer McLain?

I could think of two who might qualify.

Jarrajarra Caravan Park.

"I'm not giving you his number, Chrissy. He would crack the shits with me for sure." Wally Mellish was not about to give me the contact details for his other son, Justin Mellish. The only son who was still alive.

"We are not exactly on good terms at the moment, if you know what I mean," said Wally.

"He knows about Jason's death?" I asked.

"Yeah, he knows his brother is dead," said Wally.

We were sitting on the timber bench outside the Caravan Park reception area, enjoying the sunshine while Wally smoked a cigarette. One of many. I was sitting upwind, but the wind wasn't strong enough to blow away the fumes.

"When did this start, Wal? This rift between you and Justin?" I asked.

"I dunno exactly, not like Juzzy's the kind of boy who tells you what he's thinking. Not in words anyway."

I always considered Justin the smarter of the two Mellish brothers. Justin and Jason were both wild as hell. Big, tough country boys. He was dangerous when drunk, but at least Justin had a set of brain cells that could occasionally be persuaded to behave if you could catch him when he was sober.

"But, when Jason went to jail," said Wally. "I might have said something like 'might do him some good'. Yeah, I said something like that, and Juzzy cracked it with me. 'As if Jail does anyone any fucking good', he told me. He was pissed off when he said it. Haven't really spoken since, except when he told me he was going North to get a job on the rigs. Didn't even know that was a thing anymore. Oil rigs? Fuck that."

"It's a thing," I said. "Thought about it myself after I got out of the army. Before I joined the police."

I had thought about it for at least five minutes, till I realized they don't take too kindly to guns and fast cars in the hands of their staff. Not on any oil drilling rig I knew about. But it was something to say, something to keep Wally talking about his absent son.

"Where did Justin go to get this job?"

"I dunno," said Wally.

"I know the mob I spoke to recruit out of Toowoomba and Darling Downs in Queensland."

"Don't go doing that to me. I know how you work. Get me talking, and I let slip where he is. Fuck me, Chrissy, you're busy being a copper, and here I thought we were friends. Fuck me."

Wally looked set to cry.

"We are friends, Wal, but I am a copper, and I am worried Justin could be in danger from the same person who killed Jason."

Wally visibly shook at the mention of his murdered son. The older generation of the Mellish family had a complicated history with regard to who fathered who, but Wally had raised Jason as his own and was clearly still grief-stricken with Jason's death.

"Well, I don't know who killed Jason, do I?" Wally looked at me as he spoke. Not so friendly himself right now.

"I only have your word, wasn't you," he said.

That was harsh, but then, I wasn't the one who'd lost a son.

"Wally, Jason's death is recorded on police video. Any time you want to see it, let me know."

"Yeah, I reckon they can make videos do anything these days. Fake news and all that bullshit."

Wally looked away. His focus had moved back to the demolition of his cigarette.

Real evidence had no value in the post-truth world. Video evidence doesn't count unless it confirms what you already believe. Wish I'd thought of that in the hot seat of the Wodonga Magistrate's Court.

I went to leave. This was pointless, and Wally's sadness was not something I could fix.

Wally spoke before I reached my truck.

"Wait a minute. I'll call Justin. Give him your message. Tell him you reckon he could be in danger."

"Thank you, Wal."

I waited on the outside bench while Wally went into his office and made the call. He came back in five minutes and handed me a piece of paper.

"Alright," said Wal. "I wrote it down if you can read me writing."

I read Wally's note. Justin was working on a rig just south of the Barrow Island oil fields. I checked Google. Barrow Island was located off the northwest coast of Western Australia, about as far from Jarrajarra as you could be and still be in Australia.

"Says he's been doing fly-in-fly-out from Fremantle for the last six months. Gave me the name of his employer, big crowd from Perth. Says, call them to check he's been nowhere since he took the job in January."

"OK," I said, checking to confirm the phone number was there.

"Says he doesn't know nothin' about Jason's death, heard nothin', done nothin', and if he does do sumthin', told me to tell you, you'd be the last prick he would be tellin'."

I took a minute to let that all sink in.

"Wally, mate, I didn't shoot Jason. If I had, I would have told you when you asked me."

"I know," he said. Long pause. "I suppose."

We left it at that.

It was late. It was Friday of a long week, and I was heading for a weekend away with my girlfriend.

Sunday, June 19, 2022

Jarrajarra Hotel.

Wendy and I walked into the Jarrajarra pub around 6.00 pm Sunday evening, just in time for the roast dinner. We were happily exhausted and couldn't be bothered with home cooking. We ordered our meals and took a jug of ice-cold beer to a table for two near the open fire.

We had done some serious miles over the weekend, carrying our full packs all the way. From our home in Jarrajarra to the Cudgewa Bluff Falls, then back to the Bluff Creek Camping grounds, where we set up our tent, lit a fire, cooked our marshmallows, cuddled up in our sleeping bags, went for a long run on Sunday morning along the trails around the place, cooked a huge lunch, ate the lot, packed up the kit and walked the five hours back home.

Now we were in bush pub paradise, just around the corner from home, cold beer on the table and steaks to come and a beautiful, crackling fire.

Tired and happy, I couldn't imagine anything that would make the weekend better.

"Time we made a baby," said Wendy.

Wow.

I couldn't think what to say, but I made all the appropriate facial moves. I smiled broadly because her words made me happy.

"Say something," said Wendy.

"You want to make a baby right here and now?" I asked.

"No," she said. "Tell me what you think, no jokes."

Knowing my beautiful girlfriend, I knew I had to get these words right.

"It makes me very happy to hear this plan," I said. "And I wish to add I am extremely glad I have been chosen as a member of the production team. Proud, in fact, very, very proud. Delighted even. Couldn't possibly be happier."

"Anything else?" Wendy was smiling. I had ticked the box for an appropriate response.

I decided I could risk a bit more humour.

"I am assuming my first role on this team is the official sperm donor."

"Yes," she said. "That is correct, though normally we don't encourage assumptions."

"Absolutely," I said.

"Good," she said. "Let's keep ourselves on the same page here. Any specific questions?"

"Is there a wedding involved in any of this process?" I asked.

"No," she said. "Don't want a wedding, don't need a piece of paper. You're the one for me."

She stared at me awhile.

"And you're the one for me," I said quietly, a happy little tear in my eye.

Wendy had a happy cry herself just as our steaks arrived. They looked perfect.

Hell of a day. Can't imagine a better one. Maybe could have had the mushroom sauce on the steak, but the gravy did the job.

Monday, June 20, 2022

Jarrajarra Police Station.

Another week and Constable Tim was still with us in Jarrajarra. There had been no word from Tim's boss, Sergeant Will Walker, telling him to come home to Wodonga, so Tim stayed.

Suited me. I was over my injuries, but if Wodonga left Tim with us as an assist, I was not complaining.

I was relishing the idea of a few days at home. More time with Wendy, work fun with Barney. I was fast losing interest in commuting to Melbourne Homicide with court appearances in Wodonga on the side. How did my peaceful little town attract these bursts of criminality? Where was the live and let live in these people.

Barney and I spent the day on the office computers. Barney was looking for anything we could find about Penelope Fenwick while I was trying to track down the elusive ex-police officer, Mr. Ken Carruthers.

Barney scored first.

He came into my office, reading from his laptop.

"Right," said Barney. "Social pages of the Melbourne Age, Saturday, November 4, 1967, Victorian Racing Club Ball, Mrs Penelope Savage, President of the 'Victims of Thalidomide Ladies Auxiliary', with her husband, Doctor Phillip Savage."

Barney turned the laptop so I could see the picture.

"Handsome couple," I said.

"As far as you can tell from these ancient newspapers," said Barney. "But yes, they look good, and they are smiling."

"She would have been mid 30's by then?"

"In her prime," said Barney.

"President of the Thalidomide Ladies Auxiliary," I said with a flourish.

"1967? Auxiliary?" said Barney. "The women still had to be reminded of their place?"

Barney fiddled with his keyboard for a while. "There was a child, Irene, born in 1960, Photo here from 1964. A beautiful little girl."

Barney turned the screen on his laptop to show me the photo of Irene Savage.

Barney was right. Irene was beautiful, she also had no arms. Her hands appeared to emerge directly from her shoulders.

"Gosh," I said. "Thalidomide poisoning."

Barney read some more from the article that accompanied the photo.

"Says here, Irene died in 1965 in the Royal Melbourne Hospital. She was admitted to for an operation related to her condition. Didn't survive the operating table."

That was sad, but nearly sixty years ago, how could that be relevant to murders in 2002 or 2010.

"I'll keep digging," said Barney. "Something might emerge."

He went back to his desk, and we both battled on through the digital archives.

I found a few glimmers of Carruthers' existence.

Then I found his name, buried deep in Police Records.

"Barney," I shouted. "Got some Carruthers stuff here."

Barney wheeled his chair to sit beside me while we scanned the Police Archives.

Carruthers had served a twenty-year stint, ending in 2010. His time included the year Virginia Savage disappeared and the year the Savage men went missing. He had served fifteen years alongside my late nemesis, Superintendent Robert Anderson Hughes. Hughes and Carruthers had worked together in Homicide from 1995 onwards.

"This puts the Hughes and Carruthers together around the time of Virginia's disappearance," said Barney.

"I'm the investigator here, Barn," I answered. "You should allow me to make the verbal observations."

"I'm sorry," he said. "I'll try to remember next time."

"It says here Carruthers birth date was April 3, 1972," I said.

"Marvellous observation," said Barney. "You really are amazing."

"I wonder if he is dead?" I observed aloud.

Barney nodded at the computer by way of a hint.

I searched the Victorian Government Records for Births, Deaths and Marriages. I found only one Ken with the surname Carruthers, born on April 3 1972, but there was nothing in the death's section in his name for the period after 2010, the year he resigned. Eight years after Virginia died.

"So, he's not dead as far as we can tell," I said.

"Is that another verbal observation?" asked Barney.

"Yes."

"It was a very good one," said Barney, " even better than the birthday."

I don't know why I started sarcasm wars with Barney. I always lost.

"Look up the dates for Carruthers' parents," said Barney.

I had to think. We had the birth certificate for Ken Carruthers and the full names of his parents were on that.

Barney bumped my chair with his to push me aside. I was always too slow for his liking when we worked the computers.

He pounded the keys in his lightning style and quickly had the birth and death certificates for Carruthers Mum and Dad aligned on a split screen before us. They had died on the same day, November 2 1976. Melbourne Cup Day.

"I think it's time for a verbal observation," said Barney.

"Ummm," I said, "Died on the same day. Maybe a car accident on the way home from the cup?"

"And?" said Barney, eyebrow raised.

"Drink driving?" I was grasping.

The eyebrow was still up.

Long thinking pause.

"Kenny was only three and a half at the time?" I offered.

"Tragic," said Barney, "which made him?" The eyebrow was still up. Bloody hell.

"An orphan?"

"Honestly, Chris," he said, happy at last. "These observations of yours, I don't know how you do it."

"What have I done?" I had to ask.

"You have highlighted that our man Carruthers is an orphan. Which means he was, probably, in the Child Care system. Which, as you well know, means he was likely in Foster Care. Which means, of course, we might be able to find out if he had any foster parents. Who they were and where they lived."

"Yeah, yeah," I said. "I was just about to make that observation."

"Of course you were," said Barney.

"We'll need a court order for the foster care stuff," he said as he walked back to his desk. "I'll get it done."

I loved being home. Home at home and home at work. There had not been much joy in Jarrajarra since the drunken duck hunters fell down the hole.

I no longer carried any doubt that Virginia Collins was dead. She had not just disappeared. She had been murdered at the hands of the filthy rich Fenwicks. The best I could do now for my friend and mentor, Rusty Collins, was to find his daughter's body. I am sure it wouldn't hurt Rusty's state of mind if I put her killers behind bars as well.

Or put them in the ground.

My phone rang. Detective Pete was on the line.

"Can you put your make-up on and pretend you're Sir Laurence Olivier for me?" asked Pete.

"Where and when?"

"Two o'clock, this arvo, at the place you found the bodies of Phil the dill and his dad," said Pete. "And I take it you are pretending you know who Sir Laurence Olivier is."

"I know who he is," I said, "the first and best Mister Darcy in the 1948 Pride and Prejudice, Hamlet 1940, and who can forget his crazy doctor in Marathon Man 1976. Is-it-safe? Is-it-safe? All that stuff.

"You're on the Google," said Pete.

"No, using the brain. Save yourself a thrashing, and don't go down the movie trivia path with me, you fading old relic. You have no chance."

"Bloody hell, how the fuck did a whipper snipper like you come to Olivier."

"My Nan's third favourite actor, if you don't mind."

"Third? Olivier third? Bloody hell, she must have been a harsh judge. Who came first and second?"

"Tony Bonner first, daylight second, of course, and yes, she was a harsh judge."

"OK, well, at 2.00 PM, can you get yourself to wherever it was."

"Mellish paddock on the River Road. I can get there. What about you?" I asked.

"Don't worry about me, young apprentice. I have got it well and truly covered."

"Maybe drag along Constable Tim with all his muscles as well, and maybe the crew in the fire truck. I think they will all be very pleasantly surprised."

"Are we talking Angela Adams and a helicopter?" I asked. Adams was Australian television's greatest news personality, and Detective Pete had used her before to push a case along in the direction he wanted. Publicity and promotion. Detective Pete's two commandments.

"Don't think, Christopher, just do."

Mellish Paddock, Jarrajarra Region.

By 2.00 PM, the better part of Jarrajarra's emergency services had answered the call. They were assembled at Mellish Paddock in much the same configuration as the day of the duck hunters.

Even Wally Mellish was there to be sure no one else fell down any of the deadly holes that dotted his land. Having one batch of tourists drop to their deaths in your paddock was terrible luck. A second set would be downright rude.

Wally was in his element, telling people what to do, giving directions and giving voice to his frustration with people, just like any other day in the caravan park.

"Not there, left, left, Fuck me. Left," he shouted to anyone setting up or walking through. "Right, right, for fuck's sake. Jesus Mary, yeah, yeah, that'll do ya."

The area had already claimed four people we knew of, but today, something was working. We hadn't lost a soul. Yet.

Wally had even waved at me as he went about his business. I took it as a sign we were still mates.

In fact, the whole fire and emergency services community were mates.

Good people.

It felt right to be among them rather than chasing murderers among the rich and greedy or being ridiculed in court for trying to do your job, for telling the truth, or, in my case, singing the truth.

Most of the crews had assumed rescue positions and were ready to pretend they were looking for more dead bodies. Which was not a bad idea, something I intended to do myself when I had the chance, but not like this, not with so much fanfare and fakery.

The ambulance from the Bush Nursing Centre was present as a

precautionary measure. Our superstar paramedics, Jack Farrell and Jody Taggart, had heard there was some possibility of television exposure at the Mellish Paddock and were not about to miss out. What with Jody being the one who found the freshly dead duck hunters and the long-dead Savages, she could well be in for a speaking part.

News travelled fast in Jarrajarra.

With the hint of television megastar Angela Adams in the air, our temporary cop, Constable Tim, needed no encouragement to come along. He did insist we stop by his motel room on the way, where he changed from his long sleeve uniform to his short sleeve version, which had to be three inches too narrow in the biceps.

Tim may have hoped to be the significant beefcake on set, but with paramedic Jody present, it was inevitable Scotty Farrell would be there as well. Tim had good guns and a tight-ish waist, but Scotty was another level altogether. Muscles on muscles, a smile a mile wide, and a heart filled with love.

Scott and Jody were leaning against the side of the fire truck, chatting to each other, laughing, smiling and soaking up the afternoon sun while we all waited.

And waited.

Waited for Detective Pete and his big surprise.

My police truck was parked on the grassy verge beside the road, next to Wally's battered old ute. We were the only vehicles not assembled on the yet-to-be-confirmed movie set. Standing beside me was Greg Farrell, the local fire chief.

Greg was tending the legendary Jarrajarra CFA BBQ, probably the most critical item in the Jarrajarra fire brigade's arsenal of heavy equipment. It could cook about anything a human could conceive, but the food always costs at least two dollars to collect. If you didn't have the dollars, you'd go hungry. Jarrajarra community fund-raising was relentless and essential.

As the centre point of the town's fundraising, the BBQ was too important to risk in Mellish Paddock. It was here on the verge, sheltered by the fire truck, gassed up and cooking. The table was prepared, the donation bucket was out, and the sign was up.

'$2 minimum donation'.

If Detective Pete and his television crew didn't arrive soon, they'd miss the sausages and onions.

"Ain't love grand?" said Greg, turning the snags and onions, looking across the paddock to the lovebirds.

"Is she too old for him?" I asked.

"What? Five years difference? No way. God, Chris, look at him. Let's be honest, mate. My nephew is a stud. Jody will work that out sooner rather than later. Smart girl like that, just a matter of time."

I could see they weren't alone at the fire truck.

"What's Doctor Newton doing inside the truck?" I asked.

"He's probably coaching Jody," said Greg. "They are out and about every day. Scotty drives, Doctor Newton sits in the passenger seat shouting instructions via the megaphone at Jody, and Jody rides as instructed. It's a plan, and apparently, it's working."

"She's improving her riding."

"Yes, she had room for improvement on her downhill, so I am told by the expert."

"Scotty?" I asked.

"Yes."

"Good use of the truck," I said.

"Suits me," said Greg, "Scotty does most of the truck maintenance and never charges for it. I figure he wants to go for a spin; he can go for a spin. No complaints here."

A good deal all around, especially approaching winter when the fire risk was next-to-non-existent.

We were interrupted by the sound of an incoming helicopter.

First, we heard it, and then we saw it.

The prominent red-on-white Channel 7 symbol on the side. It had to be Angela Adams and her entourage.

The chopper arrived quickly, and we all held our breath as it landed just over the fence, inside the paddock perimeter, the potential danger zone. Fortunately for the town's reputation, the chopper touched down and managed not to disappear into a new hole in the ground.

The doors opened, and the A-team arrived.

First came the impeccable Detective Pete, followed by Dazzling Darren Everett, his muffin belly exposed beneath his too-short t-shirt, hanging over his too-tight shorts drifting well below the line of decency. Daz was smiling like the cat that bought the cream as if his brief stay in the Wodonga cells had never happened.

Emerging behind Daz was the star herself, the incredibly glamorous Angela Adams. Television news superstar. The long wait for our lead actress to arrive was instantly forgiven. Angela touched the earth, perfectly dressed, coiffed, and made-up. The only nod to the local terrain was her Doc Marten boots. No doubt Daz would shoot above the waist. The star had arrived, and we were soon to roll.

Pete wandered over to me for a chat while Dazzle organized the human and mechanical assets before him into something that pleased his photographic sensibility and looked like a believable search for missing bodies.

Constable Tim hovered near Daz, ready and willing to lift and carry. Flexing the guns at every opportunity.

I bought sausage and onion rolls for me and Pete and moved to the other end of my truck so we could chat in private.

"Does Miss Adams know that this is all fake?" I asked.

"Chris, Chris, Chris," sighed Pete, "instead of being so negative, ask yourself this. Does our superstar reporter believe this will be the first of a long series of news events focussed on the dirty secrets held by one of Australia's wealthiest families? I would say, Yes, she most certainly does, and she welcomes it."

"Does she believe an arrest in these matters will serve the promotion and glory potential of both our careers? Hers and mine? I would say that knowledge is a given. In fact, I would call it a happy certainty."

"Does she know," he continued, "that I am trying to convince some particularly nasty, very rich murderers that we, the police, know a teensy-tiny bit more than we actually do about these murders? Definitely, yes. I know she knows because I told her, and she is happy to oblige our little deception."

"And finally, does she know that the tiny bit of real information we have came from totally illegal surveillance performed by my over-enthusiastic young apprentice, namely you? The answer here is definitely NO. I will never tell her this, and I suggest you don't either."

"Any further questions?" Pete asked.

"Nope, you've covered it," I said

Leaning against the truck, I enjoyed my sausage and onion roll in the morning sun and watched Dazzling Darren Everett approach the moment of 'action'.

The trucks, the vans, the actors and all their gear were in place. We were set to roll.

Facing the camera, the beautiful Angela Adams shrugged her shoulders, patted her coat, did one final lip-pucker, braced herself and then smiled with the power-of-the-sun.

"Showtime," whispered Pete. He finished eating, wiped his chin and crept toward the camera zone.

I was sure he'd have his rugged head on camera at the very first opportunity.

Daz called for "Quiet, please," then, instead of silence, there was a scratchy, static sound, like fingernails on a blackboard, but worse.

"Testing, testing," so loud it drowned the sound of the workers, the BBQ and all surrounding noise. I looked toward the fire truck. Within the truck's cabin, I could see Doctor Newton had the microphone to the public speaker in his hand.

"Jeez, I wouldn't mind a sausage and a cup of tea," boomed the voice of the truck, drowning out anything Angela Adams or Daz might have to offer.

"I'll handle this," I shouted to Daz. I tossed another two-dollar coin in the BBQ bucket and compiled another sausage, bread, and onion concoction. I then sprinted down the safe path to the fire truck before our auteur and his muse could have a mental collapse.

I did it all in less than thirty seconds, years of military and police training. I was a barbeque weapon of war.

"Thanks, Chris," Doctor Newton was most grateful. "I thought we were doing a training run, but here we are, just standing in a paddock. What's going on?"

What indeed?

I had only known Doctor Newton for a couple of years. He'd become a regular customer once he'd started calling Barney regarding his various confusions.

Every couple of weeks, Barney would get a worried call and off I'd go on a mission of calm. It was never much trouble, though his recent effort in taking Darren-the-droney hostage, holding him in the outdoor dunny, might be seen as an escalation. A court of law might have been persuaded that Dazzle deserved it.

Daz had copped a spate of incarcerations lately, what with the

Doc's dunny and Magistrate Holland's subterranean cells beneath the Wodonga Court. Somehow, the Dazzle kept getting free. Maybe next time, I would let him sit and contemplate a bit.

Chatting quietly with Doctor Newton was fun if I followed a few rules. His short-term memory was totally stuffed, but he was a knowledgeable bloke. His long-term memory was still good, and it was easier for both of us if I kept my questions focused on what he retained. His mind still had a good output channel, but the input channels were thin.

"How's the bike training going, Doc?"

"Good, good, I love the coaching. I have been working with, umm, young aah, gosh."

"Jody."

"Yes, Jody and her young bloke."

"Scott."

"Exactly, Scott."

"We go out and follow her. He drives, and we've got this thing here," he pointed at the microphone I had confiscated in exchange for the sausage and onion roll.

"The mike."

"Exactly. Anyway, she is an excellent young athlete. Just needs to work on her downhill. Way too timid. Too timid."

"You think Jody is timid?"

"No, no, no. Fearless, brave young lady. But the thing is, most amateur riders are way too cautious going downhill. Way too cautious. Lack of experience, really. I told her, 'Watch the professionals'. They go hard downhill. It's a skill, a learned process, Chris. You have to push past what frightens you. Only way to learn. Like your, umm, what is it? The boxing thing."

"Muay Thai?"

"Yes, yes, exactly. You don't learn this without coaching, without facing your natural fear. And practice and repetition. Repetition. Stop me if I am repeating, won't you? Bloody Alzheimers. Practice and repetition. Downhill, you have to go hard."

"Do you think she can make the Olympic team?" I asked.

"Don't know, don't know," he said. "It's bloody hard that next step, bloody hard. Hardest thing I ever did. I got there once and couldn't hang on for the next one, lost my spot to younger riders. You get old. You get pushed aside by the young ones coming through. Life, I suppose."

He drifted away for a moment, forgot me, the microphone and his untouched sausage and onions. Eyes to the horizon, somewhere in history.

Then he was back in the world with me. Took a bite of the sausage.

"So why are we waiting?"

Usually, I wouldn't discuss a live case with a civilian. But, hey, he was a retired doctor and would likely forget everything we discussed by tomorrow.

Why not?

"Well," I said, "we were looking down one of the caves here for some missing duck hunters. We found the duck hunters but also stumbled on some murder victims. From the look of them, they'd been there a while."

"Murder victims?"

"Yes," I said. "So, now the newspapers and television are here and want to know who else is down these holes."

"These bloody holes," he replied, "all over the place around there. It was never a problem till some idiot cleared the bush to run his cattle. His cattle kept disappearing. He reckoned he was being robbed till he fell down one of the holes himself. A shallow one, thankfully. He survived. Broken leg."

"Well, Doc, the duck hunters fell, but our murder victims were dumped post-mortem."

"How did they die?"

"Well, when we found them, they'd had their heads bashed in, but further examination indicated thallium poisoning prior to the bashing."

"Thallium, my goodness, evil stuff that. You know it's rat poison?"

"So I am told," I answered.

"They call it the poisoner's poison," he continued, "odourless, tasteless and cumulative. Bloody stupid choice if you ask me."

"Why is that?"

"It's an element, Chris, a chemical element. The symbol is 'Tl', and the atomic number is '81'. It doesn't break down, ever. It is hard to detect, but if I killed someone with Thallium, you could come along one hundred years later, and if there was still a hair or nail or some part of you, I could still find the thallium."

"That's exactly what happened," I said, "Forensics found it in a toenail."

"Deadly stuff, horrible," he said. Painful way to die."

"What about small doses over a while?" I asked.

"Oh goodness, that would be even worse. There were people in history who've done that. Evil, evil people. Oh dear, Chris, be careful if you catch up to this person. They are dangerous."

"OK, I'll be careful. Anything else?" I asked.

"Well, if you were killing someone that way, I would guess you are the type that enjoys their victim's misery. Maybe some deep-rooted anger, combined with an extreme sense of entitlement perhaps. I don't know, Chris. I didn't deal with many murderers."

Doctor Newton was doing a bloody good job of amateur profiling.

He tucked back into his sausage and onions and drifted away again. We sat quietly. The Doc was enjoying his meal, not threatening the microphone.

He was there talking to me, then he was gone, and then he was back.

"Say hello to Wendy for me," he said out of nowhere. "Great girl, that one. You should marry her. The best nurse we ever had around here."

He might have elaborated, but that was it.

"Doc," I asked, "is there any relationship between Thallium and Thalidomide."

He stopped eating, looked at me for a moment, then returned to his sausage. He was either thinking like the Doc Newton I once knew, or my question had failed to register.

"No," he said after a while. "Nothing to do with each other."

Fair enough.

More silence, then more information.

"They are adjacent in most of your old-style medical dictionaries. You know, Chris, people used to have dictionaries for their work before we had all this Google business. So, just say you were reading about thalidomide and its devastating effect on the foetus. The next topic in your medical dictionary is Thallium, where you could read about the terrible effect that could have on your body or your victim's body. If you were planning a murder, for instance."

"OK," I said.

"So you are interested in thalidomide, you are reading about it, and remember, these books are very tightly printed. Before you know it, you stumble into the section on Thallium, and bingo, you're looking at one of humanity's oldest murder weapons."

"Right," I said. Let Doc know I was listening. Keep him rolling.

"So, Chris," he asked, "would your murderer have had access to any old medical dictionaries?".

"Yes," I said, "most likely she would."

"Ha!" he laughed, "Poison, they used to call it the woman's weapon. Lot of wife beater's thoroughly enjoyed their favourite meal, not knowing it was their last. Wasn't much help around for battered wives in my day. Still the case, I suppose."

Having said all of that, it was back to the last of his sausage and onions.

Then he drifted away again.

A few minutes later, we were disturbed by a knock on the door of the firetruck. It was Scotty Farrell.

"You got your microphone there ready to go, Doc?" Asked Scott, opening the door and standing back to allow my exit.

"Yes, yes," said Doc Newton, "I just finished this lovely roll." He crunched the wrapping in his hands, wiped his chin, and passed the soggy paper to me as I climbed out of the driver's seat.

Scott winked at me. "Good job, Chris. Take care of that, can ya?" He said, smiling at the squashed sausage wrapper in my hand. "Want to come for the ride? See how it's done."

"I'll pass, thanks, Scotty," I said.

"You read the Bugle this week?" asked Scotty, laughing at his own question.

"The 'Ducks 4 – Humans zero' thing?"

"Nah, mate, I mean this week's effort, it's a ripper," he had a twinkle in his eye, shouting over the noise of the starting truck. "You're gonna love it." He could barely contain his delight with the latest edition of the Jarrajarra Bugle.

What was that about?

Scotty and the Doc pulled out on their training mission, and I headed back along the safe path toward the helicopter. It was revving up to leave as well.

I could see Dazzle strapped in, seated beside Angela Adams. They were smiling, so I assumed Angela had a story and Dazzle had good sound and pictures.

Detective Pete was climbing into the chopper as I approached. He almost seemed like an afterthought, climbing in late as the helicopter prepared to leave. Was his lust to make the news as transparent to the newsmakers as it was to his colleagues?

The chopper was too loud and too far away to say goodbye, but Pete caught my eye and made a thumbs-up that suggested all had gone well. Then he held the hand thing to his ear and made lip movements that suggested he would call me, then he pointed at his watch, which suggested bugger all, really.

Then he held up nine fingers, which I assumed meant 9.00 P.M.

Bloody hell.

"Text him, you idiot," screamed Greg Farrell, as loud as humanly possible, from just behind me. He was shouting at Pete. "Jesus Christ, pricks got more hand signals than your air traffic controller."

I think Detective Pete smiled and gave another thumbs-up. It was hard to tell with the Channel 7 chopper pulling up and away. Quick and loud, like Afghanistan, plus no active shooters here.

"Do you think he heard you?" I asked.

"Who cares," said Greg. "Guy's a show pony."

"Well, he is," I said, "but he's more than that."

"Here, mate," said Rob, still wearing his official Jarrajarra CFA BBQ apron, "have a sausage and onions with a soda water."

I took it gratefully.

"Two dollars, thanks," said Greg.

"I thought it was a cop freebie," I said, genuinely surprised. " A community reward for excellent service."

"Dream on, Constable," said Greg, hand out, palm up.

Nothing was free in life. The closer you got to the Jarrajarra CFA barbeque, the more that rule applied.

I paid up, still a bargain.

All the fake searchers and heavy equipment were moving out of the paddock and heading back to town.

It was all very orderly, with Wally Mellish at the gate waving the various trucks and utes through to the road, each in their turn.

Probably half of the local footy team had joined the fake searchers. They would need to be back to Jarrajarra for footy training, which, on Monday nights, started dead on time at 5.00 P.M. Monday night was running night and was typically brutal.

I saw Jack Farrell behind the wheel of the ambulance. Jack was leaving alone. His paramedic partner was otherwise occupied.

The last asset out of Mellish Paddock was the firetruck with Scott Farrell at the wheel and Doc Newton on the mike. As the truck emerged on the road, Jody Taggart took off from the verge and pulled in front of the truck. The training team were heading away from town, toward the eastern ranges and some heavy hill work.

Jody's bike had appeared from the back of the firetruck, and she had changed into her hi-vis racing gear. By the time the truck passed Greg and me, Jody was already racing away, a few hundred meters ahead.

"Testing, testing," boomed the truck's external speakers as it passed us.

Olympic training was now in session.

"Faster, faster." I could hear Doc Newton's voice fading into the distance as the bike and the truck disappeared toward the ranges.

Wally Mellish had closed the gate to his paddock, jumped in his car and was off back to his caravan park with only a slight wave in our direction. Still had the semi-shits, I guessed.

"How's Wally, you reckon?" asked Greg.

"Not too good, far as I can tell," I answered. "Thinks I should have captured Jason alive."

"Well, you didn't," said Greg.

Long pause, then he added, "Maybe the dumb prick should have stayed in that country club jail for the last few months of his sentence."

"Too late for maybe, I reckon."

We stood against Greg's truck in the afternoon sun, enjoying the BBQ leftovers and the soda water. Neither of us was into the alcohol.

"I won't miss him," said Greg after a while. "More pain than pleasure, Jason."

There was no denying that.

Eyes closed, soaking up the sun and the sudden peace and quiet of an empty country road. Peace and bliss, take it when you find it.

The peace was broken by the scratchy sound of Greg's radio.

"Greg, love," it was Norma, Greg's wife, the unofficial lady Mayor of Jarrajarra. "The boys are talking about heading back to the fire station after footy training to watch themselves on the news, told me you have the BBQ in your truck."

He reached into the cabin to grab his mike.

"No worries, darl. Chris and I are having a moment here in the sun. Finishing off the onions."

"Hi, Chris," said Norma.

"Hi, Norma," I answered, eyes still closed to the warm May sunshine.

"You coming?" asked Greg as we resumed our onion-eating sun-baking session.

"Nah, heading home, catch Wendy, we're on a project," I said.

"Making a baby, according to Norma. Think she is right on the money," said Greg. The guy was a freaking mind reader. What was it with this town? They knew your business before you even told them. Before you knew it yourself.

Another minute of perfect sun and deep country silence. Not a breath of wind.

"You read this week's Bugle yet?" Asked Greg.

"No, mate," I said. "After 'Ducks 4 – Humans 0', I'm giving Saxon and his bugle a miss going forward."

Famous last words. Greg just laughed. Said nothing.

Home, Jarrajarra.

I arrived home to an empty house. There was a lunch box for me from Wendy on the kitchen table, and there was a note.

> *Problem birth in progress.*
> *Twelve weeks premature, trying to hold back the tide here.*
> *Sorry mate. Cya when I cya.*
> *Love you. Wendy xxx"*

Inside the lunch box was a majestically thick chicken and mustard sandwich and a pictorial-worthy array of freshly cut fruit. Blueberries, apples, strawberries and even one peeled grape. What a show-off.

With a new mother-to-be in the wards, still twelve weeks premature, Wendy would fight to delay the birth in every way possible. It was unlikely we would be seeing each other tonight.

I sat on the couch with my lunch box. I had missed the first run of Angela Adams and the 'hunt-for-something' in the wilds of Jarrajarra. I settled in to wait for a later version.

My last conscious thought for the evening was that Greg and Norma Farrell were wrong for once.

No baby-making tonight, not here and, with any luck, not in the Jarrajarra Bush Nursing Centre.

Tuesday, June 21, 2022

Home, Jarrajarra.

I woke up around 4.30 AM, still on the couch. Wendy had thrown a blanket over me and somehow placed a pillow under my head without waking me. I'd slept through the Angela Adams television spectacular. Barney would have to fill me in later.

I checked our bedroom, and Wendy was sound asleep. It was impossible to tell how things went for her last night or her patients. It had obviously been a long night, and for Wendy, at least, it was over. If it wasn't, she'd have still been at the hospital.

Before my run, I went to the kitchen and attempted a breakfast plate for Wendy that would match her dinner effort for me.

I went for the fruit and toast option. The toast would be OK cold, and the fruit, nicely washed and cut, would be good for a day at least. I finished the job with the three biggest grapes and peeled them. I'd won the peeled grape count, even if my cut fruit never looked as professionally done as hers.

After that, I took off for my morning run, followed by thirty minutes on the heavy bag.

With Jennifer McLain free and roaming the town at will, the murderous Fenwicks at ease in their mansions, and this mysterious ex-cop Carruthers all still free as birds, I really needed to punch the shit out of something. Pity the poor old heavy bag, with nothing to defend itself other than a lot of padding.

When I left for work, Wendy was still asleep, and my arms and shoulders had the warm burn of exhaustion.

Jarrajarra Police Station.

"Oh, Chris," said Barney. "Did you see it? Oh my god."

"No, I fell asleep. Any good?"

"Good? Oh my God, it was brilliant," Barney approved.

"Everyone looks good?" I asked.

"You all looked magnificent," said Barney, "though I only caught a glimpse of you hiding in the firetruck with Doc Newton. But yes, old Darren certainly takes a wonderful picture."

"Did you save the link?"

"Yes, yes, be patient."

As Barney spoke, he searched through the Channell 7 news highlights on his laptop.

"And don't worry about that Bugle article either," he said as he searched, like an afterthought. "I spoke to Joanne, and she took it down. Apparently, Saxon had posted it without consulting her. Anyway, it's gone."

"The Bugle is gone?" I was confused.

"No, not the website. I meant the latest article about you is gone," said Barney. "Saxon is such an idiot. Sometimes, I wonder what Joanne sees in him."

"Joanne and Saxon? No way," now I was shocked, as well as confused.

"Yes, way." Barney did the bemused eyebrow thing. "Honestly, Chris, you can be so blind sometimes. Why do you think she left here to work with him."

"Better money, I guess?"

"Oh, for heaven's sake," more withering eyebrows and a deep sigh, all aimed at me. Barney found what he was searching for and turned the laptop screen toward me to watch.

"Grab a chair," he said. "I'll do first coffees."

Great result for me. I settled in to watch the Angela Adams and dazzling Darren Everett show.

Barney was right. Angela Adams and our Daz had put together a magnificent five-minute epic. The Mellish paddock looked magnificent, with the hills in the background against the clear blue sky. The locals all shone in their roles, Scotty at the centre of the screen, pulling Jody Taggert by hand from the pit where we'd found the dead duck hunters and the two murdered Phillip Savages, Senior and Junior.

Goodness me, Scotty looked like Superman.

The big surprise was the coverage of the Fenwicks and the detective Carruthers. They were all shown in photographs.

The Penelope Anne and Albert James headshots were lifted straight from the Melbourne Society pages, with additional photos lifted from their charity websites.

The missing ex-policeman, Ken Carruthers, was not so prominent. His onscreen headshot was taken from police files. No doubt this was done with the assistance of our star of the moment, Detective Sergeant Peter Jordan.

On the telly, Detective Pete cast an imposing figure. He spoke like a media veteran. With his voice, the tailored suit and the perfect silver hair, he practically glistened.

Angela Adams was her usual magnificent self. Perfection was pretty much standard performance.

> *"According to police sources, relatives of the two murdered men are hiding behind a barrage of expensive lawyers in order to avoid answering questions from the investigating officers."*

Cut to the body searchers in the background, looking as if they were searching, not acting. Detective Pete's voice trailed in over the background shots,

> *"I wouldn't say people are avoiding us, Angela. These are very wealthy people and very old, and it takes time to arrange a formal interview."*

Cut to Pete's rugged, perfectly groomed head.

> *"We have been listening to various people, some have provided us with new and crucial information."*

Which was not really a lie. He just forgot to mention I had jumped the Fenwick fence and listened illegally, and then Pete had quite legally listened to me tell him all about it.

Angela continued,

> *"Would it be fair to say, Detective Sergeant, these people coming forward have inside information and are looking to make a deal?"*

To which Pete answered.

> *"You could say that."*

Which, again, was totally true. Not only could Angela Adams say it, she just did.

Pete was walking a fine line between slander, calling out the two Fenwicks for murder, and total bullshit. He was pretending we had a case.

Piling on fake pressure, hoping one of our bad guys might break. Fascinating stuff, but I couldn't see either of Fenwicks crumbling and if we couldn't find Carruthers, we had nothing. Still, Detective Pete looked good on TV, and I am sure people would remember that even if he had to remind them.

Then, by the magic of television, and no doubt with the transport assistance of the Channell 7 chopper, my two forensic buddies were on the screen.

Constables Carole Johnston and Glenda Johnston, standing outside Seymour's Crime Services Unit, looking very scientific, wearing clean white lab coats over their police navy blues.

They were talking about the two Phillip Savages, Senior and Junior.

> *"The remains of both male victims," said Carole, "show evidence of Thallium poisoning, delivered in a small dose, sometime prior to their murder.."*
>
> *"The Thallium would have been highly debilitating," added Glenda.*
>
> *"But the cause of death appears to be the blows to the head," said Carole.*
>
> *"Most likely by a rubber mallet," said Glenda.*

All of this information, the forensic stuff and the detail from Pete, was customarily reserved for a Coronial Inquest, but this show was trial-by-television. Detective Pete was loading up the public with all we knew. Pete loved the high-profile cases, and the Fenwick brother and sister were as high as you could fly in the city of Melbourne.

He was trying to pressure the evil old farts.

But pressure them into what?

Confessing? Highly unlikely.

Convincing them we had a case, maybe turning one against the other? Maybe.

Flushing out Carruthers? That seemed a reasonable possibility. Maybe he would turn on the Fenwicks if it kept him out of jail? But was he still alive?

Then the office phone rang and broke the spell.

"Jarrajarra Police Station," I said, almost as polished as Barney.

"Chris, can you please come to the Bugle Office?" It was Joanne Farrell, our former police admin assistant, now the power behind the journalistic throne at the Jarrajarra Bugle.

"Is this a police matter, Jo?" I was not inclined to spend work hours on social visits to the Bugle.

"Yes," she said. "I am worried about Saxon."

Fucking hell, I was not too impressed with last week's reporting of the dead duck hunters. Plus, there had been another famous effort by Saxon in this week's edition. Hadn't seen it myself, but it was the talk of the town.

Slight exaggeration. Three people had mentioned it.

Nevertheless, I wasn't sure why I should help the author of these satires avoid self-harm if that was the issue. If I got there quickly, maybe I could add to the injury.

Barney was back with our coffees. I put the phone on speaker so he could listen.

"Jo, can you give me a brief description of the problem?"

"Saxon has locked himself in the print room, and I am scared he might hurt himself."

"You're scared he'll hurt himself?"

"Yes."

Barney looked dubious.

"This is Saxon we are worried about?"

"Yes, Chris, Saxon." She sounded shirty at me now as though I'd personally locked him in the cupboard.

"OK, I am on my way."

My lack of enthusiasm for the mission came through in my phone manner.

I ended the call, sipped my coffee and made ready to leave.

"Saxon self-harm?" said Barney. "I don't see it."

"No, me neither."

"Lover's tiff, I am thinking."

"They're not lovers, Barn," I said. "She is ten million miles too good for him."

"We'll see," he said. He resumed his seat and sipped his coffee, all smug and satisfied as if he'd already won the ridiculous argument. "The heart wants what the heart wants."

"What is that supposed to mean?"

"Joanne wants Saxon."

I gave him a 'wanna-bet' type of look.

"I am not accepting bets," said Barney. "I'd rather you save your money to spend on Wendy."

I was almost out the door.

"And don't ask or tell Rob Farell either," Barney shouted after me. "He's as slow off the mark as you are."

I certainly would ask Rob Farrell when I got the chance. He was Jo's father and my friend. He would know if Jo and Saxon were a thing.

Wouldn't he?

Office of the Jarrajarra Bugle.

"Saxon, mate, come out, or I will have to come in."

"Go away."

This was going well.

I was speaking to a door that separated me from Saxon Tyson-Howard, publisher of the local paper, the Jarrajarra Bugle. Except it wasn't a paper; it was a website, totally online. An internet thing and well-read around the town, as far as I could tell.

Saxon had locked himself in a room that Jo Farrell, my former assistant, now Saxon's, called the printer room. Why would a web-based news organization need a printer? Who knew.

"What else is in there?" I asked Jo.

"It leads to the kitchen," she said, "and after that, there is the toilet."

"Fridge in the kitchen?" I asked.

"Yes."

"Food in the fridge?"

"Yes."

OK, if it came to a siege situation, I could see Saxon was far better prepared than me.

"Any weapons in there?" I asked.

"Saxon? Weapons?"

"Right," I said, "no weapons."

Bugger this. Time for direct action.

"Saxon, for your own safety, I advise you to go and stand in the kitchen."

"What?" asked Saxon from his side of the door.

"Go and stand in the bloody kitchen," I shouted.

Through the door, I heard him shuffling away from me towards the kitchen, I presumed. More importantly, he shifted away from the door.

I stepped back and kicked in the door.

It sounds impressive, but it wasn't. A two-ply door on a door-frame kit from a hardware store. The whole thing hung in five minutes by a handyman and cheap-as-chips from the local hardware. Like most of the building it was flimsy and existed within what might be liberally termed the Jarrajarra Industrial Estate. More trees and tin sheds than real industry.

Plus, I was limbered up from my bag work this morning and wearing my steel-capped boots. Me? The door? No contest.

Neither the emergency caller, Joanne, nor the target of my rescue, Saxon, were all that impressed with my destruction of the door.

"Shit, Chris," said Saxon. I noted his plans for self-harm included a sandwich he'd made himself and was now holding half-consumed.

"What the hell?" said Jo.

"You wanted him out," I said to Jo, a bit defensively, "and I warned him, and now he's out."

"Safe," I added as a final justification.

"Oh Jesus," said Jo, putting her hand to her mouth, turning green, then pushing past me, running toward Saxon, then pushing past him and heading into the toilet.

She slammed the toilet door, and a few seconds later, Saxon and I could hear her heaving into the toilet bowl.

Bit of a pause, a flush of the loo, another pause.

More heaving.

This went on for a few minutes.

"Are you OK, Jo?" I asked. Through the dunny door this time.

"Yes, fine, thanks," she answered. More heaving. "And don't kick in any more bloody doors, alright," she added.

She didn't sound fine at all.

It took another ten minutes to extract Jo. She was leaning forward as she came out from the loo into the kitchen, and I noticed something I had never seen before.

Joanne Farrell had acquired a muffin belly.

Oh.

As I was observing, Jo clasped her hand to her mouth and hurried back into the toilet.

Oh dear. A policeman's work is never done.

"Jo," I asked, " will you be OK for five minutes? I just need to talk to Saxon outside."

"Yes," she gasped amidst the new round of throw-ups.

I took Saxon outside for a quiet word.

"Saxon, mate, why did Jo call me?"

"I guess she was worried I would hurt myself."

"Why would she think you would hurt yourself?"

"I guess I was very upset. The whole town, it seemed like, calling up and abusing me, all the nasty letters-to-the-editor we received yesterday."

"Why all the abuse?"

"You know, the thing on you, It was supposed to be funny. I thought you'd get a laugh out of it. It made me laugh."

"I haven't seen it," which was true. "Can you show me?"

Saxon fiddled with his phone for a moment, then handed it to me, "Just press play," he said. It is playing from my video archive. Jo made me take it down and print an apology, which I did, but that didn't seem to make anyone any happier."

His bottom lip was quivering. His eyes were already red. He looked set to cry again.

"OK," I said, trying to sound reassuring.

I watched the video. It was me in court, on the stand during the Jennifer McLain bail hearing. It was the really good bit that practically guaranteed she got bail.

I was singing. Again.

> *"Don't forget to remember the time we had together.*
> *When we promised us forever."*

All that stuff, but on the video, you could hardly hear it because the packed courtroom was laughing out loud. Even the Magistrate was laughing louder than I recalled.

"Bloody hell," I sighed. "Geezus Saxon, you filmed in a courtroom?"

Bad enough, he was making fun of me in public. I could get over that, but the idiot had also broken the law.

"No one noticed," he said.

"No one noticed, so you put it up on the internet? Good one, Saxo, you idiot."

"I'm sorry, Chris. I thought you'd see the joke."

"Yeah! The joke? Me! Hilarious. Show it to your new cellmate."

Jesus, this kid was an idiot. This was contempt of court, which was almost as bad as mocking me, though that was just my own opinion. If the Magistrate saw this, Saxon was in trouble.

"You've taken this down, right? Is it off the web entirely?"

"Yes."

"No one downloaded it or shared it? Can you tell that?"

"No one downloaded it, Chris," said Saxon, a bit angry. "Downloads are disabled on the web site."

"What about screen recorders, Saxon?" I said, getting angry myself. "Someone could watch the video and record the screen, "Same as a download, right?"

"Yeah, well, possibly," he conceded.

Bloody hell. It only needed one person to dob him in and the young idiot would be facing contempt of court charges. Not a great prospect for a kid with multiple counts of property damage in his past. Of course, he always called that art. I would say graffiti. The court would just see a vandal, a repeat offender.

He was such a mixed bag, so smart he was stupid.

"Listen," I said, "can you tell if anyone outside of Jarrajarra saw this video?"

"Well, the site is password controlled, and we mostly have locals, but there are some from Wodonga and some from wider."

"OK, OK."

I handed him back his phone.

"Show me the apology," I said.

He fiddled with his phone again and handed it over. I read the apology. It was good.

"You mean what you say here?" I asked. "Not just saying something to get everyone off your back?"

"I mean it, Chris. I am really sorry. I thought people would get the joke, but it made everyone angry, especially Joanne."

Whoops, here come the tears.

"Alright, mate, apology accepted."

I patted his shoulder in a fatherly fashion, though, to be honest, I had no idea what a real father would do, not having experienced one. I thought of what Rusty Collins might have done in similar circumstances. Shoulder pats seemed appropriate, with a gentle squeeze on the last pat.

"Just don't ever film inside a courtroom again. It is against the law, OK?"

"OK. Joanne already told me that."

"And if you're going to run a local newspaper, why not go for something a bit more community-minded than your recent efforts? You're not Rupert Murdoch, mate, sitting up there in a super yacht, private plane, ivory tower, safe behind high walls and a bunch of muscle-bound security staff, hanging shit as he pleases on who he pleases."

"You're a local boy, Saxon. Your news is local. You slag off someone in town, and there's a fair chance they'll have a piece of you in the supermarket the next day. Could be a lot worse than a nasty phone call. Would you make fun of Ricky Chalmers like that?"

"Shit. No," he said.

"Exactly."

"Ricky and I aren't really friends like you and me."

Ouch. The Saxon I knew didn't really have a lot of friends. Now, I felt guilty.

"Well, that's a lovely thought," I said. "Thank you."

"Seems like everyone in town likes you," said Saxon, "and now, no one likes me."

"Perfectly understandable," I said. His shoulders slumped even further. Too soon. "Saxon, it was a joke, relax."

We stood there in the morning sun while Saxon regained his composure.

It would have been a good time to go back inside and check on Joanne, but there was one more thing.

"So, how far down the track is Joanne?" I asked.

He looked at me, suspicious. Maybe shocked, I'd worked out a secret. His eyes widened. Please, God, he knew she was pregnant. Was she pregnant?

"How did you know?" asked Saxon.

"Mate, it's not half obvious."

"Oh no," he cupped his face in his hands. Looked like he was ready to swoon. "Oh shit, I don't know what to do."

Oh dear, tears welling up again. Stressful times at the Bugle.

"Let's go inside and have a cup of tea and talk, hey," my Nan always fell back on a cup of tea in times of moral crisis and indecision.

As luck would have it, there was tea in the kitchen, and Joanne had emerged from the dunny.

I made the tea.

"So who else knows?" I asked.

"Only Wendy," said Joanne.

"She didn't tell you, did she?" asked Saxon, still shocked that I recognized a woman having a baby.

"No, mate," I said. "Wendy wouldn't discuss the private business of her patients with me or anyone."

"So what's the plan?" I asked. "Do you have a plan?"

"I'm having the baby," said Jo, "and raising it myself. Alone if necessary."

I looked at Saxon to hear his plan.

Nothing forthcoming.

Waited. Still nothing. His whole body was trying to talk, but nothing was coming out. If he didn't say something soon, he would lose Joanne forever.

"Let me guess," I said, trying to put a shine on Saxon. "If I were you, Saxon, I'd be thinking, I would like to marry Joanne and raise our baby, but right at the moment, I am shit scared of what the army of massive Farrell men, including her father and brother, not to mention her uncles, will do to me when they find out Jo's in the family way, and I am the dad."

They both looked a bit puzzled, so I soldiered on.

"In addition, I'd be thinking, this girl is so far out of my league and so beautiful; why on earth would she want to marry someone like me."

"Yeah, that bit, exactly," said Saxon with serious enthusiasm. I saw the hint of a smile on Joanne's face. "Plus a little bit about the brother and the Dad.

Jo's smile disappeared.

"Does your Mum know, Jo?"

"No."

Bloody hell, I was so out of my depth.

"Hang on," I said, "I need to call someone for advice."
"Don't tell anyone, not yet, please," said Jo.
"I am just going to talk to Wendy, OK."
"OK."
"Give me five minutes, have another cuppa. Rehydrate."
I went outside and phoned Wendy.
"Hi, beautiful."
"Hi, handsome," she answered. "What's going on?"
"Well, I just found out Jo Farrell is having a baby."
"Thank God," she said with a small laugh. "At last, now I don't have to keep it a secret."
"Not a problem," I said. "Guess how I found out."
"How did you find out?" She asked.
"Well, Joanne called me down to the Bugle office. On a bullshit reason if you asked me."
"OK," she said.
"It appears Saxon had locked himself in the toilet."
"The toilet?" she asked.
"Or thereabouts," I added. "To be specific, it was more the printer-kitchen area that alluded toward the toilet facility."
"Right, said Wendy. "A facility?"
"Let's call it the printer room. For the sake of brevity and decency."
"Alright," said Wendy, "So Saxon is in a facility and won't come out. I get the picture."
"Good, good," I said.
"And, for the sake of jurisdiction," said Wendy, "can I ask, how do locked printer-kitchen-toilet facilities become a police procedural issue within the Jarrajarra region?"
"Well, in this instance, Joanne was worried Saxon was going to hurt himself."
"Right, got it," said Wendy.
She had a think.
"Listen, mate," she continued. "The only two people likely to hurt Saxon are Jo's Dad and her brother. Are they likely to? I doubt it very much. Is Saxon likely to self-harm? No, never. Take it as fact. I am a medical professional."
"OK," I said.

"Are the many people around town who take to the 'Letters' section to vent their annoyance at Saxon's weird, unfathomable opinions and positions on local events likely to attack him physically? Nah, keyboard warriors mostly, and the really angry ones are too old."

"I am big in the older section of the community," I said. "They would be outraged."

"Yeah, yeah," said Wendy.

"So, what do I do?" I asked.

"Well," she said. "Saxon is right to worry about getting hurt, but not physically. He is facing the biggest decision of his short life, and if he stuffs it up, he will never get over it. No one is going to punch him up. He is in danger of wrecking his life all by himself."

"OK," I said. Wendy had been thinking about this for a while.

"They called you out for a reason, Corporal. It is my highly trained expert medical opinion that Joanne called you to be the intermediary in their mutual crisis." Wendy laughed.

"Bloody hell," I said.

"Listen, love," said Wendy. Do them a favour. Jo is having her baby, and she is still very young. She needs to tell her mother as soon as possible."

"OK," I said.

"And Saxon, you can tell him it is time to man up," said Wendy. "If he is still locked in the toilet, you can tell him it's time to shit or get off the pot."

"OK, OK," I had been briefed by former Australian Navy nurse Lieutenant Wendy Acheson. My mission was clear.

Before I ended the call, I asked, "How did your baby case go last night?"

"Still touch and go." She said. "It was more than we can handle here. I got her stabilized, and then we had the air ambulance come to collect them. They're in Melbourne now and in good hands. The young dad's feeling useless, the mum is holding on, and the baby's still in the pocket. If we can keep them just like that for another four weeks or more, it should be good. Just keep your fingers crossed.

We exchanged exaggerated kisses over the phone and then ended the call.

I turned back toward the bugle office only to find. Joanne and Saxon standing right behind me, listening to every word. Oh dear.

Small towns. No secrets.

How much did they hear? I wondered.

“Let’s go see Mum.” Said Jo.

They'd heard the lot.

“Do you want the window seat?” I asked Jo.

“Good idea,” she answered.

We arranged ourselves across the bench seat in the police truck. I was driving. Jo was against the passenger door and her head out the open window. Saxon found himself trapped in the middle seat. No escape for the father-to-be.

“Mum does the books on Wednesdays and Thursdays,” said Jo. “Let's go to the garage.”

“Will your dad and Scotty be there?” Asked Saxon”

“Yes, love,” she answered. “That's where they work.”

Saxon was white with fear.

I put a fatherly hand on his knee.

“Mate,” I said, “don’t look so worried. The day I met Wendy, I was in a hospital, and I was almost dead.”

Saxon looked at me. He was pale as a sheet.

“Think of today as, hopefully, the first day of the rest and the best part of your life. You’re going to be a Dad, mate.”

His mouth moved, but no audible words came out.

“If you survive,” I added.

“Chris,” said Jo, her head still pointed out the window. “Don’t be such a prick.”

Rob Farrell's garage, Jarrajarra.

“I think you lot need to talk,” I said.

I stood on one side of the office desk inside Farrell’s Garage, facing the joint proprietors, Rob Farrell and his wife, Mary.

Mary was seated behind the desk with her laptop, and an array of bills and paper laid out before her. Rob Farrell was standing behind her, wiping his grease-stained hands on an equally greasy towel. The grease wasn’t disappearing, but it was definitely moving around.

When we arrived, they were staring at the laptop and, most likely, discussing financial matters or maybe they were composing a letter to the editor of the Bugle, complaining about my recent turn as a karaoke singer.

Well, I thought this would definitely change the topic.

Rob looked at me.

"What's this about? He asked.

"Well, mate," I said, "it's really none of my business. I'm just the taxi driver here." I was hedging, should I even start down the long journey of the next sentence.

"Mr and Mrs Farrell," said Saxon, as if he'd been rehearsing it for a while, "Joanne is pregnant and going to have a baby, and I am the father."

Good, strong start.

"I would like her permission," he continued, "sorry, I mean your permission to ask her to marry me."

"You haven't even asked me if I want to marry you," said Jo.

"Joanne," said Saxo, not missing a beat. "Will you marry me?"

"Well, yes, I suppose," she said and definitely smiled the smile of love. Most definitely.

And that stopped the show for a bit.

Eventually, Rob looked at me.

"You were right, mate," he said. "This is none of your business."

"Right-e-o then," I said. Absolutely none of my business whatsoever.

And I took my leave. I might have heard a whimper of fear from Saxon as I left, or maybe it was my boots squeaking on the linoleum floor.

Whatever, I was out of there. It is a fact that, sometimes, people do shoot the messenger, and Rob was the best man with a rifle in town.

No laws had been broken, the truth was out, and some private family matters needed to be discussed.

Time for me to go.

Jarrajara police station.

"I can't believe they're a couple," I said.

"I told you," said Barney. "You never listen. You always have to see it for yourself. What did your Nan always say? 'You can't be told.'"

She did say that. Didn't make it so.

"She also said, no one likes a smartarse," I replied.

"No, she didn't," said Barney. "You just made that up."

Which was true.

We resolved that Barney was right and that I was wrong, and we both agreed I had no clue in matters of the heart.

Peace reigned, and without any post-it notes calling me to action, I took up the comfy chair at the front desk.

I was on my third viewing of the Angela Adams extravaganza when I received a call on my mobile from Detective Pete.

"Have you watched it? He asked.

"Couple of times now," I said. "Pretty impressive."

"I thought so," said Pete.

"I would say you looked terrific, except I don't wanna blow your ego up any further," I added.

"No need, mate," he said. "I know I look good. Your Dazzle, the camera guy, he did well."

"He usually does when he sticks to his lane," I said. Detective Pete never hesitated to share the glory, so long as he had the first bite.

"Well, mate," said Pete, "do you want the bad news or the bad news?"

"Maybe the bad news?" I answered.

"We received an injunction today from solicitors acting on behalf of the Fenwicks. We must cease and desist our harassment of Penelope Ann and her good brother, Albert James, Master of Laws."

What the hell.

"How can anyone tell a police investigation to cease and desist investigating?" I asked. "We're acting on behalf of the good people of the State of Victoria. We are in hot pursuit of murdering criminals, aren't we? That's our job, isn't it?"

"Oh, my idealistic young apprentice," he said. "Anyone can sue anyone, you know that, and if you got the money, well dammit, you can sue as many people as you like, or as many as you can afford. This is chump change for the Fenwicks, mate. Small potatoes, really."

"So what now?" I asked.

"Hmm, well," said Pete. "We go back to court, I guess. The whole thing becomes a marathon and not a sprint."

"We can do marathons," I said. "Can't we bug their phones, put listening devices in their cars, maybe in that smoko area they use."

All worthwhile suggestions from my ninja manual, I thought.

"Chris, Chris, Chris," he said, exasperated. "We can't go bugging the ultra-rich bad guys while we fight their injunction, claiming harassment. Jesus, I'd bug their backyard dunny if I could get a judge to approve and to get that, I need to show just cause. For Penelope Anne, just being the wife and stepmother of the deceased isn't enough."

"From what I've heard, it was plenty."

"We'll fight," he said. "Don't worry. The state government is probably the only organisation that could afford to go against this mob."

"Do you want the good news?" Pete asked.

"Lay it on me," I said.

"Their acting Barrister, it's NOT your old mate, Jeremy Oakley QC."

"Ah, well, that's something," I said.

Thank God for small mercies.

We lapsed into silence. Our cases were not going well.

"We need to find Carruthers," I said.

"Yes," said Pete. "If we don't mate, we are stuffed."

We ended the call. I must have slumped in my chair.

"Are you alright?" asked Barney.

No secrets in this cop shop.

"We've got two cases going nowhere," I said. "Jennifer McLain, running around Jarrajarra, free as a bird, and now these two Melbourne murderers hiding behind a dirty-great pile of their inherited money."

"And you do hate inherited money," said Barney, almost sympathetically.

"Bloody oath," I answered. "But not as much as I hate murderers."

This was a nightmare. My cases were cursed. I had become the crime solver with no solutions.

I moped around the office for the rest of the day. No yellow post-it notes to distract me. No crooks I could hunt down around town. Not even a graffiti artist to chase, not since Saxon Tyson-Howard had put away his spray cans and gone straight.

I couldn't even sneak off and go shooting with my good friend, Rob Farrell, me being the man who delivered the news of his daughter's unexpected pregnancy. I thought it best to stay away for a day or two.

Late in the day, I fell asleep in my office chair. Barney was kind enough to shut my door and let me snooze. I dreamt of good cops getting the right medals and all the bad guys behind bars where they belonged. I had a snippet of a dream about Jennifer McLain saying sorry to Wally Mellish for murdering his son.

I dreamt of Penelope Anne Fenwick confessing to the crime of kidnap and revealing Virginia Collins, still alive and well, and held in a basement in a Fenwick mansion.

Good dreams.

Then, I realized as Virginia stepped into the light she hadn't aged in the twenty-plus years since I'd seen her. It was then I knew it was just a dream and woke in disappointment.

All dreams, all fantasies.

My cases were as dead in the water as Virginia Collins was dead in the ground. Lawyers and judges were deciding the fate of the crooks around me. Meanwhile, Jarrajarra was as quiet as the grave.

Jarrajarra police station car park.

By the time I closed up the station, it was well after sunset. I walked out the back door to head home. I turned left toward the side street and the short walk to my house.

Stepping out into the darkness, I was met by two large men.

Their torn sleeveless denim jackets, their jeans and boots were a uniform screaming bad intentions. The tattoos down both of their arms were, for the most part, skulls, spider webs, and naked women, none of whom looked very friendly. Their prison-pumped, steroid-boosted muscles were just icing on an angry cake.

"Chris Taylor?" asked Number One, standing a foot in front of his Number Two. The tone of his voice and the placement of their feet and hands suggested my answer would determine their next actions.

"That's me," I said as I sized them up.

Number two moved a fraction to my left, still behind Number One. I caught a glimpse of a steel knuckleduster on Number Two's right fist. No wonder he was hiding at the back.

Oh dear.

By the time I absorbed that information, Number one had commenced his wind-up for an overhand right. His signature approach, I guessed. He was big, ugly and heavily inked and whiskered. His lack of style and speed suggested more back yard bully than trained martial artist.

Shop early, Rusty Collins always said. First in, best dressed, if you asked my Nan.

I punched Number One hard. A straight right, feet anchored, starting from the bent knee, legs, hips and shoulders working together. Landed flush on his nose, exactly where I aimed. What can I say? If the punch had been any better, he'd be dead already.

Number Two had a few options at this point, fight back, turn and run, or maybe claim a misunderstanding. Maybe suggest they weren't together. There were probably other choices.

Number Two chose the worst possible of all his options.

He caught his unconscious mate, Number One, as he fell backwards. Caught him with both of his arms under Number One's arms. Like the catcher in one of those trust exercises you'd do at a self-improvement course, maybe.

Number One kept falling, as if in a dream. Number Two was dragged forward, taking the weight of his teammate as best he could. This left 'Two' leaning forward, straining to lift back, chin just out there like a great big melon. Perfect.

I did my Rusty Collins perfect left hook. Slight sway to the right, circular sway to the left, small step right on your right foot and through comes the left, like a train. Rusty had watched a slow-motion video of the great Joe Frazier to understand why Joe's left hook was the greatest of all. After that, we practised till our shoulders ached.

Two best punches I'd thrown since forever.

I just hoped they weren't here collecting for the Salvation Army.

Number Two fell back, his arms still wrapped around Number One. Both of them, now all floppy and subdued. I cuffed 'Two', who was still cuddling 'One', then before they could wake up and untangle, I rolled them over, joined as they were, dragged One's arms behind both him and his mate, and then zip-tied the pair of them in a weird spoony embrace.

Try and get out of that arrangement without a knife, and an extra pair of hands.

I did a quick check and found they each had flick knives in their pockets and a pistol tucked away in the back of their jeans. Number Two was wearing knuckle dusters on both fists.

Pretty sure now they weren't collecting for charity.

Their little arsenal carried penalties of four years for the guns and two years each for the knives and knuckle dusters. Assaulting a police officer was another five years.

All things considered, I certainly felt assaulted.

What to do with them now, lying entwined on the cold winter concrete of the Jarrajarra Police Station car park? They were big blokes. Now, I had them hog-tied. There'd be no way I could lift them.

I needed help.

I stepped to the side street and saw a light shining in the garage over the road.

* * *

"They're big buggers," said Rob Farrell.

He was staring down at my two assailants, still cuffed and zipped on the cold ground. Now awake and grumbling.

Rob had been working late and was still dressed in an oily coverall.

"They'd be around three hundred kilos all up, I reckon," said Rob. "Third of a tonne."

Lot of weight to drag or carry, when you say it like that.

"If we help you to your feet," I said, " can you blokes promise to behave and walk to the cell politely?"

"Get fucked," was the clearest statement from their various answers.

"Let's take that as a no," I said to Rob.

"I've got an idea," said Rob. "Killed a wild pig once at the bottom of a the Deddick's Creek valley. Winched him all the way back up and into the truck."

"How'd you winch it around trees and obstacles?" I asked.

"Easy, mate, easy-peasy, just gimme a minute."

* * *

It was fifteen minutes before Rob was back and ready to go. He had it all worked out and just needed to hook up the prisoners to start the drag.

My two prisoners were now fully conscious, sore as hell with aching heads, I suspect, and whining like big babies.

"You fucking touch me, I'll fucking kill you," Number One shouted at Rob. Spluttered a bit with his bloodied, broken nose and busted front teeth.

"Shut up!" said Rob. Didn't need my help. He then did a neat trick with one of his work blankets. Throwing it over the two bad guys' legs then, while he stood on the edges, tucked it under them and folded it like a tight, going nowhere nappy.

"Neat," I had to comment.

"Mate," he said, "Five kids, ten million nappies. With a kid like Scotty, you learn some tricks.

My two prisoners were done and dusted, ready to roll.

One end of the plastic-wrapped drag chain was wrapped around their legs.

The other end of the drag chain was hooked to Rob's battery-driven winch. The winch was secured to the bars of the Station's indoor cell. We only had the two back stairs and a right-hand turn along the passage to deal with on the path to incarceration.

Rob stood and took the remote control of his drag chain out of his pocket.

"And away we go," he said, pressing the green button.

The two prisoners took off as though shot from a cannon.

Number Two, the bottom of the pair screamed in agony. His jeans shredded in an instant on the rough concrete. Number One bounced on top of him, screaming in shock or sympathy.

"Whoops, my bad," said Rob and pressed the stop button. He fiddled with the controls of the device, ready to try again.

"We'll walk, we'll walk," said Number One, emerging as the spokesman.

"Damn," said Rob.

We unhooked the chain and helped them to their feet. No sooking now.

Walked them to the cell, still cuffed, moving like an awkward four-legged baby elephant, very compliant now. In the cell, I threw them one of Rob's oily blankets and locked the door.

"Job done," said Rob.

I locked the cell door.

"Nice bluff, mate," I said.

"I wasn't bluffing, Chris," he answered, quite serious. "Works like a charm for pigs."

We walked out the back door, turning off the lights as we went.

"Hey, what about us?" shouted Number One. Sounding a lot more polite.

"See you in the morning," I said. "Get yourself some sleep."

* * *

My conscience got the better of me.

I was back within half an hour. Clean blankets, coffee and some left-over chocolate cake from the Station fridge.

"Get close to the bars, and I'll do the cuffs first," I said.

Number Two was in the cuffs, and Number One was zip-tied. I uncuffed Number Two, they turned around, and I cut the zip ties off Number One, then I stepped back in case they were angry.

They weren't. Looked pretty forlorn, to be honest.

"Go and sit on the bunk, and we can talk," I said.

They sat on the bunk. They could see my pile of goodies.

"OK," I said, "blankets, cake and coffee, all yours. I just want to know who sent you?"

They looked at each other. Said nothing.

"I could even throw in a sandwich each." That worked.

"We don't know," said Number One. The talker. Said it straight up, no thinking, no little signals. He was probably telling the truth.

I put both cups of coffee just a few inches outside the bars and waited till the coffee was collected and my two new guests were back on the bunk. I still had the blankets and cake.

"We usually do debt collections. We got a website that gives you the idea. Gambling stuff, drug stuff, most clients book us by phone and put a deposit in our account. We do the job, and they send the balance."

I passed over the cake with the same careful process. Tell me more and you get more being the hint.

"We've got cheese and ham and bread in the fridge," I said. "Could do a couple of cheese toasties, maybe."

"Some bloke calls us, gives us your name," said One.

"Did you ask extra for visiting a cop?" I asked.

"He told us extra wasn't a problem."

I was vaguely flattered.

"Any message for me? Or wasn't it a message-type visitation?"

"Nah mate, no way, we just collect money or send messages. Nothing more. No way. You were a message visit, that's all."

I threw over the blankets.

"And the message was?"

Now, they hesitated. What did my Nan say about arguing with idiots?

"You're going to jail for the message," I said, "might as well finish the job."

Nothing.

"Toasties? Going once, going twice." They were suckers for a bargain.

"Stay away from McLain."

"And you claim you never met this bloke McLain?" Trick question.

"Never met him, just the phone call and the deposit."

McLain was not a bloke. They really did not have a clue what they were doing, why they were doing it, or who they were doing it for.

"I'll go get your toasties."

Wednesday, June 22, 2022

Jarrajarra Police Station.

"They didn't have much to say beyond what they told you."

Sergeant Will Walker had come over to Jarrajarra with Constables Tim and Joycey to collect my prisoners and put them on the long, slow train to prison.

"I think they are telling the truth," said Will.

"Arm's length bashings," I said. "Fabulous business model. Punch-up by proxy."

"I did ask why there were only two of them." Will was smiling as he spoke.

"Lay it on me," I said. He was laughing now.

"Apparently, they had the word you can't fight to save yourself. You'd been done over by some local bloke a couple of years ago, right here in the police station. Knocked out cold in your own reception area."

Deep sigh from me on that one. The legend of Jason Mellish. Get over it.

"A fantasy," I said, "which likely came from the late Jason Mellish pumping up a victory he never scored to his girlfriend McLain, who wouldn't know either way, who passed it onto the mystery bloke who hired our two bash-up artists. Maybe this Ken Carruthers, maybe McLain and Carruthers know each other. Maybe all of this stuff is just one big crime organised by two bad people."

"Why do you say that?" asked Will.

"Because it's Jarrajarra. We don't have that much crime. The only time we've ever had stuff this big, turns out it's all connected.

"Yes, maybe," said Sergeant Will Walker, the voice of wisdom. "It is all possible, but it's not evidence. Life would be a lot easier if we could find Carruthers."

"Will," I said, "Jennifer McLain's just teed up two random heavies to come and give me a belting. Can't you, at least, revoke her bail."

I was getting annoyed by the way Jennifer McLain seemed to waltz through the justice system, doing as she pleased.

"Chris," said Will, "I know you're angry, but she has complied with all of her bail conditions, and we have no evidence at all that she organized these two biff merchants. They don't know who booked them. To revoke bail for murder we have to go to the Supreme Court."

"What, it's a budget problem now?" This was pissing me off.

"Yes," he said. "My word, it's about money. No one gets a free ride up at the top court. And what if she is actually innocent? Maybe she really was a kidnap victim, and now someone is trying to make her look guilty."

Bloody hell, even my own team weren't sure she was a murderer.

"Chris," said Will, "be patient. We know where McLain is. She is not going anywhere. She will get the justice she deserves, I've no doubt. Let's find Kenny Carruthers and sort out who put those two Savages down the hole."

Disappointed. Frustrated.

Finding freaking bloody Ken Carruthers. It would have made a good movie title, except the show would be dull as dog biscuits. Nothing ever happened.

* * *

After the Wodonga crew had taken away our prisoners, Barney and I assembled around our computers to pursue our mysterious Kenny Carruthers.

We used the online Police records to make a short profile of the man. We didn't get much. His birthday, 1970. The year he joined the police force was 1991, just after his twenty-first birthday. The year he left, 2010, and the list of police stations he'd worked in between. There weren't many of those either.

His cop years were not impressive. A single promotion from Constable to First Constable. No mentions, no awards, not a single attaboy from anyone. He joined up, did stuff, and then left with barely a trace.

Trained at the Waverley Police Academy, same as me, but twenty-plus years before my time, in 1991. Kicked-off there with the obligatory six months of learning the up and down of being a police officer. Didn't take more than one call to establish there was not a single person there now who'd been working there back then.

Worked at Reservoir Police Station between 1992 and 1995. Wow, interesting, less than a mile from where I lived with my Nan.

Buggered if I could remember any cop from Reservoir Station, I steered clear of them. In my memory, they weren't your caring, sharing, community-minded country cops, like me, for example.

Reservoir was a housing commission station full of hard men. No women in blue, according to the records Barney found.

We worked through the list of names from the station back then. Some were dead, and some were missing. Couldn't find any that admitted to being a close mate of Carruthers.

We did have one small victory.

We found three old-timers who were still alive and still mates. They happily took our calls.

After a bit of to and fro, Barney put together a Zoom call with himself, me and the happy trio, Gerry, Brad and George.

Front desk, Jarrajarra Police Station.

"He was always game for chucking punches when things were willing with any of the local gangs," said Gerry, a former Constable at the time. "Could fight alright if he was in a good team. Punched hard, fought dirty."

"Bit of a bully, I'd say," said Brad. "He was OK belting kids around when there was a couple of us for backup, not so upfront when it looked like it might go either way."

"Pretty quick to get the gun out, I suppose," from Gerry.

"He was an arselicker," said George.

The three of them laughed.

"Yes, definitely a bum kisser of the first order," conceded Gerry.

"That's how he got to Saint Kilda Road," said Brad. Saint Kilda Road referred to Victoria Police Headquarters, the mothership, a place all ordinary people avoided like the plague.

"Ended up a gopher for that bloke who went down a while ago, some Superintendent in there,"

"Hughes," said Barney.

"That's the one," they all agreed.

"I didn't know old Ken that much. What I knew I didn't like," from Gerry.

"He was a prick," said Brad, the happy team's hard-liner.

We didn't get much beyond that. It was all just a friendly chat.

Where Carruthers had come from before Reservoir, they didn't know.
What did he do at headquarters? They had no clue.
Where might he be now? They had no idea.
Still alive? Absolutely no idea whatsoever.
In the end, I couldn't help myself.
"Did any of you blokes know Rusty Collins?" I asked.
"Rusty Collins? My goodness," said Gerry. "A bloody saint, that one."
"My word," said George.
"Jesus, how many wild boys did we push Rusty's way? Turned a lot of them around old Rusty," said Brad.
"Tragedy what happened with his daughter, still missing," said George.
"I reckon he topped those blokes myself."
"No doubt at all."
"Good luck to him if he did."
"No ifs and buts about it."
"Bloody Hell, how'd you like Rusty Collins coming after you in the dark of night."
"Holy shit, don't even talk about it."
"Bloody hell, he was one tough unit, Rusty."
"Great bloke, though."
"Yeah, Great bloke."
"Turned out some good citizens from that club he ran."
They were three ex-cops, mates from back in the day, fun to talk to. They would have been good cops, and they would have chatted all day if we'd tried. But Barney and I thought we had to keep moving, make more calls, and dig down further.
Turned out that the Zoom session was as much as we learned about Carruthers for a while.
I called Detective Pete with the little news I had obtained about Carruthers.
He informed me that he'd found a Carruthers' acquaintance still working at Saint Kilda Road, who had told Pete pretty much the same as my three happy retirees. Carruthers was a bully, a bum-kisser, and brave enough when the odds were in his favour.
Sly, cunning, and slippery were extra words Pete had saved from his chat. A suck-up to the late and crooked Superintendent Hughes

was also confirmed.

That's what we had, and that was all we got for the next few weeks.

Discovery calls between Pete and me regarding the various murders dropped off to nothing within a week.

Nothing to see here. Ken Carruthers was a ghost.

Thursday, June 23, 2022

Home, Jarrajarra.

Crime solving hadn't gone too well in the previous week, but home life was more wonderful than ever. After all of life's twists and turns, war zones and cop postings, I had concluded that Jarrajarra was heaven and Wendy was an angel.

We had been out for a morning run. Now, Wendy was showering, and I was side-kicking my heavy bag in the backyard of our home. The bag was swinging nicely in the shiny new heavy-duty frame I had built last night with the help of Scotty Farrell and his now permanent side-kick, Jody Taggart.

Wendy had insisted I move the bag from the rafters of the back porch. My bag-directed hostilities had shaken the shit out of our old weatherboard house, and the bag needed a sturdier home before the house fell down around us.

Scotty Farrell loved to give the bag a whack and occasionally spar a bit with me, so he was only too happy to help me make the move. With a Farrell on board for the construction, I had little to do but pass the hammer and work the concrete mixer. Jody ran the wheelbarrow.

"Good for the legs," she had said on the day.

We had a few more bricks than necessary, so we ended up with a punching bag frame beside a brick barbeque. Then we went the extra yard and surrounded it with a concrete base to keep the mud out of the cooking area and the whacking area dry for martial artistry.

To top it off, Scotty had gone on a rummage through Farrell Motors and found a flat iron of appropriate heft to serve as the cooking top of the BBQ.

Somehow, it all came together with time to dry off overnight.

A wonder of bricks and cement. A unique mix of outdoor entertainment and athletic rehearsal. I could even use the crossbar for chin-ups. Incredible. And the old wooden house was safe. I could leg kick all day if I felt like it.

And I might have, but Detective Pete called me halfway through my two hundred right leggers. I did a remarkable job of getting through the "Hello" bit without sounding like I was puffing.

"I feel like the Pony-express messenger in F-Troop," said Pete.

"F-Troop didn't have Pony-express messengers," I said.

"Humour me, please," said Pete

"OK. What is the deal with the non-existent F-Troop messenger? I feel compelled to ask."

"Every day, he arrives at the fort, got arrows from Indians in his back, bullets from outlaws in his front, his horse is dead, he's on foot, he staggers into the fort to deliver the fortnightly message with his last dying breath."

"What's the message?" I asked.

"No news today," said Pete.

"That's a joke?"

"It's all I've got, Chris. Jokes."

"You haven't found a Ken Carruthers, crooked cop, wandering around Melbourne?" I asked.

"Not around here, mate," he said. "What about you?"

"No," I said. "How about my other case? What's the take on Jennifer McLain at world headquarters?"

That gave him a pause. He let out a long, resigned sigh.

"Chris, my lovable young up-country ninja, nobody cares about Jen McLain anymore. She's monied up and lawyered up way beyond our pay grade. You and Sergeant Palmer are the only two on our side who give a stuff. Everyone else is singing from the victim handbook."

"She is not a victim Pete. She's a murderer and a cattle thief. You can chuck in kidnapper with all that as well."

"Constable Taylor," said Pete, a bit tetchy now, "it's her word against yours. You say she was driving the killer Bedford. She says she wasn't, and the lovely old Magistrate, whats-his-name, from Wodonga, leans toward the pretty girl. You have to admit she scrubbed up better than you in court with your black eye and bruised head."

"Pete, she will have that money from the cattle sale hidden somewhere. I want to find it, and I want to lock her up."

"Chris, listen to what I'm saying. The tide is rolling out on McLain. The whisper is our good mate, Assistant Commissioner Jerrod Harrison, will drop the case. He doesn't want any bodycams from you or young Constable Joyce ruining his nephew's posthumous glory."

"No mate, you listen. I want to put a GPS trace on McLain's

motorbike. I want to know where she goes when she collects her blood money."

"Holy Mary, mother of God," said Pete, "Hello, Jarrajarra. Is anyone listening down there? It is a dead case, mate. Let it go."

I was angry, and he was getting angry. Too bad for him.

"Let me get this straight," I said. "You're happy to take what I learn jumping fences and hiding under bushes when you're after some rich, high-profile murder suspect? But there's no glory and promotion in a minor bush murder or two."

"You're absolutely right," he said, the glib prick. "Nothing in it for me when a bunch of redneck shitheads kill each other."

"So, to be clear, you've stopped helping me on the murders of these cattle thieves in my backyard?"

"Mate," said Pete, "get it through your head. We don't have infinite capacity down here. I am welcome to any developments, but when it comes to priorities, there's no glory or promotion for anyone hunting down a couple of blockhead bushwhackers. The last cattle rustler I know became famous was Ned Kelly. The only cops I know got any lasting glory out of Ned were the ones he murdered."

"Thanks for clearing that up, Detective."

"Chris, if I were you, I would find Carruthers and forget McLain, but you're down there all on your lonesome, no one looking over your shoulder, just how you like it. You go and do what you gotta do."

"I will," I said and ended the call, totally pissed off at the world of law enforcement.

Three Melbourne socialites murdered. One of them, Virginia, still missing, three prison escapees dead, plus a cop dead as well. I knew who the killers were, yet I'd failed to put any of them behind bars where they belonged.

I went back to my last hundred right-side leg kicks. They didn't help my anger, just put a slight dent in the heavy bag and made my leg ache for a bit.

After our argument, Detective Pete stopped calling. The Fenwick case was going nowhere until we found the private detective, Ken Carruthers.

Saturday, July 2, 2022

Jarrajarra Region.

"This is definitely, absolutely, and categorically the last time I will do this till February," I said.

"You are such a great wuss bag," said Wendy. "I thought you were made of sterner stuff. I am so disappointed."

"I can feel the ice particles on my feet," I said.

"Bullshit," she said, floating on her back twenty metres out. Flirting with the current, knowing if she was swept downriver, I'd be love-and-loyalty-bound to go in after her.

We waited while I thought about it.

"Disappointed," she sang out loud in case anyone within a hundred miles missed her point.

I really had no choice. Wendy was relentless. I girded my loins and dived in. My girded loins froze to death within two seconds. To complete the show, I screamed out loud, as much to make her laugh as any real need to make a noise.

It was early. We had run to our secret spot, past the Caravan Park, then a few kilometres along the Murray River. It was private. It was beautiful. Our own hidden swimming pool.

And it was so damn cold. My girlfriend was insane, but it was Saturday, and we had a day off, and this was what she wanted to do.

Life had settled back to a normal routine. Constable Tim had been called back to Wodonga. Barney and I were running the station on our own again. Barney was doing most of the work per usual. I was only required to attend to Barney's occasional yellow Post-it notes.

Apart from morning exercise and baby-making with Wendy, the other current attraction in town was shooting practice with Rob Farrell. No one from the extended Farrell family had as yet bashed up Saxon Tyson Howard. It may well come to pass that could happen, but generally speaking, the Farrells had accepted Joanne was going to make a baby and as unlikely as it seemed, she was making it with Saxon.

As for my murderers, absolutely nothing had moved along.

The Fenwicks were, for the moment, safe behind their money pile.

Equally offensive to me, Jennifer McLain was still free on bail.

There was no evidence linking her to my recent encounter with two hired thugs, which meant there was no change to her bail conditions.

“Suck it up, Princess,” Wendy said when I had a sook to her.

Even worse, McLain was back at her old job, selling hot pies, cakes, and doughnuts at the local bakery just across the road from the police station. Most likely watching everything I did. Which would have been boring for her because I wasn't doing much at all.

Any anger the town might have felt for her murdering a local was tempered by the fact that no one had ever liked Jason Mellish. He was a junkie and a bully, and only Wally mourned his loss. Worse than that, it appeared some amongst the townfolk thought McLain was indeed a kidnap victim.

I wondered if I was the only person who saw through Jennifer McLain.

After a brisk thrashing around in the frozen waters of the Murray for what felt like an hour, long enough to prove my manhood, I swam briskly to the bank of the mighty river and exited.

“That wasn't even 10 seconds,” said Wendy with a strong hint of mockery.

“Bullshit,” I answered. “It was at least a minute and a half, closer to an hour.”

“Ten seconds tops,” she replied loudly, never one to concede.

“OK,” I said, “maybe a minute, counting drying time.”

She was not impressed. Agree to disagree and all that.

“Disappointed,” she yodelled again as she swam out. I think she was laughing underneath all her bluster.

We ran home and shared a beautiful hot shower.

Later, in our bathroom, minding my own business cleaning my teeth, Wendy came into the bathroom and held the testing stick from her pregnancy kit.

Right there, in front of me, for me to look at.

It was shining two crystal-clear pink lines at me.

Wendy was smiling.

I was smiling.

“We're having a baby,” she said with a smiley hug.

“Well, I said, “I guess there's another thing I won't be doing until next February.”

“We'll see,” said Wendy. “Where there’s a will, there’s a way.”

We laughed.
I'd never seen her so happy.
And with Wendy happy, as night follows day, I was happy too.
A baby? Goodness gravy beef, my Nan would have said.
Goodness indeed.

Friday, July 8, 2022

Jarrajarra Police Station.

"I told you I wouldn't let you down." Dazzling Darren Everett, the whiz-kid videographer, was in my office.

"You did," I answered. Did he promise that? I was guilty of switching Darren onto mute half the time we spent together.

"What's this about?" asked Barney.

"Well," said Darren to Barney, "when I appeared as an expert witness at the bail application for Jennifer McLain, the judge turned on me. God knows why. I'd done nothing but try to help. Anyway, he was a nasty pig of a man, and I told him."

"The magistrate, Mr Holland?" asked Barney. Incredulous.

"Yeah, him," said Daz. "Anyway, he lost his cool and sent me down to the cells. I have no idea why."

Daz was almost breathless just thinking about it.

"Really?" Asked Barney, faking sympathy.

"Yes, really," said Daz. "Turned on me for no reason other than being a cranky old fuck. They sent me down to these dark, miserable cells in the basement of the Wodonga Magistrates Court. It was like being in the gulag."

"That's truly terrible," ventured Barney. Barney never gave much real emotion to the Daz. He was immune to the mental roller coaster that constituted a typical Daz day.

"You know I am lactose intolerant," continued Daz. "I actually warned them before they served lunch. Honestly, it was as though they enjoyed inflicting pain. Lunch was a glass of milk with a cheese sandwich. Hello world, are you people listening? Honestly, it was primaeval. Cheese sandwich be buggered, I refused to touch it."

"A hunger strike," offered Barney.

"Exactly," said Daz.

"I can't even begin to imagine," said Barney. "I'm amazed you survived."

"I doubt I would have made it if Chris hadn't rescued me. Another 12 hours till morning, I doubt I would have lasted."

"Well," said Barney. "you're out now. What have you got for us?"

"Just have a look at this," said the Dazzle.

He unfolded his laptop to display his efforts on my behalf.

"Great show you did with Angela Adams," I said by way of making conversation.

"I know," answered Dazzle. "We nailed it. She's a talent, Angela. We work well together."

Dazzle's near demise in the cell below the Wodonga Magistrates Court had not dulled his rampant self-esteem. Right now, he was as high as I'd seen him.

"OK," he said when he was ready to roll. "This is from the video from the night, whats-his-face, Ralph Davey, got himself shot. This is just after Davey was struck and right at the point that bloke Jason Mellish was about to shoot you."

The computer screen was paused on a picture of Jason Mellish. Taking aim at my good self.

This was from my bodycam. Apparently, Daz still had a copy from his one day as an expert witness.

Not sure retaining the evidence was legal, but hey.

On the left of the screen, peeking around the torso of Jason Mellish, was the face of my nemesis, Jennifer McLain.

McLain would have you believe that face belonged to her fellow cattle rustler, Carl Agnew. In her statement, she claimed it was Agnew, there beside Mellish.

Sadly for our team, her barrister had almost convinced the Magistrate that was so. But it was McClain, no question.

I hadn't seen her in that exact position on the night. I had been wholly focused on the shotgun barrel as it rose toward my head.

"Now," said Daz, "let's watch this for the next three seconds in slow motion."

Which we did. The action progressed to the point where my saviour, Constable Joyce MacDonald, started shooting at Jason, saving my life in the process.

The whole thing played as you would expect. The vision was scary enough, but the slo-mo sound was something else, downright evil. A cacophony. An ugly mixture of noise, the idling truck, Jason shouting at me, McLain shouting something, I couldn't tell what.

There was a thumping I didn't recognise at first. Holy Jesus, it was my own heartbeat. Beating out of my chest, I was so scared.

He played it again, and the effect was the same.

“So,” said Barney. “What does this all mean?”

“This, on its’ own,” said Dazzle, “means absolutely nothing, but have a look at this.”

He clicked his mouse, hit some keys, and we were now looking at the sound files as they appeared on the timeline of a video edit. I had seen these types of files before.

“These are sound files,” said Daz, “and these waves you see are the various noises you can hear. They look like waves, and that’s why they are called ‘waveform files’. Any typical soundtrack looks exactly like a set of waves on the sea.”

“An ocean of noise,” said Barney.

Barn knew wave files as well.

“Yes, what you see here,” said Daz, “is a combination of a lot of different sounds, each with their own wave file, and what you can do with the latest computer software is you can identify and then separate these different waves.”

He then proceeded to show us what he was talking about.

“See here,” he said, waving the computer mouse about the screen. “When no one is speaking, no lips are moving. That rumble is the sound of the truck idling.

Dazzle then selected a little splice of that noise where there was nothing but the rumble. He played that section on a loop, over and over again, and sure enough, played at normal speed, we could identify the sound of the truck idling.

“Wonderful,” said Barney. “What does that mean?”

“Well,” said Daz, “it means once you can identify a consistent sound, you can remove it entirely, just like this.”

Darren hit another button, and lo and behold, the whole wave file seemed to change shape. He hit play, and the audio was now cleared of the truck sound.

We could still hear Jason Mellish shouting obscenities at me, informing me of my pending doom, but now, you could also hear something coming from Jennifer McLean.

This was good.

“But,” said Dazzle, “there's more.”

He then went through the same process. This time, removing the loud, consistent beat of my frightened heart. Neither Barney nor Daz commented on my obvious terror.

"You can also isolate a pitch and a volume, same as a consistent noise," he said, "Like where Justin is shouting. Justin's pitch is high. His volume is high. That means it's in a range we can isolate, and if we can isolate it, then bingo, we can remove it."

Which he did, with just a click of the mouse and Jason's ranting was gone.

He had now removed the sound of the idling truck, my heartbeat, and Jason Mellish yelling.

"And all we have left," said Daz. "Is the voice of Jennifer McLain."

The wave file had been reduced significantly in height.

"Watch and listen again," said Dazzle, proud of himself and what he was about to show.

He hit play, and there it was.

The Jennifer McLain on video sounded exactly like the real Jennifer McLain and not some bloke who was, most likely, already dead in the back seat of the Bedford.

It was clear as a bell. You didn't need a lip reader to know what she was saying.

"Shoot him," she screamed to Jason. "Shoot him."

She was talking along the barrel of the shotgun, right down the lens of my bodycam. Around the side of her boyfriend, her ex-boyfriend, her dead boyfriend, Jason Mellish.

"Play that again," said Barney."

"Shoot him! Shoot him," screamed Jennifer McLain again.

"Tell me, Darren," said Barney. "Is a person's voice like a fingerprint? Does it produce a wave file that will always be the same? If it's from the same person saying the same words."

"Different circumstances, different situations," said Daz, sounding like an expert witness at last. "The voice could sound different, but yes, the same person saying the same words will produce a near identical wave file."

"Right," said Barney. "We have her saying those words, Chris. Remember her deposition with Detective Pete."

"You're right, Barn," I said.

"I'll go get it."

Barney disappeared, then returned and handed a small USB stick to Daz.

"That is the audio recording of Mclain's statement to Detective Pete," said Barney. "It was taken here in Jarrajarra when she was first brought in after her arrest. After she murdered Jason Mellish."

Barney had never doubted my version of who did what. God bless him

Dazzle took the stick and did his magic. Barney quickly guided him to the spot where McLain denied murdering Carl Agnew.

There were the words.

> *"How the fuck would I shoot him?" Said Jen McLain, on the screen-grab taken from her deposition video. "I didn't have a fucking gun. When are you going to get it in your head? I am the victim here, not the fucking cattle thief."*

All lies and bullshit, if you ask me.

"There's the words we need," said Barney. "Shoot him!"

Yes, said Darren, excited.

More magic, more computer slicing and dicing.

Eventually, the wave file of Mclean's deposition and the wave from my body Cam were aligned.

"The moment Chris looked death in the eye," said Barney, a bit dramatic. A bit sarcastic.

After some stretching and squeezing of the interrogation wave file, it was apparent that the files were almost identical.

It was the same person, the same voice.

Jennifer McLain, calling for my death from the safety of the big Red Bedford.

I called Sarge.

Barney managed Sarge onto a Zoom call, and Darren walked him through our new evidence.

"We finally have something to go back with," I said.

With Sarge watching wave files and expanded videos on our computer screen via the magic of modern software, we made our new case.

"I must say, it's compelling," said Sarge. "I'll give you that, but I don't know if voice print identification is accepted in the court as a positive. It's not exactly fingerprints, Chris."

"It's as good as fingerprints," said Daz with the usual hint of aggression and topic ignorance that crept into his voice when challenged.

"Yes, Darren," said Sarge, "I may agree with you, and it is excellent work, but it's not currently accepted in the courts. Not on its own."

"But there's an evidentiary element here," said Barney. "McLains claiming to be a hostage, but here she is, clearly giving orders to Jason Mellish a few days before murdering him. That's worth putting before the Magistrate, surely."

"True," said Sarge. "You can hardly argue it is a man's voice. It rules out their alternative."

"It certainly does," said Barney.

Barney loved being in on the cop talk. Plus, he was bloody good at it.

"I think it's a breakthrough," I added. Keen as mustard to go out and make an arrest. Put her back behind bars where she belonged.

We all had a think.

Daz was borderline bristling yet again. God knows why. Maybe he wanted to do the arrest. I patted him on the shoulder.

"Good work, Darren," I whispered, just for him. "Great job."

I could feel him relaxing as I spoke. Jesus, what a diva, but a clever one.

"Well done, Darren," said Sarge, seconding my boost to our frail droney. "Let's see if we can make a case with this, hey lads."

Yes indeed.

We signed off. I was happy. Daz was happy. Barney was thinking something.

Daz packed up and left. Barney lingered at my desk for a talk.

"What's going on with you?" He asked.

"Me?"

"You've been like a dog without a bone for the last few weeks. Since your argument with Detective Pete?"

"No," I said.

"Yes," said Barney, "Grumpy, but today, you're floating on a happy cloud. What's going on?"

Wendy and I were having a baby was going on, but that was still private.

"Something at home?" Barney was looking at me with narrowed

eyes.

I said nothing, but he was a mind-reader.

"Wendy?" He said.

I still said nothing.

"Oh my God," said Barney, "you two are getting married."

I was a sphinx.

"No," he said, then had a think.

I accidentally thought the word 'pregnant'.

"Waaaaaaaaaaaaaaaaah!" screamed Barney. "You two are having a baby."

He leapt forward and hugged me, then kissed me on the cheek.

I admitted nothing. It didn't seem to matter. I hadn't spoken a single word during the interrogation.

Barney was crying happy tears.

"Congratulations," he said. "Of course, it is still a secret. I know. I totally understand. Not a word will pass my lips, I swear. Oh, my Lord."

He released me from his happy cuddle and returned to the front desk, whistling.

"Goodness gravy beef," I heard him say as he left.

"I'll get the cell ready for our lady guest," he added, and I knew it would be done.

It had been a great morning.

The slow wheels of justice were turning again, on my McLain case at least.

Little did I know, my other case was also about to burst its banks.

Never rains, but it pours.

Home, Jarrajarra.

"I've told you before," said Wendy, "you should never look Barney in the eye when you're trying to keep a secret."

She was teasing, not serious.

We were lying in bed. It was 10:00 PM, but we were still so excited with baby thoughts we couldn't sleep. Just talking. I had confessed that Barney had guessed our secret with only five minutes of astute observation.

"I didn't blab," I said. "Barney telepathed me. Again."

"Telepathed?" she was dubious. "Is that even a word?"

"And how can I not look him in the eye? It's a bigger tell than looking."

"Look, but don't engage," she said. "And for you, never think of the word. Your face is like a typewriter to your thoughts."

She was smiling. It was all fun. Barney wouldn't blab. I could trust him on that.

Somewhere along the way, we fell asleep.

I was dreaming happy dreams of Wendy and babies, plural, as in more than one, and sunny days by the river.

I was as sound asleep as a man can be.

* * *

4:00 AM or thereabouts.

Flat on my back, deep asleep.

"You've become a real pain in the arse, my friend."

That wasn't a dream, and there was a hard metal object pushing into the middle of my forehead. I assumed it was a gun.

I opened my eyes, and, yes, it was a gun pressed hard. Very painful in comparison to my blissful sleep.

"Friend?" I croaked. My voice was barely working.

I had a good idea who my visitor was, and he was no friend. He was wearing a balaclava over his head. Only his eyes were visible.

"I assume," I said, "I am speaking to Mister Carruthers? Yeah?"

"Correct," he grunted and gave the gun a painful push deeper into my flesh.

Why wear a balaclava and then admit who you are?

Probably because you don't want anyone to see your face after you shoot me.

Shoot me? I'd prefer he didn't.

Shoot Wendy? Not an option.

As I spoke, I slid my hands from under the blankets and raised them, palms up, in abject surrender.

Meek and mild.

This is Bas Rutten 101. YouTube defence advice from the master, aimed at the armchair warrior. But Bas is scary real, and his words work best if you've been belted around the Muay Thai gyms of the world.

Belted around enough to remember 'Plan A' before and after you get punched in the face.

Meek and mild, very placating, nothing to see here, Mister Carruthers, Sir. Yes Sir. No Sir.

"Well," I said and drew a trembling breath to show I was scared and trying very hard to control my fear.

I moved my mouth to speak, so timid the words could hardly come.

Then, with my left hand, very quick, way quicker than Carruthers, I swept the gun away from Wendy's side of the bed and away from the line between the gun barrel and my head.

I had the barrel of the gun squeezed tightly between both of my hands.

My hands were off the bed. The gun was now pointing at the wall. I was not letting go.

The pointy end was not coming back toward Wendy or me.

With his gun hand swept from beneath him, Carruthers crashed forward. Landed heavily on me.

I managed a half-head butt as we collided.

"Fuck," he shouted. He was a talker.

"Prick," he screamed.

I was a bit trapped with the heavy bastard now on top of me and blankets skewing everywhere.

The gun barrel was tight in my right.

That part was good.

I didn't feel the cut the barrel left across my brow. I'd already forgotten Carruthers' head crashing into mine.

Two solid whacks to my face, but I was still on Plan A.

The tangled blanket situation was not good.

Kept my right hand clenched tight on the gun barrel. Released my left. Threw some left elbows towards Carruthers' head.

You have to do more than just defend.

Damn, this was messy. On my back, no leverage.

I was catching him on the side of his head, with the fleshier part at the back of my bicep. Not ideal.

Stupid bloody blankets.

Elbows. God's gift to the wicked.

I hurt him enough to make him pull back and turn away. Wrong move, Kenny. He'd been inside my swing.

Another try, more room this time. I caught him high on his temple with the sharp point of my elbow, the hammer. That hurt him like fuck.

Wendy was on his back now, appearing out of nowhere.

She had been faking sleep.

Both her hands around his face, over his stupid balaclava.

She gouged fingers into both his eyes.

Hard and deep. Nasty.

"Aargh!" he screamed. "Fucking Bitch!"

The gun fired. I don't know who hit the trigger.

Him or me? Didn't matter.

The shot was loud as hell in our bedroom.

Wendy hung tight. Dug in harder with her fingers.

Carruthers screamed louder still.

Holy hell, that would have hurt. Blood was now running down the front of his balaclava. Wendy had gone downright mediaeval.

Carruthers forgot his gun. He let it go. It was now in my hand. A cop standard, point-four-zero calibre Smith and Wesson semi-automatic pistol.

I knew them well.

I wasn't firing it at Carruthers, so close to Wendy, I ejected the magazine with one hand, clever me, and shot the lone bullet in the chamber into the floor.

I threw the empty gun over the end of the bed, through the bedroom door, and out of our bedroom.

Both hands were now free.

I used my left arm to shield Wendy and punched Carruthers with my right.

Caught him in the neck. That hurt him, so I did it again.

"The blankets," I shouted at Wendy.

She leapt off Carruthers and the bed.

I pinned him around the neck with my left arm. Pulling him into me. Tight.

Still punching with my right.

Messy but landing hard. Top of the blanket toward his kidneys.

Wendy had jumped off the bed.

She was standing on my side, on the floor. Holding the edge of the blanket in both hands. She lifted one foot onto the mattress beside me, then leapt over the bed.

Bloody hell. Superwoman. She flew over both of us.

Poor blinded Carruthers was now swaddled in what was left of our king-sized woollen blanket, not exactly fighting gear. He was wrapped tight.

Swaddled, but not for comfort.

Wendy was now over her side. One foot on the floor, one foot on the bed, pulling hard, tug of war on the blanket.

Carruthers, somehow, had a free leg, kicked out at Wendy, caught her in the chest, and knocked her backwards hard into the wall.

"Fuck off," he shouted, "I will kill you, you fucking bitch."

Signed himself a death warrant right there.

Finally, I was free of the blanket.

I slid out from under the blanket-swaddled lump of Carruthers. Landed on top of the pile in a solid mount.

I hit him with two of the hardest elbows I've ever thrown. Maybe three. Dead centre on his bloodied balaclava.

Wendy was on her feet, still moving, thank God.

"Get rid of the gun," I shouted.

Not sure she needed advice from me.

She moved fast, found the gun in the hall and disappeared.

I was going primeval myself, slipping into the dark place. The black mist was descending. The electric buzz in my head like a chainsaw screaming at me to kill Carruthers.

He had kicked Wendy. Threatened to kill her.

I was definitely going to kill him.

Moving very fast. I wanted this human pile of shit dead and out of the house I shared with my darling.

I was still punching. Carruthers' face was squelching through the bloodied balaclava.

I'd been told he was scum. Here he was in the flesh, worse than I dreamed.

Don't kill him, an inner whisper.

Carruthers was a bloody mess.

Don't kill him.

I stopped fighting and stood on the bed, straddling him.

I twisted the blanket till it wrapped him tight, like a straightjacket.

I held the blanket in one hand and ripped off his stupid balaclava with the other. Took a chunk of his hair and scalp with it.

He had a good head of hair, a sort of grey, nineties mullet.

Great.

I grabbed a thick clump of mullet in one hand and a bunch of twisted blankets in the other. I heaved the big ugly shit off my bed onto the floor.

I kept a hold of the mullet and kneed him in the face about three times. I let him go on the third knee.

He fell backward through our door, landing against the wall on the other side of the hall. Facing me, but with his bloody eyes shut tight.

He was totally and utterly defeated.

I calmed down a bit. Took a breath.

Definitely don't kill him, the inner voice, no longer a whisper, especially not in our bedroom.

Another deep breath.

'Put some clothes on', A logical thought, not animal instinct.

Bit of composure, more deep breaths.

T-Shirt, shorts and runners. That will do. Semi respectable, apart from blood dripping down my face.

Secure the prisoner. More solid cop logic whispering through the rage.

Carruthers, framed in our bedroom doorway, a portrait of pity. Half slumped, half unconscious, half dead, slumped against the hallway wall.

He was still out of it. Extremely beaten.

The knees to the face had crushed his nose. Burst a rich vein of blood there.

The damaged scalp thing was not helping his appearance.

Punches hadn't done much for his complexion.

I didn't care. He came into our home with a gun and got what he got.

I stepped toward him, mentally prepared to drag him by his bloodied, greasy, hideous mullet all the way to the station.

From the door frame left, Wendy emerged at a sprint.

Oh dear.

She was back, still in warrior mode.

She'd found the old guitar that had leant against the kitchen cupboard, a legacy of my last failed attempt at musicality.

She had the guitar by the neck, in both hands, swinging like an axe.

Swung it above her head and smashed it to pieces on the hapless skull of our utterly defeated home invader.

She'd lifted what remained of the guitar, now more a stick with wires than a musical instrument. She was going again. Overhand axe style this time, when I just managed to catch it. A moment before the descent.

Probably would have killed him.

"I think we got him, love," I whispered.

"What?" she grunted.

"He's done," I said, giving my layman's diagnosis to a medical professional with several year's war-zone experience.

I put an arm around her. Gave her a hug. Kissed her on the top of her head. Gently.

I was worried she was still thinking 'domestic weaponry'.

"Maybe get some clothes on, love, before the guests arrive."

"Yeah," she said, smiling a bit at 'guests'. I let go of my end of the dead guitar. No more Neil Young on this one.

Wendy waved my broken guitar in Carruthers' busted face. "You did this, you animal. This is your fault."

Kenny was past arguing with the Amazon.

"Secure the prisoner." I reminded myself.

I took some ties from a kitchen drawer. I zipped his hands and feet tight. Cutting tight.

Zip ties? I'm a cop. I keep these things around.

Done.

I found my phone and dialled triple zero for an ambulance.

Triple zero would get me Wodonga. I was not going to wake the local paramedics, our friends, just to store this piece of shit in the Jarrajarra Nursing Centre.

Plus, Wodonga had a secure ward.

Ken Carruthers was going cattle class.

I arranged the ambulance from Wodonga. Then, I called Sarge. Have him send some of the team for the cleanup.

He answered pretty quick, but it took him a moment to wake up and grasp the story.

"Carruthers, hey? The crooked policeman?" he said after he was up to speed. "I'll be buggered."

He had a think.

"I'll bring a team," he said.

'Bring' meant he was coming with them. I didn't argue with that.

"We better let the superstar television Detective in on the news," he added.

"Can you do that?" I asked. "I need to focus on here and now."

"Of course," he said, "of course. Wendy? She's OK?"

"Better than him," I answered.

"Thank goodness,' he said. "Carruthers, he's secure?"

"Zip tied to pussy's bow," I answered.

"Good, good," said Sarge. "Keep him that way."

A moment of silence for both of us. What else was there?

"Good work, son," he said. That was nice. Sarge never forgot the attaboys.

We ended the call.

"Sarge wants to know if you're OK," I shouted to Wendy in the bedroom behind me.

"I'm OK, love," she said. "You just get that animal out of here. I don't want him in our home."

True enough.

I dragged him by the mullet and, with a bit of effort, threw him in the back of the police truck.

He was still unconscious. Jesus, he might be dead or faking it.

We had given him a severe touch-up.

As a courtesy, I left him the bloodied blanket from our bed. Wendy and I would not be using it again.

I went inside, checked Wendy was OK, found my keys and prepared to drive Carruthers to the cell.

I was just about to move when Wendy opened the passenger door. She was dressed in puffer jacket and jeans and held some jeans and a jacket for me.

"I'm coming," she said, "and you'll need these before long."

She put my warm clothes on the bench seat between us, then smiled. I smiled back. God, I loved her.

"You're bleeding," she said.

"So's Ken," I answered.
"Smartarse," she said.
And off we went to toss Carruthers in the clink
I called Barney on the way.
Someone had to do the admin, poor Barney, there'd be a lot.
Five minutes after I had Carruthers locked up in the cell, I sat with Wendy in the Police Station kitchen. She'd made us both coffee. We were holding hands across the kitchen table. The electric heater blowing hot from the corner.
Life was cosier for us than Mister Carruthers.
Wendy was safe, and I was happy.
The cavalry was on the way.
"He hurt you?" I asked.
"Just a flesh wound," she smiled, rubbing her ribs. "Mother and baby are both fine."
We sipped our coffee.
"We'll have to start locking the doors, I guess," she said.
"Whatever you want, but he's a one-off, I reckon."
"We'll lock 'em, Corporal," she smiled.
She was feeling better.
My phone rang, it was Detective Pete.
"So, Carruthers, he's locked away? Yes?" He asked.
"He's not going anywhere," I said.
"Bit battered, I hear," said Pete.
"Yes," I said, "some of that."
"Well, mate," said Pete. "I suppose this makes us friends again."
I wasn't sure about that, but it didn't need saying.
"See you when you get here," I said.
"I'm on my way." Call ended.
No doubt Pete would bring the reporters, probably arrive by chopper.
Wendy read my mind. She was looking at me, holding my hand.
"I'm taking today off work," she said. "Stick with you for the rest of the day."
"Okay," I was smiling, but Wendy was serious.
"Make sure you don't punch anyone else."
"Sounds perfect," I said, and she was.

Saturday, July 9, 2022

Jarrajarra Police Station.

10:30 AM, outside the station, police cars everywhere, a couple of ambulances and a few TV reporters who'd arrived from Melbourne in their station-identified vans.

The word was out.

Dazzling Darren Everett was there in his rugged old Toyota Corolla and his grungy low slung jeans, but his Channel 7 camera gear looked shiny and new.

Daz was outside with the media maul today. No special access when you weren't the expert witness.

Of course, the Jarrajarra emergency vehicles were all around, and the CFA barbeque was up and running and making money. I hadn't seen the Barbie on the main street before. Bit blatant. Pretty sure the owners of the cafe on the west side of the road and the bakery on the north would be pissed at the amateurs stealing their income.

It was the full scrum.

Rich people, murder and now a suspect in custody.

Big news for a small town.

* * *

Inside the station, it was borderline mayhem. All the cops had gathered for a gawk. Angela Adams had made the mysterious Ken Carruthers a criminal celebrity, and here he was, in the battered flesh. It might have been wise to hold back on those knees to his head, given half the major media were there to get a shot of his ugly mug.

Too late for restraint.

Wendy and I were in my office relaxing. My door was open.

Jarrajarra's unofficial Lady Mayoress, Norma Farrell, walked in with a tray containing hot soup, sandwiches, sausage and onions from the barbeque, and a thermos of coffee.

The two sets of cutlery suggested it was all for Wendy and me. We were fulsome in our praise and gratitude.

"Give me your keys, Christopher," said Norma, "I'm heading down to your house to clean the place up."

"It's a crime scene, Norma," I said carefully. "Have to leave it for the Crime Services ladies to have a run-through."

"Oh," she said.

That was as close I had ever come to saying 'No' to Norma. The results were unpredictable.

Norma had to think about this. Someone said 'No', goodness. She had to think for a very long moment.

"Very well then. When it's not a crime scene, you let me know immediately. I'm not having Wendy face up to that mess in her condition."

I was bewildered. I had not discussed Wendy's condition with Norma. The whole town was telepathic.

"That'd be great, thanks, Norma," said Wendy. "Maybe get the boys to burn that bed and the linen for us while you're at it."

"Done," said Norma.

"Barbeque," she said to herself, then headed outside to resume tossing sausages on the streetside barbie.

"We can stay at the Nursing Centre digs till this blows over," said Wendy.

"How the hell did she know you were pregnant?" I asked.

"Who knows?" Said Wendy. "Direct line to God, maybe."

"God and Norma? I wonder who makes the call?"

* * *

Sarge was at the front desk with Barney, running the cop side of the show. My two favourite fill-ins had been assigned to us for a few days, Constables Tim Silver and Joyce Thompson, and of course, our media superstar had arrived from Melbourne and had found Wendy and me sitting together at my desk in my office, sipping hot soup.

"So, Wendy, How are you feeling?" Detective Senior Sergeant Pete Jordan sailed into my office smooth and charming as ever.

"Better than the other bloke," said Wendy.

"Great, great," said Pete. "I know bugger-lugs here can survive anything, so that means no casualties on our side. Good news, good news."

There were only three of us in the room. I guess that made me bugger-lugs.

"You know I have to ask, Chris," said Pete. "He's never contacted you before? Right? He's not going to play the victim, paint you dirty?"

"No, never," I said, "I have never met the man before this morning."

"No communication with him in any form?" asked Pete.

"None," I said.

I could feel Wendy bristling beside me.

"Sorry, Wendy," said Pete, showing rare sensitivity. "Cop question had to ask."

"All fine," I said.

"Yes, all good, all good," said Pete. "I just need to speak to Carruthers himself now. Cross fingers he doesn't die on us before we chat."

"Die?" said Wendy. "He's not going to die, trust me."

Wendy hadn't really dealt with Detective Pete before. A man whose every second thought was on how the previous thought or action would play in the media.

Even proxy actions like Wendy belting Carruthers might theoretically bounce back on Pete's shining glory. Pete Jordan was fun when we were chasing crooks, but his passion for appearances could wear thin.

"Yes, yes," said Pete. "You've seen dying men before, of course. War zones, yeah. I will bow to your expertise," he said, smiling. Always smiling.

I could feel a grey mist descending.

I wanted my mate, Pete, to just bugger off. Just go away before I throw him out. I liked him, but not this media stuff, not now. How to find the words?

I didn't have to worry. Enter Barney.

"I'm sorry, Detective Senior Sergeant," said Barney, "but Chris and Wendy have just survived a terrifying home invasion at the hands of an accused murderer. Could I ask you to wait outside till they have both seen the paramedics?"

"Oh, yes, of course, absolutely," said Pete. "They look alright to me."

"Let's leave that to the professionals, shall we," said Barney, smiling that front desk smile of his, holding the door to my office open. Open for exit.

Pete hadn't quite got the idea.

"I don't know if you are familiar with the local acoustics," said Barney. "I am guessing that sound in the distance is the Channel 7 chopper."

That threw some motivation into Pete's thought pattern.

"Time for your close-up," added Barney, still smiling sweetly.

Pete walked to the door. Barney held it open. Pete left, and Barney followed. Barney threw a wink and a smile over his shoulder to Wendy and then closed the door behind him on his way out.

"I love that man," said Wendy, meaning Barney, not Pete.

"Pete has just been Barnied," I said.

We had a laugh and resumed sipping our delicious CFA soup.

"Didn't we already see the paramedics?" I asked.

"Jody and Jack?" said Wendy. "No, mate, that was just a social visit. The real examination comes later. Tonight."

* * *

Barney was correct.

The Angela Adams chopper arrived at the footy ground. The big show was back in town.

'Dazzling' Darren Everett stuck his head in the front door of the police station. Before anyone could push him out, he said, "Turn on Channel 7. We're going direct."

Miss Adams had arrived outside the Station, and the show was almost ready to roll.

Inside, Barney was like lightning. He had Channel 7 streaming live on his computer in a heartbeat.

We all grouped around the screen like cows at a trough. Who could resist? Angela might be just outside the front door, but everyone preferred watching her on TV.

Barney gave Wendy the comfy work chair. Barney, Sarge and I sat on the ancient wooden stools, and the rest of the tribe stood in the back row.

We did not have long to wait.

Channel 7 Live Television Broadcast

Angela Adams Shared a split screen with the studio host, Tom.

"Good afternoon, Australia. I'm Tom McGregor, and we're interrupting our normal broadcast for breaking news. We cross now, live, to Seven's crime reporter, Angela Adams, in the small country town of Jarrajarra in North-East Victoria. Angela, what is going on up there?"

Handsome Tom nodded, and Angela continued.

"Thanks, Tom. There has been a breakthrough in the mystery surrounding the murdered high society millionaires, Doctor Phillip Savage Senior and his son, former Melbourne-based business entrepreneur Phillip Savage Junior."

"Local police have arrested former homicide detective Ken Carruthers," said Angela. "According to my police sources, Carruthers has been missing since the disappearance of the Savage father and son in 2010."

"And the bodies of these two men were found recently," interrupted Tom.

"Yes, Tom." Said Angela. "Since the discovery of the bodies of the Savages only six weeks ago, Carruthers has emerged as one of the chief suspects in their murder."

"How did police find this fellow?" asked Tom, determined to have his share of the conversation.

"Good question, Tom," said Angela, "In a strange turn of events, Mister Carruthers has revealed himself. At around 4:00 AM this morning, Ken Carruthers went to the Jarrajarra home of the local policeman, Senior Constable Chris Taylor. Carruthers was armed with what has been described as a police pistol. He broke into Constable Taylor's home. At some point, after entering the residence and threatening Constable Taylor and his partner, local nurse Wendy Acheson, Carruthers was disarmed and then overpowered. He is now being held in the Jarrajarra Police Station, which

you can see behind me."

"Does anyone know why Carruthers went to the policeman's home, Angela, and why carrying a gun?" Asked Tom.

"I can't answer those questions yet, Tom, but I understand there was a scuffle inside the policeman's home and during that fight, Carruthers received several injuries and has since been transferred to the Wodonga Hospital, where he is being held under police guard."

"How badly injured is he?" asked Tom.

"The injuries have been described to me by police sources as severe but not life-threatening. The situation is unfolding here, Tom. I can promise our viewers that tonight, on the 6:00 PM news, I will have an exclusive interview with the lead detective on this case, Detective Senior Sergeant Peter Jordan of Melbourne Homicide."

"Thank you, Angela," said Tom.

"Tom," said Angela with a nod, and the television screen reverted to a full shot of the impeccably groomed Tom McGregor.

"Well," said Tom, "murder, mayhem, high society billionaires, a rogue policeman and now a home invasion. Is this the break police are looking for in the decades-old disappearance of the wealthy Toorak divorcee, Virginia Savage and the subsequent murders of her ex-husband and father-in-law? Find out more on Channel 7 news tonight at 6:00 PM."

Jarrajarra Police Station.

"Gosh," said Sarge, "that was quick".

"Geez, that woman is beautiful," said Constable Joyce.

"I carried her bag last time she was here," said Constable Tim. "You reckon she'd remember me if I went outside and said hello?"

Strange looks from everyone, nothing that Tim noticed.

"Don't know, Tim," I said, "you've added ten pounds of muscle since she saw you last. What are you on, mate?"

"Steroids," said Constable Joyce, laughing.

"Testosterone," came a voice from one of the cops in the back row.

"No way, I'm clean," said Tim, always serious, never joked, and didn't understand teasing.

"It's OK, Tim," said Joyce, "only teasing."

"They didn't show Detective Pete," said Wendy.

"My goodness," said Barney, "he will be devastated."

"Pete will be waiting for the bigger audience at 6:00 PM," said Sarge.

"Be still my beating heart," said Barney, and everyone laughed.

Cops talking shit. Much more fun than waking up to a gun in your face and seeing your beautiful girlfriend and unborn baby being kicked across the room by a cop gone bad.

Hearing him threaten to kill her.

Ken Carruthers. We will meet again.

* * *

The day rolled on, and Wendy was true to her word. We just stuck together as the day proceeded. No one raised an eyebrow as to how and why a cop would have his girlfriend by his side during a working day and why would they? Anyway, I wasn't working. Technically, Wendy and I were the victims, though we were carrying significantly fewer scars than our attacker.

As the day wore on, Sarge and his crew of Wodonga cops all filtered away, except for Constables Tim and Joyce, who would hang around another week to help. They would be very handy if another random bad guy came around pointing weapons in faces at ridiculous hours of the morning.

Tim was like an old glove and slotted back into Barney's system of yellow Post-it notes without a second thought. He even tried to explain how it all worked to Joycey.

"Barney takes the calls for police assistance, he writes the guts of the message on the post-it, then we go and do the assist, and then Barney does the paperwork," said Tim.

Joyce struggled with that concept. "A station where the cops have no paperwork?"

"Exactly," said Tim, "just do what Barney tells you, then tell him what you did and leave it there."

"So Barney does the incoming calls, the Post-its and the papers?" Joycey was still confused.

"Yep," said Tim. "Just trust me, mate, it works like a dream. Once you get used to it, this place is a holiday."

* * *

Later, still hanging in my office, Wendy looked ready for home. We were sipping the last of the cold soup.

I received a phone call.

"G'day Killer," only two people called me that. Constables Carole Johnston and her sister, Glenda Johnston, from the Seymour Crime Services Unit.

"Love what you've done with your bedroom," said Carole. They usually called on the speaker and worked through a call like one person, filling each other's gaps.

"What's that striking shade of red?" Asked Glenda. "Blood or guts?"

"They're in our bedroom?" Wendy whispered to me. I shrugged. It didn't pay to be too sensitive when talking to the forensic sisters.

"Nice bit of nose splatter we've got going here from the bed to the backyard," said Carole. "What the hell did you hit him with?"

"This thing halfway down my leg, I said.

"What?"

"My knee."

"Oh, OK," said Carole.

"We were told he bought a gun to the party," said Glenda.

"He did," I answered. "Where's the gun," I asked Wendy.

"It's in the barbeque, next to the punching bag," said Wendy.

"Oh, G'day, Wendy," said Carole. "Didn't realise you were there, mate. Sorry about the bedroom jokes."

"No problem."

We listened as Glenda took the phone and headed for the barbeque. "Nice setup," she said. "Who'd have thought cooking the snags and kicking the heavy bag? What a guy."

"It's Wendy's bag," I said. "Hurts my fists."

"Not surprised," answered Glenda. Sounds of fossicking, "Here we go, one standard police issue .40 calibre Smith and Wesson."

More sounds of fiddling about.

"And the magazine? That would be the one from the bedroom floor?"

"Yes," I answered.

And so it went.

"The gun will have my fingerprints and Wendy's all over it," I said. "But, check the magazine and the shell casings. They should be Carruthers prints only, if we're lucky."

"Roger that," said Glenda.

"We've also got his car," said Carole. "It's a Ford F150, utility truck, parked around the corner, out of sight. He's got guns in the boot, a couple of spare shell packs, same brand as those in the magazine from the bedroom by the look of it."

"Truck was stolen from Safeway, Wodonga yesterday around 11:00 AM," said Glenda.

"Lot of mud on his boots," said Carole. "I've got a trail from the car to the house. He checks out your bedroom, outside looking in. We've got his boot prints outside your window. Then he goes in the back door, straight through the kitchen to your bedroom and then to the side of the bed."

"Don't suppose your doors were locked?" asked Glenda.

"No," I said.

"No," they harmonized in disappointment. "Would have been nice to get him smashing a lock," said Carole.

"Anyhow, I found the two bullet holes," said Carole, "one in the floor beside the bed and one in the wall."

"Got a very bloody balaclava here. Some strands of long, grey hair. Not yours, I reckon, Chris."

"No," I said. "Not mine."

"I think we've got him covered," said Glenda.

"Steals a car. Drives here fully armed," said Carole, summing up. "Hides his car. Loads up on weaponry, comes in through the backyard, checks out the house, wearing a balaclava, then in the backdoor straight to the bedroom and discharges the weapon. Then, cops a father of a hiding from the hero cop and his girlfriend. Strike a blow for the good guys."

"A hidden car," added Glenda. "A trail straight to the target, gunshots in the bedroom, cartridges match between the car and the bedroom wall. A home invasion gone wrong."

They were no longer talking to me, just shorthand between themselves.

"Can't see how he's gonna argue anything else."

"Goodbye freedom, hello prison."

They stopped talking for a moment.

"I'd say you're in the clear, mate," said Carole. "You can get back to your music lessons with a clear conscience."

"No assault charges on you here," said Glenda. "Not for this one, at least."

I laughed. They had seen the guitar and chosen not to mention it. Cop covering cop. Good for our side, not so good for bad guys.

"Thank you, ladies," I said, sincerely grateful.

"Ladies?" said Carole.

"Dunno about ladies," added Glenda.

"Talk later," and they were gone. What a summary.

Ken Carruthers, he came to my home in secret and with serious intent, the evil bastard.

Definitely should have killed him when I had the chance.

Temporary Home, Jarrajarra.

Wendy and I called it a day. We went to my house and collected our stuff, then moved ourselves to Wendy's apartment in the Nursing Centre.

I called Norma Farrell to let her know the house was no longer a crime scene. Just a mess.

"Don't you worry about it, Chris love," said Norma. "By lunchtime tomorrow, I will have it shiny and new."

"Two bullet holes in the bedroom," I added.

"They are as good as gone," she said.

Norma had spoken. It would be done.

Wendy and I settled into her apartment, locked the doors and went to bed. We had a lovely cuddle and went to sleep.

The phone rang at 9:30 PM. Holy Mother of God, who would phone at such an hour.

Detective Pete.

"Did you catch the interview?"

"No, mate, long day, went to sleep."

"Shit, sorry, mate, should have realized, sorry. Anyway, Carruthers is awake and whingeing like a baby, apparently."

"You're breaking my heart," I said.

"Thought you'd be sad. So, anyhow, doing the interview in the hospital ward tomorrow at 10:00 AM. Can't have you in the room, I guess, him screaming police brutality and you being the perpetrator, as it were."

"Fair enough," I said.

"I can do the honours and maybe take Will Walker in as backup. Will knows him from way back, save us having to wade through any Carruthers bullshit about his time on the force."

"OK."

"I can set up Zoom for you to watch. Yeah?"

"Yeah, sounds good."

"It all worked, mate," said Pete. "The television, the power of suggestion, it all worked. We smoked him out, and you cooked him. Well done to you, Constable Taylor. You got Carruthers. Now let's nail those other scumbags to the wall and find your missing Muay Thai mate."

"Detective Jordan," I said. "I am truly shocked. You actually said, Muay Thai."

"Oh yeah, well, OK. Brazilian Mumbo Jitsu, whatever you call it. You've done extremely well, Chris."

"Thank you."

"Zoom you tomorrow with our new mate Kenny."

End of call.

Detective Pete was euphoric. He'd had his fifteen-minute dose of television glory and was back to being a real cop with one suspect behind bars and two to go.

I was so excited for him that I went back to sleep without another thought.

Sunday, July 10, 2022

Security Ward, Wodonga Hospital.

"It's police brutality is what it is."

Ken Carruthers was speaking from a single-bed in the security wing of the Wodonga hospital. The hospital didn't run to private rooms for bad guys. Lucky for Ken, Wendy and I had guitared the crap out of him on a quiet weekend, so Kenny had the secure room all to himself.

Kenny was cuffed by his hands and feet to the iron frame of the hospital bed. He was going nowhere, and if he was itchy anywhere under his bandages, he was in dire straits.

Detective Pete and Wodonga's Senior Sergeant Will Walker were asking the questions, but Carruthers was too busy complaining about me to listen.

Pete had set up a Zoom arrangement that allowed me to watch the interview from the comfy chair at the front desk of the Jarrajarra Police Station. He had a Wi-Fi camera posted somewhere on the wall behind him, so I could see Pete's laptop screen, the back of Pete's head, the back of Will Walker's head and the battered face of Ken Carruthers.

Kenny didn't look too good. He had a plaster splint on his nose, held in place by white hospital adhesive. Under all that, his eyes were swollen to slits, red, bruised, and battered. Something was going on bandage-wise on the top of his head. This would be the result of Wendy's guitar solo.

Nevertheless, our Ken was alive and breathing, awake and talking. All up, he could have been worse. The other side of dead, perhaps.

Detective Pete had also turned off my microphone at his end, so I couldn't accidentally speak to the room from the clouds during the interview. Wise move since I wasn't technically allowed to participate.

"I just went there to talk to the dumb bastard," said Kenny on his angry roll. "I go there to give over some information that could help all of you blokes. I went to talk, negotiate, not have some cowboy country cop beat the shit out of me."

"What did you want to talk about?" Asked Pete. Had to love his focus, though it looked like Kenny hadn't finished his list of grievances.

"No, no, no," said Ken, "not talkin' now, not after this. This is a whole other thing. Look what he did. Look at me, for fuck's sake."

Pete leant forward to his computer and spoke.

"Interview terminated at 11:13 AM."

With that, Pete and Will Walker stood up to leave. Just like that, no sideways glances, just good old cop telepathy.

Pete picked up his laptop without closing it. The interview was over, but the Zoom session continued for my benefit.

Pete and Will moved out of camera view toward the door.

"Ken," said Pete, "call the nurse when you're ready to tell us what this is all about. They know where to find us."

"How can I fucking call the nurse?" Ken shouted back. "I'm cuffed here like an animal. How can I reach the fucking buzzer, you stupid prick?"

Ken Carruthers was in angry victim rant mode.

Will Walker came back into view and put something in Carruthers' hand.

"There you go, Kenny," said Will.

It looked more like a television remote than a hospital buzzer.

"Fucking smartarse, Walker," shouted Kenny, "I remember you, always the fucking cock-sucking smartarse."

The veins on Kenny's neck were bulging angry red. He tried to fling the object in his hand back toward the departing Walker, but with his hands cuffed, he didn't send it far. It landed further down the bed, closer to my camera feed.

Yes, it was definitely the television remote.

"Fark!" screamed Kenny in frustration.

Straight-arrow Senior Sergeant Will Walker had made a joke, a good one.

First time for everything.

The two cops left Carruthers alone in his room, closing the door on the way out.

Sergeant Pete sent me a text in the chat window at the side of the Zoom session. Carruthers couldn't see or hear us, so it was an excellent way to talk behind his back.

"Anything to add?" asked Pete in the chat window.

"Not yet," I typed.

"Walker is enjoying this," typed Pete. "He told the nurses here that Kenny has been arrested for the attempted murder of your Wendy. They all know her, I assume."

"Yes, they do" I answered. "I am sure they will remain totally professional."

"I hope not," typed Pete.

Everyone in the region knew my beautiful girlfriend, Nurse Practitioner Wendy Atcheson of Jarrajarra. She was a local legend of the good kind. Attempted murder was not a wise prelude to Kenny's care and attention at the Wodonga Hospital.

"Why would he come at you like that if he only wanted to talk?" asked Pete.

"No idea," I answered.

The chat window paused a while.

"I'll call you when he is ready to go again," said Pete then ended the Zoom session and the chat.

Jarrajarra Police Station.

"It's a good question," said Barney. "If he wants to negotiate, why come at you masked, armed and in a stolen car? And why involve Wendy?"

"I don't know, Barn. We'll find out soon enough."

"Yes," said Barney. "I don't see him holding out for long."

"It's weird that it comes after those two blokes tried to warn me off McLain," I said.

"Especially given they didn't really know her," said Barney.

It was closing in on 5:00 PM. Barney and I were sitting in my office thinking about the failed interview and strange visits from standover types. Constables Tim and Joyce were at the front desk chatting between themselves.

Not much was happening in Jarrajarra. All the yellow post-it notes had been attended to. To fill out the day, Joyce had sat on the highway and collected half a dozen traffic violations during the afternoon.

Two of the tickets were issued to local farmers. One driver was over the speed limit. The other was driving an unregistered tractor on the road. Sometime this week, I would have to make the charges disappear from the system without hurting Joycey's feelings.

I knew both families, and they were both cash-broke. With large supermarket chains selling milk and meat cheaper than it can be produced, our smaller farmers were struggling. Not just in Jarrajarra but all over. Loss-leader was the biz-speak bullshit the corporate types used to cover the unfair pricing. Bugger that. The Jarrajarra justice system would survive without further funding from the local milking community.

The phone rang. Detective Pete.

"Apparently, Mister Carruthers is ready to talk. Just resume that same Zoom session, and you can watch the fun. Anything you want to pass on, just type it in the chat box. Give us 10 minutes to get over there and set up."

"Roger that," I said.

Barney and I made ourselves ready around the front desk computer. Tim and Joycey stood behind us to watch. Within fifteen minutes, we had disposed of all the digital and legal preamble. We were back in business.

Security Ward, Wodonga Hospital.

Detective Pete and Senior Sergeant Will Walker were in the room facing Carruthers. Barney and I were watching via Zoom from Jarrajarra. Our two visiting Constables, Tim and Joyce, were sitting behind us in the back row, looking over our shoulders.

"This is good TV," said Tim.

"Shoosh," said Barney, Joyce and me. All one voice.

All that mattered was what Carruthers had to say.

"How are they treating you?" asked Pete.

"Terrible," said Carruthers.

"Is there anything I can do to help?"

"You could at least un-cuff one of my hands, so I can scratch my fucking itches and use the button to call the nurse. That would be good."

"I think we can do that," said Pete and uncuffed Carruthers' left hand and placed the Help button where he could reach it.

"Thank you," said Carruthers. Quite polite.

Next, Pete confirmed that our prisoner did not want a lawyer present and was willing to talk without a representative.

Pete then went through a few identification questions, asking Carruthers for his full name, date of birth, and current address, which Carruthers refused to reveal.

All pretty standard stuff, essential even, but Pete, the experienced interrogator, was also laying down a control track. Straight questions, no reason to lie, getting a picture of Kenny's behaviour when he was telling the truth.

Then Pete changed the pace.

"So," he asked, "can you explain why you attacked Constable Taylor in his home?"

"I didn't attack him," said Carruthers. I disagreed on this particular point, but no matter.

"I went there to talk," he said. "I saw the television show. I knew you blokes had found the bodies of the two Phillip Savages. I knew from the TV that Taylor was a part of the investigation, so I thought I could get in there, get my point across and get out. You know, element of surprise, get my message through and be away before anyone had time to think."

He hadn't said much beyond the obvious. So far, he was still telling the truth.

"A surprise visit?" said Pete.

"Yeah, mate. Think about it. If I just showed up at a police station in the middle of the day and said hello, I'm the man you're looking for, there's a fair chance I wouldn't be getting out of the place on my own volition. Not anytime soon."

"You didn't want to be detained, under arrest?"

"Absolutely no fucking way, No."

"So, that's why you fought with Constable Taylor?" Asked Pete. "To avoid arrest?"

"Well, yeah, but I wouldn't call it a fight. Your fucking constable attacked me out of the blue for no reason. After he started belting into me, I was just defending myself."

While Carruthers was talking, I was typing a message into the Zoom chat box for Pete's attention.

"Why wear the balaclava?" I wrote.

"So, Ken," said Pete. "Why the balaclava? Why the stolen car? Looks to me you were intending to use the gun and get away without being identified."

They'd found Carruthers' transport, the stolen car. The team had been busy.

"No," said Carruthers. "The gun was to keep Tatylor under control."

"That worked well," said Tim behind me.

"Shoosh," said Barney and Joyce.

Carruthers continued.

"The balaclava and the car were so I could stay away from you blokes. No one has my photo for the last ten years or so. I've changed a bit. Plus, no one knows where I live. I want to keep it that way."

He looked directly at Pete, and then his eyes briefly flicked at Will, "People around this case of yours tend to die unexpectedly," said Carruthers. "I don't want to be one of them."

I wasn't sure if that was a lie.

I typed something for Pete to upset Carruthers' rhythm.

"Ask him why he kicked and threatened to kill Wendy."

"Didn't even know she was there. I thought Taylor was a single bloke. Then, the shit hit the fan, Taylor starts belting me for no reason. She comes up from under the blankets. I never kicked her or swore at her. Never said anything. She just got out of the way, under her own steam." He did that eye flick, back and forth between Pete and Will again.

"Total lie," I typed.

Pete didn't react.

"So the whole visit was about sending us a message and not getting arrested."

"Yeah."

"So what was the message?"

"Well, you know, you blokes want to talk to me, but you can't find me. I know stuff you want to know. So, like, what sort of deal are we talking about here? If I tell you what I know? What's in it for me?"

"You want to trade information you have in exchange for some level of exoneration for any crimes you may have committed?"

"Yeah, that, but not saying I did commit any crimes."

"Well, last time I checked," said Pete, "entering a police officer's home, uninvited, with a loaded weapon, and shoving it in his face, is still a crime in the State of Victoria.

"Maybe, maybe," said Carruthers, not much bothered by Pete's recitations of the morning's events. "But, who knows what you guys might skip over if I give you what I know. Maybe there might even be a reward if I gave you what I have on some very well-known, filthy-rich third parties. Maybe you'd be interested in some other dead bodies that may be out there in the countryside. It's all negotiation, isn't it?"

"The only rich third parties we are interested in is the Fenwicks," said Pete. "The only missing person we are looking for is Virginia Collins. Anything else, and we are not interested in a deal."

"You need to focus, Ken," added Will.

"Yeah? Well, I saw on TV where you were looking for that woman, Collins," said Carruthers. "Mate, you are not even close."

He looked smug. I wanted to hit him again, one more guitar solo on his smug-ugly head.

"So you are admitting to me," said Pete, "that Virginia Collins is dead, and you know where she is buried."

"Maybe," said Carruthers.

Pete just stopped. I could only see the back of Pete's head, but from the look on Carruthers' face, I guessed Pete was giving him a very disappointed stare-down.

"Mister Carruthers," said Pete, "at this point, I suggest that you find yourself a legal representative. If you have information that you wish to trade, a lawyer might help that process. I am not prepared to play twenty questions with you on every single item of discussion."

"I thought we were working together here," said Carruthers.

"Will," said Pete to Senior Sergeant Will Walker, who was seated beside him.

Will spoke for the first time in the meeting.

"Mister Ken Carruthers, I am informing you, pursuant to the Crimes Act of 1958, section 77B, you are under arrest on the charge of 'Aggravated home invasion' in that you entered the home of Senior Constable Christoper Taylor as a trespasser with intent to commit an offence involving damage to the home and to property within the home and that you entered the home in the possession of a firearm."

Will was so unemotional he could have been reading a recipe for banana cake. It was fake. He cared a lot. He wanted Carruthers in jail for a long time, but interrogations are theatre, and Will was playing his part.

"So, Kenny," said Pete to Carruthers, "just in case you've forgotten your Crimes Act, any person found guilty of 'Aggravated home invasion', with a gun, on a cop no less, is looking at level 2 imprisonment, which you might remember puts you behind bars for up to 25 years."

"Or thereabouts," added Will Walker.

"I thought we were negotiating," said Kenny, sounding nervous.

"We're cops, Ken, not car salesmen," said Pete.

"Could've fooled me," said Carruthers.

"Interview terminated," said Pete, then gave the time and clicked something on his computer. It wasn't the Zoom session, as it was still open.

"Listen," said Pete, standing now, looking down on the battered prisoner. "Stop wasting everyone's time. Get yourself a lawyer, one who understands how this works. Let your lawyer know what you can give us, and we will work with them on what we might do for you. Keep mucking us around like this, and you are going to jail."

"For twenty-five years, an ex-cop in the general population," added Will Walker, playing nastier than I'd ever seen him. "That's a long time watching your back. Your old boss, Hughes, didn't survive a single day. Not one."

Pete closed his laptop, and the Zoom session closed down with it.

Jarrajarra Police Station.

"Goodness," said Barney, "they are quite the team."

I was still staring at the empty screen when my phone rang.

"We are done with Carruthers for the day," said Pete, "let him stew on it overnight. You be right for tomorrow?"

"I will," I said.

"Did you notice anything?" Pete asked.

"Yep," I said. "Getting a read via Zoom is not ideal, but when he is telling the truth, he just speaks to one person, focused eye contact and all that. But, when he is lying, his eyes flick around, off to the horizon, then back to both of you in the room, judging the reactions. Looking to see if you believe him, maybe. The bigger the lie, the more he does the eyeball wandering."

"Yeah," said Pete, "I think you're right."

"Replay the bit where he talks about Wendy," I said. "He's definitely lying about kicking her. No question."

"Yeah, I agree," said Pete. "Now, why do you think he called on you?"

"Well, he was lying about just wanting to talk and then leave," I answered. "But if 'trying to stay free' is not Kenny's motive, what is?"

"The obvious, mate."

"What am I missing?"

"Think about it," said Pete. "Up till yesterday, we didn't even know if he was alive. He goes to your place in a stolen car with a gun and wearing a balaclava to hide his identity."

"OK," I said.

I was waiting for a penny to drop.

"He went there to kill you, Chris, and since Wendy was there too, he was probably going to murder her as well."

"Why me?"

"He probably planned to blame someone else, plant the gun somewhere. If you'd turned up missing or dead, who would we look at?"

"The two Fenwicks, or maybe even Jennifer McLain," I offered.

"There you go," said Pete. "Three suspects already. He's a crafty bugger, our Kenny."

Wednesday, July 13, 2022

Jarrajarra Police Station.

It was Wednesday before we got back to Ken Carruthers. By then, he'd recovered enough to be moved to the holding cells of the Wodonga Police Station. I'd heard the transfer was not without protest. Kenny was a bit of a complainer.

Barney and I were at the front desk watching Barney's computer screen.

We were back on Zoom, but from a different location, the interview room at Wodonga Station. Stark and much less friendly than the security ward at the hospital.

Kenny looked right royally pissed off. Sulking. Eyes, down, not speaking. Didn't have to say a word this time. He had taken the advice and found himself a lawyer, some young bloke from Wodonga, Lachlan Holmes.

The new lawyer gave me pause. While the two officers, Sergeant Pete and Will Walker, talked through the introductions and the legal preamble, I wondered how Carruthers had found this Solicitor fellow, Lachie Holmes.

I stepped away from the Zoom and called our local Solicitor, Eddie Doolan. Eddie and his QC mate, Jeremy Oakley QC, were representing our alleged cattle rustler and murderer, Jennifer McLain. I couldn't ask Eddie anything about McLain, lawyer-client privilege and all that.

But Eddie was a mate. Surely, I could ask him about Carruthers. Didn't mean he would answer, but worth a try. Debbie, Eddie's personal assistant, Debbie put me straight through.

"Eddie," I asked, "were you asked to represent a Mister Ken Carruthers over the last few days?"

Eddie had a think before he answered.

"Why would you ask me that question, Constable Taylor?" The fact he didn't call me by name indicated we had gone official.

"Well, I know he has a lawyer representing him. I know it's not you, and I wondered if he asked you first. Since I know he is not your client, I thought it wouldn't be breaking any privilege to ask." I offered.

"You know, without asking, I wouldn't break client-lawyer privilege for any reason. I wouldn't even tell you if someone was or was not my client. It's the principle, Chris."

We were back to first names. Eddie was relaxed.

"Would you ever consider him as a client?" I asked.

"Well," said Eddie, "if we are speaking about the Ken Carruthers that has been in the news lately, and it is the same Ken Carruthers who invaded your home on Friday night, I don't think I am betraying any principles, if I told you that I would not represent anyone who was accused of attacking Wendy in her home, in such a manner. Not under those circumstances. Not for all the money in the world."

"Doesn't concern you that he was also attacking me?" I was a little bit miffed.

"Chris, you're a policeman. It goes with the territory. I could be hired to oppose you. You know that." I suspected he was partly joking.

"OK," I said.

"But, yes," said Eddie, "with you, in a case like this, off-duty, in your home, I would not want that person as a client."

"Thanks," I said.

"Mind you," said Eddie, "if he called me beforehand, I might have advised him not to invade your house for his own safety."

"Did Carruthers call you, or was it someone else?"

He almost spoke, almost, almost, almost said 'someone' but stopped himself, took a moment, and then laughed over the phone.

"Not answering trick questions today," he said.

"Thanks, Eddie," I said and ended the call.

I returned to the front desk where Barney was watching the Zoom session into the Wodonga interview.

"Did I miss anything?" I asked.

"Still on the introductions," said Barney, "they're almost ready."

Interview Room, Wodonga Police Station.

"Gentlemen," said Carruthers Solicitor, Lachie Holmes, "I have an unsigned document prepared on behalf of my client, Mr Carruthers. He has indicated that he would be willing to sign an affidavit to the facts in this document if certain arrangements can be made to his benefit."

"A trade?" said Pete.

"Exactly," said Holmes, who then handed the document to Pete.

Pete had a quick read while Will Walker read over his shoulder. The Zoom camera didn't cover it. Barney and I just had to wait.

"OK," said Pete, eventually.

He spoke while reading from the document.

"So, if we make a deal with our Ken, here, he admits to the disposal of three bodies. Those being Phillip Savage Senior, Phillip Savage Junior, and Mrs Virginia Savage nee Collins. All of whom were deceased when he collected them. He was not a party to the murders of any of these three people and had no foreknowledge of their deaths."

"That's it," said Holmes for Kenny.

"Your client is just the cleaner," said Pete.

"Yes," said Holmes.

"Now, to assist police in the solution of these crimes, you are offering us a diary, written in the hand of Penelope Anne Fenwick, in which Ms Fenwick makes various statements regarding the murders of her husband, Phillip Savage Senior, and her stepson Phillip Savage Junior."

"Yes," said the Solicitor.

"You are also offering one audio tape of a conversation between your client and Albert James Fenwick, Master of Laws, in which Mr Fenwick solicits the permanent disposal of the dead bodies of Phillip Savage Senior and Phillip Savage Junior."

"Yes," said the Solicitor. Again.

"You are offering another audio tape of an earlier conversation between your client and Albert James Fenwick, Master of Laws, in which Fenwick solicits the permanent disposal of the dead body of Mrs Virginia Savage nee Collins."

"Yes," said Lachie Holmes.

The room went silent for a moment.

Carruthers kept his head down.

Pete and Will Walker just stared at him.

"Kenny, Kenny, Kenny," said Pete. "Haven't you been the naughty boy?"

"Frankly, I'm not surprised," said Will Walker. A rare

interruption. No jokes today from Will.

"So, Virginia Collins is dead, and you buried her?" Pete was speaking directly to Carruthers.

Solicitor Holmes interrupted. "My client is not answering any questions until we agree on the matters discussed in the document."

"OK," said Pete, "Let me put it this way. You have no evidence at all regarding the actual murder of Virginia Collins?"

"No, we don't."

Pete turned his attention back to the document.

"OK, to sum up, your client had no part in any murders. He did dispose of some bodies, and he now wants absolution of all his sins for any crimes he may have committed relating to the disposal of these bodies."

"Yes."

"And absolution for any activity during, and leading up to, his recent attendance at the home of Constable Chris Taylor of Jarrajarra."

"Correct," said Holmes.

"So, no charges, none at all, on the home invasion or the theft of the car he used for transport to the officer's home?"

"Correct."

"Well, we need to run this by the Director of Public Prosecutions, but you know that already. We will also have to run that past the police officer whose home was invaded and his partner who was also assaulted."

"Understood."

"What do you propose we do with your client while we wait on the DPP and Constable Taylor?"

"I suggest," said Holmes, "my client be released under his own recognisance."

"Out of the question," said Pete.

"In that case, may I suggest he be returned to the security ward of the hospital?"

"Can't go there," said Pete. "He's not sick, and they don't run a security service."

"They're a hospital, Kenny," said Will Walker, "not your fucking holiday farm."

I hadn't heard Will swear before. Another first.

"If you send me to wait in jail, the deal is off," said Carruthers.

"I think you can appreciate my client's attitude to prison, being an ex-policeman," said Holmes.

"I don't think appreciate is the right word," said Will Walker.

"I thought we were no-commenting today, Kenny," said Pete.

Carruthers didn't bite. He went back into his shell, head down, eyes on his cuffed hands folded on the table.

"No comment," said Holmes.

There was a pause for a think then Pete spoke.

"I will see if he can stay in the cells here for a few days while we talk to the DPP. After that, no guarantees."

"Accepted," said Holmes.

I quickly typed a question for Pete into the Zoom chat window.

"Ask him if he knows Jennifer McLain?"

Pete did that little body shift of his as he read my message. He tapped his fingers on the table for a moment. It was a distraction. I doubt anyone on the other side of his laptop would have guessed he was reading my messages.

After thinking and tapping, Pete did a sly little halt gesture with his hand. He wasn't going to ask my question.

"Interview terminated," he said, then went into the closing waffle that legal convention required after every taped interview. The courts required it all, but it made for boring television.

Jarrajarra Police Station.

"He wouldn't ask Carruthers about McLain," I said to Barney, stating the obvious.

"Might be too early," said Barney. "There is another question, though."

"Which is?"

"I'm wondering where this evidence is."

"You're right. Kenny came to my place uninvited."

"He invaded your home, Chris. Bit further up the scale than uninvited."

"Yes, he invaded and with a clear intention of leaving unimpeded. Didn't think much of my defence capability."

Barney laughed then had a think.

"So, where are these tapes and diary entries?"

"They could be digital," I said. "Ken gets his deal, and then he points the DPP to an as-yet-unknown location on the internet."

"Is he that smart?" asked Barney.

"I don't think Kenny Carruthers is that smart," I said. "Rat cunning, brutal, a vicious bully, yes to all that. But smart enough to hide his evidence in the Cloud? Don't see it, Barn."

My phone rang. Detective Pete.

"OK, does Carruthers know McLain?" he said, "I will ask him, but not yet. OK?"

Pete had obviously ended the interview with Carruthers and his Solicitor and called me as soon as possible.

"Why not?" I asked.

"Mate, it's too soon."

Barney was right again.

"I get your line of thinking," continued Pete. "Hell of a coincidence, two major crimes appeared in your sleepy hollow barely a month apart. No offence to your lovely town. It is kind of dull, crimewise."

"Maybe to a fat-arsed couch-potato urban dweller," I said in defence of Jarrajarra. "How can it be too soon to learn something new? The sooner we know, the sooner we can act on it."

"Christopher, my budding criminologist, This is not like you. Maybe you're too angry at our Kenny boy to think straight."

Damn right, I was angry at Ken Carruthers.

"Just hold the steam coming out your ears for a moment and listen for half a second."

Bloody hell, he could be patronising.

"Listening," I mumbled.

"Let's say I ask him your question today," said Pete. "Right now, before we have a deal. Let's say they do know each other. And, yes, maybe they were in cahoots on the cattle. What if he alerts McLain while she is out on bail? It would be goodbye to her. Again. Off she goes, poof into the wind. Again."

"OK," I said. Maybe Pete had a point.

"We ask your question," Pete continued, "and we try and tie Carruthers to the sleepy town missing cattle. Where does that leave the deal he is offering? He will not do a deal on the Fenwicks and Virginia Collins if some upstart young copper from the back of beyond is trying to jam him up for a bit of cattle duffing in conspiracy and another murder."

"OK," I said. Maybe Pate had another point.

"If this deal falls through, where does that leave your dead friend Virginia Collins. Still buried somewhere, we know not where. Correct?"

"OK, Correct," I said. Maybe Pete had yet another fucking point. Smartarse.

"We do the deal. Then we find your missing friend, we put the Fenwicks behind bars, and then and only then, we go after both Carruthers and McLain for the cattle and the murder of whats-his-name Mellish."

"OK," I agreed.

"Frankly, my dear, " said Pete. "I don't care if he was a cow-co-conspirator. Let's pin it on him anyway."

"My dear?"

"It is a movie reference. Before your time, my young apprentice. And 'pin-it-on-him-anyway' was a joke, sort of."

"The movie reference was to Clark Gable, speaking to Vivien Leigh at the end of 'Gone with the Wind'. I've told you before. Don't even attempt to beat me on movie trivia. I trained with the best. For instance, what were their character names?"

"Ummm, Clark Gable and Missus Gable?"

"Exactly," I said, "you are embarrassing the both of us. Have you ever seen the movie?"

"No, but it's on my list."

"So you just looked it up to be able to pretend you're a movie buff?"

"It sounds strange when you say it like that, Constable Taylor."

"Not half as strange as doing it."

"OK," he said, "Looks like we all agree on waiting to pop the question about the true love-gone-wrong between McLain and Carruthers? Yeah?"

"Sounds like a plan," I said. He was right, of course, the smarmy bugger.

"Meanwhile," said Pete, "how is McLain driving back and forth on her check-ins to Wodonga Police?"

"Motorbike," I answered.

"Right, I will get a warrant and see about getting a tracker placed on her vehicle. Shouldn't be too hard now that your mate, Assistant Commissioner Jerrod Harrison, is out of the mix."

"What, Harrison is gone?" That was a genuine surprise.

"Didn't your boss tell you?" said Pete. "Your Sarge and Harrison fronted Professional Standards Command after they both submitted complaints about each other."

"And?"

"And? End result, Harrison has taken early retirement, and for your Sarge, life goes on as normal."

"Harrison gone?"

"Retired, gold watch, thanks for your service, hoo-roo, out the door, goodnight, sweet prince. Plain old Mr Harrison now, he took on more than he could chew with your boss."

Typical of Sarge to keep his victory to himself.

"I didn't know any of this," I said.

"You were probably too busy getting bashed up by Carruthers."

"In his dreams, maybe."

"Anyway, there will be no medals for Harrison's poor departed nephew, what's-his-name, Senior Constable Davey. And no more political interference in the unique crime-solving capacities of you and me, me mostly. We are henceforth unfettered. We can go after the Fenwicks, Carruthers and McLain, but all at the right time, Chris. Timing."

"OK, OK, I get it."

"We are a champion team, you and me, Christopher. They will make podcasts about us one day. Movies even, like your 'Gone with the whatsit'. Might even make 'em myself. I'm getting so bloody good at the media stuff."

Detective Pete was feeling good. Then he remembered something.

"You don't mind letting Carruthers walk on the home invasion, do you?"

"Wondered when you'd get to that?" I said.

"And the answer is?"

"I'm OK with it. I'll have to ask Wendy how she feels."

"Of course, mate, of course."

Assistant Commissioner Jerrod Harrison was out of the way, Jennifer McLain was back on police radar, and Detective Pete would get a warrant for a GPS tracker on McLain's motorbike.

Better to have a warrant than not. Nevertheless, I decided not to wait on the paperwork. I'd get the tracker on the motorbike tonight.

My town, my rules.

Rob Farrell's Garage.

"I've got a stack of 'em," said Rob Farrell. "They cost about thirty bucks from Amazon. You can track your car from your phone worldwide if you need to. Battery lasts about six months. They are good, mate, getting cheaper and more powerful every day."

We were sitting on the bench at the back of Rob's garage, sipping his perfect coffee and staring at a small magnetic black box half the size of a matchbox.

"It's tiny," I said.

"That's the point, mate. Small, discreet, no one knows they're attached. Don't see 'em, so they don't remove 'em."

"Why have you got them?" I had to ask.

"Because those idiot footballers who run with the fire brigade over summer leave my equipment lying all over the bloody countryside. Cheaper having hidden trackers, quicker too, not having to hassle those young fuckwits to strain their brains to remember where they left the four-wheeler or the water carts or even the fire truck, which they lost up past Toowong last summer. With these doo-dads and spare keys, I just send Scotty to go and retrieve."

As well as running the local motor repairs, Rob ran the town's equipment hire business in the space next door to the garage. He had heavy machinery, trailers, water carts, plus a wide collection of renovated trucks. He had tippers, flatbeds and two old buses. Anything that could be bought cheap, repaired, buffed up and rented out.

"Could I borrow this one?" I asked, bouncing the tracker in my hand.

"Borrow?" Rob was bemused. "Mate, these things never come back. I lend it to you, then you stick it on Jen McLain's motorbike, and I don't see it again, ever."

I looked at him. How the fuck did he know what I was going to do with it.

"Mate, you do this without a warrant. You better make sure it stays a secret. You can't tell anybody. I wouldn't even tell Barney if I were you."

"Was Barney who told me you had a bunch of these."

"Well then, we might have to shoot Barney as well."

"I won't be a party to shooting Barney," I said. "You can't either. Joanne has asked him to be Master of Ceremonies at the wedding."

"Holy Mother of God," said Rob, closing his eyes and shaking his head. "Saxon Tyson-Howard, my future son-in-law. Father of my grandchildren. The world's gone mad."

Rob was faking, I hoped. I felt the need to cheer him up.

"How about we do some shooting?" I asked. "Maybe pistols? Yeah?"

He didn't say a word, but his eyebrows said, "yes."

We finished our coffee, then retrieved his pistols and a stack of ammunition from the locker in his shed.

"Shootin' with Chris!" he shouted towards the office.

"Be back by 3.00," shouted his wife, Mary, straight back at him. Then, we stole away from our separate duties for an hour to go and shoot up the targets at the Jarrajarra Rifle Range.

* * *

We returned from 'shootin', and as the truck pulled up in the drive, Mary shouted from the office, "Who won?"

"Not everything in life is a competition, Mary," Rob said.

"Well done, Chris," she shouted back.

Rob went into the office and then returned with another two GPS trackers.

"Might as well have some extras," he said, handing them to me. "Give me your phone."

I handed over my phone. Rob fiddled for a moment, then we watched as the necessary application downloaded.

"How did you know my password?" I asked.

He just laughed. "Postcode," he said.

After a few moments, he returned my phone with the app running.

He then took one of the trackers and turned it on. After a moment, a locater appeared on the phone app, showing a flashing dot right outside Farrell's Garage, Main St Jarrajarra.

"There you go," said Rob. "The app tells you it is on. There is no light on the device, so it doesn't spill the beans, so to speak. Battery should give you six months. Even keeps a history of the movements."

"Incredible."

"And there's more," said Rob, warming to the subject. I had the phone. Rob jogged down the street for forty metres, at which point I received a notification on my phone.

'Subject in motion,' it said in a metallic voice. Oh, my goodness.

Rob returned and handed me back the GPS.

"You're in business, Chris. Now go and track like the wind."

Rob was laughing as he handed me the gear. A bit of shootin' and some equipment fun. Our friendship was restored. It wasn't my fault his daughter was marrying Saxon Tyson Howard. He might even get to like it once the baby arrives.

Jarrajarra Cafe.

I was having lunch at my favourite table outside the Jarrajarra cafe. It was Barney's idea I have lunch in the sun.

"You're recovering too quickly," he said. "They'll call our extra constables home. I enjoy the extra staff."

Technically, Constables Tim and Joyce were in Jarrajarra to cover for me while I recovered from the home invasion. Truth was, apart from the surprise, Carruthers had barely left a scratch on me.

I was as good as gold, back in uniform and, in my own mind, back on deck. Barney just didn't see the need to let Wodonga know.

"Go and have lunch in the sun," he said. "Try and look weary, at least."

We both loved having the two reserve coppers around. They were fun, and if it meant more time for me to soak up the sun in my favourite seat outside the cafe, I was all for it.

Tim and Joyce had taken off on their post-it note adventures. Tim had a barking dog dispute to sort out. Barney had made it clear to Timmy that he was not to shoot the dogs or the owners. Definitely not the owners.

He sent Joyce to meet the farmers she had ticketed the other day. Barney asked Joyce to go to the farms, meet the families and tell them not to worry about the traffic fines. Give them warnings about speeding and driving unregistered, but forget the penalties. It would be a good afternoon for Joycey, life among the locals.

Being a cop in a small town was different. Give a two-hundred-dollar speeding ticket to a person one day. You might meet them the next day in the supermarket without enough money for groceries. Worse, you might be penalizing someone you had to ask for help down the track.

Small-town cop work was different.

I was seated at a sunny table outside the cafe. From my vantage point, I could see the whole main street of Jarrajarra.

I watched Scotty Farrell pull out of the CFA garage in the fire truck. Next, he stopped at the bus shelter, and old Doc Newton jumped up from the shelter's bench and climbed into Scotty's passenger seat.

Further down the main drag, the truck stopped outside the Ambulance station. A moment later, Jody Taggart rode out of the Station on her racing bike, dressed in yellow lycra, heading toward the river. Riding fast. She waved to the fire truck as she passed.

Another training run. Now in progress.

Even from a distance, the Doc looked revitalized, and from the little I could see, in smiles and waves, it seemed Scotty and Jody were as close as ever.

Young love. It was all so energetic and innocent.

Someone emerged over my right shoulder, took the chair opposite and sat down facing me. My visitor had caught me totally by surprise. Moved like a real ninja.

"G'day, Chrisso. How's my young warrior?"

Rusty Collins.

In the flesh. Out of nowhere.

Thick grey hair, cut short, older in the face, still built like a brick shithouse. Bit of a beard. He had to be seventy years old, surely. Still as rock-hard as muscled concrete.

Chiselled.

He reached out and grabbed my hand in his massive mitt and smiled.

"Bloody hell, it is good to see you," he said. "Dressed in blue, who'd have thought? I suppose I had to get one copper out of the batch of badasses I raised in that gym."

"Rusty," it was all I could think to say. I suspect my mouth stayed open and wobbled a bit, looking for words.

He laughed.

"Caught you by surprise, yeah?"

"Yeah." The shock evaporated. I smiled back, and we did a double-hand grasp across the table. Then we stood up and did a real hug. I might have shed a happy tear.

I ordered a tea for Rusty, and we stared at each other until it arrived. I smiled till my face hurt and saw he was as fascinated by the new me as I was by the new-old him.

"Good to see you are keeping yourself fit," he said.

"Same for you," I replied.

"I've been keeping an eye on you," he said. "SASR, army give you some serious medals, you earnt some cop medals as well. Bloody hell, mate."

"Well, you know what most army medals get you," I said.

"Not a lot," he laughed. "But, you must have done something good," he said, still smiling.

"Got blown up is most of what I remember. Learnt some good stuff before that. Lots of guns, lots of shooting. Great training."

"We didn't do guns at the gym," he said. "Probably for the best with you lot."

More silence, more smiles. Over twenty years. What to say?

"Where have you been," I asked, eventually.

"Off-grid, I guess. After Virginia disappeared, I knew she was dead. I hung in around Melbourne, waiting till someone sorted out what happened. No luck there."

"Seems to me no one was trying too hard," I said.

"No, they didn't. Then that piss-weak long drip of a husband disappeared. And Ginny's father-in-law disappears as well. Your mob thought I'd offed the both of them. Time to disappear, I thought."

"I know you didn't do it," I said.

He laughed. "You'd have known it wasn't me, I am guessing."

"Yes," I said.

"If I thought that prick had murdered my daughter, he'd have been dead within a week. Wouldn't wait eight minutes, let alone eight years."

"How did you know it wasn't him?" I asked.

"I paid him a visit."

"You got to the truth by asking him?" I smiled. If you want to know, just ask. A Rusty Collins commandment.

"Asking? Yeah, you could say that," said Rusty. "Phillip didn't do it and had no idea who did. If he knew, he would have told me. Not much of a man, Phillip Savage Junior."

"Why did she marry him?" I asked.

"Money, I suppose," said Rusty. "After her mother and me, I wouldn't think Virginia had a high opinion of love ever after."

"There are worse things in life than marrying for security," I said.

"True."

He thought for a bit.

"Her mum and I, bloody hell, it was just a couple of nights before I was sent off to Vietnam. Neither of us even thought about a permanent thing. Never."

"Briefly in lust?" I said. "Never in love?"

"No," he said. "Never in love."

"So, that was around 1969?" I asked. The great detective me. I knew Virginia was born in early 1970. I did the sums.

"Yeah, around then."

"They didn't have contraception, way back in olden times."

"He gave me that look known to wither lesser men."

"You ever heard of the rhythm method?" he asked me.

"Not one I've used myself."

"Good," said Rusty. "Don't."

He had another think. I could tell, despite the circumstances, he was enjoying just hanging with me for the moment."

"Tell me about Virginia's mum," I asked.

"She was a good woman, a beautiful person, like her daughter. And a great Mum. Losing Virginia killed her. Died of a stroke, only fifty-nine. Sadness and stress got to her. Not knowing, always hoping. Fuck it."

Silence. Head down for a moment.

Rusty was an old-time tough guy. I'd never seen him cry or even get very emotional. I had learnt to read him as a kid, his student. The father I dreamt of having.

"You got kids yet, Chrisso?" he asked.

"Not yet."

"I was a better parent to you and all those other Muay Thai

larrikins than I was for my own daughter."

"You tried."

"Yeah, not hard enough. She didn't enjoy the Muay Thai that much, only did it to keep me happy. After she quit the gym, we made a regular running date. Ran around the park a couple of times a week with Tina. The three of us. Kept me in touch, kept us fit."

"Never saw you as a runner, Rusty," I said.

"Bloody Hell, mate, I hated running. Ginny was good."

"But, not much of a fighter," I said with a smile.

"No, mate, never really into it."

Another silence.

"I left a message with Richard Martin about a month ago," I said. "You are off the hook as far as the cops are concerned. No need to hide."

"Yeah, got the message, thanks. I wasn't really hiding. I was just keeping scarce. I might stay that way permanently now. Might need it soon."

That sounded ominous.

"You in touch with Virginia's kids," I asked.

"Yep," he said. "Great kids. Surfers. Hippies, really. Rich hippies, thanks to Richard Martin screwing every last dollar out of those Fenwicks."

"Are they in touch with the Savages or the Fenwicks?"

"Nope," said Rusty. "There are no Savages left, and as far as the Fenwicks are concerned, the kids are not 'of the blood', so to speak."

"Of the blood? Holy hell." I had to laugh.

"Feeling goes both ways. Kids barely remember them, and the memories ain't pleasant."

"But they love their maternal granddad?"

"They don't say it out loud, but yeah. They love their one surviving granddad. I treat 'em like I treated all you young head-kickers, only more."

That brought a quick smile to his face.

"So why come out of hiding now?" I asked.

"Why?" He was shocked. "To see you, of course, you idiot. To catch up, check you're alright. Need some money? Need a backup? Just see my little mate, who's not so little anymore. All that stuff."

"Well, that's genuinely lovely, but I don't need anything, really," I said.

"No, I can see that."

Long pause.

"I also wanted to catch up," he said. "Say hello and give you a hug before things get interesting."

"Before what?" I asked.

"You know what," said Rusty.

"I can't talk you out of doing something stupid."

"What was that saying your Nan used?" he said, smiling at me again.

"Let me guess which one," I laughed. "Old enough to know better, too stupid to stop?"

"That's the one," said Rusty. "Great lady. your Nan."

"She was."

Another pause. Rusty drank his tea. I finished my coffee.

"So, this Carruthers bloke," said Rusty. "He wasn't the one who murdered my daughter?"

"No," I said. "Pretty sure it wasn't Ken Carruthers. He was just the cleaner, so to speak."

"But he handled her body after she died?" he asked.

"Yes," I said. There was no way to sugarcoat it, and I was not about to fall back on 'ongoing investigation' style answers. Rusty had filled the role of surrogate father when my own had walked away from the job. I would tell him what I knew.

"Well, keep clear of him if you can," said Rusty. "He's for the high jump, that one."

"Rusty, he's in police custody. He is offering information. I am hoping he leads us to Virginia's body."

That made him angry. He looked away.

"I'm sorry, Rusty, but right now, I need Carruthers alive and talking. Don't do anything stupid, please."

"I won't," he said. "Not yet."

What to say? I could see Rusty killing people and ending up in jail himself.

"So, who killed Junior and Senior," he asked.

I paused.

"Rusty, listen, you might not care about landing yourself in jail, but I do, and I am not the only one."

"Yeah, yeah, I hear ya. But, last time I checked, I'd have to get caught to go to jail. Even if they catch me, they have to prove something."

My old coach was not for turning.

"So, Chrisso, I will ask you again. Who killed Junior and Senior?"

Fuck it.

"Carruthers claims to have evidence it was the brother, Albert Fenwick, Master of Laws. There was some poison thrown in. We are guessing that came from the sister, wife, stepmother, Penelope Anne."

"I always knew they were fucking off the planet, those two," said Rusty. "I picked them as spoilt rich fuck heads, never picked them for batshit crazy murderers."

He stopped. Went back to his thousand-yard stare, then looked at me.

"So one or both of them killed Virginia," he asked.

"Looks that way," I said. Which one did it? I don't know yet."

"What is this evidence Carruthers is touting?"

"He claims to have a diary and some voice recordings."

Giving out this information to a member of the public would get me sacked. If any of the people we were discussing were hurt or injured as a result of this information, I could end up in jail myself.

Rusty knew that. A moment passed.

"A diary?" Rusty was talking to himself.

"Thanks, Chrisso," he said, then stood. Looked at me for a moment. "You've turned out well, mate. Your Nan would be very proud."

"I hope so."

"All class, your Nan."

He reached into his pocket and pulled out an envelope. Gave it to me. It contained photos of Virginia, some with Rusty, some with Tina. They were all in running gear and looked magnificent.

"Virginia is wearing Nike clothes and Adidas runners," I said.

He smiled at the memory. "Always wore the same gear," he said. "Always."

"OK."

I know she went running on the day she disappeared," he said. "She would have been wearing these clothes or something very similar. OK?"

"OK?"

"I want you to have these. Help you identify her when you find her. Take care of them, mate. I want them back. OK?"

"Wait a moment. I don't need to take them," I said. "Modern technology."

I took out my phone, lay the pictures Rusty had given me across the table, and re-photographed each of them individually.

"I wouldn't expect you to follow this process, old timer," I said. "It is very scientific."

"Still a smartarse," said Rusty.

I finished up, replaced the photos in the envelope and handed it back.

"Thanks," he said.

"These will be a big help when I find her," I said.

"I've been waiting so long," he said. "I'd like to have her back, bury her with her mother."

Silence.

"I can wait a bit longer," he said, "just get it done, hey?"

"I will, I promise you," I said.

Why the fuck did I say that? Never make a promise you might not keep. Fucking hell.

Rusty stood up and gave me a sad smile, then a hug.

It was like hugging a slab of concrete.

With that, he was gone. I didn't try to stop him. He walked away, turning down the side street just past the cafe. A minute later, I heard a motorbike take off and disappear out of town.

I had just committed half a dozen sackable offences. Bloody hell.

The things you do for love.

Thursday, July 14, 2022

Home, Jarrajarra.

My alarm went off at 2.30 AM. I rose and quickly dressed in my black long johns, shorts and long-sleeve winter running top, all black. I grabbed a black beanie to go with the ensemble.

"What are you doing?" asked Wendy.

"Striking a blow for the good guys," I said.

She opened one eye.

"All ninja'd up again," she observed. "Oh dear."

She rolled over, heading back to sleep.

"Don't get caught," she whispered.

Was I making too much of a habit of this stuff? Even Wendy was getting casual about it.

Jarrajarra Motel.

The local Motel was an old flat-roof brick thing built alongside the hotel. For paying customers, it was cheaper than the caravan park, and you didn't need a caravan.

As a tourist location, there were better options around. Even a cheap tent in the caravan park would be better, but that was hardly an option for the woman who put a bullet through Jason Mellish's rain.

For Jennifer McLain, it was a short walk to her job at the Jarrajarra Bakery. I knew she used her Harley to get to Wodonga for her bail check-ins at 9:00 AM on Monday, Wednesday and Friday. Apart from those appointments, I had no idea where she went when she took off on her bike. After today, I could track her with the GPS. Hopefully, I wouldn't get caught before the paperwork came through from the DPP.

I had an excellent cloud cover, very little moonlight, and it was now 3:00 AM and pitch dark.

Jen McLain's Harley Fatboy was parked near the rear of the motel, away from the street. I came in over the back fence. The back border of the property was covered with thick, shrubby ti-trees.

I crawled through the ti-tree, keeping in the line from McLain's motorbike to the motel. There was a small light nearby, on the motel wall, but I was crouched in the shadow of the bike and damn near invisible. I had done a lot of sneaky stuff in the army. I loved it, and I was good at it. Much more fun than being shot at.

I placed the GPS tracker among the nuts and bolts that held the rear suspension in place. The flat disc-like GPS just melted into the shape of the machine, hidden behind the very stylish twin exhausts. It stuck in place so well it could have been part of the design.

Within thirty seconds, I was back in the space between the fence and the bush. There, I waited and watched. Fifteen minutes, no sound, no movement. I was good. I slipped back over the fence and disappeared into the darkness. Now, we would wait and see what we would see.

Jarrajarra, Out and About.

By 5:00 AM, Wendy and I were out running. We had reached the river and powered along the riverside trail toward her favourite swimming hole. It was July already, but she was still determined to go in and under the freezing water.

We arrived at the swimming hole, and I was contemplating my frozen, watery doom when my phone vibrated in my pocket.

'Subject in motion.'

5:00 AM, and Jennifer McLain was up and about.

"You coming in?" Asked Wendy.

"I need to watch this," I said. Wendy looked dubious but left me to my illegal observations.

The GPS dot on my mobile screen showed McLain leaving Jarrajarra, heading north for one kilometre, then turning left at the highway, heading toward Wodonga.

I knew she was due at Wodonga Police Station around 9:00 AM, for her bail check-in, but 5:00 AM was far too early for the ninety-minute ride to that appointment.

I watched, transfixed, wondering.

Wendy appeared beside me, fresh from the river. She wrapped her wet arms around me and made me jump.

"Holy shit, you are freezing," I yelped.

"Wussy," she said.

We both watched the screen on my mobile as the GPS dot

progressed toward Wodonga.

"Does this have a history thing?" asked Wendy. "Or will you watch it like this, all day and all night?"

"Good point," I said. I put the phone away, and we headed home. Wherever Jennifer McLain was going, theoretically, I would find her as long as she went there by motorbike.

Jarrajarra Police Station.

"Why didn't someone tell me that murdering bitch was working in the Bakery?" Constable Joyce had just walked into the station with a bag full of jam doughnuts. It was Joycie's go on the goodies and Tim's turn at coffee.

Tim's efforts on the coffee machine usually meant lukewarm rubbish, so the onus was on the person in the 'goodies' column to get it right.

"I don't bloody believe it," said Joyce.

No one had thought to tell Joycie that the Jarrajarra Police Force no longer patronized the Bakery across the road.

It may have been a whole thirty metres further to the Jarrajarra Cafe, but the coffee at the cafe was better, and the jam doughnuts as good, plus the slight matter of not employing a woman who shot people in the back of the head when it suited her.

"Chris," said Barney, a hint of accusation in his voice.

"Sorry, Constable," I offered. Bit lame.

"Well fuck her," said Joyce, "I turned around and went to the cafe."

"Language, please," said Barney.

"Here we go," said Tim, walking in with a tray holding four large cups of frothless cappuccino.

"Doughnuts look good," said Barney.

"You two Wodonga interlopers, take a look at this," I said, waving them around the counter to look at the screen on Barney's computer.

What they saw was a Google location image. The location in question was where Jennifer McLain had stopped first on her journey to Wodonga earlier this morning.

Barney and I knew that, but we weren't telling Constables Tim or Joyce. No need to bring them in on my legally questionable ninja stuff.

McLain had gone to the new shopping strip I had up on screen. She stayed there for less than thirty seconds and then headed back out of town to a roadside cafe where she waited over three hours. From there, Wodonga local Police Station at 9:00 AM.

The shops on the screen were empty. I can't imagine McLain making a nighttime dash to an empty shop. What was she doing?

The date on the Google image showed January 2020. Google street views were often a few years behind. Hard to imagine, but it appeared Wodonga was not at the forefront of Google map development.

"Do either of you know if these shops are now occupied?" I asked.

"Yeah," said Tim, "The one on the left is a new cafe, and the two on the right are the offices of the new Solicitor in town. Whats-his-name?"

"Lachie Holmes," said Joyce, "seems a nice bloke. Got a girlfriend, unfortunately. My luck."

"Yeah," said Tim, "he's alright, for a lawyer."

"Thanks," said Barney.

"What's it about?" asked Tim.

"Personal matter," said Barney.

"What?" said Tim.

"He means mind your business," said Joycie, clearing the mist as she often did for our Tim.

Tuesday, July 19, 2022

Jarrajarra Police Station.

"Well, gentleman, it seems Mr Carruthers has his deal." Sergeant Pete had the floor. Actually, it was a computer screen. We were back on Zoom. This was the modern police force. We all looked at each other on computer screens and talked about stuff.

"Thank heavens for that," said Sarge. "It is driving everyone crazy having him in the cells here. He truly is an awful human being."

Sarge was sharing a chat window with his second-in-charge, Sergeant Will Walker.

"You know, Sarge," I said, "you don't have to share an office with Sergeant Walker to do a chat session. It's a marvel of modern science. You can do this from the comfort of your own desk. You could even have your own little window on the screen and not need to bump heads."

I knew damn well why Sarge was doing it from Will's office.

"This blessed technology business is alright for you young blokes," said Sarge. "I can never get it to work. Can't be bothered." Sarge was an unabashed technophobe.

"We're a team here at Wodonga," said Will. "We love sharing." Will was smiling. In the last few months, he had acquired a sense of humour. It suited him.

"If you yokels can concentrate on the task at hand," said Detective Pete, "there will be two officers from the AFP arriving at Wodonga Thursday morning to take Kenny into witness protection."

In Australia, witness protection was handled by the Australian Federal Police. They took care of the whole show. We would get him when we needed him for court appearances and interviews.

Kenny Carruthers was about to start down a road leading to a new identity, a new location, and many other things he'd done well enough by himself for a long time until he was arrested.

All he had to do now was hand over his evidence and tell the truth. It was that or jail.

"OK," said Will Walker.

"What I would like to do, starting this afternoon till the AFP takes Kenny offline, is give him and his lawyer their good news and have a face-to-face with our boy. Collect his evidence and get Kenny's statement locked down and signed."

"OK," said Will Walker.

"So, we do that at Wodonga," said Pete. "If that's alright with you blokes?"

"Fine, fine," said Will.

"Absolutely," said Sarge.

"Now he has his deal." Said Sarge. "I assume Chris can join the party. Yes?"

"Absolutely, yes," said Pete.

So it was on. Kenny Carruthers had a deal.

The slimy weasel.

Interview Room, Wodonga Police Station.

"What the fuck is he doing here?" said Kenny Carruthers, not a happy home invader.

We were back in the Wodonga Station's interview room, but I was present in the flesh this time, not hiding in a Zoom chat window. I would even be allowed to speak if I felt the need.

Kenny wasn't pleased at all.

"Constable Taylor has, very generously, agreed to drop the home invasion charges, Kenny," said Detective Pete. "I'd be polite if I were you. It is up to me to determine the officers in the room, not you."

"You can always pull out of the deal, Ken," said Sergeant Will Walker. "Your choice."

"We have no objections to Constable Taylor's presence," said Lachie Holmes, Carruthers solicitor, deftly putting that little outburst to rest.

"Alright, Kenny, let's get started," said Pete

Pete started the recorder and quickly waffled through all the welcome-to-interview stuff the law required.

Then, we kicked off the 'discovery' with the diary.

Lachie Holmes handed over an old leather-bound notebook.

"The key page is marked with a yellow tag," said Lachie. "on that page, you will find Penelope Fenwick discussing the murder of Phillip Savage by her brother, Albert Fenwick.

Pete took the diary, and then he and Will leaned in to read the relevant page. I just looked at Carruthers, who did everything he could not to look back at me.

Eventually, Pete and Will finished reading and handed the diary to me.

"Can you bag this, please, Constable," he asked.

I took the diary. I didn't have time to read it now. I noted it was white leather, about six inches tall by four inches wide, 150 by 100 if you work in centimetres. On the cover was the year '2010' in gold italic letters. It had a little leather strap about two inches long. The strap was permanently attached to the back cover. It folded over and joined to the front cover via press stud. I hadn't seen a diary like this in a long time. It looked lovely and expensive, but who wrote by hand anymore.

"Well," said Pete, talking to the Solicitor. "I think we can use that. Let's have a listen to your other offerings."

Lachie Holmes reached into his briefcase and came out with a USB data drive. It was barely an inch long. These things were getting smaller by the minute.

"There are several audio files on this stick," said Lachie. "The first set of files are all prefixed by the year 2002. The second set is prefixed by 2010."

"Right-eo," said Pete.

Will Walker took possession of the USB drive and plugged it into his laptop.

"The first set," said Lachie, "the 2002 files, these relate to the disappearance of Virginia Collins. The 2010 files relate to the missing Savages."

I looked at him. The gossip was right. Lachie Holmes was a fair sort of bloke. I like that he referred to Ginny by her chosen name and not the married name of the family that had brought her so much unhappiness and then death.

I also liked that he'd avoided words like 'disposal' where he could.

His eyes flicked at me, and he caught me staring. I returned to my designated role of staring death daggers at Kenny Carruthers.

"Ready," said Will Walker, and we all settled in to listen as Will hit play.

The first audio file in the 2002 set was a phone call.

"Mister Carruthers."

"Miss Fenwick, what a pleasant surprise."

Pause.

"What can I do for you, Miss Fenwick?"

"My brother is at our old house in Toorak. I think you know the location."

"Yes, Miss, I do."

"He would like to meet you there as soon as you are able. He has some rubbish he needs to dispose of. I am cleaning the place out, you understand."

"Yes, Miss Fenwick, I understand."

"Good, and don't let him quibble on price. He always does. I find it tiresome."

Then Miss Penelope Anne Fenwick ended the call.

No one in the room spoke. Pete was staring at the desk in front of him, listening. Will was looking at his computer, listening. I kept staring at Carruthers, who kept his eyes firmly downward dog.

The second audio was another phone call. Short.

"Mr Fenwick."

"Kenneth, old boy, how are you?"

"Good. I understand you need a removal."

"Yes, yes. You spoke to Penelope Anne, I assume. She told you where?"

"Yes, Sir."

"Good, good, I am standing outside of the location right now, old chap. Supervising, so to speak, though at this stage, I have no one to supervise. My managerial skills are totally wasted."

"I will be there in thirty minutes."

"Wonderful, wonderful. I look forward to your arrival."

Call ended.

Albert James Fenwick, Master of Laws, was 'outside the location' as he spoke.

I had to think.

What was the state of mobile phones back in 2002? I remembered several people back at Rusty's gym sported those massive brick-like things. Not the digital marvels of today, but you could take a call anwhere you had coverage.

That was in the nineties. So 2002? Fenwick would have been on a mobile. Carruthers could have been taping the calls from his office phone.

What would a jury of reasonable people make of all this?

I was certain there'd be no trouble convincing a jury who we were listening to. Pomposity and entitlement have a certain tone.

I was also sure a jury would believe that whatever happened inside the 'location', someone had made a mess, and Carruthers' job was to clean it up.

So what had happened?

Audio number three of the 2002 set.

> *"You're not doing anything stupid like wearing a recording device, are you old chap?"*
>
> *"And if I was?"*
>
> *"Then I'd have to shoot you and add your corpse to the dead pile inside."*
>
> *"I don't need to tell you I am perfectly expert at using this."*
>
> *A gun, most likely.*
>
> *"I am not wearing a wire. Search me if you want."*
>
> *A pause.*
>
> *"I guess if you find a wire and shoot me, you'd still have a couple of bodies to get rid of."*
>
> *"I certainly would."*
>
> *"And if you shoot me, I suppose I won't be getting paid for any of this."*
>
> *"True enough. No, indeed, I would NOT be paying you. I think we could consider your death a termination of your employment. But, believe me, I'd miss you, Kenneth. You and your Inspector Hughes are entertaining characters, I must say. But you're not cheap, are you? And at your prices, I am sure there would be others*

willing and able."

Another pause.

"Well, are you going to search me or not?"

"Oh my god, no, couldn't bear it, old boy. Touching, touching. Oh no. Just show me something or other. Anything to make me believe you. Give me a look at your belly. There you go."

More rustling sounds. Clothing?

"Good, good, wonderful. You are in fine fettle, old chap. My word, I wouldn't like to wrestle with you. I've never seen so many bulging abdominals in one space. My, my. Do a spin for me. Hoik your back bits, will you? Good, good."

Another pause.

"Done?"

"Yes, yes, let's get on with it then."

What to make of that? Definitely, Albert James was doing most of the talking. Not a voice you forget. Showing awareness of guilt? Maybe? Didn't want to be recorded, pulled a pistol on our Ken and admitted to paying Carruthers and his Inspector for previous undisclosed services.

Guilty of some fucking thing.

Pete put a hand on Will's arm to stop playing for a moment.

"How did you convince him you weren't wired?" Pete asked Ken.

"He was looking for wires and secret microphones," said Kenny. "I had a simple little recorder. A dictation thing. Tiny, powerful little fucker tucked in my pocket. Set it to record. Worked like a charm. He had a mobile size of a house brick, plus I knew he wouldn't want to get close enough to physically search me. Too polite, old Albert James. Too far up his own arse."

"What if he had searched you and found the phone in your pocket?" asked Will.

"Well, I had me gun in me other pocket," said Kenny. "I wasn't too worried about him.

We moved on.

Audio number four of the 2002 set.

"Here she is then. Dear departed Virginia, nicely packaged, as you can see. My dear sister would be delighted with her lack of spillage. Not a skerrick of blood anywhere. Not outside the tarpaulin, at least."

Detective Pete raised a hand. "Stop there. Play that from the start again. Could you please, thanks, Will."

I knew what Pete was listening for. The key sentence.

"My dear sister would be delighted with her lack of spillage."

Whose lack of spillage? Who was the 'Her'? Was it the perpetrator? Penelope? Or was Albert James referring to the victim? Virginia, whose blood did not spill because the poor woman was dead and wrapped up in some form of drip-proof shroud.

I was getting angry. Needed to focus on the job at hand.

Pete raised an eyebrow in my direction.

I think he was telepathing at me, "Stay calm."

I was good for the moment, at least.

"Let it roll," said Pete to Will.

We listened from the start again. There was nothing there to prove Penelope Anne was the killer, but what followed clearly indicated a murder had occurred.

"Do you mind if I look inside the tarp?"

"My God. Not here, old chap. Carpets, remember. Take her away to your secret hiding place. Make sure she is placed where she will never be found. Between then and your exit from here, do your damnedest with her. Fuck her lights out if that floats your boat. Though we've already put her lights out, so to speak, haven't we?"

Laughter.

"Just want to know who I'm burying on your behalf."

"Not my behalf, old boy. My sister's behalf, her house, her mess. Leave her to rot right there for all I care. But, I suppose that could prove rather incriminating in the longer term, what?"

Pause.

"I think dear Virginia has caused enough trouble for my family. I, for one, will be glad to have her gone for good as soon as possible. Thank you very much."

"What's that thing?"

"The bulge? Some tin or other. Full of photographs and a book belonging to Virginia, of no value to anyone. Let's just call them supplements for the afterlife, shall we? Very ancient Egyptian, don't you think? Pictures to ponder as she floats down the Styx. Isn't that what they did back then? Package up the corpse with something to play with for the remainder of infinity. Very thoughtful. Penelope's idea, not mine, but, you know, time is of the essence, Mr Carruthers. Time is of the essence."

"I'll need my trolley."

"Yes, yes, very clever idea. Looks heavy all wrapped up like that."

"I think we will take a break at this point," said Pete.

"Interview terminated," he said, then ended with all the end-of-interview blah-de-blahs.

We left Kenny and his solicitor in the interview room with a junior constable ready at the door to cater to their needs and make sure Kenny didn't do a runner.

Kitchen, Wodonga Police Station.

Pete, Will and I made our coffees, found some century-old biscuits, and shared our observations.

We were all mostly, on the same page.

"OK," said Pete, "I think we can finally discard any doubt that Virginia is dead."

"No turning up in some backwoods religious cult," agreed Will.

"But we still don't know which one of them actually murdered her," said Pete.

"No," said Will.

"So," I interrupted, "can I ask him about Jennifer McLain?"

"No," said Pete, very emphatic. "I do not want to go there today.

Definitely too soon."

"Let's concentrate on putting the Fenwicks behind bars," said Will, agreeing with Pete, the turncoat.

"Yes," said Pete. "Once Albert and Penny are in the clink for good, we can circle back to the prison-escape-cattle-theft-murders business. Wrap up Kenny and Jenny and dress 'em both in prison stripes."

"But we have the evidence in hand," I said. "We are not compromising the Fenwick case if we connect him to McLain."

"Really?" said Pete. He was not impressed.

"Chris," said Will, "we could probably get there with the evidence. But, ideally, we have Kenny being Kenny up there on the stand, just for us. If he's facing cattle theft and murder as well, why would he bother?"

"You've seen how easily he tells lies, Chris," said Pete.

They were convinced. I could see that. McLain and Carruthers would remain unconnected criminal floaters for a while yet.

"OK," I said, "but remember I told you today, those two are connected somehow. The escape and the cattle theft were three weeks after we discovered the bodies of the Savages. It was a diversion."

"Ok, you told us," said Pete. "But, you tell me, my young apprentice, how is one crime a diversion from another? It is not as though we only ever investigate one crime at a time, or is that how it works up here in the wild green jungles of Ruraltania."

We headed back to the interview room.

Interview Room, Wodonga Police Station.

Pete did the 'start-of-interview-rigmarole" and then we went straight into the audio files. It was the 2010 set this time.

The first two 2010 audios were similar to the 2002. Penelope Anne was not involved this time. The phone calls between Albert and Kenny were definitely incriminating for both of them. Showing intent to clean up a crime-related mess. Duration? Short.

The third tape, referring to the bodies of the Phillips, Junior and Senior, was the strawberry jam of the 2010 set, enough to put them all in jail for murder.

But Kenny had a deal, while Albert and Penelope did not. Not ideal for the Fenwick dynasty.

The voices on the third 2010 audio were of Penelope, Albert and, occasionally, our Ken.

It started with Penelope screaming at her brother.

> *"No! No! No! I don't want anything to do with this. My God, they would have been dead next week. Why the rush, Albert? Why the blessed rush? I've told you before my house is not your playground."*
>
> *"Well, I could hardly invite them on a picnic, given their condition. I had to kill them somewhere. You wanted them dead and gone, Penelope, and now you have it, well dead at least and soon enough gone."*
>
> *"Every time you do something like this, these murders, we end up more indebted to your chosen third parties. I don't enjoy my freedom being dependent on a pair of corrupt policemen. No offence, Mr Carruthers."*
>
> *"None taken, Miss. I'll go and get my trolley."*

That was the end of the third 2010 audio.

Detective Pete waved his finger in a circle to tell Will he should keep the sound files coming.

"Last one," said Will.

File number four of the 2010 set. The only voices were Kenny Carruthers and Albert Fenwick.

> *"How do you want to do this?"*
>
> *"I don't intend to do anything, old chap. That's what you're being paid for, or so I intended."*
>
> *Pause.*
>
> *"I'm going to have to use the sheets and blankets to wrap him. Is that OK?"*
>
> *"Your choice, Kenneth. I dare say my darling sister will not be using them again. I don't believe they have co-bedded for many years."*
>
> *"Right."*
>
> *Some sounds of activity.*
>
> *"Quite the tableau, isn't it? Death really becomes you,*

Phillip, dear man."

"Lot of blood."

"Yes, blood indeed. Apart from grizzling like a baby, he actually tried to parry my first strike. Did not go quietly into the sweet beyond, as it were. I felt the need to strike him again, a punitive blow, if you will. Quite hard."

"Looks like it."

"Very decorative."

Pete raised his hand. "That will do, thanks, Will. We've heard enough."

We all took a breath. Pete was the boss, so he spoke first, and he spoke for all of us on our side of the table.

"My goodness," Pete was speaking to Carruthers. "All that while you were a serving police officer. Ken Carruthers, you are an absolute disgrace."

Pete took a long pause and then officially ended the interview.

"Mister Holmes," said Pete after the recording had ceased, "I'd suggest you help your client get his written statement up to scratch. We get that sorted tomorrow, have a bit more chat, and then we can all sign off on the deal, and you, Kenny, old boy, you can toddle off to your lovely safe house with your federal minders."

We left Lachie and Ken in the interview room with the young cop outside the door. They'd work for a bit, and then Kenny would be off back to his cell for another evening.

"Let's get out of here, lads," said Pete. "I fancy a pizza. My shout."

"Sounds wonderful, old chap." Will Walker with an exaggerated impersonation of Albert James Fenwick.

"What a fucking murderous, pretentious ponce," said Pete. "I am gonna love shoving his disgusting arse in the back seat of the divvy."

"Alert the media?" I asked.

"Smartarse," said Pete. "I'll tell you when," he added as an afterthought.

While the crew went ahead to the pizza parlour, I used my mobile to photograph the 'guilty' pages from Penelope Anne Fenwick's diary.

I texted those pages to Barney. I didn't want to leave the best detective in Jarrajarra out of the loop.

I had a quick read on my way to dinner.

At first glance, Penelope Anne had plenty to say about everything. She had filled the entire diary with tiny cursive script. Every page was chocka block.

The pages in question were dated January 4, 2010.

Well, Albert came over, as he said he would. I am truly tired of dealing with my younger brother. Sadly, he is the one man in my life not so easily disposed of. He is my only remaining blood family. How appalling.

My idiot younger brother is now more certain of himself in all his endeavours than ever, the very same boy that father proclaimed should have been strangled at birth. But blood and water, I can't help loving him. There it is. It disgusts me, he disgusts me, but it is so.

It was 3:00 AM when Albert finally arrived, in all his pomp, his intention clear from the moment he walked in the door. Mallet in hand.

I had to ask him why that thing had not been disposed of after its previous use. He replied that he rather liked it. It was a memento for him. A trophy, if you please.

He paraded up the stairs, holding the mallet poised on his shoulder like a woodsman with an axe, heading to a forest to commit a day of honest toil. My God, he would die if ever required to perform a minute of manual labour.

He stopped halfway up the stairs and leered back toward me.

"Let's put an end to all this bellyaching, shall we," he said.

Then he just stared at me for a long moment in time. Then asked If I hadn't enjoyed his little joke.

I had no idea what he was talking about.

He explained his joke to me. Bellyaching? Thallium? Bellyache? Don't you get it?

"Bellyache from the poison, dearest," he had said. Oh my God.

Well, yes, I suppose I got the joke once he'd explained. Even then, I didn't think it was funny. And what did

Father say about the need to explain one's humour?

Then, Albert actually asked me if I wanted to come with him. One can only describe his manner as sarcastic.

I said nothing, and eventually, he resumed climbing the stairs.

He did say something I found meaningful. 'Leave it to me, Penelope. I shall surely enjoy their release almost as much as you enjoy your consequential freedom.'

And off he went to the task at hand.

Whilst I didn't want to watch the carnage, I did go to the foot of the stairs where I could listen.

I could hear Albert's voice so clearly. He was always loud, whatever the occasion.

He attended to my stepson first. I could hear a mumbled exchange. Poor, pathetic Junior was much too sick to say anything of interest. I believe I heard him beg.

Eventually, I heard the tell-tale whack of the mallet, after which Albert emerged from Junior's room, heading to Senior.

The mallet was back on his shoulder, so cometh the axeman. Mallet-man, in this case, and he was whistling. Whistling? It occurred to me then my younger brother was a psychopath. A murderous psychopath.

He entered Senior's room, and I heard Albert's voice clearly. "Now then, Phillip, old boy, sorry to keep you waiting," or words to that effect. Oh my goodness, the casual, unnecessary cruelty.

'Just do it,' I thought. Why do men talk such rubbish at each other in moments of conflict?

God only knows what Phillip replied. He mumbled something, I am sure. I could have told him to save his breath. When Albert was in a mood, he never listened. Not ever.

I heard a thump, followed by a frail, pathetic scream from Phillip. This was followed by a second decisive whack of the mallet. It sounded surprisingly crisp. I imagined I might have heard a squelching sound, but no.

Eventually, Albert emerged from Phillip's room.

Marched down the stairs, stood before me with his mallet shouldered, and said words I shan't forget.

"Call Carruthers. Tell him two this time."

Bloody Hell. What a pair of psychopaths.

All I could think of was my long-lost friend, poor, sad Virginia. Married for money and landed in this circle of psychopaths.

Wodongo Bongo Pizza, Wodonga.

The pizzas were great. Even better, Sarge had joined us.

I loved watching the uneasy tension between Sarge and Pete. Big city glamour boy versus the best country cop that ever was. I could be biased.

"I think Chris is right," said Sarge.

"Not saying he isn't," said Pete. "Kenny and Jenny, even the names rhyme."

"Chris, I suspect you are right," said Will Walker, never afraid to speak his mind. "There has to be a connection, so let's keep looking, but we have to concentrate on getting these murderous scum Fenwicks where they belong, and then we do McLain and Carruthers for the cattle."

"Personally, I think it's a bit of a stretch," said Pete. "Find dead bodies down a hole, then suddenly go cattle rustling and murdering for fun and profit."

"Not for profit, for diversion. Maybe?" I ventured. Even I wasn't so convinced about diversion as a motive.

"How is it diversion, Chris?" said Pete. "Look at us. We have them all lined up. McLain is going down. The Fenwicks are off to the hospital ward in the big house. Some fucking diversion."

"OK, not a diversion, maybe quick cash for a getaway, maybe a cover-up, maybe insurance."

"What? Your Pendergasts were in on it for the insurance money?"

"No," I said. "I'm sure the insurance money was welcome. But Ben and Irma Pendergast were lucky they didn't die."

"Maybe they were meant to," said Sarge.

Why kill Ben and Irma Pendergast? Holy shit, a vague memory flickered past.

I called Barney.

I put him on speaker. We were in a booth at the back, safe to talk. I gave Barney a quick brief. He had an audience of more than just me.

"Barn, how did you go with the Carruthers and the Orphans people?" I asked.

"It is the Foster Care Association, to be correct," said Barney.

"That's the one," I said. I really had no clue.

"They were happy to confirm Carruthers was one of theirs," he said. "Not so keen on confirming who he was fostered out to."

"Barney, I remember I saw some Foster Care award at the Pendergast Farm." It was when I was pumping up their cattle insurance claim. No need to say that out loud now, in the present company. "Is there any chance at all Ken Carruthers was fostered down here, and Irma might know something?"

Barney had a long think.

"Oh, Chris," said Barney. "We are such idiots. The Pendergasts were heavily involved in Foster Care for a long time. In fact, I think Irma might have been President of the regional Foster Care Association a while back. I think they gave it up when they scaled back. Age-related, most likely."

"Barn, mate, could you call them? Run the name Ken Carruthers by them."

"I'll do better than that," he said. "I'll get Irma to call you. You know what she's like. It will all be in her head, and she will have photos."

"Run it by her first. If she has a photo, just ask her to send that."

We ended the call. Ate pizza and waited on the results of the Barney and Irma discussions.

"He does a lot for an admin," remarked Pete.

"Best cop in Jarrajarra," I said and I meant it. "Just doesn't like confrontation."

"Could have fooled me," said Pete.

Pizza was good. Portions were huge and stacked. We'd ordered enough for the whole station, then polished off the lot.

Eventually, my phone pinged.

I had a message from Irma Pendergast. It was a photograph. With text as follows.

Kenny, summer of 1984, 12 years old, a lovely boy.

> *A little bit wild. He loved the dirt bike. Used to sneak off to roam the area when our back was turned. We didn't see much harm in it. He used to follow Ben around like a puppy.*

I expanded the image to full screen and showed the others. A photo of a photo. Framed. Our Ken. Tanned, healthy, almost shining, so young but unmistakably Ken Carruthers. A foster care kid with a trail bike living less than three kilometres from Mellish Paddock.

I called Barney.

"Barn, Carruthers is connected to McLain somehow. Get Tim or Joyce out to the Pendergast farm. Immediately. Let them know Ben and Irma are in danger. Keep a watch for McLain."

I ended the call.

"Good thinking, son," said Sarge.

Maybe a bit dramatic, but better safe than sorry.

Dirk Gently would be so pleased. The whole crime was connected. Coming together.

Synchronicity. But Synchronicity was Carl Jung, not Dirk Gently.

Never mind, I had my connection.

Wednesday, July 20, 2022

Wodonga Police Station.

"I'll be glad to be rid of this bloke," said Sergeant Will Walker. We were standing in the kitchen having a quick coffee and brief before the interview.

It was Ken Carruthers' last day as a guest of Wodonga Police. Everyone in the station was sick to death of him.

"Will, mate," said Sergeant Pete, "You will look back on this and realize this is a career highlight. You've solved a twenty-year cold case and put away the two richest psychopaths in the country's criminal history. Kenny Carruthers is your ticket to glory."

"Yes, well, I think the price is too high to ride that train, and Chris solved this by the way, certainly not me and not much help from you, to be honest."

Oh, Will, he was truly getting more like Sarge every day. I just soaked up the praise, trying to look humble. I always did a lovely humble. Not sure Pete was so keen on Will's summary.

"He is poison," Will continued. "I don't believe he will ever live up to his end of the bargain. I don't think he knows how."

"He fucking will," said Pete. "He will get his arse on that witness stand, and he will bury the Fenwicks, or, I swear to you, Sergeant, I will bury him myself."

"I will help you dig if it comes to that," said Will. "But let's assume we get him there. You get a bloke like Carruthers into court. First, the defence will make a meal of him. He is worse than a jail-house snitch. He was part of the crime now he's a turncoat, a dobber. Juries hate tattletales, especially with something to gain."

"OK," said Pete, listening.

"Second, they will tear the clemency deal apart. Make him look like the sleaze bag he is. Trying to unload his own guilt onto others. Thirdly, personally, he is just repulsive. The jury will hate him, and I am worried they might even sympathise with the Fenwicks."

"Will," said Pete, "no one will sympathise with the Fenwicks, not after they hear the audio, they just won't. Trust me."

They were not quite in agreement, but getting there.

I noticed a young policewoman walking toward us, smiling at Pete.

"Here, she is," said Pete. Both Pete and Will greeted the young woman approaching. Beaming smiles all around.

"Chris," said Will, "meet Constable Evelyn Craig, Wodonga's newest Police Prosecutor."

Evelyn was a very neat-looking young lady. Her uniform was perfect. It practically shone. Squared-away was the military term.

"Hi Chris, Call me Evie."

I said, "Hello, Evie," and we all marched off to meet Ken Carruthers.

Interview Room, Wodonga Police Station.

"Gentleman, Evelyn," said Lachie Holmes.

"Lachie," Evie answered. They obviously knew each other.

"Here is the documentation you asked for," said Lachie, placing several documents in front of Pete's chair before we'd even sat down.

"Firstly, a police statement stating Mr Carruthers' version of events. Signed."

The police statement ran to quite a few pages. Lachie Holmes had done some serious work. I can't imagine Kenny could fill a single page without help.

"Also," continued Lachie, "a signed acknowledgment that my client understands he may be subpoenaed to appear in court on any matters contained within the statement at police discretion. And should he be required to appear, he commits to do so."

I hadn't heard of that particular piece of paper, but yes, why not? He was super efficient, this young lawyer.

"Finally, a document detailing our understanding of our agreement. In particular, a list of what you gentlemen have offered regarding the immediate housing of my client and his obligations to be met before his release from custody, and of course, police obligations regarding his health and safety."

"You know we can't sign health and safety agreements for the Federal Police," said Pete. "They're the ones handling his protection."

"Yes, we know that, Detective Senior Sergeant, but we're not there yet, are we? Who knows what could happen before the AFP gets here."

Did Lachie look at me when he said that? He did the cheeky

bugger. I liked him more every minute.

Lachie handed over copies to Evie and Will. No papers for me and no reason was given. I assumed I was still on Kenny's shit list.

Everyone had a quick read. I could have read over Will's shoulder, but I sat back and stared the bad vibes at our boy. Ken was a bit more confident today and stared right back.

Eventually, it was all read and digested. We were ready to talk.

"Alright then, Kenny," said Pete, "the young lady in attendance today is Police Prosecutor Constable Evelyn Craig. Today, I want to give you a taste of the questions you will face once we present your evidence to court. We want to see how you hold up. OK with you?"

"Fine by me," said Kenny.

I noticed Pete had said nothing about putting Police signatures on any documents yet.

"Mr Holmes, you good with this?" asked Pete.

"Happy to try, Detective," said Lachie, "Though we do have plenty of time to rehearse if we don't nail it today."

"Absolutely," said Pete. Very animated about it all. "OK, Evie, over to you."

"So, Mr Carruthers," said Evie. "You're what they call a snitch?"

"I'm no snitch," said Ken.

"What would you call yourself then? A fink? A dobber? A dog?"

"Get fucked, you bitch," said Kenny.

This was going well. We were off to a flyer.

"Oh, none of those then," continued Evie, totally undeterred. "So you're just a poor guy who acted in a conspiracy with others to murder three people, one of them a beautiful young mother in the prime of her life, in exchange for money. So what does that make you? A murderer-for-hire? A contract killer? Who got caught and now makes a deal with the police to save his own sorry skin and bury his co-conspirators just like he buried his victims. Is that better?"

She said all that without a breath or a break.

"I didn't kill anyone, you dumb cow, get that through your fucked head," said Kenny to Evie. "Do I have to listen to this bullshit?"

"I think so," I added. Not sure who Kenny was asking. No harm in venturing my opinion.

"Fuck you, you king-hit merchant," said Ken, quite angry now. "You'll get what's coming, and that bitch of yours."

“Whoa,” said Pete, probably aimed at me. But I wasn’t getting angry at this scum, not here.

“I understand you’ve met Constable Taylor before,” said Evie. “He arrested you, didn’t he? Naked and asleep in his bedroom? Quite the effort since you had a gun and he didn’t. Put you in hospital, I am told?”

“I thought all that home invasion bullshit was off the table?” Kenny was asking Pete.

“Tell me, Mr Carruthers, how was it you came to leave the police force. Forced to resign, is that the term?”

“Fuck off, fuck this shit,” poor Kenny had wilted, like a shrivelled flower, in barely two minutes.

“OK, that will do,” said Pete. “I think you’ve got some work to do, Kenny, old son.”

Pete was disappointed, and Will Walker’s body language screamed, ‘I told you so’.

I loved it. How good was it having a serious prosecutor on our team?

Pete took the last of the documents prepared by Lachie Holmes and handed it back to him.

“We won’t be signing this one, Counsellor. Safety in police custody is a human right. But it doesn’t come with a written, money-back guarantee. Who's to say your boy won’t hang himself in his cell, what with all the guilt he must be carrying.”

No one laughed at the joke.

“I will sign the handover to the AFP,” said Pete. “You can go with them today, Ken.”

“And the other documents?” asked Lachie Holmes.

“I want to have a meeting end of next week. Kenny, you need to have another interview with our police prosecutor. You are going to have to do way better than you managed today. Do that, and you get our signatures on your get-out-of-jail card. Plus, I want a map with a big fat ‘X’ showing me where I can find the body of Mrs Virginia Savage.”

There were grumbles from the other side. We had Kenny’s evidence. The DPP had agreed to the deal, but no one promised that our Ken would be any good in court. He’d been a shit cop, now he was a shit witness.

I knew Pete would sign eventually, but he'd take his time to keep Carruthers in line.

The interview was terminated. We left the room.

Said my goodbyes and headed to my truck to drive home to Jarrajarra.

With an ounce of luck, I thought, I might never have to lay eyes on Ken Carruthers for a long while.

Will Walker followed me to the car park to say goodbye.

"Chris," he said as I set to leave, "I am starting to worry. I don't think we will ever get that bloke into a courtroom."

Wise man, Will.

Friday, July 22, 2022

Jarrajarra Police Station.

Penelope Anne and her brother, Albert James, were arrested first thing Friday morning.

I had an invitation from Detective Sergeant Pete Jordan, my self-appointed mentor in the art of homicide investigation, to go to Melbourne and join the circus.

"Be in for the kill," Pete had said.

I certainly had a right to be there. But I couldn't face the hours of driving just to stand in the glow of Pete's lust for the limelight. Instead, I stayed home in Jarrajarra and watched the whole shebang on Barney's computer from the front desk of the station. There was plenty to see.

Angela Adams, live on Channel 7 breakfast news, crossing with a news bloke called Roger.

> *"Hello, Roger. Yes, we are here, live in Melbourne as prominent legal identity, billionaire, and philanthropist Albert James Fenwick is being taken into custody by Victoria police for alleged involvement in a triple murder.*
>
> *Dramatic scenes here in the city and in Toorak as both Mr Fenwick's home and his inner-city office are raided by police.*
>
> *We understand from police sources that Mr Fenwick is being arrested on charges relating to the disappearance of Mrs Virginia Savage, nee Collins, twenty years ago, and the subsequent disappearance of her ex-husband, Phillip Savage Junior, and her former father-in-law, Phillip Savage Senior.*
>
> *Three murders and two bodies.*
>
> *The bodies of the two men were discovered recently, approximately two months ago. Virginia Collins remains missing, but police now, sadly, presume she is dead.*
>
> *You can see behind me absolute chaos as police lead Mr Fenwick, who is in handcuffs, down the stairs from his truly magnificent office here in the heart of Melbourne.*

Mr Fenwick is being led to the police divvy van by Detective Senior Sergeant Pete Jordan through a melee of cameras, reporters and curious onlookers.

This is bigger than the football, Roger, and there is a lot more to come. Today, here on Channel 7. Stay tuned."

"I can't believe you knocked back the chance to be there," said Constable Tim.

Barney, Tim and Joycey were seated beside me at the front desk, watching the live news on Barney's laptop.

"Chris is too busy," said Barney.

"Here you go," he added, breaking a small batch of yellow post-it notes into two. "One for you," he said, passing one bunch of messages to Joycey, "and one for you." He passed the second crop to Tim.

"Off you go," I added in motivation. "The criminal heart of Jarrajarra awaits your interventions."

"Yeah, while you two sit here and watch TV all day," Tim felt aggrieved.

"Timothy, honestly, sometimes," said Barney. "You know how busy I am with admin, and you can see Chris is still recuperating from being invaded. Now scoot before I re-consider school crossing patrol."

They left without any further audible grumbles. Perhaps a slouch of the shoulders.

"School crossing patrol?" I asked once they'd left.

Barney waited till he heard their cars leave the car park, then took a paper bag from his desk.

"These were the last two in the cafe," he said. "They are too perfect to pass over and not enough to share."

He placed a paper plate with two magnificent apricot slices from the cafe over the road. Absolutely perfect. Real, fresh apricots, stewed and squeezed between perfect layers of soft pastry, topped by a thick bed of sugar.

"Oh, Barn."

"You need your little comforts while you're getting better," he said.

I took a bite, and, yes, I felt better already.

"Perks of high office," I said, feeling a shred of guilt at not sharing with Tim and Joyce.

"I've ordered four for tomorrow," said Barney. "You can pay then, so you don't feel so guilty now."

We ate our slices and argued over whose turn to make the coffee.

"I'm feeling tired from my invasion," I said, and Barney surrendered to guilt.

We waited by the laptop for the next instalment of 'The Fenwicks go to jail'.

An hour later, the studio frontman, Roger, crossed to our on-site reporter, Angela Adams. We were back for more.

Angela was standing outside a Toorak mansion. Last time I'd seen this place, I was up close and hiding behind a hedge.

> *"I am outside the well-known Toorak home of leading Melbourne socialite and a former board member of some of Victoria's most important Children's Charities, Miss Penelope Anne Fenwick.*
>
> *I tell you, Roger, the drama, in this case, is never-ending.*
>
> *I understand that police arrived fifteen minutes ago to arrest Miss Fenwick on the same charges applied to her brother Albert earlier this morning.*
>
> *It appears the ninety-year-old Miss Fenwick collapsed before she could be escorted from her home. An ambulance has been called. We can hear it approaching now from the city end of Saint Georges Road, one of the most prestigious addresses in Victoria, if not the whole country.*
>
> *We have just been told Miss Fenwick is under arrest. She is conscious and aware of the charges laid against her.*
>
> *It is not yet certain where she will be taken next. It may be to a cell, or it may well be a secure hospital ward nearby.*
>
> *You can see the ambulance arriving now. It is waiting for these huge, secure gates to open.*
>
> *Hard to tell how long the next stage will take.*
>
> *Rest assured, the Fenwicks will have the best representation money can buy. It is hard to imagine these*

people spending any time behind bars. But, this case has a way about it. It twists and turns in directions you can never anticipate.

Strange days indeed. Back to you, Roger."

"My goodness," said Barney, "an ambulance."

"Faking it, I reckon."

"Chris, you are such a cynic."

"You read the diary page?" I asked.

"I did," said Barney. "It left me in no doubt about the type of person she is."

"No, it did not."

"It also raised a question," he said.

"Where is the diary for 2002," I finished his sentence.

"And who killed Virginia?"

"And where is her body?"

"Oh, Chris," said Barney, "it is all so terribly sad. I have to remind myself she was a friend of yours. A real person."

Virginia 'Ginny' Collins, friend, mother, and one-time Muay Thai buddy. As real as a person can be.

"You know Barn," I said, "my Nan always told me every life is a story. Beginning, middle and end. You just never know which part hurts the most."

Virginia's end had hurt a lot of people, some of whom were more than capable of murder. This was not a new thought.

My cop conscience got the better of me.

I called Detective Pete.

"Mate," he answered, "Let me guess, you are jealous of all the attention I'm getting."

"No," I said.

"You're jealous," he continued as though I hadn't spoken. "You're only human."

"I think Penelope Anne could be in real danger, right now," I said. "I hope you're keeping her hospital location secret."

"Bit late for that, mate. There is a media throng outside the Alfred right now. We are heading to a secured private room. I've got cops on the door there. We're tight as a drum, mate."

"How many of your blokes guarding her?" I asked.

"Two. Chris, she's 90 years old, mate. She's not getting out."

"Pete, it's who gets in that worries me. If Rusty Collins has been watching your head on TV, he will have her down for the murder of his daughter. If he decides he can't wait to say hello, two cops won't stop him."

"Chris, mate, I value your concern, I really do, but your bloke Rusty must be in his seventies. Bloody Hell. How much of a threat can he possibly be?"

I didn't want to mention I had spoken to Rusty in person just over a week ago. Truth was, Rusty looked more threatening than ever. And angry.

"Pete, if you lose one of your accused, after all the publicity you've had over the last few weeks, you will look a total dickhead. They will write songs about it."

He thought for a minute.

"If you're so concerned, you should join my guy in the security ward. Double the guard, and it might be good for us to have you there."

"Good?"

"Yeah. Good. The collapse is totally fake. Penelope Anne is fine. Talks to anyone who'll listen. She will love you, won't have any trouble getting her to talk. But, yes, I had to put her in the hospital. As you infer with your totally unwarranted criticism of your superior officer, I must be careful about the optics."

Optics? He said optics. Dear God in heaven.

"Three things," I said.

"They are?"

"One. If you need to remind someone you are their superior, you're probably not."

"Yeah?" he said. "And two?"

"Two. Anyone who uses the word 'optics' is most likely a wanker."

I paused for effect.

"And three?" he asked.

"I'm on my way."

Security Ward, Alfred Hospital, Melbourne.

“Another young policeman, my Goodness. I hope you are more communicative than that other fellow. Can barely get a grunt out of him.”

Penelope Anne Fenwick was sitting up in her hospital bed, giving me the once-over. The other cop she referred to was a Constable from the St Kilda Station named Fred. Not a hard name to remember, but Penny Anne hadn’t bothered.

Penny Anne was in a talkative mood, flirty in fact.

“I’ll do my best not to grunt, Miss Fenwick.”

“Oh, for heaven’s sake, call me Penny, and I know who you are.”

“You do?”

“You are Constable Chris Taylor.”

“That’s me,” I said. “Guilty, your honour.”

“So, tell me, Chris, I don’t fully understand the terms of my incarceration. I am new to all this nonsense. Would it be totally un-prison-like to request a cup of tea? Pretty please.”

“I will see what I can do, Miss?” I smiled, totally fake.

“Penny,” she emphasized again.

I moved the young cop from outside the wardroom to sit inside while I went to find the kitchen.

“Weak black, no sugar, extra hot, thanks, Chris,” she said through the closing door. “Tea bag is acceptable.”

I was sure there would be nothing but tea bags in a city hospital kitchen. Penny had a few lifestyle skills to acquire if we managed a conviction.

* * *

“Chris Taylor, I’ve been reading about you online.” Pete was right. Penny loved to talk.

“You’re a user of the internet, Penny?”

“Oh, yes, very much so. As you might imagine, I took a keen interest in the young officer who rescued the bodies of my late husband and stepson.”

“We were a bit late for a ‘rescue’, Penny. More like we fell down a hole and accidentally landed on top of them.”

She laughed, “Yes, what was it? ‘Ducks 4 – Humans 0’. I do love your little newspaper. Jarrajarra Bugle, what a hoot. And what a wonderful idea for a magazine. Totally on the web. No paper, no printing costs. Young people today are so clever. I might invest in their company once all this nonsense is sorted. Do you know the proprietor?"

"Yes, I do, as a matter of fact, Saxon Tyson-Howard. But his assistant, Joanne Farrell, is the brains of the outfit."

The discovery of the dead bodies had clearly not upset her. Not in the slightest. She took a careful sip at her tea. She wanted it hot, so I'd boiled the kettle twice.

I read her face as she took her first sip.

"Yum," she said, and she meant it.

I'd nailed the teabag mission.

"Lovely tea, thank you, Christopher. Perfect."

More sips of tea, a moment's diversion.

She was thinking. She had something to say, maybe wondering how far she could go.

Direct eye contact. Something special.

"Tell me, how on earth did you capture Mr Carruthers?"

"You didn't see the news?"

"I want to hear your side of it."

"OK, finding him? I never did. He found me. I suspect he came to shoot me, get rid of me, shut down the trail. Unfortunately for Kenny, my girlfriend broke my old guitar over his head. Sent him to sleep, almost permanent."

"Good for her, and what a pity she didn't hit him harder. I suspect I'd be at home now. Enjoying a brewed tea. If she'd only hit him that little bit extra. Caved his head in, perhaps."

Penny Anne smiled. Took another sip of the tea.

"How did you know about Mr Carruthers? That's what I am most curious about? I always thought he was Albert's secret weapon."

She was so casual, looking at the cup in her hands. Quite a good interrogator.

Why not? What harm could it do to tell?

I could just deny it later.

"About five weeks ago, I was out running in Melbourne. I do a lot of running, keeping fit. I ran past Virginia's old house. Nothing to see there. Then I ran to your place, the mansion."

"You liked my home?"

"Liked? No. Impressed? Yes. Great building. Beautiful gardens. Just not my idea of a home."

She thought for a moment.

"And you jumped the fence, and you hid over there under the pine hedge, listened to Albert and me, out near the garage, with his revolting cigar, discussing Mr Carruthers?"

I shrugged my shoulders and paused for a beat.

"Yep."

"Oh my God, We heard an alarm. The next day, I found your footprints under the hedge. That was you?"

"Yep. That was me," I said. "Guilty again, your honour."

Penny looked at me for a moment. Then she laughed so hard she had to put her cup of tea on the drawers beside her bed.

"Oh, my goodness, how incredibly bold," she kept laughing. Snorting.

"Loose lips," I said.

"Sink ships," she answered and kept laughing for another minute.

"I don't recall saying anything very incriminating."

"You mentioned his name, Carruthers," I said. "I took it from there, looked him up on the web. He had worked on the original investigation into Virginia's disappearance. Most people thought he was just not very good as a cop, never realized he was on the take."

"On the take? Goodness, we are sharing police lingo now. I love it. What else do you fellows say to each other when you're alone in your stations."

"Want another cup of tea?" I asked.

She laughed, thought it was a joke, then realized it wasn't.

"Oh, could you, please. That would be so lovely."

I went through the chair swap with Fred at the door. Wanted him 'in-the-room'. Didn't want Penny Anne topping herself on my watch, though it did not seem likely.

"Hotter this time, thank you, dear," she added as I went to make more beverages.

This round, I found sweet biscuits, Scotch fingers, no less. I stole two from the pack. Just for my new best friend, Penny.

* * *

"Biscuits. Oh lovely, dear boy, you wouldn't consider a position on my security team? Would you? Once we get this all tucked away. You are such fun, Christopher."

"Got a job, thanks, Penny. Happy with it."

"And a girlfriend up there in Jabberwocky?"

"Yes."

"You are very dogged, aren't you? A persistent policeman. All the way from Woop Woop to Melbourne, jumping fences into Toorak mansions. No legal standing, I assume. Just you and the need to know, yes?"

"Pretty much."

"Our very own Inspector Javert."

"Javert is not my cup of tea. I go more for Dirk Gently."

"Oh. My. God. A Douglas Adams fan? And a Plod? I can't believe it. Impossible."

"I am not Sherlock Holmes," I said in my best North American accent. "I refuse to eliminate the impossible?"

She laughed. She knew the reference. She really was a Gently fan.

"But why this case?" she asked. "Why this sordid little tale, why these people, and why my brother the psychopath?"

"Well," I said slowly, staring at her. "I hate to dampen our fun, but even though I was very young, even though she was fifteen years older than me, Virginia Collins was a close friend of mine. I intend to convict her killer and find her body, and you are right. I am very dogged."

It was as if I'd struck her. A punch to the gut.

I really had put a downer on the tea and biscuits.

Saturday, July 23, 2022

Security Ward, Alfred Hospital, Melbourne.

Pete assigned a few extra officers to protect Penelope Anne while she was in hospital. The new roster included four constables, two of them female, so someone would be with Penny the whole time. There would be no deaths in this custody.

I moved out of Penny's room for the night, and I was back in there after breakfast. I had slept. I had run around the Tan in South Yarra. I was feeling good.

Penny would not be so happy. Second day in police custody for one of the richest women in the country. Front page of every newspaper, lead item on every TV news bulletin, for murder. That had to hurt.

I bought a cup of tea for Penny, just the way she liked it.

"Thank you," she said.

"My pleasure," all very formal, me.

"You must hate me," she said.

"You are not number one on my hit parade, Penny. That's a fact."

"I didn't like Virginia, it's true," she said. "Then again, I didn't like my stepson much either. In fact, it would be more honest to say by the time Virginia was on the scene, I loathed both Phillips, junior and senior. Your friend, Virginia, was just a part of that horrible mix of money grubbers as far as I was concerned. Just another financial leech."

Don't hold back, Penelope.

"Virginia didn't want your money, Penny," I said. "I doubt she could even imagine or need the sort of wealth you've enjoyed."

That earnt a look of reproach, but no stopping now. Might as well poke the bear while I had the chance.

"Virginia married for security," I continued. "She was raised by a single mum in poverty. Didn't know her father till her teens. She wanted children, and she married someone she thought would have sufficient means to raise them right."

"She should have looked elsewhere," said Penny. Angry.

"Yes, dead right," I said. "Virginia wanted someone safe, and look where she landed."

"She should have done some research," said Penny. "She should have looked past young Phillip's nice car. She married a man who couldn't protect himself, let alone a family. Never had a job of his own, nor a penny of his own to scratch himself with."

Phillip Junior broke? No money? That was not the legend we had all believed.

"You couldn't possibly understand Virginia's concept of financial security," I said.

I was really pissed off now and curious. This was more an argument than an interrogation.

"Phillip had a good job," I said. "Who cares if he worked for his father? And between them, Virginia and Phil Junior, owned their own house. That was true wealth in Virginia's mind, not the sort of pampered existence you've endured."

I wasn't sure why I said 'owned'. I knew Virginia and Junior had been gifted their home. I sensed that level of gift, the transfer of so much dollar value, had irritated Penelope. I wanted to rub it in. It was worth a jab in a joust.

I watched her closely.

My little outburst hit a nerve. Penelope did a flick of the eyes. Toward me for just an instant, then away from me. She even did a sort of gentle shoulder roll, looking for a more comfortable position, getting ready to deliver something. But what?

"Phillip Junior," she said. "Own a house? You have to be joking."

Did Virginia and Phillip own the house on St Georges Road?

Virginia thought they did.

So, who owned the house? Dirk Gently would have called that a clue.

I might have lost Penelope's goodwill, but maybe I'd learnt something. Mights and maybes.

Penelope's eyes returned to mine. Maybe we were still talking.

"I generally don't like the police," she said. "I thought, for a moment, you might be different."

"So you don't like the police. Who do you like, Penny?" I asked as gently as I could manage.

She took a long think-break. Maybe wondering if she was still talking to me.

Turns out she was.

"I had a daughter I loved very much, and she loved me. Make no mistake about that."

"Irene?" I said.

"Yes, you have done your homework."

"A thalidomide baby. Died in hospital," I said,

For a moment, I saw a softening of her face. Hadn't seen that before in our short acquaintance.

"Yes," she whispered. "Over sixty years ago."

She stopped and seemed to disappear into her own thoughts again.

"My Nan had lost two of her children along the way," I said. "My mum and a daughter who only lived a week, my aunty, I guess."

"Oh," said Penny, suddenly out of her reverie and staring at me.

"Nan told me 'Every life is a story. It has a beginning, a middle, and an end.' They all leave a trace."

"Some stories don't get enough time," said Penny.

"Nan believed we're only here for a blip. Up against infinity, even the longest human life is barely more significant than the shortest."

"Did she believe in heaven?"

"Well, according to my Nan and Einstein, if you believe in infinity, then you have to believe in every possibility that could ever exist. That's the definition of infinity. So yeah, with infinite options, she settled for heaven."

"I am hoping for heaven," she said.

"To see your daughter again?"

"Yes."

"Is that why you started all those charities?" I asked.

"Hah," she almost snorted. "Pay my way into heaven, you think?"

"Maybe."

"No, it didn't work like that, not in my mind."

She took a long moment before she spoke.

"I truly wanted to help. Very few people saw the beauty and the intelligence in those damaged children. Irene was such a wonderful girl. Smart, resilient, and so clever. My husband and stepson never saw that, but then I met other mothers of children just like Irene, with different disabilities, perhaps, but just as beautiful. And the mothers were people I could talk to. They understood. This was before the internet, before computers, really. There were no online friendship groups and no forums."

"Just people," I said.

"Yes, people who needed help, and I used my money to get that help and, you might say, purchase their friendship. Their admiration. It was comforting. I did that for a long time. Then I stopped."

"Why?" I asked.

"Why indeed?" She said. "You get old. You outlive the few genuine friends you made. The inspiration to help others evaporates. All that's left is the pain and the memory."

She had a moment to think.

"I was tired, I suppose," she added.

Penelope Anne's eyes travelled with her mind. They wandered about as we spoke, from full eye contact to faraway horizons. She didn't move her body or her hands much at all.

If she was lying, I couldn't pick it.

She looked at me again.

"So you are well acquainted with Virginia's father?" she asked.

"Yes, I trained with him in Muay Thai from age seven until I was old enough to join the army."

"I would imagine he does not look kindly at me."

"You're equal first on his shit list, I'd reckon."

She laughed.

"More police jargon, is it? Shit list? Oh my."

"Are you still in touch with him?" She asked

"Yes," I said. "Indirectly, but yes, I can get him a message."

"Tell him, please, I did not murder his daughter. I didn't ask for it, I never wanted it, and I never approved of it. I have never murdered anyone in my life, nor would I consider it."

I believed her.

Barney was right. Again. Penny Anne Fenwick, the rich bitch from Toorak, was not a murderer, just a grieving mother.

"If your friend, Mister Collins, is set on murdering me to revenge his daughter, tell him to go right ahead. I would welcome it."

"I would do it myself," she added, "except suicides don't go to heaven."

We sat in silence. Eventually, I had to ask.

"So, who did kill Virginia?"

She looked at me a long time.

"You want me to, what is the word, be a snitch? Like Mr

Carruthers? Tell you all I know for a better arrangement? For myself? The devil take the rest? Are you the good cop, Constable Taylor, sent to soothe me before I have to deal with that ridiculous Detective Sergeant Jordan?"

"Penny, you are in a hospital bed, recuperating from a collapse. I haven't made you aware of your rights. I have no recording devices operating. There is nothing you can say to me now that a judge would accept as evidence in court."

"So you say, but then you are not obligated to tell me the truth, are you?"

"No, I'm not. It is up to you to decide if I am."

She paused again for a long time. Looked away to some distant memory.

"I'm tired," she said. "I think I will take a nap."

She turned, closed her eyes, and turned her head. It was as subtle a 'Fuck-off' as I had been delivered.

"Penny," I said. "I hope I never have to go through the death of a child. I can only imagine how painful it must be. At least you know how she died and where. You know where she is buried, and if you want to visit her grave, you can."

I was getting no response from Penelope Anne.

"I would guess you even have photos of her somewhere," I said. "You can see her as she was when she was still with you."

Still nothing.

"My friend Rusty has none of that. Virginia is lost to him forever. He doesn't know who killed her, where she died, where she is buried. He doesn't even have his photos of her."

Her eyes remained closed, but she could hear me.

In for a penny, in for a pound.

"You talked about meeting Irene in heaven. If you want to get there, maybe do the right thing while you still can."

She was listening.

"I need to know who killed Virginia, and I need to know where her body is buried."

I left it there, then swapped myself out with one of the other officers. I moved so quietly I doubt she heard me go.

Penny Anne Fenwick, what a joy-killer. The morning that had started so well was now depressing. I badly needed more coffee and exercise.

I was in Melbourne. I had my truck. I knew just the place.

Police car park, Alfred Hospital, Melbourne.

"Mate, of course, I can get you in the gym. I own the fucking joint. If I can't get you in, nobody can."

I had called Richard Martin, once a budding Muay Thai fighter, now a middle-aged suburban lawyer with a rugged suburban clientele. I was in the small area in the hospital car park set aside for emergency vehicles.

"How did you end up owning the place," I asked.

"I bought it when Rusty wanted to disappear," he said. "He needed money. He didn't need a gym, so we did a deal. Now, I own it, and Tina runs it. I get my kicks for free. If he ever wants it back, he can have it."

I shook my head and smiled in admiration. He was incredible.

"You can still send Rusty messages? Yeah?"

"Of course, What's the message, Constable Closeau?"

"Penny Anne Fenwick did not murder Virginia."

That stopped the banter for a moment.

"So, who did?" he asked.

"Meet me at the gym in thirty minutes, and we can discuss it while I humiliate you in the ring."

He didn't bite.

"Not Penny? Bloody Hell, Chrisso. First, I thought it was Junior, then when he and his old man vanished, I assumed it was the mother-in-law-from-hell."

"It wasn't her."

"Well, Chrisso, the only one left is that disgusting prick, Albert James, Master of Lunches, or maybe one of those crooked cops on Albert's behalf."

I had no intention of discussing it further on the phone.

"Rick, old mate, I need a workout."

"See you in thirty minutes," he said. "If we are going to do a few rounds, try and stay conscious till I've finished my questions."

"You just remember to send my message," I said. "See you in thirty."

I ended the call.

Hopefully, Rusty would now be warned before murdering the wrong person. Or, maybe he would just murder the lot of them. Who knew?

Rusty's Gym, Reservoir, Victoria, Australia.

"Bloody hell," I said. "I must be ten years old, maximum."

Richard and I were looking at your bog-standard gym photos on the wall. There I was, in a fighting stance with a medal of some sort, miles too big, hanging around my neck.

"Most determined," said Rick, reading the caption under the photograph. "Must be some sort of mix-up. I'd have had you down as 'Least likely'."

Richard Martin's first rule of fight gym, talk shit to show someone how much you love them.

"Before we spar, let's go into the office," he said. "Run you through my files and theories."

"You keep your files in the gym office?"

"No," he said. "Holy hell, the modern policeman, what hope do we have. I have thirty years of files digitized and indexed to the cloud, Constable Closeau. The cloud, the computer cloud, not the fluffy one in the sky. You've heard of it? Of course not. And before you ask, the paper stuff is in permanent storage."

So we sat down and went to the 'Cloud'.

"This is all cone-of-silence, right?" I asked.

"Give me a dollar," he said. "Make it official."

I reached out and pushed forward my empty hand.

"Oh God," he said. "Nothing changes."

He took a little cash book from the desk drawer and wrote me a receipt for one dollar. Dated and signed. He then took a dollar from his pocket and, rather dramatically, threw it in a cash tin in his drawer. Did an eye-roll of fake exasperation.

"You are now my client. Our conversation is now privileged, so fire away," he said as he handed me a copy of the receipt.

"I think Albert did it," I said. "Murdered all three."

"Do you want me to pass that on to Rusty?" He asked.

"No. Not yet. Just tell him Penny didn't do it. OK?"

"Already done that."

We sat in silence for a moment.

"I should have known Phil Junior wasn't up for it," said Rick.

"Yes," I said. "So, your next candidate was Penny. She told me she didn't do it, and I believe her."

"OK, that leaves this ex-cop Carruthers or Albert, Master of what-the-fuck."

"Carruthers is just the cleaner," I said.

"Which only leaves Albert and the big question, Chrisso," he paused for effect. "Why?"

"I think it has something to do with Virginia's house," I said.

"The house? The mansion, you mean," said Rick. "Ginny was planning to sell it, take her share. I was her anointed lawyer and was about to start up her legal work when she disappeared."

"Yes, you were," I said. "and maybe Albert wasn't so happy with either of you."

"Fuck-me-hooray," said Rick. "Bit of a stretch, mate. Kills half his family over a land deal?"

I shrugged. "Sex, money, or houses?" I said. "Maybe Uncle Albert doesn't like sharing."

"I don't think Albert is capable of sex. He's got a gut the size of a baby elephant and can barely move out of a chair," said Rick. "And the Fenwick's have so much money, plus the house wasn't his. It doesn't make sense."

"Everything makes sense to a psychopath," I said.

We both had a think for a bit.

"Did Albert ever show any anger to Virginia while you were there, in meetings?" I asked.

"Bloody hell, mate," said Rick. "Such a long time ago. The two Phillips, Junior and Senior, always had their undies in a twist with Ginny. From memory, she did antagonize Albert in the last meeting. She didn't understand how someone so involved could represent her husband. Told him to his face. I just assumed old-school Albert didn't like being spoken to by a modern woman. I recall he did get ridiculously angry for a so-called objective representative."

"Maybe," I said, "you were getting too pushy on the property sale."

"Hang on a minute," said Rick.

Rick powered up the computer on the gym desk.

"LANDATA," he said. "Solicitor types like me, good citizens, we can track who owns what, which you normally do when selling property or borrowing against it."

He mumbled the names of the two St George's Road properties as he typed. Virginia's former house and Penny's.

"You always speak out loud the words you type?" I observed.

"I usually pay someone to type it while I say it," he said. "Since you probably can't spell, I will have to do this lot myself. Big words, Chrisso. I know you'd struggle."

"How long does it take to get this LANDATA?"

"For a yobbo like you, couple of weeks, for an important man such as myself," he said, "bingo, got it already."

He turned the computer screen sideways so we could both see it.

"Albert, Albert, Albert. Holy fuck," said Rick. "The Master of Laws is the only name on the official titles for both properties. He's owned them since nineteen-bloody-ninety. Holy shit."

"He swindled his own sister," I was incredulous.

"Today's prices," said Rick, "that's fifty, sixty million dollars. Holy-snapping-arseholes."

He played with the computer some more.

"Virginia had copies of all the property documents for her own place," said Rick. "She gave copies to me and to the real estate agent. Everything got pushed to the side when she disappeared. The actual sale never happened. It never really got started."

"The money you dragged out of Albert in 2010 for Virginia's children, that was purely a settlement?"

"Exactly," said Rick. "Just cash to go away, which we took and went." He was still focused on his computer.

He searched through folders and files and quickly found what he was looking for.

"There you go, mate," he said. "One forged property title and one original."

Rick had put two documents side by side on the computer screen. They both purported to be the title of the home Virginia shared with Phillip Junior.

"Wow," said Rick, "Virginia, the estate agent, and yours truly. We all thought the Toorak mansion was half Ginny's. Meanwhile, Penny

Anne thought it was all Penny's. Back in the real world, the great man, the Master of Breaking the Law, owned it all."

"Murderer plus forger," I said.

"It's more than that," said Rick. "This is stuff that gets you disbarred in about two minutes flat. Disbarred forever. Add fear of exposure to your list of motives. Whenever someone wants to sell these Fenwick houses, they threaten to expose old Albert's forgeries. Bloody hell."

"Albert doesn't like the idea of being disbarred and disgraced," I said.

"Virginia wants a divorce and a property settlement," said Rick, "so she disappears before Albert's fraud is exposed. With Virginia gone, no need to sell, no need for the paper work."

"Everyone assumes it was Junior," I said.

"A convenient patsy," said Rick.

"Eight years after all that kerfuffle, Phil Junior is restless," I said. "The kids are off his hands, living with Virginia's mum. Junior has no ties. He wants his big dollar share of a Fenwick property."

"So, around we go again," said Rick. "Jesus. I suppose old Albert reckons you're killing one Phil Savage might as well kill 'em all. Three murders over forged paperwork and a few million bucks. And everyone blames Rusty for the disappearance-presumed death of the Savages. I guess it makes some weird sense."

"Rusty becomes another convenient patsy," I said. "Dear old uncle Albert. Patsies everywhere. He probably topped JFK."

"He's thought this through," said Rick. "Three deaths, no bodies and always someone else to blame. Cunning as a shithouse rat."

The same description I'd heard for Ken Carruthers.

"Add a couple of paid-up crooked cops to help paint the required picture," I added.

The front doorbell dinged, and in walked my other Muay Thai buddy, Tina Harris.

"You two finished yet?" she asked.

"Done our best," said Rick. They kissed.

"Hang on, are you two together?" I asked. "Like as in 'lovey-dovey-together'?

"Nothing gets past you, Poirot," answered Rick.

Tina hugged me, smiled, kissed me on the cheek and said, "Hello, gorgeous."

I felt welcome.

"Enough smooching. Time for some serious sparring," she said, looking at me. "Gloves and shinnies on the back wall for you out-of-towners."

And so, in the middle of an investigation, we changed into our Muay Thai gear and turned back the years.

We sparred happily, trash-talking, punching and kicking for the next two hours. About seventy per cent power, nothing too lethal if you knew what you were doing. Three-minute rounds, one person rotates in, and another rotates out. We kept at it until we were all too stuffed to take another turn. The last few rounds were more slap and giggle than serious training.

Exhausted. We lay flat on our backs in the centre of the ring.

"Well, that's one way to maintain a relationship," I said.

"Works for us," said Tina.

Rick was gazing at the ceiling. Running the case in his head.

"I think that's your best answer, Chrisso," said Rick. "Albert James, the often-irritated, money-obsessed, swindling psychopath. Holy mother of God, he played us all."

"He lost to you in 2010."

"Well, it felt like a win at the time," said Rick. "But it wasn't, was it? He'd already stolen millions of dollars with his gold-plated pen."

We all thought about that for a bit.

"How did Albert ever think he would get away with it?" I asked.

"How does anyone get away with any swindle?" said Rick. Talking slow, exhausted from the sparring. "Create a story and tell it the way you want it told."

"A story?"

"Like defending someone in court, Chrisso, especially when they're guilty. It's not just the story, mate, but how you tell it and the bits you chose to push."

"Spin?" I said.

"Exactly," said Rick Martin, old mate, great bloke, defender of the wicked.

The three of us were all laying flat on the canvas near the middle of the ring.

I had another thought.

"Rick, mate, do you have a printer here?"

"I do."

"Awesome," I said. "Can you print me those titles please?"

"Yeah, why?"

"It's what we in the policing forces call evidence, mate. As a defence lawyer I doubt you'd understand."

"Evidence," he mumbled. "Remarkable."

Sunday, July 24, 2022

Security Ward, Alfred Hospital, Melbourne.

Morning. Run, push-ups, shower, then back to the hospital with the usual cup of tea for Penelope Anne.

One more try.

I had no intention of telling her about the full extent of Albert's financial trickery. Not straight off the bat, at least.

I didn't really care about who owned her various houses. I wanted to catch Virginia's killer and find her body.

"Thank you for the tea," she said as I placed it on the table beside her bed.

She took the cup and sipped at the tea. There was a flicker of satisfaction. I'd got it right.

She looked across at me.

"Albert murdered Virginia," she said. "Though I am sure you've already worked that out."

"Yes," I said, "I thought as much, but thank you for confirming it.

We both took a moment to sip our tea. This triple-boiled water on the extra-strong teabags was addictive.

"Why do you think Albert did that?" I asked.

"Because of the house."

"Virginia and Phillip Junior's house?"

"Yes and No."

"Can you explain?" I asked.

"Yes," she said, "I am talking about the house Phillip Junior and Virginia shared during their marriage."

"OK," I said.

"But, you must understand, it was never theirs. It was mine. Phillip Senior had insisted that we gift it to them for their wedding. According to my husband, we should then buy a better house more suited to our rank in society. A place that he would half own. Oh, my Lord, he was so transparent. He would transition from a mere doctor to a millionaire overnight. His son would own half of my family home, and he would own half of something new. Millions of dollars to his family benefit, taken directly out of my pocket."

"An argument over a house?"

"Yes. Phillip Junior and Virginia were about to be divorced. Virginia wanted her share of their mutual assets. That included the house they lived in. She wanted to sell it, of course. It wasn't theirs to sell. It was mine."

"The transfer of the old house and the purchase of the new house never happened?"

"No," said Penny Anne. "Going back to the wedding, when Phillip Senior insisted on gifting my home to his son and new daughter-in-law, he was like a broken record. He became a nagging, greedy child. Night and day, I was so depressed I told Albert to do something. So, in typical slap-dash fashion, my brother faked the transfer to the children. Then, purchased the new home in my name, thank you very much."

"How did Albert explain these fake dealings to the Savages?" I asked.

"He didn't really. It was more 'show-don't-tell'. He told me later he forged the transfer documents for the original house and the purchase documents for my new house. Then got them all to sign meaningless bits of paper. I presume the newlyweds were happy. They thought they'd received a house for free. My husband was happy because he was suddenly wealthy. I was happy because I still owned everything."

"The Savages and Virginia didn't own a thing," I said.

"Correct. They owned nothing. Knew nothing," said Penny Anne. "As their lawyer, Albert kept control of all the original documents. He just showed them the forgeries. My husband, my stepson, and my daughter-in-law all believed the property transfers and the purchase of the new property had happened according to their wishes."

"He showed them these?" I said.

I took out copies of the fake property titles Richard Martin had printed for me last night.

She carefully put down her tea and then took the titles.

The top page was the fake title to Virginia's place, showing Virginia and Junior as the owners. Their names were highlighted in yellow.

The second page was the forgery for Penny's castle. Showing Penny and Phil Senior as joint owners.

"Yes, yes," she said as she read. "I don't usually deal with paperwork, but I presume these are the forgeries."

"They look authentic," I said.

"My husband and stepson were handsome men, but they were both weak and stupid. They would never have the sense to see through Albert's bluster."

"But it all came unstuck when Virginia wanted to sell the house?"

"Yes, unstuck indeed. There were several meetings during the months following the separation. According to Albert, Phillip Junior was pathetic in every meeting. A snivelling little toad. Pathetic. Not much of a man."

"Seems to be a general opinion," I said. Keep talking, I thought.

"At their last meeting," she continued, "Virginia and her Solicitor, this Martin fellow, met with Phillip Junior and Albert at Albert's offices. Virginia insisted they sell the house as part of her settlement. She had already been speaking to a real estate agent. For Heaven's sake. Planning to sell a house that wasn't theirs."

"So, pushing to sell the house. That was Virginia's death warrant?" I said.

"Yes. Virginia was dead and gone within the week. Phillip stayed in the house with the children. According to Virginia's current will, written by Albert, at the time of the wedding, everything she owned went to her children. Sadly for the children, she didn't own as much as she thought."

"Albert wasn't trying to protect Phillip Junior?"

"Oh," she laughed. "Heavens no. As if Albert would do anything in concert with the Savages, he hated them. Never wanted me to marry Phillip Senior."

"But you did?"

"I did. More fool me. One year's love and a lifetime of regret."

Silence. I let it hang, hoping she would continue.

"Anyway, Virginia insisted the house was theirs to sell. Phillip Junior didn't care. He'd never paid a penny for anything in his life. Phillip Senior certainly didn't care. He thought half the sale would go to his son, the fruition of his unholy swindle. Against me, his wife."

"But Phillip Senior wasn't as clever as he thought?"

"No," she said.

"And neither of the newlyweds were as wealthy as they imagined."

"No, not by a fraction."

"When did you know about this."

"About the fake property deals, I knew in advance. I wanted Albert to make my husband stop nagging me. I didn't care how."

"And Virginia's murder?"

"Not in advance. My goodness, no. But, of course, Albert was so arrogant, so proud of what he'd done. He could keep the secret from the world well enough, but he felt so clever he simply had to tell me. Called me to come over. Have a look at what he'd done."

"You saw Virginia's body before Ken Carruthers took her away?"

"Yes, she was wrapped in a tarpaulin at that stage. I could still see her face. Despite all the damage, I concede my former daughter-in-law was a beautiful young woman."

"So why did Albert kill the Savages?"

"Questions, questions, don't you get tired of being a policeman? Your nose in everyone else's business."

"Dirk Gently, Penelope, the whole crime or nothing at all."

"Well," she smiled, "Dirk and Douglas Adams would have loved this." She was stifling a laugh. Ironic, considering we were discussing three murders at the hands of her brother, the serial killer.

"Virginia's children, the oldest fifteen years old or thereabouts, took it upon themselves to go and live with Virginia's mother. Good riddance, I thought, not my family, not my blood. This leaves Phillip Junior alone in the big house. He decides it might be a good time to sell the house he thinks he owns and retire to the country."

"Oh," I said.

"Oh, indeed. Retire? At his young age, on my money. Naturally, Junior visits his Solicitor to discuss his plans, as any vendor would. Unfortunately for Phillip Junior, his solicitor is my dear brother."

"Sadly, for both Savages, Albert arrives at the same conclusion he achieved the last time someone wanted to sell the house. Time for the trusty mallet. If you're going to kill one Phillip Savage, why not kill them all."

That was almost, to the word, what Richard Martin had said.

Two for the price of one.

"OK, so why the Thallium?"

"Good question, Constable Taylor."

She closed her eyes. She was getting tired of the discussion. I had worn out the welcome of the few cups of tea I'd made for her. I was losing her, and she had well and truly lost me.

"It was meant to be a salute to me," she said. "A toast to my particular sadness. My brother, in all his wisdom, believed that Phillip had unintentionally poisoned me and my child with Thalidomide, so it was only right that he should suffer the same fate."

"So he fed him Thallium?"

"Yes, with champagne to celebrate the upcoming sale of the house, as both Phillips believed."

"But Thallium is not Thalidomide," I said.

"No," she laughed out loud this time. "Nothing like it. I know that, so do you, apparently. Try telling that to my brother, the lawyer and self-appointed chemical genius. Laughable."

"And he didn't get the dosages correct?"

"No, not even close, leaving me to nurse the pair of them till he finally decided to end their misery. And mine. Fortunately for me, they were both so incapacitated they weren't that difficult to contain."

"I guess not."

"Then, of course, the wonderful Mr Carruthers was employed, yet again, to clean up another Albert-created disaster."

"So Virginia, your husband and stepson, all dead for a house?"

"Yes, I suppose they are."

My disgust must have been obvious.

"Oh, Constable Taylor, you can canonize your sweet Virginia Collins as much you like. She and my husband were of the same ilk, greedy. Married for money, not love. They compounded their sins by poking a stick at a psychopath."

I couldn't think of anything to say.

"Look," she said, "I am terribly sorry for your loss. I truly am, but I didn't murder anyone."

She wasn't the slightest bit sorry. Her first lie to me. She did a look-away with a turn of the head and a half-close of the eyes. Her first signal of complete dishonesty.

"You know," she said, "If Virginia had asked me, I would have paid her to go away myself. But she didn't."

"But Virginia's solicitor, Rick Martin, kept at you," I said. "You still had to pay out your own grandchildren. That must have hurt."

"Albert refused to pay them out. I told him, 'Your mess, your money'. But he refused. He said the property advantage was mine. I had approved the forgeries, so I had to pay the piper."

"How much did you pay?" I was guessing it was more than the four million each that Rick Martin received on the kids' behalf.

"Five million," she said. Dramatic pause. "Each."

Oh, Albert. What a guy. No wonder he and Carruthers partnered up.

"In the end, the children took my money and went away," she said. "Never saw themselves as my grandchildren, I suppose. Their father was my stepson, that is all. It all boiled down to the money."

"They were kids, I said. "They'd lost their mother. You were the adult. You could have made any relationship you wanted."

"Why would I do that? They were never blood of mine."

"No," I said. "Obviously not."

A life of wealth and entitlement. Never able to see or feel any side except her own.

"You're judging me, I can tell," she said.

"It doesn't matter what I think, Miss Fenwick. You've still got the courts to worry about."

"But I told you I did not murder anyone."

"I believe you," I said. "I will tell Detective Jordan that, and he will probably believe me. But, he may still pursue other charges."

"What other charges?"

"Accessory to murder. After the fact with Virginia. Plain old Accessory to murder for your husband and stepson. You were there. They were still alive. You could have called the police at any time. You didn't. Any one of those gets you up to twenty-five years."

That set her back in her bed.

"Oh my God," she said. "I am going to end my days in prison. After all I've been through."

Score one for selfish misery, empathy zero. She actually started to weep.

"You'll have company," I said. Bit cruel, I suppose. But I'd had enough of the heartless Fenwicks. And this one wasn't even the murderer.

She was not impressed.

"Don't fool yourself, Constable. You and your detective will never get Albert into prison. He is too clever for your lot."

"You can put him away yourself if you don't trust the police," I said. "You could probably make a deal to escape all charges. If you are brave enough."

"Why on earth would I do that?" She looked at me.

"All of those property titles I gave you are forgeries. Not just the ones Albert gave Virginia."

She looked at the titles in her hand. Didn't get my meaning at first. Not a clue.

"Here are the real titles," I said. "If we can't get Albert for murder, we can sure as hell send him down for this."

I handed her the titles to both the multi-million dollar Toorak mansions. The houses she thought she owned. The property titles with Albert James Fenwick's name in all the relevant places. The real titles.

Albert's name was highlighted in blood red.

"Virginia wasn't the only one, not quite as rich as she believed," I said.

It took Penny Anne a while to work it out.

"Oh my God," she said as it finally dawned. Hand to her mouth. Crying harder. Breathing harder.

Faking? I didn't think so. I hit the button for the nurse and then stood to leave.

"I am sure Detective Jordan will be in touch," I said. "If you don't want to go to prison, you should tell him everything you told me."

Pete would probably go for a deal with Penny Anne in exchange for sending Albert down. He might want to avoid punishing the distinguished-looking old lady, the charity queen. What with the optics.

It was still pre-lunch. If I left now, I could be home in Jarrajarra with Wendy for dinner.

The road home, Melbourne to Jarrajarra.

On the road, I played phone music through the Bluetooth, a mix of John Denver and Jim Croce.

Fuck the Fenwicks and the Savages. Fuck all their money and privilege. Fuck their ridiculous, loveless houses.

We'd solved the murders. Still needed to find a body.

The truck radio played 'Country Road' by John Denver, followed by Jim Croce's 'Operator', which reminded me I had to make some calls.

I called Wendy, no answer.

She'd be on baby delivering duty, most likely.

I called the Sarge. Got him at home on his Sunday off work. Talked him through the whole solution. Sarge said he'd pass it on to Will Walker. Will would be pleased.

Called our glamour boy, Detective Senior Sergeant Peter Jordan. He was going to be a hero. He'd love that.

No answer. Left a message.

"Hi Pete, I'm heading home. I've quit the Penny Anne protection team. No need to worry about Rusty Collins paying her a visit. Penny didn't do any murders. And, she has a ripper deal you might well consider. If not, she's good for accessory-after-the-fact if jailing ninety-year-old ladies floats your boat. Anyway, Albert's our murder guy. Should be easy-peasy from here. Talk tomorrow."

I drove home singing along to John and Jim.

Just had to talk Ken Carruthers through the location of Virginia Collins' body, and this sorry saga would be over.

Famous last words.

Wednesday, July 27, 2022

Jarrajarra Police Station.

Three days at home, total bliss. I was on a frustration destruction mission. Trail running with Wendy every morning.

Mental calm through body exhaustion and a civilized batch of Barney's yellow post-it notes. That was the plan.

Monday at lunchtime, I went to the rifle range with Rob Farrell. We did pistol practice on paper targets. There'd been complaints from neighbours downwind of the range about the constant bangs and dings they could hear when the steel targets were in place. The gun nuts preferred the hit-confirming ding of the steel targets. The feel of the steel was the local jargon, but small-town compromise reigned supreme, and we'd all returned to paper targets for a bit. Some club members had suggested I get to the farm next door, in uniform, and run the new yuppie-owners out of town.

Seemed a bit harsh on the newcomers. We all agreed the previous owner, Bert Ashmead, was a far better option. Bert had gone to God a year back at age ninety-six, near blind and deaf as a post. Bert never complained about the noises from the range. He'd even mowed the club lawns on occasion. Usually, when no one was shooting. Usually, not always.

Whenever Bert mowed the club lawns, I wondered if he was just being a good neighbour or if he'd forgotten he'd sold his north hundred acres to the rifle club.

Hard to tell. Too late to ask.

On Tuesday evening, I went on a bike training session with the new Jarrajarra triathlon team of Jodie on the bike, with Scott, Doc Newton, plus me in the firetruck. The old Doc looked tired by the end of the session. He drifted off and went a bit quiet on the megaphone. No problem. We all swapped seats. I drove. Scotty shouted instructions to Jody from the passenger seat while the old Doc sat quietly on the back bench, ruminating.

All good fun, no harm done, light years away from Melbourne, murderers and blackmailers.

* * *

Wednesday afternoon, sharing a coffee at the front desk with Barney.

"Chris, do me a favour. Please call Detective Jordan in Melbourne."

"Why?"

"You're tapping your foot so hard you'll put a hole in the floor. It is driving me insane. Sorry."

I stopped tapping my foot.

"I called him Monday, and I called him Tuesday. Left messages both times."

"Call him again and leave him a proper message," said Barney. "Say 'fuck' twice if it makes you feel better."

"Can't say that. I promised Wendy I'd stop swearing," I said. "Not suitable for children."

"You've stopped swearing?" asked Barney.

"Yes," I said.

His expression said, 'could have fooled me', but he made no outward sound.

He grabbed my coffee, withholding my caffeine, and nodded toward my phone on the desk.

"OK, OK."

I made the call. Put my phone on speaker so Barney could listen.

"Let me guess your question," answered Detective Pete. "Have we asked Kenny boy where your friend Virginia Collins is buried?"

"Well, have you?"

"Chris, I'll be honest," he said. "Right at this minute, we are focused on getting all our evidence lined up for next week. The Fenwicks and their football team of lawyers want an urgent bail hearing on Monday, and we are all hands on deck getting all our ducks in a row to keep these two fuck-heads in custody."

"So that's a long drawn out, roundabout, hard no."

"Yes, mate, it's a no. We will find Virginia after we use Ken Carruthers to put the Fenwicks in prison for good. He'll have to tell us then, else he won't be going free."

"So Penny is going down as well?" I asked.

"Aiding and abetting," said Pete.

He hadn't even included a sorry in all of that waffle.

"OK," I said. "I guess I will bloody have to bloody wait."

I looked at Barn and got a nod of approval for avoiding the two F-bombs.

"Talk soon," I said and ended the call.

I stewed on all of that for a moment.

"I am really starting to dislike that fellow," said Barney. "He's forever using you for his own benefit."

"It's the police force, Barn. It's hierarchical, and it's collaborative, all at the same time."

"What does that mean?" he asked.

"It means the glory flows up, and the shit flows down. Just like the army, really. Only not so much.

That got a smile.

"Well, I'm not in the police force or the army, so you can be as philosophical as you like about Detective Senior Sergeant 'Where's-the-camera' Jordan. I choose to dislike him."

"I wonder why all the reluctance?" I said.

"What do you mean?"

"After giving up all the stuff on the two Phillip Savages, why do you reckon Carruthers gets all defensive about Virginia?"

"Why is he so coy about two murders but not the third?" said Barney, putting it into the words I was looking for.

"Yeah, exactly," I said.

Barney handed me back my coffee and we had a long collaborative, non-hierarchical think on that one.

"I can only surmise," said Barney, after a minute, "a self-serving, evil swine like Carruthers knows something we don't know. Something darker he wishes to hide. Something that might be exposed by the location of Virginia's body. Perhaps something that our ever-compromising, Peter 'let's-make-a-deal' Jordan could not conceivably excuse."

"Maybe," I said.

"Or, perhaps," added Barney. "Just as likely, there is something so evil it would make a bigger headline than jailing the Fenwicks. That would not be good for Kenny."

"Yeah," I said. "Could be that, possibly. Maybe. Perhaps."

As time would reveal, my admin assistant, Mr Barnaby Trail, had done it again.

Two guesses. Right, both times.

Thursday, July 28, 2022

Home, Jarrajarra.

12:40 AM.

Being home, in my own bed, three nights in a row with Wendy. Heaven.

Sound asleep. My mobile phone rang. Detective Pete.

This could not possibly be good. Nothing good ever came from a phone call after midnight, especially from a man who'd been dodging my calls.

"Our Ken has disappeared from protective custody," said Pete.

"Disappeared?"

"Gone, vanished, escaped, whatever. There one minute, not there the next."

"That went well," I said. Waking up very slowly. "Gotta love the optics."

"For once, can you not be a smartarse?" said Pete, sounding truly shattered.

Silence.

"So what happened?" I asked. Trying to sound a fraction less smartarse-y.

"Kenny told his minders he was heading to the backyard of the safe house for a cigarette," said Pete. "They looked, and there he was smoking. Looked again a minute later, and there he was, gone."

"Just walked out?" I asked.

"He might have had to jump a fence, but yeah, out the door with no farewells. No goodbye from our Kenny.'

"So, who will wear all the humble pie?" I asked.

"To be pedantic, it's the Feds' fault. They run witness protection and relocation." He paused for a moment, maybe for a dose of reality. "But we both know they are just one more anonymous fucking bunch of grey suits. If Kenny stays gone and Albert and Penny walk free, it'll be me looking the dickhead."

"Sounds like our recent escapees up here," I said. "Mellish and McLain and the rest. Let's all meet in the car park and run away together."

"That's what I thought," said Pete. "I was hoping you might have jumped the gun and put a tracker on McLain's vehicle."

"You were going to get me a warrant, as I remember."

"Yes," he said. Long pause. "Still waiting on the DPP for a response on that one."

"It was you," I said, "who told me no one cares about McLain."

"They will if she's with Carruthers," said Pete.

The poor bloke sounded despondent. If and when Kenny's vanishing act hit the media, we would all look like idiots. Pete, most of all.

I put him on speaker, and while we were talking, I opened the GPS tracker app on my phone. Was McLain on the move as well?

She was.

Jennifer McLain had been to Melbourne, the northern suburb of Pascoe Vale, to be precise. She had then waited a while, then turned around and headed back out of Melbourne. It had to be a pick-up.

"Tell me," I said. "Do you know where Carruthers' safe house is located?"

"Not officially, no. Unofficially, I'd say Pascoe Vale. Why?" he asked.

"Just curious," I said, which was not untrue. Strictly speaking.

So, according to the illegally planted GPS, McLain had been near the safe house. After that massive coincidence, she had left Melbourne going east, then northeast. She had already passed Bairnsdale, a good three hours out of Melbourne. She'd stayed on an eastern track for a while and was now heading North to New South Wales.

Looked like she was doing a runner as well.

Travelling fast and most likely not a coincidence at all.

I was watching the GPS tracker on my mobile phone while talking to Pete. The wonders of modern science.

Great stuff if you had a warrant.

"Please tell me you didn't wait for the warrant," said Pete.

"I can't tell you that, sorry." I could but I didn't want to. Once again, the way I said it wasn't really a lie. Close maybe.

"Fuck," he said. More sad than angry.

I had other considerations beyond Detective Pete's sterling media reputation. With Ken Carruthers lost in the wild, I would never find

Virginia Collins' body. And, even more important, there was always the chance he would follow through on his angry threats against Wendy.

After the Jason Mellish-Jennifer McLain fiasco, I didn't want to engage the full Detective Pete machine, Special Ops, drones, and media helicopters. Too many moving parts and too much uncontrolled mayhem.

"I have an extremely strong hunch where to find McLain," I said, "but it will only help you if our Jenny and Kenny are together. I'll check it out."

"OK, mate, OK. Do that," said Pete. "Holy Jesus, escaping custody with Jennifer McLain. Surely, he isn't that stupid."

"He probably is."

"If I were him," said Pete. "I'd be taking the passenger seat on the Harley."

The drone vision of Jennifer McLain sitting on the passenger seat of Justin Mellish's motorbike, taking the pistol out of Mellish's waistband and then, before he could react, blowing a hole through his brain was as vivid in Pete's mind as it was in mine.

"I'll get back to you after I find McLain," I said. Not a lie. Didn't offer a time estimate.

"Thanks, mate," he said.

We ended the call.

Wendy was sitting up beside me in the bed.

"You didn't tell him about your locator thingy," said Wendy.

"No," I said.

"Corporal," she said, "you call Barney and Sarge right now and let them know what's happening, or I will."

"Oh," I said.

"Yes, oh! You're not running around in the middle of the night murdering scumbags like Carruthers on my account. You'll never forgive yourself, plus it's against the law."

"Oh," I said again. I was good at debate, when I'd had a day or two to think about what I wanted to say.

"Oh indeed," said my darling Wendy. "I'll make you a thermos for the trip."

"Good thinking," I offered.

12:55 AM.

I called Barney and Sarge to let them know I was off on another hunt. I would call them back when I had located our targets.

I told Sarge about the illegal GPS tracker. He was personally pleased but not officially impressed. Pragmatic.

"With any luck it might disappear in the process," said Sarge. "Before we get to the fine print." Which was about as off the books as Sarge ever went.

I was going after McLain and Carruthers immediately, I made that clear. No one objected. Sarge was equally happy not to let loose the city-based circus of cops too early in the pursuit.

"Don't want another dead escapee if we can manage it," he said.

Detective Pete might have to wait for an update.

Sarge said he would prepare the troops in anticipation of me finding our absconders. He would also inform Detective Pete once we had a fixed location.

Both Sarge and Barney were adamant if I found our baddies, I should hold back till support arrived.

"Of course, of course," I lied.

Rob Farrell's Garage.

1:15 AM.

"You can borrow the rifle, but I'm coming with it," said Rob Farrell.

Five minutes after I'd called him, he was already dressed in his camo gear, standing beside his truck. Both his truck doors were open, which I took as a second-level hint.

"Sorry, mate," I said. "You can't come on this one."

"Says who?" said Rob. "Anyway, how is 'this one' different from the visit to the Pendergast's farm?" he asked, sounding a bit sarcastic on 'this one'.

"Rob, mate, the visit to Pendergasts was a rescue. This is an arrest, very likely to involve weapons," I said. "I already know McLain is a murderer and pretty sure Carruthers is capable. We shoot at these two, and they will shoot back. Guaranteed."

“Correct me if I’m wrong,” said Rob, “but we didn’t know what was going to happen at the Pendergast place till we got there.”

Which was true.

“You can’t come,” I said. “The higher-ups find out I took a civilian I lose my job.”

“I am not a civilian. I am the head of the local chapter of the State Emergency Service.”

“Since when?”

“Since the other day. Big meeting. Pity you couldn’t be there.”

He was making it up.

I was there to borrow Rob’s Steyr Scout Rifle. Having a loan of the most accurate and reliable rifle in the district was becoming a habit. I really needed to buy my own. Victoria Police weren’t too enthusiastic about purchasing fully-fledged sniper weapons for one-cop stations like Jarrajarra. It was more shotguns and pistols for cops like me.

“Steyr’s good at eight hundred yards,” said Rob. “I’ll stay back. If Carruthers shoots you, I’ll hide in the bushes, and when the opportunity arises, I’ll shoot him. He won’t even know I am there. Easy-Peasy.”

“Eight hundred yards?” I was dubious. “Can you even see that far without your glasses?”

““OK, four hundred, smartarse.”

This was so totally wrong. I was already in the crap zone with this plan. If things went bloody, taking a civilian along for backup as opposed to calling for a police team would get me sacked with extreme prejudice.

“If you call your mates in Wodonga,” said Rob, “you’ll be waiting an hour, at least, before you get moving. Probably two hours. Mate, let’s go, now, you and me. Who else you got can do this?”

I had no one else in the district as good at this stuff as Rob. Ex-army, twelve years of service, multiple tours to Iraq and Afghanistan. Tough as nails. Still as fit as the day he de-mobilized. Fabulous shot. Sarge was the only cop within an hour’s drive nearly as good. But he was over sixty, not here now, and would never approve of my dark intentions.

Plus, we were the only two people I knew who loved their army training so much that we still practised our assault drills at the rifle range. Weekly, at least.

Two grown men. As silly as each other.

"Did you tell Mary about this plan?" I asked.

He reached into the front seat of his truck and pulled out a large paper bag.

"She made the sandwiches," he said, holding up the bag. "Beef and chutney mostly, plus a couple of chicken breast and salad. She said you'd prefer the low-fat chicken."

The road to Jindabyne.

2:45 AM.

We were in Rob's truck, so he was driving while I navigated.

He had a highly modified Ford F150 Utility. A four-wheel drive, almost a tank. He drove it like a race car. We were flying. I had the passenger safety strap firmly in hand, watching the GPS tracking app on a navigation tablet Rob had rigged on his dashboard.

I had Google Maps open on my phone, checking the best directions to our moving target.

McLain's motorbike, hopefully with her and Carruthers on board, had crossed the border into New South Wales. Just a minor violation of my jurisdictional authority.

Not to worry.

"So, what's the real plan," asked Rob, "now we are actually doing it."

He was shouting above the noise of the F150.

"OK," I shouted back. "We follow them at a distance till they stop. Then we ninja up and sort out what's the go. See what we see and do what we have to do. OK?"

"So, I cover, and you sneak up and make an arrest?"

"Yes."

"No intercepts or ambush?"

"No, definitely not. My intention is to find the body of Virginia Collins. I need Carruthers alive and talking."

"What if he doesn't want to talk."

"He'll talk."

"I love your plans, Chris. So detailed."

"Yeah, well, some details will reveal themselves within the flow of events while others remain forever obscure. It's the Zen of the situation."

"Mate, you should have been a general."

Which was meant to be funny, but we both had years of training and experience sneaking up on people a lot more armed and dangerous than McLain and Carruthers. Enemy soldiers who knew we were coming and were armed and ready.

Once we found these two greedy fleeing fuckwits, we both knew what to do.

The main question was where would we be doing it?

All this while Rob was driving at speed along the tight, never-ending curves of the road around Australia's highest peak, Mount Kosciuszko.

Near Jindabyne.

3:25 AM.

Rob and I were coming up to a place called Jindabyne. It was meant to be a three-hour drive from Jarrajarra. He had cut it to just over two in a truck not normally associated with high-speed pursuit.

"You reckon they're on one bike or two?" asked Rob.

"I don't know. Long way to go riding passenger."

"Do you reckon McLain has collected her cattle money?" he asked.

"Buggered if I know," I said. "Can't see her leaving it behind."

"Did you ever see Heath Ledger in Batman?" he asked. "The bank robbery bit."

"Yeah," I said. "The robbers kill each other, one by one, till the last one left alive is our Heath, the Joker."

"Maybe that's Carruthers?"

"I don't think our Ken is that smart, and he certainly isn't as handsome as Heath. Even with the make-up."

I thought about the idea for a moment.

"But he is that devious," I added. "Jen kills the cattle rustlers one by one, then Ken kills Jen and gets the rustlers money."

"I thought you killed one of them," said Rob.

"Yeah, but not without provocation, and she put them there, so technically speaking, it was her fault."

"Dubious," he said.

We went through a string of serious curves at ridiculous speed.

"Do you reckon they're heading to a hide-out or just running to catch a plane?" Rob had questions upon questions.

"In these hills, I am guessing, hideout," I said.

I had a question of my own.

"How the hell can you talk so much and drive like this?"

"Takes my mind off the risk."

"Reassuring."

3:35 AM.

"They've stopped," I said.

Our escapees had reached the New South Wales town of Bombala and stopped for a short break.

Or they'd found the tracker and chucked it. Or they'd found it earlier, and the tracker was on a decoy truck. The negative options were endless. I put them out of my mind.

Control what you can.

Bombala was hours and a mountain range away from our current position.

"Pull over, mate," I said.

Rob slowed to look for a safe spot, then pulled over into an empty truck stop just short of Jindabyne. The lights of the town shining through the trees ahead of us.

Now, we were both looking at the GPS tracker on his dashboard screen.

According to our magic GPS app, they'd been on the move for six hours. They'd made a short stop in Bairnsdale for petrol, I guess. It was a big country town with half a dozen all-night garages. It would take days to check the CCTV in all of them. We didn't have days.

Hopefully, we'd prove they were together within the next few hours.

"They've probably stopped to refuel again," I said.

"What have they done so far, over six hundred kilometres?"

"So would they get three hundred plus on a loaded-up Harley

Fatboy?" I asked.

"Rob, the mechanical genius, took a moment to think.

"Yeah, that would be right. Should get three twenty easy."

I was checking Google. "Bombala, New South Wales, has a no-frills, twenty-four-hour petrol depot. Can't see any cameras on the Google Street cam."

"They'd like that."

"Yes," I said. "They would."

"They are surrounded by a lot of mountains and a million options," said Rob.

"I think we wait here for a while," I said.

"Good thinking, number one."

"We could wait till they start moving," said Rob, "give it two minutes and call the petrol station. Ask if there were two riders? Yeah?"

"Nah, mate, what if the operator knows them? Makes a call. We blow our biggest advantage."

"Just a thought," he said.

"What did Ricky Chalmers say to Scotty at halftime in last year's grand final?"

"Don't think, it's bad for the club."

Scotty had played brilliantly in the second half and Jarrajarra had won another flag. For a player of Scotty's size and strength, finesse was not essential in bush footy.

"Leave the thinking to me, mate," I said. "I'm in the zone."

We broke out Wendy's coffee and Mary's sandwiches. I opted for the chicken breast. We watched the stationary light of the Harley Fatboy on the GPS tracker.

It blinked on the spot at the Bombala petrol depot. Maybe Ken had his hideout there, maybe they were having a coffee break as well.

Leaving Bombala, they had a lot of options.

Our coffee and sandwiches were perfect.

The dashboard screen was the most riveting television I'd watched in ages. Nothing happened, but we couldn't take our eyes off it.

The road to Wulgulmerang.

3:50 AM.

"Here we go," said Rob.

The Harley was on the move. We watched for a moment.

"Bloody Hell," he said, "they're heading back to Victoria.

They'd curved into Bombala from the southeast and had made a ninety-degree turn.

"Southwest," I said.

They were on the move, gaining speed, heading southwest, back to Victoria, but on a different road.

Our original plan was to catch their trail around Cooma, New South Wales. They'd screwed that notion by turning around. Not a total one-eighty, but they'd gone from heading north-west to going south-west.

Back toward my legal jurisdiction. Legal, if you didn't count the illegal GPS tracker on McLain's bike.

Minor detail.

They were heading into mountain terrain that had never been cleared or cultivated. Some of the roughest bushland in the country.

"Gotta be heading to a hideout," said Rob.

We watched for ten minutes.

Watching them move west, it was clear that whatever option they chose, it would be south of our present location. There was only one road out of Jindabyne going south.

"OK," I said, "We don't lose anything by moving further south."

We put away our picnic and moved out.

"No great rush," I said. "They still have a lot of options."

"Same plan?" asked Rob.

"Same plan," I said. "We don't try to catch them on the move. We follow till they stop. You hang back, cover me, I move in."

So, plan in place, we moved forward, mostly south, while Jen and Ken moved mostly west.

"If we all keep going in these directions," I said, "we arrive at a conjunction of roads near Wulgulmerang East."

"Yeah, I've heard of it," said Rob.

"Ever been there?"

"There is no there. It is just a T-section."

Rob was still driving. I was still navigating. It was working.

"They are heading toward a place called Bonang, then a region called Deddick Valley. Heard of that one?"

"Yep, a road in the middle of a river flat, mountains on both sides. Call 'em valleys."

"Who names these places?" I asked.

"It's a mix, mate. The First People had great names, like Jarrajarra or Wulgulmerang, then some explorer named Gordon Ded-dick comes along thirty thousand years later and names it after his mum."

"Makes sense."

"When they get to the T-section at Wulgulnerang East," said Rob, "they can turn north towards us or south going away. Not a lot of options from what I remember."

"Satellite map agrees," I said.

We headed south. At civilized speed this time.

If they went all the way to Wulgulmerang, we'd beat them there by an hour.

If we get to the T-junction before them, anywhere we can hide?" asked Rob.

I checked the satellite maps.

"The junction is wide open. We could end up in a car chase gunfight, and I don't get my chat with Kenny."

I kept looking.

"Google has a bush reserve about five kilometres north of the junction. We'll be there an hour before them."

"If they're still coming," said Rob.

"Yep," I agreed. "If they're still coming."

The hideout, if it existed, could be between us.

"We might as well speed up since we're gonna get there first anyway."

"Might as well, maybe have a nap," I said.

"Sounds good," said Rob.

It was as though someone had ignited a rocket in the trunk.

Rob was back on the racetrack, and I was holding onto the safety strap as tight as I could.

Wulgulmerang Bush Reserve.

4:20 AM.

“Where are you blokes?”

Sarge had called on the mobile. He said ‘blokes’. He’d guessed Rob Farrell was with me but made no comment.

I put Sarge on speaker so Rob could hear.

“Parked at a place called Wulgulmerang Creek Bush Reserve,” I said. “Check it on the satellite.”

“Where are the absconders?”

“Well, they went north into New South Wales, took a break at Bombala, then looped back toward Victoria. They are now heading towards my position. Could be here in half an hour.”

I was carefully avoiding plurals, not using ‘us’ or ‘we’. Wasn’t going to admit to bringing a weekend warrior, even one as good as Rob.

“OK,” said Sarge. “I have a convoy of cops and paramedics set to roll here.”

“See you soon,” I said.

“Take care, Chris,” said Sarge and ended the call.

“OK,” I said to Rob. “The Google gives us four and a half hours to find our bad guys before the cavalry arrive.”

So, we waited at Wulgulmerang Creek Bush Reserve, while the blinking light of McLains GPS moved closer. I slept until Rob’s voice interrupted.

“Here we go,” he said.

Rob was watching the tracker. Carruthers and McLain had just stopped at a place called McKillops Bridge, then turned off-road onto Deddick’s track.

“Do you know that track?” I asked.

“Not really. I’ve been over that bridge, though. It’s a wooden thing, no tarmac, just a wood-bridge.”

“Will it take our weight?”

“Yeah, absolutely,” he said. “Hope so. Maybe. Probably.”

“Let’s go see.”

Rob drove while I looked up what I could find about our bridge. There was plenty.

"The Google Maps says it’s 255 metres long and is very high above the Snowy River. Opened in 1936, after the original bridge washed away in 1934.”

“Encouraging,” said Rob.

McKillop's Bridge – Deddick's Track.

4:55 AM.

The bridge was a masterpiece. Nothing to worry about.

Deddick's track started a few metres past the bridge on the eastern side.

According to our GPS tracker, Ken and Jen were now approximately ten kilometres along and had come to a stop. They hadn't moved for twenty minutes.

The early part of the trail looked rugged, but there was nothing immediate that Rob's four-wheel drive F150 couldn't handle.

We stopped at the head of the trail.

"How far out before they hear us?" asked Rob.

"We've got the sound of the river," I said. I licked my finger and held it out the window to the breeze? "Barely any wind, and it's blowing towards us. How loud is your truck?"

"On this road in four-wheel, no more than 90 decibels."

"Let's go to the Goog," I said.

You can look up anything on Google, even plan an assault on two escaped murderers.

"Ninety decibels carries 800 feet, it says."

"That's too close," said Rob.

"We stop a kilometre short. Go the rest on foot."

"Yeah," he agreed.

"Vests on?" I started our checklist.

"Yes."

"Mobile sounds off."

"Yes."

"Ammo?"

"Yes."

"Bodycams off?"

"I haven't got one," said Rob. "I don't want to be seeing your arse running through the bushes on next week's Bugle."

"Me neither," I said.

There were a lot of reasons I didn't want my bodycam in

operation. I'd think of a good excuse after. If I needed one.

Rob re-started the truck and flicked into four-wheel drive."

"What about Carruthers?" he asked. "Maybe he has some cameras in place."

"It's a public trail, and he is hiding here. He wouldn't be putting a camera this far out."

"No, maybe he has them closer."

If it were my hideout, I might risk cameras and booby traps, but they would be closer to home. Not out here where some curious passer-by might stumble across them.

"If I built a hideout," said Rob. "I'd just have a warning camera hidden somewhere within my boundary, on the last bit of road before the door."

Great minds think alike.

I called the Sarge.

"Chris, where are you?"

"Place called McKillop's Bridge. I'll send you the coordinates and a picture of the GPS."

"Good. Where is our target?"

"Just down the road, around the corner."

"Good, Good," said Sarge. "We are on the move."

"OK," I said. "Sarge, if it turns out we need paramedics, we might be better with a chopper. Satellite doesn't show any easy way to get an ambulance in."

"Right, OK."

I posted the location and the photo of the target location.

I waited a bit.

"Oh, my Lord," said Sarge. "I see what you mean. Rugged country. My goodness. And we are still three hours away."

Three hours.

"See you then," I said.

We ended the call.

"Time to go," I said to Rob.

Ready or not, Mister Ken Carruthers, here we come.

Deddick's Track.

5:40 AM.

"Now we walk," said Rob.

We were roughly six kilometres along the trail, and it had shrunk to almost nothing. The bush had closed in, leaving a rugged track barely three feet wide over sharp rocks and gum roots. Hardly a trail at all. Wide enough for a bike, no room for Rob's F150.

"I reckon we back up and park the truck out of sight," I said.

Rob obliged. Found a spot, backed in about five metres, parked and turned off the headlights.

Hidden from the track.

We were four kilometres short of our destination. The GPS tracker had not moved in close to an hour.

Looked like Kenny was at home, at least for now.

Sunrise was about sixty minutes away. The early dawn light made it easy to see without torches or headlamps.

The bush around us was mostly tall, high country snow gum. Thick canopy, but the trunks and branches were bent and battered from the mountain winds. At this altitude, there'd also be occasional snow load as well. This morning, there was dew on the ground, and a bit of ice here and there, but we were lucky, no snow.

The ground was walkable, even off the trail.

Rob took the Steyr out of its frame inside the truck cabin and handed it to me.

"What about you?" I asked.

He opened the large steel case he kept welded to the tray of the utility.

"Got a new toy, another Steyr, with a tiny modification," he said.

He pulled a suppressor out of the steel case with a bit of flourish.

"He won't know what hit him."

"Have you practised with this thing?"

"I have," he said. "Plenty. Don't worry, I know the rules, no new gear on race day."

"How come this is the first I've seen it?"

He gave me a look. Laughed.

"Possibly because you're a cop? What do you reckon, Constable?"

The reason I hadn't seen it before was that a suppressor modification on a high-powered sniper rifle was highly illegal in the hands of a civilian.

"How long have you had it?"

"Christmas present from Mary. Found it on eBay."

I shook my head. "You Farrells are a different breed."

"Can't argue with that."

"If you feel the need to start shooting, remember I need to talk to this bloke."

"I'll try and remember."

"Try hard."

We checked our weapons, one rifle and one pistol each, backpacks full of ammo.

Ready to go.

"Feeling tired?" I asked. Joking.

"Mate," said Rob. "What do you think?"

"Wired, not tired?"

He smiled. Didn't need to answer. He was ready.

"Four thousand metres. We do the first thirty-five hundred quick but quiet. You keep back about one hundred."

"Got it."

"I didn't find anything about Carruthers being an expert with a rifle," I said. "Nothing special on his police record about weapons, but he likes to make people disappear. Don't forget."

"I won't."

"I've seen McLain in action. She is definitely a murderer. She will shoot you if she gets close, so don't get close if you can avoid it."

"Keep it safe, stay in cover," said Rob.

"And don't trip on that path," I added.

Last words.

"This goes south. You move back at wait for the cops, OK?"

"OK."

"Thanks, Rob," I said. "I'm glad you're here."

"No worries, mate," he said.

Pause.

"Yeah," I said. "Those sandwiches were bloody sensational."

The last few kilometres of track were not so smooth.

The dust-covered rocks and tree roots were almost invisible. Sharp and totally random. Parts of the trail opened on one side to a steep fall to a wide creek that fed the Snowy. Apart from the cliffs, most of the trail was bordered by thick bushes and sharp branches invading your head space.

Moving forward, it was a constant trade between watching your foot placement and keeping a wary eye on what was ahead.

We didn't speak or check on each other. We didn't trip or stumble. I could barely hear Rob moving behind me, but he was there. He kept about fifty metres back. Closer than we'd discussed, but he wanted me in sight. Any further back and bends in the trail and the scrub around the tall gums would make me invisible to him.

He couldn't help me if he couldn't see me.

Thirty minutes in, we found a spot with enough space to stop and confer.

We were four hundred metres from the target, which was off to the left of the track. East. No trail showing on the mobile app. We'd be bush-bashing from here.

"Geez," whispered Rob. "Not somewhere you'd nip out for a pint of milk."

"Long way for store-bought coffee."

"The bikes made it through alright," he said.

"Probably felt safe. Not thinking about sneaky bastards and GPS trackers."

The trail was dusty, and there were fresh motorcycle tracks on the ground ahead and behind.

"Definitely two of them," I said.

"One looks more like your bog-standard trail bike," said Rob. "The Harley came behind. Looks like it struggled a bit in this rubbish."

"Good old Kenny, not waiting for his girlfriend."

"Always the gentleman."

"He's a thug and a bully," I said, "and he's most likely got a gun or two."

We smiled at each other.

"We've seen worse."

"We have indeed." Rob liked that. I would put our army training and combined tours against anything these two had to offer. Plus, we were the wild men from the Jarrajarra Rifle Range lunchtime sessions. Look out, Kenny.

The light was getting better every minute.

This was a strange place. It had similarities to Afghanistan. Same topography, steep slopes, thin bush-cluttered ravines, but all at lower altitudes, huge trees, but different species.

Nowhere near as cold here.

Under the tall canopy, in the July morning mist, it was cold, beautiful and drippy wet.

"It's not the sort of place you deliver building supplies," said Rob.

"Can't be a long-term hideout," I said. "Too rugged."

"I'd reckon."

"Maybe a camping space and a dumping ground?"

"We'll find out soon enough," he said, and he was right.

Three gunshots.

The first two, really close together, high-pitched clatter, quick sound like clanking tin cups, followed by a single deeper, more resonant thump.

"The first two sound like a .22," said Rob. "The third sounded bigger, like a Glock."

Either someone else beat us there, or the lovebirds, Jen and Ken, were shooting at each other.

"The show has started," I said.

"Hand signals from here," said Rob.

I nodded.

There was nothing more to discuss.

I moved out, and Rob followed twenty seconds after.

The Shelter.

6:20 AM.

If the two fugitives were trying to kill each other, I needed to get to Ken Carruthers while he still had breath in his body.

Ken and I were going to have a talk.

I was moving fast, and Rob was not far behind.

Thirty metres on, the bike tracks led us to another trail. Off to our left, heading west and uphill.

Thinking on the run.

Were there Booby traps? Mines? Trip wires? None of them made sense on a government-owned bush trail, no private property here. Traps were just as likely to expose your location as keep you hidden.

Maybe a warning camera? But they'd hardly be monitoring a CCTV while shooting at each other.

I kept moving as fast as I could, taking the risk.

The gunfire had ceased. Someone had won, or maybe it was a draw. Both dead? Please no.

"Come on, Kenny," I thought. Don't die on me now.

Moving forward, after another hundred metres, the tight, narrow trail widened into a cleared space. Oval-shaped, about thirty metres wide and forty metres long. Rough but level ground, well-grassed. The whole thing was hidden from above by the tree canopy. It felt like a cave among the trees.

At the other end of the clearing, a shed-like structure made from half a dozen thick upright timbers cut from the surrounding snow gums, supporting longer, thinner rafters cut from the same trees.

Rough cuts, nothing square, the roof basically a tarpaulin over close-laid timber rafters. Covered in soil, with a grass roof.

Whoever made this was quite the greenie but no carpenter. Made from the earth and surrounding timber. They'd had the right idea but little finesse. This had been bashed into place using material at the ready. More a shelter than a shed.

I moved closer, staying in cover.

The whole structure almost filled the far end of the clearing. The left-hand end merged into the surrounding hill. The right-hand end was an earth-made wall. Looked as though it had been pushed into place by an earthmover.

At that end, under the roof, leaning into the earth wall was a decrepit caravan. Next to that, a massive ancient bulldozer, a three-metre-wide blade on the front, and a large bucket on the back. All of it, the bulldozer and its implements, covered in rust.

Shed, machinery, caravan.

I couldn't see deeper into the structure. Too dark.

How the fuck did any of this get here?

Rough. Effective. Solid.

You could hide here forever if you didn't need comfort.

I was behind a large snow gum, thick enough to stop a cannon.

The shelter thing was pitch black inside. Hard to tell how deep it went, hard to tell if someone was hiding there waiting for us.

If they were, I was not offering a good shot.

I signalled to Rob to come forward and join me. Twenty seconds later, he appeared behind me. Hardly a sound.

We kept going with the hand signals. Didn't risk a whisper this close to whatever it was.

I disarmed the Steyr rifle and handed it back to Rob. I was heading in close and would be better served by my pistol. Rob hid the empty Steyr about a metre into the surrounding bush.

I gave him a 'cover-me' signal, and then off I went to discover what was inside the mystery structure.

I went left and through the surrounding bush, using the thick, tall trunks of the gum trees for cover. I was on the high side of the open front in less than twenty seconds.

I slid quietly down the last of the hill into the massive grass-covered shed from its northern edge. I would be on Rob's left.

The light was improving rapidly. I could see deeper into the structure. It was about three metres high on the inside. I was on the opposite end of the building to the crappy old caravan.

There were water carts, petrol drums, and assorted machinery, most of it rusted. None of it could possibly be working. Plenty for Ken or Jen to hide behind.

But they didn't know I was coming. Couldn't know.

A "Parks Victoria" sign was stamped on the back or side of most of the gear. That made sense. This was some abandoned works shed, put together for some forgotten government purpose, then left to rust till a parasite like Carruthers found it.

I couldn't see Kenny having the ability to put any of this together. I could definitely see him finding it and taking it over for himself.

I moved inside and quickly worked my way through the place. It was filthy but all clear of bad guys.

The caravan.

Dirty, covered in dust and bird shit. A green bush mould, thick on the roof, descended the aluminium walls till it blended with the muck and spotted rust.

I made it to the side of the caravan undetected.

Listened. Nothing.

The windows were covered by rotting, grey canvas curtains. I took a quick look through the filthy glass portal in the caravan door.

I saw someone on the floor. Could only see legs and feet.

I signalled to Rob. One body. I'm going in.

I saw Rob scoot low across the clearing, then back into cover, giving himself a better view of the caravan door.

I didn't knock. Just stepped up to the door and front-kicked the shit out of it. It swung open hard and fast, half disintegrating in the process.

I followed in fast. Gun ready.

No Kenny, but there was Jennifer McLain. On the floor of the caravan. Shot through the chest, upper right.

Naked.

She was lying flat on her back. Her hands cuffed above her head to the metal base of the caravan bed.

A small amount of blood pooled around her right shoulder.

Alive, but barely.

Holy Jesus. What the hell happened here?

I stuck my head out the van door and signalled Rob to come forward. He sprinted to my position.

"McLain," I whispered. "Shot, alive, do what you can. I'm going after Carruthers."

I had to find Ken Carruthers now and neutralize him. If Rob stayed to look after McLain, I was leaving them both vulnerable.

You or me, Kenny.

Where was he?

I slipped out of the shed the way I came, onto the north side, the high side. I'd seen from my approach that the area beyond the shed led to higher ground. More of the colossal hills that overlooked the Snowy River below us.

Moving past the outer structure of the shed, I could see a wider area with no trees, the space protected from above by the canopy of massive gums. Another clearing, but longer and thinner. Maybe Carruthers had kept it clear enough to live without exposing it to mapping satellites above.

I could see fresh machinery tracks. Maybe another rusted-out mechanical digger.

Against the back of the shed was a pile of sand. Partly covered in weeds. Been there for years by the look, but still in use. There were recent bite marks from a digger.

I kept moving. Stayed to my left, north of the trail. Upwards.

Steady climb, not too steep. Used the enormous trunks of the snow gums as cover. I would be a hard target unless Kenny had heard me coming and had taken a position behind me.

Not likely.

A minute or so along the track, the trail narrowed, and right there was my man.

Ken Carruthers in the flesh.

Dammit, he was inside the cabin of an ancient backhoe. It had a sabre-toothed digger on the front, and Kenny looked to be digging a body-sized hole in the ground. This was presumably the intended grave of Jennifer McLain.

I could shoot him easily enough, but I wanted a talk. Hard to chat with someone wounded. Harder still if they were dead.

I was certain, now, he had no idea I was there.

What with the digger going full hammer and under Kenny's control, just walking up and asking for a chat did not seem a smart choice.

When in doubt, do nothing.

I took cover deeper in the bush, kept eyes on Carruthers and waited. Watched.

There was a pile of sand dropped near the grave. Beside the sand, there was another pile. This one was dirt, freshly dug.

After about five minutes of digging, Kenny took a break.

He jumped down from the digger, then reached back into the cabin and took out a small steel case heavily wrapped in clear plastic. He put the case on the ground beside the grave, then took a pack of cigarettes from his back pocket and lit up for a drag.

Taking a smoko. Jesus Christ.

Dig a grave, kill someone, have a ciggy, then chuck your victim in the ground. Talk about 'the banality of evil'. Kenny was beyond banal, downright fucking pedestrian.

I moved through the bush, further along, on my secret path beside the trail. The ground was soft. Black parrots were shrieking away with the early morning light.

Confident he couldn't hear me, I came out of the bush on the north side of the digger. Carruthers had his back to me, checking out his handiwork as he puffed away on his cigarette.

I used the large body of the digger as cover while I moved through the gap between us. I came around, left of the digger to be standing about five metres behind him, east side.

I spoke very quietly, didn't want any surprises, no sudden moves.

"OK, Kenny, put your hands on your head and turn around slowly."

He froze.

"Fuck me," he said, then paused.

"Constable fucking Taylor," he said without turning around. "You are a serious fucking pest. Should've done you while I had the chance."

"Why didn't you?"

"Didn't realize you had your girlfriend sleeping there. Had to stop and think what I was gonna do with two of you."

"Well, I'm glad you stopped for a think. Now, do what I told you. Put your hands on your head and turn around slowly."

He did as he was told, hands on his head, and turned very slowly.

The bulge of his weapon, stuck in the back of his belt, hidden under his shirt, was totally obvious.

"So, you came to my house to shoot me?"

"That was the plan. I must have gone rusty all those years out of the force," he said. "I'll do better next time, hey?"

He was smiling. The arrogant prick.

"Why me?"

"Wasn't really about you, Sunshine. Same reason I sent those two useless standover dickheads. Wanted to stick it on my girl Jen."

"So you sent those two blokes to meet me in the car park?"

"Guilty," he said. "Thought you'd have to revoke Jennifer's bail for sure."

"Why did you want that?"

"Stupid cow had told me where the cattle money was. Didn't need her anymore. Wasn't sure if you blokes knew about me at that stage."

"So the bashing backfired, and you upped the stakes to murder, so to speak?"

He laughed. This was all so cordial.

"Nothing personal, Constable. I was gonna do you, plant the gun on her bike, take the cattle money and be gone forever. She'd be back in jail before she'd had her WeetBix."

"Great plan for you," I said.

"My word. Ending up in that shithole Wodonga Hospital was a bit of a hiccup, you could say."

"So, you end up in custody," I said, "then McLain gets you out, gets you all the way up here to God-knows-nowhere, and then you shoot her?"

"Guilty," he said. Again. So relaxed. He was telling the truth. "Lucky for me, you dumb bastards hadn't locked her up already."

"Not so lucky for Jennifer," I said.

"If you fucking blokes had kept her in there," he continued, "stupid bitch could have lived forever, safe and sound in jail, but no, not fucking Jennifer. If she hadn't got bail, I wouldn't have needed to bother you and your missus."

What a kind thought. "Just the luck of the game?" I said.

"Exactly. Selfish bitch landed herself a real lawyer," he said. "That Oakley is too fucking good. He was gonna get her off, by the look of it, the dumb cunt."

"Shooting her was basically a 'plan B' break-up?" I said.

"Yep, and not a minute too soon. You ever spent more than five minutes in her company?"

"I have," I said.

"Well, mate, I reckon you'd know. She's bloody hard work. A great fuck but Jesus Christ, outside that, no thank you."

His eyes were fixed on me. I'd seen him interrogated before. He was telling me the truth. His own weird version of it.

"Why is she naked?"

"I just told you, mate, she is a great fuck. One last rumble in the jungle before she goes down the rabbit hole here," he nodded at the grave. "Pity to waste it, hey."

What a guy.

"You wouldn't have a gun on you by any chance, would you, Ken?"

"No, mate," he said. He spread his hands wide. "No gun. I am at your mercy, Constable."

He did that small, twitchy eye-flick I had seen before, plus I'd seen the Glock bulging out of his belt at the back of his jeans. Hard to miss it, really. Lying again, Kenny.

"Hands," I said, waving my gun. Directing him to put his hands back on his head. He sighed and did an eye-roll.

From somewhere in the bush around us came the whip-crack bird song of the Eastern Whip bird. Carruthers closed his eyes, soaking up the sound.

"Psophodes Olivaceus," he said. "Fucking beautiful, hey?"

Who'd have thought, murderer, pervert and bird lover?

He was taking a moment, looking for the right words.

"There is another way this can go," he said. "Doesn't need to be all by the book. I've got money here, a lot of it. The Fenwicks paid pretty well, and they weren't my only customers."

"How much are you offering?" I asked.

"Half a million, buried here, around the place," he said. "Maybe more. Got a hundred grand right here in the tin from the Pendergast cattle. Enough for you and your girlfriend to move out of that cop hole you live in."

He nodded his head toward the plastic-wrapped case near his feet. "It's all yours, mate. You don't even need to dig for it."

Paused, let him think I'm thinking about it.

"Why try to kill the Pendergasts?" I asked. Casually curious.

"Covering tracks," he said. "They fostered me as a kid. Old Ben knew I loved those caves. After those bodies turned up, only a matter of time before my name got mentioned. Stupid fucking Jennifer was supposed to leave old Ben and Irma dead. The cattle were just bonus money, but she fucked that up as well."

"Spilt milk now," he added.

"You'd kill Ben and Irma even though they took you in?"

"Foster parents, mate. Not like they were my real parents. Fosters only do it for the government money. Anyway, it wasn't me killing them. Jen gave it to that mate of hers, Mellish. The big useless sook went soft on the idea."

"Hard to find good help?"

"Fucking tell me about it. You reckon the dumb fuck would have been grateful she got him out of jail," he said. "Steroids, they soften the brain. Gave 'em up myself."

"Anyway," he continued, "nothing against old Ben and Irma. I was thinking of number one. You could try it yourself, mate."

He was waiting for me to accept the bribe.

"What do you say?" he asked. "You take the money, I walk. Simple. You dig around a bit, find some more dead bodies, and get a 'well-done Constable' from your bosses in Wodonga. But between you and me, you walk away rich. No one the wiser."

"How many bodies are buried here?"

"Just a few, eight, I reckon. Every time old Albert was a naughty boy, I'd clean up the mess. After that gig ended, I started doing clean-ups for others. 'Drag out your dead', I called myself. Good cash business."

"Who are all these bodies?"

"Scumbags mostly," he said. "Albert's daughter was the first I put here. To be fair, she was more your inconvenience than your typical scumbag."

"Daughter-in-law," I said.

"Daughter-in-law, whatever. Anyhow, my former boss, Inspector Hughes, was a Detective Sergeant in Homicide at the time. You know him, right?"

"Yes," I said. "I knew him."

"You put him away, if I remember?"

"I did. I put him in jail, and he died before lights out on day one."

"Well done you," said Kenny. "Anyway, when a Toorak rich bitch goes missing, cops have to get involved. Right?"

"Right," I said. Agreeing, confirming. Kenny is just telling a story here, and I am his enthralled listener.

"Albert's smart enough to know he needs old mate Hughes on-side. Apparently, they'd dealt before with some of Albert's previous naughty business. From what I gather, the daughter-in-law was the first that needed to disappear."

"The daughter-in-law, she was the first that Albert murdered?"

"Yeah, as far as I know, Albert's first kill? Maybe. I don't really know. But boy, did that light a fire under the fat prick."

"He liked it? The killing?"

"Well," Carruthers laughed. "Let's say he lost his inhibitions. Opened his eyes to the possibilities when people got in his way."

"And how did you get involved in all of this?"

"Well, mate, you knew Hughes. You met Albert. You ever see either of those lazy fucks digging a hole in the ground. Fuck me. Anyway. Hughes collected the cash, and I did the dirty work. Hughes gave me a cut when it was all done and dusted."

"Hughes and Albert Fenwick never came here to McKillop's

Bridge?"

"Are you fucking joking? Here. Fucking Albert reckoned North Fitzroy was the wilderness. Neither of 'em ever came up here. Never laid hands on a corpse. Hands-free, I used to call 'em. Lazy fucks."

That sounded about right, Albert Fenwick and the late Inspector Hughes. Neither man ever looked capable of physical effort. A fit, muscular psychopath like Ken Carruthers was their perfect lackey."

"How'd you find this place?"

"I worked up here as a kid, with a forestry crew, then the parks people took it over for a while, then they abandoned it. After I joined the cops, I checked it out and sort of made it my own."

"What about the machinery?"

"Some was left here, some I stole. I stole this digger. It is a fucking ripper. You can keep this too if you want."

He was enjoying the chat.

"Tell me why you shot through after the two Phillip Savages disappeared?" I asked.

He laughed at the memory. "I shot through alright. Hughes and me, we went all arse-up with the father and son?"

"How?"

"The usual when you deal with greedy fucks like Hughes."

"Money?"

"Yeah, money and arse-covering. The night I collect the Savage boys, I'm barely out of the city with them all wrapped up in the boot, dead as doornails. Hughes calls me. He's got a new plan. Wants me to pick him up. Gonna help me with the burial. Wants to see my private playground."

"And you smelt a rat?"

"I smelt a giant fucking rat," he answered. "I could see good old Hughesey putting me down the hole with the Savage boys, then finding the rest of my cash I buried around the place."

"So, Hughes had a plan that didn't include you?"

"Too right he had a fucking plan. He'd teamed up with some gangsters from Sydney. Didn't need me anymore. I could see the devious shithead cooking up some story that I was some serial killer, had done all the Savages on my own, just for fun. Or whatever."

"So, that's why you dumped the Savages down the cave in Jarrajarra and not up here?"

"Dead right. I was on my way out of town when he called. Jarrajarra was my best option. I got rid of the Savage boys. Quick as I could. Then I took off and kept myself out of harm's way for a bit."

"That was 2010," I said. How have you lived since then?"

"Well, mate, not here, for starters. I love the outdoors as much as the next bloke, but as a permanent accommodation, it's all a bit rugged."

"I noticed."

"So, I got a bit entrepreneurial, you might say. I just reminded old mate Albert what I knew and what I could prove about him and his fucking evil twin, the sister."

"You'd taken voice recordings every time you collected a body from him?"

"I did indeed," he said. "And not the sort of recordings the highly respected Master of Laws wanted out in public."

"How did you get Penny Fenwick's diaries?"

"I broke in and stole them, the ones I could find. I couldn't find all of them." He laughed at a memory. "All the money they've got, they have shit security."

"So, you gave them a taste of what you had, and the Fenwicks sent you rent money?"

"Rent and more," he said. "Inherited wealth, hey? The gift that keeps on giving."

"You mentioned other customers," I said.

"Just the one. AJ Davies, you probably heard of him."

"The gun-for-hire. Jennifer McLain's husband?"

"The very same," he answered with a smirk. "Did a few for him before he got topped by one of his ex-girlfriends. Hughes hired him for a couple of jobs and he outsourced them back to me. Didn't tell Hughes. Fucking hilarious."

"How'd you meet Davies?"

"Big-time party boy, AJ. Back when I was on the job. I worked in Melbourne and partied in Sydney. Couldn't miss him."

"That's how you and McLain met?"

"Yep, and one day after we met, we were fucking each other senseless in a Sydney motel while dumb fucking AJ Davies was checking the baby oil on his muscles in some gym mirror in Sydney."

"You weren't worried about Davies?"

"Didn't worry, didn't care."

He was lying. Everyone was scared of the late, unlamented hitman AJ Davies.

"Look, mate," he said. We could talk all day. Why don't we do a deal here? You seem open to negotiation. Just take the money."

He was getting impatient.

"You let me walk," he continued. "You take this lot to your bosses. Wrap some cold cases for them and collect some real cash for you."

I said nothing. Left a gap.

"I got quite a collection in the dirt here, mate," he said. "Not just Albert's in-laws. I got drug scum, debtors who wouldn't pay, and lenders who tried too hard to collect. I've even got a pair of auditors who were too honest for old Albert's books. I've got papers, pictures, all the good stuff is buried here. Bloody Hell, Constable, you'll be a hero."

Carruthers was smiling again. Selling me, he thought. I smiled back. His mirror.

I relaxed my two-handed grip on my pistol. Kept it in my right hand, dropped my hands to my sides, pointing my pistol down at the ground, away from his chest. Took my finger off the trigger.

Now, he mirrored me, dropping his own hands. I let that go without comment. Fine by me was the message.

I relaxed.

He relaxed.

"So, you and me, we do a deal," I asked, "How does it work? How do we find new business with Albert Fenwick in prison?"

"If we do a deal," he said. "I disappear. That means Albert walks free. Once he is out and about, I will milk his fat arse till it bleeds. With what I know, mate, he will pay and pay till he is dead in the ground. And that bitch sister of his, she's gonna live forever. There's a lot of milk left in those two fat tits, trust me."

Trust and Ken Carruthers, there was a difficult concept.

"You turn your back," he said. "I walk away. We share it all fifty-fifty. Scout's honour."

He lifted his hand in a two-fingered Boy Scout salute.

Making jokes now.

He was looking at me, waiting for an answer. Growing in

confidence.

Here we were, two blokes discussing a solid business venture. Standing beside a hole in the ground intended for me.

And Wendy.

But hey, ancient history now. Bygones. No hard feelings.

I tapped the barrel of my pistol against my leg, watching him.

The pistol, tapping gently against my thigh, finger off the trigger.

Thinking, thinking.

"You sure you're not hiding a gun there, Kenny. We make a deal, I relax, and you shoot me.

"I told you, no gun. Money in the tin is yours. Let me grab some of my other stuff, and I am gone." So easy.

"Kenny, I'm thinking I'll give you another deal," I said.

"Another deal?"

"Yeah, what about this? You show me where you buried Virginia Collins."

"Virginia Collins?"

He didn't even know her proper name.

"Virginia Savage, the woman you collected from Albert Fenwick. The daughter-in-law."

"Oh her, yeah, yeah. Fuck yeah, that one. Number one. Shit, what a waste, mate. Jesus, she was hot. What a body. Yeah, she's here. Got some photos of her if you're interested. They're all yours, in the caravan."

"Photos?" I asked.

"Yeah, mate, photos, fucken good ones. Pity she was dead by the time she got here, but get what you can, I reckon. She didn't complain." He laughed.

I nearly shot him dead right then and there.

I was such a shit actor. He was nervous again.

He was thinking. Might have sensed a weakening of his deal. I couldn't tell. I didn't care. From here on, it only mattered what he did.

"Where is Virginia buried?" I asked.

"If I tell you where," he said. "what's in it for me?"

"Your life," I said.

He laughed, "You? Kill me?"

"Kenny, I will kill you where you stand. I hit you just right. I reckon you fall right into that hole you dug for Jennifer."

I wasn't acting now. Kenny must have noticed the difference.

"Whoa! OK, OK. Let's keep it friendly. She's here, she's here."

He was looking at me as he spoke, not doing his signature shifty eye thing. I believed him when he said Virginia was here.

But where?

He looked at me for a while. He looked over my right shoulder.

"Let me think," he scratched his chin with his left hand. Relaxed now. His right hand relaxed at waist level.

The sun was almost up. The light was behind me, my shadow over his right shoulder. Looking at me, he'd be looking into the dawn glow. My face would be in a darker shadow.

"She was the first one I put in the ground up here." Recalling a fond memory. Scratching his chin with his left hand. Relaxed now, he'd come to a decision.

He pointed over my right shoulder.

"Over there," he said, pointing. Quite definite in his memory. "Her and a tin of photos, photos of her dad, yeah, she's right to the side of that big snow gum, top of that rise. There's a mound of earth, under that a layer of sand, under the sand, is the tin of photos and, yeah, a bunch of cash, I forgot to mention."

I started to turn my head as if to look. Still innocently tapping my pistol against my thigh.

"Which gum tree?" I asked, turning my head a tiny bit further.

"The one with the," he said. Pointing with his left.

With his right hand, he went for the pistol stuck under his shirt, back of his jeans.

Smooth and fast. Within a moment, he had his pistol by his side, raising it to shoot. Robbie was right. It was a Glock.

Carruthers was fast. A police-trained country boy. He knew his guns.

But.

I practised this stuff three times a week. I had the cop training plus the best army training in the world.

I shot Ken Carruthers dead-centre of the stomach before the barrel of his gun had passed his leg.

He managed to fire his Glock, hitting the ground about an inch in front of his right toe.

He folded in half around the hole in his gut and fell backward into the hole that he had dug for me. He fell bum first across the grave rather than along.

Awkward.

He didn't fit crossways. Way too tall. He was now stuck with his head, shoulders and legs planted firmly above the ground. Everything else, folded around his wound, was stuck firmly below.

Still alive. How long for, I couldn't guess.

Still breathing, barely conscious, and groaning in serious pain.

He'd dropped his Glock on the ground in front of him. I picked it up, disarmed it, disassembled it, and put it in the cabin of his digger, out of harm's way.

I walked behind him, grabbed him by the shoulders and dragged him out of his predicament, out of the grave.

Lay him on his back as he coma-groaned. He was in a bad way.

Gut shot. Kenny was fucked unless professional help arrived quickly.

I rolled him over. He barely protested, just a weak grunt. I cuffed his hands behind him and zip-locked his feet. Noted the bullet had hit him in the gut and gone right through. Missed his spine. Lucky for him.

I patted him down and found a small Ruger .22 in his back pocket. Turns out he wasn't lying, he didn't have one gun, he had two. I disarmed and pocketed that one as well. He had probably lifted it from McLain after he shot her.

I checked him thoroughly. There was nothing else to find.

I left him there face down on the ground. Gunshot wounds to the stomach were beyond my skill set.

A pool of blood collected on the ground under him. Not exactly gushing. He might pull through, might not. More likely not.

I was exhausted.

I walked over to the side of the digger and sat on the wheel. Took a moment to think. I looked at Kenny. That pool of blood hadn't grown much. He was going nowhere.

Did I do all that deliberately? I wondered. I didn't think so, or maybe I did. Who knew?

I wouldn't waste guilt on the likes of Ken Carruthers. I'd been loyal to my intentions, and that was enough for me.

Virginia. My promise to Rusty.

Rusty's only daughter was here somewhere. I was sure of that. I wouldn't leave this place until I found her.

Rob Farrell walked out of the bushes from the northern hillside. Silent as a ghost. He had followed in behind me and set up a perfect crossfire on Carruthers. He was so quiet, I hadn't realised he was there. I wished he wasn't.

"That was short and sweet," said Rob.

"How much of that did you hear?"

"Mate, if I heard anymore, I'd have shot him myself."

"Very glad you didn't do that."

"Yeah."

"How's McLain?"

"I think she will live if help arrives soon. I left the handcuffs on, don't think she is going anywhere."

"Will she remember you were here?"

"Not very likely. I collected this as well," he said and held up the tracking device I'd planted on McLain's Harley.

"Nice job," he said.

"You found it easy enough," I smiled. Neither McLain or Carruthers had noticed it, but Rob had managed.

"Robbie, thanks for the backup, mate, but I think you need to dissolve into the bushes about now and take that with you."

We knocked fists, and then he did as I asked, vanishing as quietly as he had arrived.

"Don't forget the other rifle," I shouted to the bushes.

"Roger that," came back.

I tried Wendy on my mobile. Still had coverage, which was remarkable.

"Hi, love," she said. "You good?"

"All good, job done," I said. "I will be here for a bit. A lot of cleanup. You'll probably hear from Sarge or Barney soon. Gonna need the paramedics and the SES team."

"OK. You're going to be a while?" she asked.

"Most likely," I said.

"I'm coming with the ambos," she said. Not a debate.

I sent the coordinates. "See you when you get here, love."

We kissed and cooed, then ended the call. I rang Sarge.

"You OK, son?" asked Sarge.

"I'm good. McLain and Carruthers are secured. Both wounded. Carruthers is in serious trouble. Need the medics ASAP."

"You're not hurt?"

"No, boss, just buggered. Sending you the location now. You're gonna have to walk the last three or four kilometres."

"That's fine, son. Just take a seat and wait. We should be there in an hour."

"Boss, we are looking at some sort of body dump here."

"Oh," he said and paused. "How many do you think?"

"Kenny said eight. Before I shot him."

"Eight," said Sarge. "Dear God."

Nothing else to say. We ended the call.

I just needed a short rest.

Sitting there on the wheel of Ken Carruthers' digger, I put my elbows on my knees and my face in my hands and fell asleep.

8:30 AM

"Hey, Chris. You OK, mate?" The familiar voice of Constable Joyce Thompson.

Woke me from a dream, not a good one, dead bodies, rotting corpses, none of them Virginia.

I stood up and stretched.

Joyce had her gun out, two-handed grip, pointing at the ground. Tip-toe-ing toward me.

"You can put your gun away, Joyce," I said. "All secure here."

She knelt down beside Carruthers. Felt his neck for a pulse.

"This one's still ticking," she said. She spoke into her lapel mike. "Second suspect down, two hundred metres along the track. The track is clear."

Joyce was in the zone, less than a year in the force and already first through the door. Or, in this case, first down the bush track. What a woman.

"Mr Carruthers is not looking too good," she said.

"He's had better days," I said. "You got any evidence bags, Joyce?" I didn't care about Carruthers. He did what he did, and he got what he got. I didn't say it out loud because I knew Joyce would have her bodycam recording.

“There is a dismantled Glock in the cabin of the digger,” I said. “That belongs to Carruthers.”

I held the Ruger out to Joyce, holding it by the barrel.

“This belongs to McLain.”

Joyce had a bag out for me to drop the Ruger. She was facing me. The bag would be caught by her bodycam. If either McLain or Carruthers died, there would be an inquest. If Carruthers died, I could be in deep shit.

Time to get my version on the record.

“I heard shooting as I approached the shelter back there. Sounded like two shots from the Ruger and then a single shot from the Glock. I found McLain badly wounded back in the caravan.”

Joyce was clever enough to see what I was doing without saying it out loud.

“Subsequent to that,” I said, “I found Carruthers here, preparing a grave. Carruthers and I had a brief interchange, and then we exchanged fire. Carruthers was wounded in that exchange. I took the Glock from Carruthers and found the Ruger in his possession.”

I had said what I needed and hadn’t mentioned Rob Farrell.

That was enough. Joyce nodded and turned to let her bodycam see the grave. Then she walked around the digger to capture the collection and bagging of the disassembled Glock.

Done with all that, evidence all bagged, she turned off her bodycam.

“So, Chris, mate. How are you really?” she said.

“Joycey,” I said. “Old buddy, old pal. I am well and truly stuffed.”

“Rather be you than Kenny,” she said. Cop Humour. Disgusting, really. We both laughed.

Wendy appeared, on the jog, out of the bend in the trail. Behind her was one of our gun paramedics, Jack Farrell, folded stretcher in hand.

Wendy gave me a quick kiss and rub on the back, then turned her professional attention to Carruthers.

“Chris, love,” she said after a moment. “Could someone see about making a landing pad, maybe near that shed? We need to get this one on the move.”

That was that. The new day had begun. First, we clear the wounded, and next, we start the search for the dead.

I headed back to the shelter to see about making a landing space for the chopper. I wouldn't be much help, but I was sure the Emergency team would get it sorted.

Back at the shelter, a few of the team were chainsawing a couple of the larger trees around the clearing on the open west side. Right where Rob and I had first arrived.

Rob Farrell was inside the shelter, in his Emergency Services gear now. Already on the job, he'd blended back into the civilian team. He had the bonnet up on the ancient bulldozer I'd seen near the rusty caravan on my way in.

Rob was standing on the dozer's front wheel track, peering into the giant engine space. His son Scott was in the driver's seat. Somehow, they had worked mechanical magic, and the bulldozer was kicking into life, begrudgingly, with a lot of cranking sounds and chugging smoke.

I walked up to Rob and tapped him on the leg.

"I'll get this going, and we might make a landing pad," he shouted. The Jarrajarra Emergency team was working together by telepathy again.

"Good job," I said. I doubt he heard me above the roar of the bulldozer.

I checked inside the caravan. Paramedic Jody Taggert was inside attending to Jennifer McLain. My boss, Sergeant Palmer, was standing over them both, watching.

McLain was already on a stretcher, cuffed to the sidebars. Covered by a sheet, I could see clean white bandages up and over her shoulder. She was in better hands than she might have expected a few hours ago.

We had to wait while the bulldozer drove out of the shelter area before we could talk.

"Wendy says this one should be OK," said Sarge. "Chopper is on its way from Wodonga. Should be here in forty minutes."

I nodded. It was all happening around me. Noise, movement, focus. Everyone in action for the benefit of two wounded crooks. The worst kind of people.

I felt like a ghost walking through the remains of a catastrophe. I kept thinking of the long-dead, buried around us. Were they waiting for their discovery? Could they hear us around them? Were they happy to be free of Ken Carruthers custody, or were they just dead? Feeling nothing, their souls having flown.

"Son," said Sarge, "you must be exhausted. Go and find a place to sit down."

"Big turnout for two lowlifes," I said to Sarge.

"Your friends aren't here for those two, son," he answered. "They're here for you."

"I'll check what Rob is up to," I said and left the caravan.

Scott Farrell had driven the bulldozer to the far end of the clearing and was already pushing over trees. Pushing out from the open space, making a hole in the canopy above us.

This area had been cleared before. Most of the snowgums here weren't old enough to offer any resistance to the bulldozer.

Rob Farrell was at the front of the shelter with his brother Greg, the head of our SES and our Fire Chief. Greg was standing while Rob was fussing over a chainsaw.

"Bloody thing won't start," said elder brother Greg.

With that, Rob tugged on the rope, and the chainsaw kicked into life.

"It doesn't like curse words," said Rob to Greg as he handed the chainsaw to his brother.

Greg headed off to his task, following the bulldozer at a safe distance. He chopped those random branches that had fallen into the intended landing zone. Making it clear. Forty minutes till the chopper arrived, it didn't need to be perfect.

Rob and I moved off to the side, safe on the high side, watching the work in progress.

"I am guessing you want this ambulance stuff all done," said Rob. "Want to start looking for your friend? Yeah?"

"Yeah," I said. "Too tired to help with this lot."

"Yeah," sighed Rob. Rob would be as tired as me, plus he'd done all the driving.

Nothing else to say. We found a spot, sat down, and watched the real workers in action.

"I love work," said Rob.

"I could watch it all day," I said, stealing his punch line.

11:00 AM

The rescue chopper had arrived, been loaded up and would be gone in a minute, taking the wounded escapees back to the Security Ward in the Wodonga Hospital or the morgue. Out of my responsibility was all I cared about.

Greater love hath no man than to shoot his girlfriend after a prison breakout, an all-night bike ride and a quick cuddle on a rotting mattress in a mouldy caravan.

Ken Carruthers. What a romantic.

Wendy and her two paramedics had secured the pair on separate stretchers at opposite ends of the chopper. Showing more care than either McLain or Carruthers could ever deserve.

The chopper door closed, and as it rose into the sky, Wendy looked out the window to give me a beautiful smile and a see-you-later wave.

If Wendy was truly concerned about me shooting Carruthers, I had clearly been forgiven. Not getting myself killed by Kenny probably helped her mood.

I was sad to see Wendy go but now, with the wounded evacuated, we could start the next stage. The search.

Sarge and Greg Farrell had led body searches before, usually for missing hikers. Sarge also had experience hunting hidden murder victims, but not this many in one spot.

This was something new for all of us.

Ken Carruthers had divulged a little of his burial techniques to me before we ended our conversation. Steel cases with cash and perverse trophies, all wrapped in plastic and buried with the corpses. The steel cases could be useful.

Metal detectors would be the order of the day.

Sarge put a call through to Barney with our shopping list. Barney took the checklist and had suggestions of his own.

"We'll need a separate command tent and a mess tent if this shed thing is a crime scene," said Barney.

"There's no footy training tonight," he continued. "Next game's at home tomorrow night. Plenty of time for Ricky Chalmers to collect what you need and do an up-and-back to Deddick's track. I'll ask him."

Ricky Chalmers? Footy coach and town hero. Only Barney would think of tasking Ricky with a mission the day before a game. Might as well call God and order a pizza.

Barney at headquarters, command tents, whiteboards, with Ricky Chalmers and some spare footballers on their way. Team morale lifted like a boat on a rising tide. The problems at hand were under serious attack.

Four of the younger emergency service kids had done the six-kilometre round trip to the parking area to collect two ice chests from the trucks containing food, sandwiches, and drinks.

We all chowed down while Sarge laid down the search rules.

Paint a search grid of numbered ten-by-ten-metre squares

Preliminary search with metal detectors.

If we think we have a hit, we mark the spot, note the grid number and wait for Crime Services.

Face masks, gloves, and protective clothing for everyone.

Do not touch anything that is not your detector or your shovel.

All good, sensible stuff. Typical Sarge, calm, confident, commonsense, with no thought of camera angles or optics.

"One last thing," said Sarge. "We do this search correctly, and we give the victims buried here their best chance of justice. Some of the people buried here may be criminals, but we believe one of these victims is Virginia Collins. A woman who was not a criminal but a loving mother and a good friend. A good citizen, murdered in her prime. Let's find her. Let's bring her back to her family. Be focussed, careful and most of all, be respectful."

That was Sarge. Word perfect.

5:00 PM

Nearly sunset, about to run out of daylight, Scott Farrell rumbled into the clearing on his new toy, the giant rusty dozer. He drove into camp on the new, wider track he'd built from the shelter back to where we'd all been forced to leave our vehicles.

Scott, being Scott, had taken it upon himself to widen the last three kilometres of trail. Now we had something like a road, in and out. No one was complaining.

Half an hour later, the first vehicle down the brand-new rugged highway was the Shire's four-wheel-drive truck, driven by our local footy hero, Ricky Chalmers. Seated in the passenger benches were another five volunteers. The tray of the truck was laden with search essentials from Barney's list.

"And all the cracks had gathered to the fray," said Sarge, quoting from his favourite poem, 'The man from Snowy River', which was exactly where we were now.

And gather we did to do the unload before the opportunity was lost to total darkness.

We now had tents, swags, ice chests full of food and drinks, two huge steel-encased plastic water tanks full of drinkable water and another two similar-sized tanks containing diesel. For the search, there were metal detectors, shovels, mattocks, lights and generators.

It was well and truly dark by the time Scott Farrell, on his unstoppable bulldozer, had created another clearing. Scotty had decided we needed a camping ground where the team could sleep safely, and now, there it was. Flat ground, safe from the danger of falling snowgum branches.

By 8:00 PM, the camp was ready. Sleeping tents, generators, lighting, and the command tent were all in place.

Less than twenty-four hours after Rob and I had crept into this place with guns drawn, and here we were, with a team assembled and already searching.

High on enthusiasm. We had a good plan, and it was in motion. If Virginia was buried here, we would find her.

Friday, July 29, 2022

The Clearing.

The first morning of the search did not go well.

No hits, nothing.

We had a full team conference at the known grave, the empty one initially intended for me. Sarge was a great believer in collaboration. If you have an idea, then throw it out there.

"Maybe this bloke, Carruthers, was lying," offered one of the younger volunteers.

"Maybe," said Sarge, "but Constable Taylor doesn't think so. Let's work with that for now."

"Maybe the graves are too deep for the detectors," said Rob Farrell. "This empty one is over two metres deep.

"How deep can Carruthers' backhoe thing dig?" I asked.

"Fifteen feet easy, said Rob.

"So he could have buried them deeper than this?" asked Sarge.

"Easy. Three to four metres, no stretch at all," said Rob. "This digger would struggle to go deeper than five metres."

"How deep can our detectors detect?" I asked.

"Two to three metres." I honestly believe Rob knew the answer to every question you could ask about machinery.

"So theoretically," said Sarge, "Carruthers could have buried them at three metres or deeper, and that could be testing the envelope on our detectors."

"Yeah," said Rob, "Exactly. These detectors are Kits-for-hire I rent out to fossickers working out of the caravan park. They're rock-solid, but they're not the greatest going round."

"Would cadaver dogs help?" someone asked.

"Would three metres be too deep for a dog?" I asked, "with the bodies wrapped in tarpaulins?"

Most of the young SES team were hunters. Some had dogs.

"Anyone have a clue?" I asked.

"Actually, Chris," said Raymond Twomey, one of the younger searchers. He'd put his hand up like we were all still in school. "A good dog can smell up to fifteen feet below ground and can pick up even a drop of blood after it has been exposed for months or more.

They might not smell the body after a few years, but they might get the tarpaulin. Might. If you know what I mean."

Raymond was a young and licensed deer hunter. Lived about five kilometres out of town

"There you go," I said. "You have a dog that clever, Ray?"

"I've got three," he said proudly, "not exactly your human cadaver dogs, but maybe worth a shot."

"Good lad," said Sarge. "Let's do it."

"My grandpa has an OKM 6000 Professional ground scanner if that helps," said Vicky Tranh, a young assistant from the Jarrajarra Library.

"You're joking," said Rob and Scott Farrell in chorus.

"Would he lend it to us?" asked Rob.

"He wouldn't lend it, but he might come up and work it for us, maybe if Chris asked him."

"I am sure Chris would be delighted to ask him," said Sarge.

That pumped my tyres a bit, and then Vicky deflated them in her next sentence.

"He'd definitely say yes if Ricky Chalmers asked him."

"Mate," whispered Rob Farrell into my ear, "they are worth about fifty grand. You have to get this. They go to about thirty metres and give you subterranean holograms. They are incredible. Fucking arrest him if he says no."

"I will," I promised Rob.

Vicky called her grandfather. There was no need for the cuffs. Mr Chang did not say no. He was happy to help. Turns out the reason he didn't lend his ground scanner, it was too complicated for most people.

We sent Raymond Twomey home to get his dogs and show Mr Chang the way up here at first light tomorrow.

Then, we resumed our search.

Then, much later in the day, we finally had a win.

* * *

At 6:00 PM, after dinner, we had our first hit. It came from one of the "old style" detectors.

There was a lot of excitement. Our 'find' went from a maybe to a yeah, to definitely. Sounded like a metal case three and a half metres down.

The bad news. If it was a grave, Carruthers had gone deeper and further out by forty metres than the grave we knew.

The general opinion amongst the crew was to start digging at our hot new site. Make sure we'd found a body.

Sarge said, "No". The plan was to wait for Crime Services, and we would stick to that. They were due tomorrow afternoon.

There were a few groans from the team.

"No digging till the Crime Services get here," Sarge was not bending.

I agreed. Some of our searchers were still in their teens. Dead bodies are a grim business for the untrained. Digging them up out of the ground can be the stuff of nightmares for anyone.

The other good news for the evening came in over the internet. The Jarrajarra Football-Netball Club had beaten Corryong in the footy and the netball. Both teams had won comfortably. Hopefully, some of the resting players would join the search tomorrow.

* * *

Late that night, I spoke to Wendy. She was busy at work, no time to miss me. Carruthers and McLain were both still alive. McLain would survive. Kenny was still a line ball, still ticking over in an induced coma in a Melbourne Hospital.

Not my problem.

Saturday, July 30, 2022

The Clearing.

I was first up at 4:30 AM. No time or space for the morning trail run. The trails here were rugged. God only knew where they went, potluck where you'd end up. Plus, they'd need full attention, or you'd be arse over breakfast before you knew what happened.

I went to the command tent, set the generator on, turned on the lights and plugged in the kettle. Morning coffee in the peace and quiet of the empty tent. All things were possible.

* * *

By 6:00 AM, the full contingent of four cops and eight searchers, twelve in all, were having breakfast. Fuelling up, waiting for the search to resume at first light, due in thirty minutes.

"Crime Services hope to be here early afternoon," said Sarge. He was sipping his coffee next to me outside the Command tent. "They're busy with a fatal crash on the Hume Highway. Will join us here as soon as they finish that."

Whenever we had murder victims to deal with, we called the deadly duo from Seymour Crime Services Unit Constables Carole and Glenda Johnston. Crime solving sisters. Whoever did what to who, up here in the Snowy, Carole and Glenda would get it sorted.

"Have you spoken to Detective Pete?" I asked.

"Yes," said Sarge. "Very relieved his key witness is back in custody. Not very stressed at all about his condition."

"As long as he's ready for the case against the Fenwicks?" I said.

"Not necessarily," said Sarge. "He seemed happy with the notion that the Federals had lost Carruthers, and we managed to catch him again. We probably have enough now with the bodies, the statements and the tapes. Carruthers might not be needed on the stand."

"Is Pete coming up here?"

"Well, son, I think that depends on his media priorities. If we find a few more bodies, he may find himself compelled to join us."

Sarge was as cynical as me about Detective Pete's devotion to his growing media profile.

* * *

By 9:30 AM, the team was out and about on the grid, scanning the ground without much early luck.

At 10:00 AM, the second Jarrajarra convoy arrived with another full load of useful stuff. Prime position on top of the equipment pile stood the famous Jarrajarra CFA Barbeque.

Following the lead truck was a line of four-wheel drive vehicles carrying pretty much the entire Jarrajarra football and netball teams. It felt like half the town had arrived to help.

The last of the convoy was a massive Toyota Troop Carrier. It had everything. Roof rack, solar panels, an extra row of high beam night lights on the grid, a row of moveable hunting lights above the driver's cabin, and even one of those river-crossing snorkel things. Driven by Jarrajarra's own media diva Darren 'Dazzle' Everett.

Beside Daz in the passenger seat was the smiling face of Victor Tranh, the owner of the vehicle and the man who owned the OKM 6000 Professional ground scanner. A device capable of deep analysis and underground holograms, but only if you knew what you were doing, according to Victor's granddaughter.

Our numbers had skyrocketed. I could have been concerned about the level of inexperience, but somehow, the show of community support just made my heart swell.

The council truck pulled up right beside the command tent. The rest of the convoy just found the best spaces they could within the boundary of the Scott Farrell improvised car park.

I was so proud, I didn't know what to say, I just thanked everyone as they unloaded. Thanked and thanked, and I meant it.

"Thank God Tim's not here," said Sarge, nodding toward Dazzling Darren.

I was watching Daz carefully. What would he bring today? He was such a variable package. 'Hope for the best, prepare for the worst,' my Nan would have said.

Daz looked ready to drive the massive Toyota past the other parking cars when Victor tapped him on the shoulder and pointed to a spot behind the arrivals. Daz complied without so much as a disgruntled shrug of the shoulders.

Sarge quickly rounded up the new arrivals to our designated

assembly point out front of the Command tent and gave them a shorter version of the search commandments he had delivered on the first day. Basically, be careful, wear the right gear, mind your own stuff, and don't put anything anywhere that it doesn't belong. Finally, above all else, be respectful.

As everyone proceeded to their business, Victor Tranh walked Daz over to the front of the tent to talk to Sarge. I wandered over for a listen.

"Darren has a computer and three large screens," said Victor. "Most important, he has a UPS. All of this stuff needs to be in the main tent so you can watch the screens while I scan."

"UPS?" said Sarge.

"You know," said Victor, "UPS, uninterruptible power supply. It is a big fancy battery that powers equipment. Protects the equipment from damage by shorting. Very useful."

"OK," said Sarge. Always reluctant when Daz was around. "So why the receivers?"

"Set them up. Everyone can get internet on their phones," said Victor, "and Darren gets the signal from the scanner into his computer. All connected."

"Oh," said Sarge, no further along in his understanding of UPS or the internet. "Why do we need all these televisions?"

"Computer screens," said Victor, "so you will be able to see what I see, only more."

Sarge looked bewildered.

"Best we stop talking," said Victor, "I will show you."

And so, it was done, and with Constable Tim back in Jarrajarra and Ricky Chalmers busy, I took over as the Daz-Controller. I was keen to see if this technology hung together.

It did. Spectacularly.

* * *

By 1:00 PM, Victor was out of the tent, working the grid, scanning the ground. Making crosscuts and three-dimensional videos down to five metres, showing rocks and hollows and whatever happened to be there.

By 1:30 PM, Victor and Daz had painted portraits of twelve of our grids. Once a grid was locked down and digitised, Daz could scan back and forth and up and down to review every part of it.

This was space-age stuff. It felt like cheating, like looking underground with binoculars.

At 1:37 PM, on the thirteenth grid, another twenty metres out from the first body, we found another. Daz shouted, "Victor! There! There!"

"Yes, yes, I see," said Victor, his voice coming through the speaker on Daz's computer.

Daz launched into a two-handed frenzy with the computer's mouse and gearstick controller.

The middle of the three screens seemed to move through the earth horizontally, zoom in on a fixed point, and then focus.

Revealing what?

"Oh, my goodness," said Sarge.

We were looking at the hollow eye sockets of a human skull.

Victor Tranh and Dazzling Darren Everett had found their first corpse.

Daz was speaking. It took me a moment to realise he was talking into his computer microphone. His words appeared as text on the computer screen before us.

"Cadaver 1," said Daz to the computer text converter thing, "contained in grid 37, GPS location, is," he clicked about five different things with the mouse. From all that clicking, the GPS coordinates appeared on the screen to six decimal places.

Daz clicked again and then turned to me, "I'm making a video record of all this as it happens," he said, wiggling his eyebrows in self-approval. Still Daz under all that expertise. Another click and he back was speaking words into screen text as I watched.

Watching the screens, it appeared as though Daz was zooming through the earth like a fish in water. Moving upwards on the centre screen, there it was a steel box. Full of cash, according to Ken Carruthers. Hard to tell from the holograms on the screens.

Where were the Crime Service team? Fuck organized patience, now. I was desperate to dig and see what, or who, we had found.

Daz zoomed back to the skull, then shifted the frame scale outwards on the right-hand screen. We now had the skull on the centre screen and the whole skeleton on the right-hand screen.

I couldn't tell what it was flashing by on the left screen. Numbers on numbers. It must have meant something to Daz or Victor.

Sarge was transfixed.

Daz was talking. The text appeared. It all just flowed.

"Skeleton is tall, approximately 190 centimetres, six foot four inches, heel to head."

Virginia Collins was tall, but not that tall.

"Can we get some visuals, please, Victor," asked Daz. "Context, mate, context."

A video appeared on the left screen. It must have been attached to Victor's head. We could see what Victor was looking at. Hard to place where he was from what we could see on the screen. The vision was all over the place. Hard to watch and not get seasick.

"I might go and be Victor's camera bloke," I offered, sick of being a spectator in the tent.

"Good idea," said Sarge, and off I went.

How hard could it be?

"Grab a headset," said Daz before I got too far. "I can guide you. Tell you where to shoot." Giving Daz control of my headset, I had to be out of my mind.

As it turned out, he was excellent. Clear and precise. Fair to say, with his patient guidance, I did some of my best work. Actually, my only work as a videographer, but who's counting. I got the mids, the wide screens and the close-ups. Every shot, every time. I flogged the autofocus to death. Even Sarge was shouting instructions by the end of the day.

"Give me a middy," said Sarge at one point, loving the jargon.

After a few hours, Victor, the scanner, the camera, and the constable were as one.

* * *

By 6:30 PM, Victor Tranh called it quits. He was tired. It was easy to forget the muscular little bloke was seventy-five years old and here as a volunteer.

The body count at the end of Victor's first day was five. Five. All men.

One was our first, the one we discovered last night. The other four belonged to Victor and Daz on their science fiction scanner and computer.

Then a call came in from Raymond Twomey who was still going out there in the dark. His three beautiful German Shepherds, Lilly, Milly, and Tilly were howling for attention. Deeper in the bush, further up the rise.

"Old blood, I think," said Raymond when we arrived. "There is a bit of a mound but I can't see anything else," he added.

The body was confirmed by Victor and his camera guy, me, with help from Daz back in the command tent.

What a day. I was as excited by each individual find as much as I was by the first. But none appeared to be Virginia. Too tall, or the scanner picked up men's belts or boots, or their skulls bore no signs of fracture. None of them Virginia.

The Crime Service sisters had texted several times, "Sorry we're late. Can't get away." Etcetera, etcetera.

We needed them. We had reached a point where we really needed to unearth these bodies. See what we have found.

We retired to the mess tent for dinner. Soon for bed, when the rumble of an approaching four-wheel drive was heard. Sounded like a big one. Sarge and I stepped outside the mess tent to welcome our new guests.

Powerful headlights bounced through bushes and tents, shining in our eyes till we couldn't see, then disappearing behind the massive trunk of a snow gum. The early evening mist caught the light, even as the truck disappeared behind trees.

It all came to a halt in front of us, and then the sound show stopped, but the lights stayed on, fixed on our faces. Behind the glare, I heard two truck doors open and then slam shut.

"Chris Taylor, where the fuck have you dragged us this time?" said Constable Carole Johnston.

Seymour Crime Services team had arrived for duty. They were driving a four-wheel drive tank with a large, refrigerated cabin on the back. The side door had a label, Crime Services, Victoria Police.

"What's this?" I asked.

"This," said Carole, "is a loaner from Detective Pete, courtesy of Homicide HQ. You can think of it as a high-quality limo service for dead people. Comfy beds for ten at a time, racked and stacked."

I must have pulled a face of some sort.

"Don't worry, Chris," said Glenda, patting my shoulder. "When we find your friend Virginia, she will get the royal treatment, I promise."

"Any chance of a cup of tea and a biscuit?" asked Carole.

"This way, ladies," said Sarge, pointing to the door of the mess tent. "I think we can do better than tea and biscuits."

Finally, a full team at last. In the highest and wildest bush in the state of Victoria where bad men roamed free, and the dead had lay buried for decades.

Command tents, Mess tents, computers, high precision ground scanners, volunteer searchers, A Crime Services team, and now, to cap it all off, a refrigerated truck.

Justice, however cumbersome, had finally arrived.

Led here by Rob Farrell and me, following an illegal device planted on a crook's motorbike with no warrant and no authority.

Hopefully, amidst all these people and their machinery, the legal system might miss the fact that I'd cheated to get us here and, along the way, put a bullet in the man who invaded my home.

Sunday, July 31, 2022

The Clearing.

"I reckon if you let the girls sniff around the first one after we dig it up, they'll find the last couple in no time."

Breakfast in the mess tent and Raymond Twomey was speaking to Carole and Glenda.

Our Crime Services Officers weren't too excited with the idea of some strange bloke and his girls sniffing around their first cadaver.

The determination with which they both chewed their toast, mouths firmly shut, told me they were not convinced.

"Raymond has three excellent hunting dogs," I said by way of explanation.

"Lilly, Milly, and Tilly," said Raymond.

"OK," said Carole.

"We usually work with police-trained cadaver dogs," said Glenda.

"The girls, that is to say, the dogs," I said, "have already found one of the bodies, and it was a long way from the base of the search. So, it was a good effort."

Our CSU was dubious. Being a trained policeman, I could detect dubious.

"Yeah, so like up till yesterday," said Raymond, "the girls have only done deer and foxes and that stuff. So, they were just basically looking for blood, which they found. Eventually."

Raymond's pitch was not getting through. Not a salesman by trade, his big idea was failing at the first refusal.

"You train a cadaver dog by exposing it to the smell you want it to find," I said, doing my best. "The dog goes out, and if it finds that smell, it gets a reward."

"OK," said Carole.

"Bit late in the game for smell training," said Glenda.

"Probably, possibly," I said, "But these are experienced dogs. They can track down animals, and after a kill or a wound, they can track the animal by the blood traces."

"OK," said Carole. Not saying no. That was something.

"From what Carruthers told me," I continued, "he wrapped the victims in tarpaulins. Those tarpaulins have been in the ground with the cadavers for years. The whole package must have some sort of specific smell."

"OK," said Carole. "We dig one up, and these ladies sniff around. How do we tell them to find that smell?"

"You don't tell 'em," said Raymond. "It's their instinct. Like a cattle dog, it's born to push cattle. No one trains 'em. Start when they're pups. Give 'em a pat when they get it right. Good kelpie, by one-year-old, best cattle hand you'll ever have. Instinct."

"Instinct?" asked Glenda.

"Yeah," said Raymond, "instinct and plenty of practice. And for sniffers, all they need is a good solid whiff of what we are looking for."

* * *

We decided at breakfast to dig up the bodies we'd found in their order of discovery. That was the plan.

Carole and Glenda had worked out a digging agenda. Scott Farrell would use the rusty old digger to gather out the top layer of dirt and rocks from the grave site. When we hit the soft sand Carruthers had laid to make it easier to find his money, I would take over the sand removal with a shovel.

"Very carefully with the shovel," said Glenda,

"No power tools for you, Constable," said Carole, enjoying herself.

"This will take forever," I said.

"Price of perfection," said Glenda.

And so we went, inch by agonising inch.

An hour into the dig, we found the steel case. It wasn't very big, six inches by six by six. It was wrapped in transparent plastic. Beneath the dirty plastic, the whole thing was heavily oiled. Kenny had clearly intended to come back for it.

Carole climbed into the hole, did a bag and tag, and then passed the case out to Glenda. All of this activity was captured by Constable Joyce using the CSU video camera.

Most of the team had gathered around. Glenda had spray-painted an orange crime scene perimeter on the ground, and the gang had faithfully remained outside the line.

Here we were, finally looking at our first metal case. A Kenny Carruthers trophy tin, in the grave the boys had found Friday night using the old-fashioned metal detector.

Curiosity. Deep curiosity was the mood of the moment.

"I think we'd all like a peek inside the money box," said Sarge, "if that is at all possible."

I was the same, another rubber-necker, keen as mustard to know what was inside the tin. Sarge, I knew, was thinking of the volunteer searchers. A reward for effort.

Glenda removed the case from her plastic bag, then carefully removed the Carruthers' plastic wrap. Finally, the mystery tin sat there on a CSU tarpaulin on the ground before us. Glenda clicked the greasy locks, and the latches sprung open. She gently lifted the lid.

Inside, the small steel case was packed to the sides and the brim with cash. Fifty dollar notes.

A collective gasp of "Wow" and "Bloody hell" from the assembled group. I checked the Google. "Two piles of fifty Australian dollar notes stacked six inches high, how much?" I typed.

"One hundred thousand dollars," according to the mobile phone of wisdom.

One steel case opened, plus the cattle money and another seven graves to go. The crew was right, that could be a lot of money.

And we still had to do the body.

"OK, everyone. Listen up," said Sarge. "This is a good result. I am glad you all saw it. This confirms our information is correct. We are on the right track, and you all deserve to know that and see it for yourself. So well done, everyone."

Stroke, stroke.

"Now, the next stage is the body, and I can assure you it will be very confronting. A job for the police, I am afraid."

"Can I ask you all to go back to your assigned tasks now and leave the recovery of the body to our experts? Let Crime Services handle this while you all resume your search for the two missing graves."

Stroke, stroke, gentle punch.

"What you are doing is absolutely vital. We are all grateful, but from this point on, none of us, police included, are helping much by standing around watching the Crime Service Unit perform these very difficult tasks."

Stroke, stroke, gentle punch, finish off with a final soft stroke. The Sarge approach.

"OK, everyone," shouted Fire Chief Greg Farrell. "Let's get back to it."

And it was done.

Everyone went back to their assigned mission except Raymond Twomey and his three girls. Raymond wasn't going anywhere till Lilly, Milly and Tilly took a good whiff of the uncovered cadaver. He'd asked if they could. No one had said yes, exactly, but no one said no either. So here they were, waiting patiently for their time to learn by smelling.

Meanwhile, Glenda carefully re-tinned the money, and after a bit of consultation, I was back in the hole, removing sand.

The hole was now so deep Scotty Farrell had lowered the bucket on the digger into the grave so I could fill that rather than toss sand randomly from the depths. When I filled the bucket or needed to swap ends, Scotty gently lifted the bucket out of the grave and dropped the sand in a pile somewhere out of the way.

From the holograms we had made with the scanner, I was looking for a body around twenty centimetres, eight inches, below the base of the steel case.

Slow going.

Commentary from my fellow police officers was relentless.

"Any time this year will be fine," from Carole, whenever I was too slow, even for the ever-careful CSU ladies.

"Easy, Killer," from Glenda, whenever my haste exceeded her required level of caution.

"Does he always need this much direction?" asked Constable 'Big-Help' Joyce.

"Always," harmonised Carole and Glenda.

"Lost without it," added Glenda.

I was in a lose-lose situation.

They were having fun with their commentary. Me? Not so much. I was now forty-eight hours without a run. I needed something as a distraction. Digging and mockery would have to do. Then, with no warning, I gently scraped the edge of a rope. It was quickly obvious the rope was tied around a very grotty, blue plastic tarpaulin.

"Here we go," said Carole, excited.

"Better get you out of there, Killer," said Glenda.

We swapped places, and Glenda resumed the dig with a tiny hand trowel.

Twenty minutes later, the full tarpaulin package had been exposed. Another twenty minutes after that, we had it out of the ground and laying on a plank stretcher.

Carole took a careful peek inside the tarp and confirmed we had a body.

"First passenger for the ice truck?" said Carole.

While we all had a think about that, Lilly, Milly and Tilly were having a good sniff around the edges of the tarp.

"Don't let them touch," said Glenda.

"OK," said Raymond, not paying the slightest bit of attention. Focussed on his girls.

* * *

Lunch-time in the mess tent.

"The girls are going well," said Raymond. "If your friend Virginia's here, they'll find her."

"I'm grateful you're here, mate," I said. "I appreciate you trying. Every bit helps."

I didn't mean to sound unimpressed, but I must have.

"I know," said Raymond. "I can count. Victor's finding most of them, but he's only human. The girls will go all day, all year, if we need to. When everyone else has given up, they will still be looking. I promise."

"I appreciate it, Ray, I really do."

"You don't believe me. You'll see."

A massive, heavy hand rested on Raymond's shoulder.

"Excuse me, Ray-man," said Ricky Chalmers, "I need to borrow the policeman for a bit."

"Yeah, sure," as if Raymond would say no.

"What's happening?" I asked.

"You got your gear?"

"Yes," I answered, "in the truck."

"Your boss has decided you need a run. Actually, Greg Farrell decided, and your Sarge agreed. Greg reckons you're looking a bit haunted."

"Haunted?"

Such is life in the Jarrajarra. The fire chief felt I looked haunted, so running it was.

"Wear your boots," said Ricky. "Your runners won't cope up here."

Who would argue with Ricky Chalmers, the king of the wild high country? Boots it was.

"And grab your backpack and put these in it." Ricky handed me a couple of wrapped sandwiches and three one-litre bottles of water."

I went to my tent and made ready, and away we went.

Apparently, I looked haunted, and a run was the cure.

You don't exactly run with Ricky, especially on mountain trails. You take your life in your hands and try your best to keep up. Heart and lungs might collapse, but you just keep going. Today, he was on a mission, so he mercifully waited for me at key points along the trail.

If Ricky lost the cop, Sarge would not be pleased.

We ran over dust-covered rocks and spiky roots that broke through the soil at dangerously random spots. The trail, if you could call it that, was a creation of water erosion and bush animals. The boots proved essential.

Turns out Ken Carruthers' hideaway was not unique to the area. We passed two more abandoned logging stations. Deserted in the bush, same rusted machinery, small clearings with remnant roads hidden below the canopy of towering gums.

Incredibly beautiful.

We stopped for a break after an hour. We'd reached a place that my map described as 'Small Unofficial Camping Ground'.

Logging had left this spot open to the sky. We found a massive tree stump beside a clear, free-flowing, rocky creek. About six metres wide and full. We took a seat on the stump to enjoy our sandwiches and water.

"It is called Mountain Creek," said Ricky.

"Original," I said.

"I did a few dugouts around here, you never found," he said. Amused.

"They still in use?"

"I doubt it," said Ricky. "Most of my patrons are dead."

"Footy is a lot safer."

"There's that," he said. "More fun as well. They're a grim lot, your drug growers."

We sat for a while. Ate our sandwiches and drank most of our water. Saved some for the run back. I might have fallen asleep sitting there on the weathered stump.

Ricky woke me with a whisper.

"Keep really quiet," said Ricky, "that's a whip bird through there." I couldn't see what he was looking at, but after a moment, the whip-crack bird song rang through the bush.

"Psophodes Olivaceus," he said.

I must have looked shocked.

"What?" asked Ricky.

"The last bloke who told me the scientific name of the whip bird was Ken Carruthers. Right before I shot him."

"Right," said Ricky, maybe a tiny bit shocked himself. "He must be quite a guy, this Carruthers."

What could I say to that? "Scum of the earth."

"Glad you shot him?" asked Ricky.

"Glad?" It was a good question. "I haven't thought about it much yet, to be honest. He tried to shoot me and wasn't good enough. I'm glad as hell about that."

"Well, there you go," said Ricky. "Greg said take you for a run and cheer you up. That's the extent of my therapeutical power exhausted."

I had to laugh.

"Mate, I will tell you what I am glad about. I am very glad you all came out to help me. I know it is my own personal quest here, and it is a hell of a stretch for everyone else, but here you all are, and I am very grateful."

"I think we need to run back," said Ricky. "You're getting soppy."

We stood up, stretched and adjusted our backpacks in preparation.

"Ricky," I said before he could run off, "this next bit is not pretty. Digging up dead bodies, all murder victims. It is going to get gruesome. I know your mob are keen and curious, but they are mostly kids. I don't want to put them through something they're not ready for. Best we get the younger ones home, hey?"

"I hear you," he said. "Leave the corpses to the cops."

"Great," I said. There might have been a better way to send them home after all their efforts, but that was the best I could do.

It hardly seemed possible, but Ricky ran us back to base harder and faster than we had run out.

In the hours we had been away, I missed a visit from Detective Pete Jordan and his travelling media circus. Helicopter, cameras, the ever-beautiful Angela Adams, wide shots, close-ups, cut-aways and talking heads. The whole extravaganza.

"You sent me off on purpose," I said to Sarge.

"Well, I knew he was coming, and Greg was worried about your state of mind," said Sarge. "I thought you'd enjoy a break."

"How was it?"

"Absolutely excruciating. Pete Jordan is getting worse," said Sarge. "Best not to talk about it. Go and get some dinner." Ending that conversation.

The mess tent was full of hungry volunteers. Filling up for the drive home. Ricky had made it look easy. Most would have to be back at their jobs tomorrow morning, and they all looked exhausted. "We've found the bodies and cracked the case," was the consensus.

While I was away on my running break, Carole and Glenda had bagged and tagged another body. Another tin case, twenty thousand dollars in this one, plus a wallet and driver's licence.

Plus, another tarpaulin wrapper around the cadaver. Ken Carruthers had a signature style of disposal.

Carole found me in the mess tent.

"G'day Killer," she said. "Hope you don't have any urgent appointments in the next few days."

"This going to take a while?" I asked.

"About a week, I'd say."

Another week to collect and account for all the missing bodies. It made no difference to me. I would not be leaving till I found Virginia.

Wednesday, August 3, 2022

The Clearing.

Midweek.

Inevitably, the search had scaled down. It had to. There is a finite limit to the time volunteers can spare for a cold case nearly two decades old.

Sarge and the Wodonga cops had gone back home to work. The Jarrajarra footy and netball teams had headed home before we got down and dirty digging up the dead. Even our mechanical beast, Scott Farrell, had returned home to work at Farrell's garage. Someone had to keep the wheels of our tiny town turning.

Rob Farrell had stayed, so we had someone on hand to drive the old machinery. Victor Tranh also remained behind with his ground scanner, and the Daz had stayed with all his computer equipment.

Greg Farrell had also stayed, mainly as our cook, and he was good. He tended toward the keto side of the equation. Meat and veg, his signature dish. No one complained. You could always cook for yourself if you wanted different. Most of us were too hungry by the end of every day to worry about the balance of the food. Volume mattered most.

Ray Twomey and his three beautiful dogs had stayed as well. Ray had set himself a rigid schedule. Early breakfast for the girls and himself, then off into the bush by 7:00 AM. Back at 1:00 PM to feed and water his dogs and himself. Dogs first, always. By 2:00 PM, he would return to the task. He would be out there till the last light every night.

Ray was as obsessed as I was but had better tools for the job a hand.

There were four cops left. Me, Joycey and the two CSU, Carole and Glenda.

Carole and Glenda would supervise the digging and the retrieval of the bodies. Do their best to determine a cause of death, catalogue the artifacts, and try and work out who these people were and how they died. It was grim, horrible work. Names and places and likely murderers were emerging from the ground.

It was an evil place.

Joycey and I were the odd pair, no special skills, just fit and keen. There was always something to lift or carry. Plus, we took turns working either the CSU camera or the Daz-Victor context camera. Always something to do.

I preferred working with Victor. As much as I loved the CSU ladies, there is only so much scorn one humble policeman can take. Especially when it is funny and mostly accurate.

Victor Tranh, on the other hand, was the most polite person I'd ever met. He was in his seventies but puttered on at a steady, deliberate pace all day, every day. Never too fast, never too slow. He just persisted.

In the days since he arrived with Daz, they had mapped our original grid plan and had extended it another fifty metres by twenty, adding another thousand square metres along the gully section where the previous bodies had been found.

We were walking and talking. Victor never took his eyes off the monitor on his scanner. I was much the same working the camera, giving Daz his 'context'.

"How do you keep so fit?" I asked while we were fossicking together.

"Eat healthy, keep active. Not difficult. Mystery to me why people get so unfit?"

"I don't know. Bad luck?"

"Yeah, and bad choices," he said. "You were a soldier?"

"I was," I answered.

"My granddaughter told me you were special forces?"

"Ummm, yeah, lowest cog in the SASR, me."

"Very fit soldiers," said Victor. "Very scary. Fight dirty. Fight to win?"

"That's true," I said. "We had the best training."

"Training?" said Victor. "We didn't get much training, more learn on the job. Learn quick or die. Better to be fit and healthy than not. If someone is trying to kill you, the fittest person usually wins."

"Depends on the type of contest, Victor."

"I've seen you running on the road. Going to the rifle range with Rob Farrell. Always training. This fellow, Carruthers, he tried to shoot you, yeah?"

"Yes, he did."

"And he goes home in the ambulance. You're still here helping me. The fittest person wins. Same with armies, same with teams. Like Ricky Chalmers, a great coach. The fittest team wins. I like Ricky."

"Which army were you in, Victor?"

He looked up from his scanner for the first time in our conversation. Smiled.

"I played for the other team," he said. "Our secret, hey?"

"Our secret, absolutely," I said.

"It's why I live in Jarrajarra. The Viet Cong is not so popular with most Vietnamese Aussies. Not popular with a lot of Aussies either," he said with a smile. It's good here. No one cares. It's all ancient history now, so long ago."

"But here we are," he said after a moment, his eyes fixed on his monitor. "Just you and me, two old soldiers. You, maybe not so old. Still going. We will find your friend, Chris. Bring her home to her father. The fittest team will win."

"Never give up," I said.

"Never," said Victor.

We would need to persist. Another day passed and still no luck in finding Virginia.

Thursday, August 4, 2022

The Clearing.

"Chris, I think we've found something," said Ray Twomey.

It was 9:00 AM, in camp. Ray had been out with the girls since 7:00 AM. I was waiting in the mess tent for Victor to finish his breakfast.

"You think? You're not sure?" I asked.

"Yeah, I think," he said. "Girls are really agitated by a particular spot. Something there they don't like. Might be worth getting old Victor to have a look with his widget."

"Victor's Widget? OK."

"Victor went pretty late last night," I said. "Have a coffee, mate. Let him finish his breakfast."

From the other end of the table, Victor had heard it all.

"I'm ready," he said. "Let's do it."

* * *

"So Carole and Glenda told me that Virginia was probably the first. Yeah?" said Ray.

"Yes," I said, "from the information gathered, I believe she was the first person buried here."

'Information gathered' was a civilised way of saying, 'What Ken Carruthers told me before I shot him." I was tailoring my story for public consumption already.

We were walking along a ridge three hundred metres further east than anywhere we had searched before and higher. It wasn't exactly the direction Ken Carruthers had pointed when he tried to distract me, but it wasn't far off.

Ray and the girls, Victor with his gear, Rob Farrell, and me. Walking and talking.

"So," said Ray, "all of the other bodies were in the wide gully behind that horrible old shed, right. Well, I was thinking about where we hadn't looked. If Virginia was the first, maybe he picked a spot that wasn't so easy."

"Sounds reasonable," I said. "Maybe the first wasn't a business yet?"

"Yeah," said Ray, "with the later ones, he was more efficient."

"Maybe just lazier," offered Rob. "Maybe first time out. He wasn't thinking too straight. Making it up as he went along."

"OK," I said.

"I reckon, first time, he used the old digger," said Ray

"You sound pretty sure," I said.

"Have a look at this."

He stopped at a broad rock that poked out of the earth, surrounded by long grasses and moss. The rock was like a broad three-metre span of poorly laid concrete. It looked like a mini mountain of grey and black. Totally smooth, except for the track marks crushed into the hard surface.

"These indentations," said Ray, "I measured them against the metal tracks on the excavator back in the shed. They match."

"OK," I said. They looked like they could match.

Ray pulled his mobile phone out of his pocket and showed me a photograph.

"Have a look," he said,

The first photograph showed the indentations in front of us. He also had a ruler displayed over the photograph so I could see the true size of the indentations.

"Didn't know you could do that," I said.

I got a surprised look and a derogatory mumble for that comment.

"Now look at this," Ray swiped to the next photo in his collection.

The same ruler thing overlaid the photo in his app. This photo was of the metal tracks that encased the wheels of the excavator.

He flicked back and forth between two photos. The indentations in the rock and the tread of the metal tracks size-matched perfectly.

"You see?" said Ray.

"I see."

"Now this," he said and showed me a photograph of a sign on the excavator. It said 'Parks Victoria' and under that a few hieroglyphics that indicated what department it belonged to plus a date, 1998.

"Finally, this," Ray showed me another photo. "This is a pic of the registration plate I took from the engine of the smaller digger. You know, the backhoe thing."

"The little digger? Not the excavator?" I said.

"Yeah, the little digger, and you can see, the year of construction was 2003."

"The year after Virginia disappeared," I said.

"That's what Carole told me," said Ray.

"So," I said, "the only equipment available in 2002 that could get all the way up here and dig a hole big enough for a body is the excavator?"

"Carruthers told me," I said, "some of the equipment in the shed was already here, some he stole.

"Exactly," said Ray. "Plus, digging a hole with the excavator is OK. It would be kind of a big hole. But how do you fill it in without crushing everything inside the hole, including your money box."

"You don't drive over it?" said Rob Farrell, who'd dug more than his share of holes.

"Exactly. You push the dirt over it using the front of the blade, then extend the blade to reach past the hole, then smooth the mound of dirt down by reversing and using the back of the blade."

"So," I said, "you don't run the weight of the wheels over the hole?"

"Dead right," said Ray. "That would get the job done, but it'd never be as smooth as the backhoe."

"So, Carruthers' first go at hiding a body, he leaves a bit of a mound, at least the width of the excavator's blade," I said.

"There's a learning curve for everything," said Rob Farrell. "Even being an evil bastard."

"The girls found a mound?" I asked.

"They did," he said, "and they know jack shit about excavators versus backhoes."

The beautiful Alsatian ladies, Lilly, Milly and Tilly, had been sitting quietly beside Ray as we spoke.

"Show me," he said and snapped his fingers, and the dogs sprinted off, further and higher along the ridge, disappearing into the bracken and undergrowth.

Two minutes later, we could hear them barking for attention.

What with working through the undergrowth and fallen branches while helping Victor with his gear, it took us much longer than two minutes to reach them.

Then, there it was, a section of ground that had been cleared and smoothed, then overgrown again exactly as you would expect a piece of land worked over by an excavator. Done twenty years ago by an inexperienced operator.

At the end of the flattened section, standing on a weed-covered mound, were Ray's girls. His beautiful, brilliant dogs.

"There you go," said Ray. He whistled, and the girls joined Ray, standing with us and looking at our target.

"And there is this," Ray walked about ten metres left of the mound area. "I haven't touched it, I promise, just cleared the brush a tiny bit so I could see what it was. The girls found it first then they got distracted by the mound."

We stood beside Ray, looking down at a cleared piece of ground within a sea of bracken.

A long-handed shovel. Old and abandoned, 'Parks Victoria' stamped on the handle.

"I reckon he might have had a go at digging with this first, then figured it was too hard, chucked it, and maybe forgot it or couldn't find it after he was finished."

"Jesus, Ray," I said. "Dunno if we've found Virginia, but this is a hell of an effort, mate."

"Very well done, young Ray," said Victor.

"Wasn't me," he said. "The girls did all the work."

"You make a very good team," I said.

We looked back at the mound of dirt, capped with weeds.

Virginia? Maybe?

Missing nearly twenty years, if this was her burial place, Carruthers had chosen well. She would never have been found in a thousand years.

"Don't think, just do," I whispered as much to myself as anyone.

"Yes," said Victor, "let's see if we have found your friend."

* * *

It took about ten minutes for Victor to get set up and make his connection to Daz back in the command tent.

I had the camera in my hand and the headphones on, which meant I had Dazzle back in my ear again. It wasn't so bad. He had behaved impeccably the whole time here at the search. He had become the technical lead, and his confirmations that we had a body under our scan had proved correct every time.

I was filming Victor, who was now on the top of the mound, from camera left to right, north to south. I had shot my mids and wides, and I was now keeping quiet, listening to the dialogue between Daz and Victor.

"OK, said Daz, "stop now." Victor stopped.

"Now pivot on the left end of the scanner," said Daz.

Victor did a full 360-degree turn, using the left end of the scanner as the centre of his turning circle.

"Now, straight ahead."

Victor followed instructions, walking and scanning back to where he had come from, except he was now one scanner width to his right. East. His new scan line was parallel to the previous.

"Stop," said Daz.

Victor stopped.

"Give it a moment to compile," Daz's computer always took a moment to catch up to Victor's scan. He had explained several times that it needed time to compile the thousands of infinitesimal two-dimensional slices taken by the scanner into a three-dimensional hologram.

Every time he explained it, I understood it less, but I was getting good and nodding with a look of understanding on my face.

Daz wanted time to compile.

Go for it.

"We've got a body," said Daz. "Two metres down, and there's another box. About fifty centimetres above her."

Why did he say 'her'?

"We're coming up there, now," said Carole over the headphones.

For some reason, I was nervous as hell. Feeling sick in my stomach.

* * *

It had taken a week, but our little team had developed a good system.

The 'new' body and the steel box were out of the ground, lying beside the grave, within two hours.

There were no jokes now. Maybe Carole and Glenda were being respectful on my behalf for a dead person who may well be my friend.

Everyone else had stepped back. The three of us were wearing the full hazard suits. Carole and Glenda had headphones on and were recording their observations.

"We've seen this rope before," said Glenda as they worked through the rope that held the tarpaulin together.

"Hemp, three-strand, no synthetics, no nylon. Same as the rope on the two bodies from under the duck hunters."

"Just about ready to disintegrate," said Carole.

Glenda laboured away with the rotting rope till the tarpaulin was unbound and a sufficient quantity of the rope had been bagged.

"The tarp is not so old, plastic or vinyl. Got a label here," said Glenda, holding up the tarp label to Carole, who photographed it. Carole then fiddled with her phone, searching for details of the tarpaulin.

"The House of Tarps, been going since 1980," said Carole, reading from her phone. "It's old enough. Same rope as around the bodies under the duck hunters. This tarp is older than theirs."

"OK," said Glenda. "Let's see who we've got here."

"Good luck, Chris, mate," said Carole.

That caught me unawares. Didn't realise my anxiety was so obvious.

Glenda slowly folded back the tarpaulin, exposing the body, starting at the feet.

She had been in the ground since 2002. No part of the body was neat and tidy.

The first thing I saw were Adidas runners. The three signature stripes of the Adidas brand were still clear enough to identify despite nearly two decades in the ground. They may have been white originally but were now a dirt-encrusted grey.

Glenda peeled the tarpaulin back further.

Our victim was wearing a yellow Nike running hoodie and grey Nike running shorts. The hoodie and shorts were dirty and covered in blood but in relatively good condition, considering. Clearly recognisable.

"Nike clothes and Adidas runners," I said. "Virginia's preferred gear." The same running outfit Rusty had described.

"She was blonde, wasn't she?" asked Glenda.

"Blonde, yeah," I said. "Cut shortish at the time of death."

Glenda reached into her kit and grabbed a pair of tweezers. She leant into the partly unfolded tarp and extracted a hair. She held it up so we could all see.

"That's not blonde," she said. "Eight inches, white and wavy."

"Our murderer," said Carole.

Albert Fenwicks' perfectly coiffed, rich-boy mullet. Fuck you, Lord Fauntleroy. You are going down.

I worked through the photos on my phone to find the images of Virginia, her dad, Rusty, had provided me. I found a photo of Virginia in her favourite running clothes.

I showed it to Carole. She just nodded.

Glenda had peeled back the last section of tarpaulin very slowly, revealing the skull.

The skeleton was around 175 to 180 centimetres. Five-foot nine to five foot eleven.

The skull lay as though the face had turned to the right.

It looked as though the skull had been encased in plastic. Strangely, the plastic hadn't lasted so well. It must have been damaged during the burial. Green and mouldy, it had partly disintegrated and the remainder had clung to the face, Virginia's face. Her facial skin had shrunken to the skull but was strangely intact around the mouth and eyes.

Glenda gently turned the skull so we could see the entire face and head.

There was a hole in the right temple, identical to the mallet wounds in the skulls of the Savage father and son who we'd found in the Mellish Paddock three months ago.

"Well done, mate," Carole whispered. "I think you've found your friend."

Glenda grabbed my hand and turned the phone so she could see it. She looked back and forth between the beautiful person in the photograph and the body before us.

"Good job, Chris," she said. "Bloody amazing, mate."

"Team effort," I said.

"She was one beautiful woman," said Carole, looking again at my photo of Virginia.

"Yes," I said. "She really was. Inside and out."
"So sorry, Chris," said Carole, rubbing my shoulder. "So sorry."

* * *

The next few hours flew by, getting things done. The victim, the process, almost a sad, horrible ritual by now.
I was devastated. No crime in my police career had ever been so personal, and here we were. My beautiful friend. No longer a mystery.
I'd phoned Sarge with the news. Daz had set up a Zoom session from the command tent. Sarge, Carole, Glenda, Detective Pete and me.
I hadn't spoken to Pete since I'd taken off in pursuit of the escapees Carruthers and McLain. That had been a week ago and Sarge had handled all communications since then.

* * *

Here we were in the command tent, Daz's world now. Zooming.
"Congratulations all around," said Pete. "Amazing result. Amazing."
"Thanks," said Carole, "I reckon I've killed it."
"You had help," said Glenda. Fake annoyed.
"I did? Really?" Pause, "OK, yeah, I suppose." Fake modesty.
"How certain are you this last person is Virginia Savage?" asked Pete. Did he just use her married name to annoy me?
"Virginia Collins," said Glenda. "As certain as I can be without DNA. Just need that to confirm. But clothing, height, the contents of the box we found with the body."
"We are certain," said Carole in over-ride. "Would like to do DNA just to tick that box, but I'm one hundred per cent."
"Yeah. Me too," said Glenda, conceding.
"I suppose this is why Carruthers was so cagey on the location of Virginia's body," said Sarge.
"Ten dead," said Pete. "Not three, kind of blows his deal."
The Zoom window went quiet while we all had a think about that.
"OK," said Sarge. "Moving along. Pete? How are the two escapees?"
"Well," said Pete, "our happy couple, in case you missed the news, Wodonga Hospital passed on taking them. They were tight on space

and, probably, still tainted from Kenny's previous visit. The Wodonga Emergency team sent the helicopter to the Alfred."

McLain and Carruthers were now bedded down in the secure ward at Alfred Hospital Melbourne, just around the corner from St Kilda Road Police Headquarters. They now belonged to the Justice System under the direct administration of Detective Pete Jordan.

"McLain is doing well. Awake, can talk, but not talking, if you know what I mean. She's going to be OK, healthwise. Judicially, her bail has been revoked."

"And forfeited?" asked Sarge.

"Yes," said Pete. "Plus, she has nothing we need, so unless that team of hers can pull another miracle, she is facing a long stint of incarceration.

"Carruthers?" Asked Sarge

"Not so good. Struggling."

"What if he dies?" said Sarge.

"If he dies, we lose his testimony. Our case against the Fenwicks gets tougher, but it is still strong. I don't think we are dead in the water. Actually, I'd say we are almost as good without Kenny. With the bodies, Carruthers' original statements, and the recordings, I'm confident."

"We have stuff here," said Glenda, "possible DNA from Fenwick. Then we've got hessian ropes, tarpaulins, and these cash boxes. I reckon we go back and search the Fenwick garages to match this rope."

"There is so much stuff," said Carole. "We've got hairs inside all of these tarps. Has to be a match to Albert somewhere in amongst it. Has to be."

"Was there a box with Virginia's body?"

"Yeah," said Carole. "Family photos, a couple of books, and ten thousand dollars."

"My goodness," said Sarge. "The man was a self-incriminating hoarder."

"He was a blackmailer," I said. "Tools of his trade."

We all stopped to think. Whatever reason Carruthers had for burying his stuff the way he did, it was clearly never meant to be found by anyone but him.

"If Carruthers dies, Chris has to face a coronial inquest," said

Sarge.

"Yeah, there's that," said Pete. Mister sympathy. "Don't hold your breath. Courts are still months behind from the pandemic.

"He'll be fine," said Carole. "Chris is safe as houses on this. "Self-defence, reacting to an attack by a known murderer."

"Murderer?" asked Sarge. "Isn't Carruthers just the cleaner in all this?"

"Yeah, well, he'd just tried to murder McLain," said Carole. "Plus, two of these corpses were shot in the head."

"We think we can match those two to Carruthers' weapon," said Glenda. "He wrapped his cartridges in the tarps, all neat and tidy."

I had no idea the CSU ladies had worked extra on my behalf. It wasn't as though they had any spare time during our week in the high mountain body dump.

"That sounds good to me," said Sarge. "Wonderful work, ladies, just wonderful. Above and beyond."

"Aw shucks," said Carole.

Off camera, I reached out and gave Carole's hand a squeeze. A friend in need is good. Two friends are better.

Got a nice hand squeeze back.

"On that note," said Glenda, "If we are done body-hunting, I want out of here. This place just creeps me out."

"Yeah, me too," said Carole. "Let's get all this stuff back to base."

"Wonderful," said Sarge. "Thank you all."

We wrapped up the Zoom call. Turned off the computers.

"Thanks, you two," I said. "I had no idea you'd done all that extra on Carruthers' shooting."

"Part of the service, mate," said Glenda, which was not true. They had been working to the point of exhaustion yet still found time to make a case for my exoneration.

"Shooting a member of the public," said Carole. "Who'd a-thought that would land you in the poo."

"You'd think being a policeman would make it OK," added Glenda.

* * *

Night time, about half way through the pack up and clean. Maybe one more day to get through.

Greg Farrell had got a bonfire started. Head of the CFA and biggest firebug I knew. The crew sat around the flames, in a mellow, job done mood.

It was peaceful watching the sparks of the fire rise into the clear night sky.

Around midnight, only the four cops were left contemplating the flames. Everyone else had gone to bed.

"OK," said Carole, "One last thing."

"Two last things," added Glenda.

"They can't both be last," said Carole.

Carole took a thick, closed envelope out of her jacket pocket.

"Photos, old-fashioned Kodak Instamatics," she said. "Found them in the caravan. Since Virginia is the only woman we found here, I think it was probably her."

"Photos?" asked Joyce.

"Not nice ones," said Glenda.

"Burn 'em, I reckon," said Carole.

"Carruthers had mentioned photographs of Virginia," I said. "Taken post-mortem?"

"Post-mortem? Barely-mortem? Who knows?" said Carole. As serious as I'd ever seen her. "They are disgusting."

"Ken Carruthers, what a guy," said Joycey.

I was ready to throw up just thinking about him.

"You don't look well, Killer," said Carole. "Executive decision time, I reckon."

Carole threw the envelope into the fire. The envelope caught fire immediately. It curled and unfolded as it burnt. The photographs were marginally less flammable than the envelope and took a few moments to flame-up, long enough to reveal what a monster Ken Carruthers was. I wished him agony in his hospital bed, then I wished him dead.

"Gone," said Carole. "Never happened, they never existed."

"What a horrible week," said Glenda.

We stood together, watching the flames for a bit.

"What was the other thing?" I asked.

Glenda lifted a plastic bag and held it up to me. Inside were a large number of small leather booklets, each with a leather closing clip.

"Penelope Fenwick's diaries, starting 1942, not all of them, but a lot," said Glenda. "Started when she was only a kid, eleven years old. Albert wasn't even born. Found 'em stashed in the caravan. No value to the case."

"OK," I said. More of Carruthers stolen blackmail inventory.

"Into the flames?" asked Glenda.

"No," I said. "Might be useful, I'll hang onto them for a bit." I shoved the package into my own jacket pocket, not sure what I would do with them.

Standing beside the bonfire. Last night at the clearing, I didn't know then I would soon need another excuse to visit my dear old mate, Penelope.

Saturday, August 6, 2022

The Shelter Car Park.

The graves and campsite had all been filled in and smoothed over. Ken Carruthers' decrepit machinery all returned to place in the abandoned Parks Victoria Shelter.

"You don't want them?" I asked Rob Scott Farrell, referring to the machinery he and Scott had revived and used to make our little temporary town in the bush.

"No, mate," said Rob. "Let 'em rot." The machinery and the surrounding area were all tainted in Rob's book. I felt the same.

Normally, there was a joy of completion at the end of any successful mission. Emergency Services, cops, army, it didn't matter. You finished, you won, you were happy.

Normally, but not this time. This time was just sad.

Rob had been the last of the citizen army to leave. He was the only one able to park the diggers. Job done, Rob departed, leaving only Joycey and I to finish the thermos of coffee Greg Farrell had milked from the mess tent as it folded to the ground.

"So, the mess tent goes back to being a Wedding Tent?" asked Joyce.

"Apparently," I said.

"Remind me not to take that option when I get hitched."

"You'll go with the Community Centres?" I asked.

"Probably, I'll need the bigger venue," she said. "Lot of friends, big family. Love to dance, my mob."

"Anyone in mind for the partner position?" I asked. I used 'partner' strategically. I had no idea of Joycey's preferences in the love department.

"I like that Ray Twomey bloke, very nice, capable, lovely smile. I like 'em big and strong."

"Ray smiles?" that was news.

"He does for me," said Joyce, "and his girls, of course."

"Plus, there's that farm he works for his mum," I said. "He'll inherit that eventually."

"Inherit? Whatever," she laughed. "You'd hardly come to Jarrajarra if you wanted to marry for money."

"True," I said.

"Don't know if you noticed, Chris, dairy farming is fucked."

"True," I said again.

"He wants six kids," she said. "Promised to house husband."

"Jesus Christ, Joycey, I thought we were on a case here. You were on the 'Married At First Sight'.

"Hardly first sight," she said. "My boy Ray was the farmer I ticketed for driving the unregistered tractor. You and Barney made me rip it up and go and apologise for harassing destitute farmers, remember."

"Jesus, Joycey," I laughed. "We sent you out to let old Mrs Twomey off the hook for her tractor, and you make off with her last-born son."

"The tractor was unregistered, Chris. A penalty had to be paid. What do you always tell me? Win-win?"

We finished our coffee.

"That's how this all started, wasn't it? Your friend Virginia, married for money?"

"Don't know about money, so much. I think she married for something better, and that's not a crime."

With everyone gone from the site and all the searching gear removed, the sounds of the bush just breathed around us. The breeze through the canopy, the dripping of the morning dew, and the bird calls. There was that whip-crack sound.

"Which one was that?" asked Joyce.

"That was the eastern whip bird," I said. "Psophodes olivaceus."

"Didn't know you were into birds."

"I'm not really. Kenny Carruthers told me, except he mispronounced it."

"So, you shot him?"

"Some things, Joycey, you just can't forgive."

The road home.

Joycey drove us out of the McKillop's Bridge district back toward Jarrajara.

In all the comings and goings to and from the shelter on Deddick's Track, everyone had forgotten I'd arrived here in a car driven by an armed civilian in hot pursuit of two armed felons. Events and discoveries had clouded minds. Rob Farrell and I were off the hook on that particular breach of police protocol.

Time for another.

I texted the sad news about Virginia Collins to our mutual Muay Thai friends, Tina Harris and Richard Martin.

> *'You will hear on the news very soon that police have discovered Virginia's body. Virginia's remains have been moved to the mortuary in the Jarrajarra Nursing Centre. Ready for release to the next of kin. Await further instructions. So very sorry.*
>
> *Love to all, Chris.'*

I did not have contact details for Rusty. I doubt anyone knew where he lived. I assumed Richard Martin would get the message through somehow. Again.

As an afterthought, I texted the GPS location showing where we had found Virginia.

> *'PS - This is the location where Virginia was buried.'*

They both texted back. We were all sad. Tina was particularly grief-stricken all over again. Richard said he'd pass the message on. Couldn't say when it would get through.

It was a quiet trip. Joyce and I were both tired. We stopped at a roadhouse halfway along to get coffee and swap drivers. Sadly, for me, Joycey was not a wheel-hog like Sarge. I was required to do my share of the driving.

Back on the road, my phone rang. It was Sarge.

"Sarge," I said. "You're on speaker. Joyce and I are on our way back from the search site. All done and dusted."

"Yes," he said. "Good work, both of you."

He paused for a bit, maybe preferring he wasn't on speaker.

"Christopher," he continued. "I'm sorry to bring you the bad news, son, but Ken Carruthers died last night. Passed away in hospital."

"OK," I said.

"There will be an inquest, not sure when. No doubt you will be asked to explain your actions."

"My actions were pretty simple, Sarge. Not a lot to explain. I shot the bastard."

"Yes, well, son, maybe you can express yourself a little more sympathetically when the time comes."

"I'll do my best," I said.

"I am going to see if I can have it heard up here," said Sarge. "Maybe a local Magistrate. Might get that through the gate, given the logjam in Melbourne."

The Covid pandemic, the year before, had played havoc with the Melbourne Courts. With most of the population restricted to working from home, the courthouse side of Melbourne's justice system had ground to a halt.

Fortunately for the rural community, most of the lockdowns did not apply. The country courts were basically up to date.

"Do I have to stand down, anything like that?" I asked.

"No, just carry on," said Sarge. "I don't expect much hue and cry once the full story emerges. No one is mourning Mr Carruthers."

"Good," I said.

"Drive safely," he said and ended the call.

"Goodness," said Joyce. "Another inquest."

"Hope I do as well as you, get myself a medal."

She laughed. There'd be no adverse judgments on my actions from Joycey.

"You worried about it?" she asked.

"No, mate. I think I'm covered."

I wasn't worried about an inquest into my actions. At worst, I could lose my job, possibly a short suspension. More likely, I'd get sent on a self-awareness course. Some sort of counselling.

Ken Carruthers could rot in Hell. I preferred to think about Virginia.

Twenty years dead and still loved. Virginia had been led to her grave by four people. Not all of them were guilty in the eyes of the law, but they were guilty as hell in my book.

Her pathetic husband, Phillip Savage Junior. Her money-hungry father-in-law, Phil Senior. Ken Carruthers, the self-titled cleaner and an actual murderer himself. Finally, Albert Fenwick, Master of Law. The perpetrator.

I didn't count Penelope Fenwick among the guilty. She was a greedy, entitled piece of work, but that didn't make her a killer. The others were just numbers now, numbers in the Book of the Dead.

Three down, one to go.

Monday, August 15, 2022

Jarrajarra.

As it turned out, I took a week away from work after I returned home. I had spent most of that time trail running, sometimes with Wendy, sometimes alone, working out on the punching bag, cooking dinners and, otherwise, sleeping on the couch.

I wasn't physically tired from the time at the body dump, just mentally drained. Drained? Hard to find the words to describe the funk that lingers from a week of resurrecting decomposed murder victims.

Hard to put the sights, the sounds and the smell out of my mind. Easier to do that at home with my beautiful partner, a former military nurse. She had some experience putting ruined bodies behind her.

"Life is for living, Corporal," she said, "and we are making a baby here, so, what do you reckon?"

"Build a bridge and get over it?" I answered.

"Sounds like a plan," said Wendy. She was standing at the kitchen sink in her undies, still sporting her runner's six-pack. I gave her a gentle hug from behind.

"Are you sure there's a baby in there?"

"Something's going on," she said, patting my hands. "Bloody hope it's a baby."

Wendy had to work most days. Her client mums don't have the luxury of a fixed schedule. But there was still time for us to spend together. Her plan was to keep running through the pregnancy, then resume after the event using one of those cross-country running prams she'd found on the internet.

Our early morning runs still came at the price of a dip in the almost-freezing Murray River. The duration of my dips was getting shorter, and the scorn invective was getting stronger.

It was wonderful being home after the days chasing Carruthers and his victims. I had no ongoing guilt about killing him. Being with Wendy, I had lost interest in the outcome of any inquest.

What will be will be.

"If you get the chop from the job," said Wendy, "you'd make a good house husband with a few minor adjustments."

She had mentioned this several times.

"I don't do ironing," I said.

"Ha! You'll learn."

Apparently, I'd learn, though I couldn't see the humour.

Jarrajarra Police Station.

Back at work, Constable Tim was happy to stay on for one more day as officer-in-charge of Jarrajarra Station.

Technically, the extra day was referred to as handover day, but really, Barney ran the place, so there was nothing to hand over. Just relax and enjoy each other's company.

Barney had sent Tim out with half a dozen manufactured Post-it notes. Make-work for Timmy while Barney and I sat at the front desk eating apple slices and watching all the television news clips from my 'Week of Glory', as Barney had titled it.

"I didn't realise Detective Pete was even up at the search," said Barney at one point. "Seems like he is everywhere."

"How's Tim been going?" I asked as a distraction.

"Timmy did quite well considering," said Barney.

"Considering he's not a people person?" I offered.

"Exactly," said Barn. "Credit to him, he tried."

"Any chocolate cake from admiring pensioners?"

"Not there yet," said Barney. "Doctor Newton dropped in a god-awful, high protein, high carb banana cake he made for Jody Taggert. Said Jody couldn't take it because she was allergic, and Scott wouldn't take it because he didn't like cake. He thought you might enjoy it, and it would help your running."

The notion that Scotty Farrell refused a cake of any sort was a solid indication that the cake tasted like shit.

"So it wasn't really for Tim? This cake?"

"No," said Barn, "But he was very respectful to Doc Newton and very graciously accepted the cake on your behalf."

"Very promising," I said.

"Yes, but it's not something that comes naturally to Timmy," said Barney. "I did have to suggest that he might avoid a missing person report if he took the time to drive Doc Newton home."

"And how bad was the cake?"

"Not as good as this," said Barney, taking another bite of apple slice while I lined up the next news report from the previous week's action.

I was well and truly back in the news, and I had to admit Detective Pete had spun me a favour or two, although that was before his star witness had died in hospital.

My name was associated more positively with the discovery of the eight missing murder victims and the hard work involved there. The Carruthers' shooting was presented as a necessary police action against a known murderer resisting arrest after his 'death-or-glory' escape from custody.

I wasn't even mentioned as the shooter.

The portrayal of Carruthers was not so kind. The news reports after Kenny died were 'gloves-off'. No upcoming court cases to prejudice. He was being painted for what he was.

Scum.

None of which would hurt my own coronial inquest whenever it arose. There was good news on that case as well. It was going to be heard in Wodonga Magistrates Court. Any luck, I'd get my old mate, Magistrate Holland.

If I landed Mr Holland, I'd probably get another medal.

Tuesday, August 16, 2022

Jarrajarra Police Station.

By Tuesday, Constable Tim had returned to Wodonga, and Barney and I were back in standard formation, me in uniform, Barney doing all the work.

Around 11:00 AM, I took a call from Constable Joyce.

"Hi, Killer," she said.

Made me laugh, as intended.

"Don't you start calling me that," I said. "Bad enough from those other two."

"I saved your life, remember," said Joyce. "I can call you any damn thing I want."

"You've been in the force less than a year, and you already sound like every second cop out of Wodonga station," I said.

"That's me, big city girl."

True. Wodonga was big city by Jarrajarrra standard, population forty thousand as opposed to our nine hundred.

"Sarge sent me on holiday for a few days," she said. "Told me I'd earned it."

"You did, mate."

"He also sent me to see the counsellor. Again."

"How did that go?" I asked.

"Remember when Maxwell Smart got a glass of water for the dead man."

"Didn't help?" I said.

"Didn't hurt," answered Joycie.

She paused for a bit. She hadn't really called to make jokes.

"I'm struggling to get the whole thing out of my mind," she said.

"The bodies?" I asked.

"Yes, that, and the way he buried them. The tarpaulins, the layer of sand, the tin cans of money and all the victims' personal stuff. Like keeping trophies. Part of some weird ritual."

"I think it was more ritual convenience with our Kenny," I said. "The tarps made it cleaner to transport the bodies. The sand and the steel boxes made it easier to retrieve his money. The personal stuff was more blackmail fodder than trophy."

"How come he never went back for the money tins?" she asked.

"Didn't need it yet," I said. "From what he told me, he was milking Albert Fenwick for more than enough to live on. The money in the ground was his superannuation, I guess. Can't leave murder money in your local Building Society."

"How long did you two actually talk?"

"Long enough," I said.

Joyce went quiet for a bit. When she spoke again, she was close to tears.

"I joined the force to help the community," she said. I never thought I'd be digging up victims of a serial killing scumbag like Ken Carruthers."

"He wasn't alone on the project," I said, "But yeah, not your everyday stuff."

"Maybe your time in the army made you tougher with this sort of thing," Joyce sounded sad. "I don't know if I'm cut out for this life."

"Mate, you, of all people, don't need to be any tougher," I said. "Carruthers was a psychopath. No feelings for other humans at all. I am glad he's dead, and I am glad you were the first person to find me after it happened. You're not like every other cop from Wodonga. That was a joke, sorry."

"I knew you were joking," she said. Joyce was crying on the other end of the line.

"Mate, listen to me," I said. "You are a great cop. If the sight and sounds from extracting those poor dead people bother you, it is because you're human."

She was listening. That was good.

"Carruthers threw them into those pits like garbage. We helped resurrect them. Joycey, you brought them back to their families. You should be proud of yourself."

She was silent for a bit. Getting a cop-style grip on her tears.

"Plus," I said. "We solved the case, mate. The bodies under the dead duck hunters, the cattle theft, and the prison escapes. We solved 'em all. Every single one."

"Plus your friend Virginia and the two Phillip Savages," she added.

"Exactly, we didn't just solve the case. We solved the whole case and all of its twists and turns."

"Dirk Gently, the Wholistic Detective," she laughed.

"Exactly," I smiled. "You should use your days off and read some Douglas Adams. That will cheer you up."

"You sound like Sarge," she said.

My phone buzzed, I had a message, it was from Richard Martin, Rusty Collins' representative.

Joyce and I talked a bit longer. By the time we ended the call, she sounded a little bit happier.

"Fake it till you make it," my Nan would have said.

I checked the message from Richard Martin.

Our mutual friend will be at the same place at 10:00 AM tomorrow if you are available.

I texted back.

I will be there. 10:00 AM tomorrow

Wednesday, August 17, 2022

Jarrajarra Cafe.

10:00 AM.

"Hi, Chrisso," said Rusty. "I'd like to see the body as soon as possible, thanks."

Straight down to business. Rusty had appeared out of nowhere, same as last time, like a ninja. Not there, then right there.

He didn't sit down at the cafe table this time around. He stood waiting for me to move.

"OK," I said. "Let's do it."

Jarrajarra Nursing Centre, Mortuary.

Jarrajarra was too small for a funeral home. Wendy had allowed us to store Virginia's remains in the Nursing Centre Mortuary. Norma Farrell and the team at the SES had thoughtfully provided a basic coffin from the funeral home over in Wodonga.

After twenty years, Virginia Collins was back with her father.

The coffin lid was open.

Rusty was looking at the remains of his daughter, crying silently. I was barely holding it together, the big tough cop. I didn't dare speak. I knew I'd start crying in sympathy if I tried.

"It's her, but it's not her," said Rusty.

"How can her face still be so intact?" he asked. He was looking at the remains of his daughter. His own face was rock hard, but his eyes were leaking tears.

What to say?

If any man deserved the truth from me, it was Rusty Collins.

"Virginia's face had been covered in a plastic bag," I said, as gently as I could, "probably used to restrain her, limit her breathing, maybe a weak attempt to suffocate her. There was no mark on the bag, so she was struck with the hammer before the bag went on. Then the bag was wrapped inside the tarpaulin before she was buried."

Looking at Virginia now, the bag and the tarp had managed to preserve her skin and hair, but her eyes were gone and the skin that remained had shrivelled to the skull. The hammer blow to the side of her head was obvious, but it didn't affect her face.

No father should ever witness this.

"Was she buried alive?" Rusty asked.

"No," I said. "I really don't know how long she lived after she was struck. But according to Carruthers, Virginia was dead when she was buried."

"I wouldn't believe a word out of his mouth," whispered Rusty. Still looking at his daughter.

"Police opinion," I said, "is that Virginia died from the hammer blow." I was struggling. Paused for a bit.

"I'm sorry, Rusty," I said. "I don't believe much of what Carruthers said. But I do believe Virginia was dead when she was buried."

Bloody hell, the jobs you have to do.

We both stared in silence for a moment.

You could see Virginia in the remnants if you wanted to, but Rusty was right. It wasn't Virginia lying there in the coffin.

"Richard Martin will be in touch," he said. "He is going to organise the next bit. I thought a cremation, then bury the ashes beside her mother. Small service, OK. Rick will let you know the where and when, yeah?"

"I'll be there," I said. "Tell Rick I'll do what he needs at this end."

He stopped crying. Wiped his face with the back of his hand.

"Thank you," he said. "I want you to thank everyone from around here who helped. I saw it on TV, seemed to be the whole town."

"Yeah," I said, "we had a good part of it."

He reached into his jacket and, brought out an envelope, handed it to me. It was thick and foldy. I guessed it was cash. A lot of cash by the size of it.

"Give this to the right person," he said. "Spend it on the town."

With his eyes on Virginia, he very gently reached out and touched her face, then closed the lid of her coffin.

I hadn't returned Virginia to her dad. We both knew that. It could not be done. Virginia Collins was gone forever. All that was left now were her body, this coffin and our memories.

"There is a lovely little spot behind the hospital," I said. "Do you want to sit outside in the sun, and I'll get you a coffee?"

"Sounds good," said Rusty.

* * *

How long does it take to realize there is no cure for the loss of a loved one?

Rusty Collins was there already.

"This Carruthers bloke," said Rusty. "I'm guessing you were the one who shot him."

I gave a nod for yes.

"I told you to stay away from him," he said.

"If I'd stayed away," I answered, "I would never have found Virginia."

He seemed to understand the truth in that, but it didn't make him any happier. He looked away to the huge, beautiful gum trees beyond the hospital boundary.

Rusty wasn't seeing the beauty around us today.

"I wanted to kill the bastard myself," he said. "Let him feel how Virginia must have felt. Whatever he knew, he would have told me."

"Carruthers didn't kill Virginia," I said, "you know that. Killing him wouldn't do anything for you."

"Don't be so sure about that," he said. "A dead Carruthers works for me just fine."

"If you think Carruthers death ruins the case against Albert Fenwick, you're wrong," I said.

"No, mate, I don't think that. I'm sure you can make your case now you have all those bodies, but that will take time."

That was true.

"Old Albert has so much money and so many connections, he won't be serving that time in jail. I promise you."

That was probably true as well.

"Fenwick will be free on his own recognizance by next week. So, pay attention this time," he said. "Stay away from him. Go on a holiday somewhere sunny with Wendy. Get yourself a tan. Albert Fenwick is a dead man walking. He is going to know pain like he never imagined. He will feel exactly what my beautiful daughter felt, I promise you."

He looked at me long and hard. Rusty was angry.

"You don't approve, Chrisso?"

"No," I said, "I don't. I thought finding Virginia would be good for you, some sort of closure. Some justice, maybe."

"Closure," he laughed. "What a joke. Justice is a game, and the winner is the one with the most money. I am grateful you found her. I am glad I know how she died."

He stopped for a breath, holding back tears, most likely.

"I love you, Chrisso, but there's no closure. My daughter is still dead, and her murderer will be free within a week."

We had a staredown for a moment then he softened. Some part of the man I had known flashed across his face.

He stood and rested his hand on my shoulder. Gave me a gentle pat.

"Thank you for what you did, but remember what I said. Stay away from Albert Fenwick."

He walked away the same as last time, no goodbyes. He didn't look back, walked around the corner of the hospital, and he was gone.

* * *

I had stayed in the hospital barbecue area, soaking up the sun, finishing my coffee, and contemplating Rusty's untouched cup.

I heard the back door of the hospital swing open. Wendy sat down beside me at the table. Together in the sunshine, she'd bought two fresh hot espressos.

"How was Rusty?" Wendy asked.

"Not good," I said.

"Not the man you remember?" she asked.

"No," I said.

"Not your perfect hero anymore?"

"Don't know, love. Was he ever really that person? Did I just see what I wanted to see?"

"You always say young blokes need a place to belong," said Wendy. "He gave you that and a lot more."

"He did."

"Don't blame the poor guy for not measuring up to the picture you painted back then. He's been through a lot."

"He has," I said, "and I think there's more to come."

We shared a smile. A little kiss, then sat there in the sun, finishing our coffee.

Part 3

Monday, September 5, 2022

Chris

Jarrajarra Police Station.

I was sitting at the front desk of the Station, reading the online news with Barney.

"Life is a shit sandwich," I sighed. "The more bread you've got, the less shit you eat."

The use of the word 'shit' got a side-eye from Barney.

The shit sandwich analogy was aimed at Albert James Fenwick, Master of Laws. Albert had enough bread to cushion a lifetime of evil.

Albert Fenwick's court process had rolled out exactly as Rusty Collins had predicted. It just took a bit longer to happen. Four weeks, not one, but the end result was the same.

With the death of Ken Carruthers, the lawyers for Albert promptly asked for an urgent bail application. It took the court a month to get everyone together. Then, it was over as quick as it began. The Fenwick team put it to the court that the death of Fenwick's accuser, my mate Carruthers, sent the prosecution's case to the toilet.

No witness, no case. Simple as that.

Not so, according to the prosecution. There was a massive array of incriminating evidence. We had Carruthers' sworn statement. The Police had the DNA of the accused, actual strands of the pompadour no less, found among various corpses excavated from the clearing on Deddick's Track.

There were incriminating diary entries from his sister, Penelope.

There were recorded conversations, Albert's voice discussing his murder process.

Literally tons of evidence, all of which spoke to the clear guilt of rich, old, greedy Albert. Our murderer.

"And where is all this evidence?" cried the defence.

"In preparation, your Honour," answered the prosecution. "Ready, very soon."

With that, it was all over red-rover.

Albert, a man of such wealth and high esteem, a leader of industry and charity, and some age, plus an invalid, what with the cane he was now sporting. A man such as this could not be expected to rot in a cell while the prosecution dawdled over the preparation of their transparently threadbare case.

Ridiculous. Outrageous. A travesty.

The judge agreed, and Albert walked. Admittedly, with a custodial ankle bracelet. Black, to go with his cane.

Ankle bracelet, whatever, Albert Master of Murders, goes home, free as a bird.

From there, from behind the massive gate and the high brick wall with all its shrubbery, from within the protection of the best private security money could buy, he promptly disappeared with barely a trace.

The very same day.

"Gone, by his own design," according to the news.

"Maybe, who knows, but yes, most likely he planned this," according to un-named police sources.

"Dead and buried, if you ask me," said my own trusted sleuth, Barney Trail, Jarrajarra's Civilian Police Administrator.

I agreed with Barney. But no one reported our opinion.

"How would anyone know this was him," said Barney.

Barney and I were looking at the video that was all over the news. The one of his Lordship, our Albert, driving out the front gate of his Toorak mansion in his sleek black Mercedes S450 with heavily tinted windows.

More gliding than driving, the car was as magnificent as a private jet, which, according to the media, is where Albert Fenwick headed next.

From then to now, God alone knows where. Albert had vanished.

"You look at the video," said Barney, "all you can see through the heavy tint is that ridiculous white pompadour."

"Could be a wig," I offered.

"Easily," agreed Barney. "Wouldn't even need to be a good one."

More videos of Fenwick, just last Friday, the day of his release, walking down the steps of the Melbourne Court, using his cane. Smiling, delighted, old, surrounded by security, walking toward his chauffeured Mercedes. His magnificent, ridiculous silver mane waffled on the breeze. The only handsome thing about him.

"Would have kept Albert in jail just for the hair," I said.

"Too late now," said Barney.

Way too late.

The media and the cops they interviewed all seemed to agree Fenwick had done a runner all by himself, fuelled by his tons of money. The gloves were off for the cops. The leaks of diary entries, voice recordings and so on had turned into a torrent. The cop leakers were already touting the DNA from the tarpaulins even though the results weren't back yet.

Barney looped back to the video of Fenwick, or his impersonator, driving out of the front gate of the Toorak mansion on the road to nowhere.

I knew in my heart Albert James Fenwick was not doing a runner, not by choice.

Oh, Rusty, I wondered, what have you done?

* * *

Nan's rules, you had to love 'em. She never delivered them as rules, just her little sayings, usually spoken in context. Half the time, she was just thinking out loud.

"If you don't know how to approach someone after a dispute, just pretend it never happened. In fact, go hard enough the other way, and you'll quickly forget what you were fighting about."

"G'day, mate," I said. A bit too hale and hearty, maybe?

"I thought we weren't talking," said Detective Pete Jordan on the other end of the line.

"What?" I said. Mystified by such a statement.

"Fuck me, you are a bull-shit artist, Chris Taylor, we were no-speaks. Remember?" he said, then paused. Sounded like he was happy with the not-talking status quo.

"OK," he said after failing to out-non-talk me. "I'm curious. What do you want?"

"How do you know Albert did a runner?"

"Videos, you've probably seen, all over the news, some you haven't and fingerprints. You know, the unique twirly-whirly thingies on the end of your pinkies. They leave little, sweaty smudges on stuff. You heard of them up there in Mayberry?"

“Fingerprints?” I said. “Rings a bell. Let me Google that.”

He laughed. At his own joke, really, but there you go, ice broken.

“We found his Mercedes abandoned at Leonwarra Airport. There’s a video we haven’t released from a CCTV camera they have in their car park.”

“Leonwarra?”

“In South Gippsland, on the southeast coast, a nice straight run on the Monash Freeway for about ninety minutes, cameras all the way. Then, another hour along the Gippsland Highway. Easy drive to a lovely little country airport.”

“OK.”

“Airport’s got a two-kilometre tarmac runway with no control tower and no Pilot Controlled Lighting system. You know what that is?”

“No.”

“OK. Google Pilot Controlled Lighting System, PCS, while you’re catching up on all these terms we use here in the real world. Basically, the pilot can use his microphone to turn on the landing lights. Very modern. Not every bush airport has them yet. So, flying in, the pilot clicks the secret code on their microphone, and the landing lights come on. Amazing.”

“So the pilot has a microphone?”

“Ha-ha,” he said, not laughing. “Still a smart-arse, I see. Anyway, Albert parks his very expensive, soon-to-be-abandoned luxury vehicle and then gets out and opens the gate, comes back to get the car, from there under the CCTV, then disappears into the darkness of the landing area. Wearing gloves at this stage, mind you, very expensive leather gloves.”

“All of this is on CCTV?” I asked.

“Yes,” he answered, “all of that on CCTV.”

“How do you know it’s our Albert?”

“How long’s a piece of string?” said Pete. “We can see the ugly fat beer gut, except it is probably not a beer gut, more your fine wine, caviar and champers. Ridiculous hair managing to bulge its way out of a hoodie and a beanie. Walking with his cane, favouring his gout-riddled left foot. Sure looks like our Albert, but hey. Could be anyone, right?”

“Right,” I said.

"But the fingerprints, Chris, hard to impersonate fingerprints?"

"Where did you find them?"

"On the base of the flares, your bog-standard army disposal flares."

"Flares?" I asked.

"Yes, mate, flares," said Pete. "Leonwarra has no Pilot Controlled Landing Lights. You might have forgotten I mentioned that fifteen seconds ago."

"Vaguely remember something along those lines, yeah."

"Clever lad, you'll make a policeman yet. Anyway, Albert set up a row of flares on either side of the runway, then drove to the northern end, shining his lights back along the length of the runway. Lit up the landing strip like Christmas. Perfect guide for his pilot, who flew in, picked him up and flew out to heaven knows where."

"They're tight old things, the flares," I said. Speaking from experience. "Albert wouldn't have been able to unscrew them with his gloves on."

"Apparently not," said Pete, "Never set one myself."

I'd set a few in my time.

"You've clearly never done traffic duty down there in the real police world."

"Traffic? What's that?" Smug bugger.

"Flares," I said. "You hold them by the base. They are real tight for safety's sake. Unscrew the top, use the tip of the top to scratch the top of the base, just like lighting a big match and off they go. Burn for as long as you like. Depends which type of flare you're using."

"There you go," said Pete, "Ninja-boy knows his flares and dumb old Albert leaves his fingers all over them."

"So, moving on," said Pete, "Sunday. We find the car parked at the end of the landing strip. We go over it. Find nothing but Albert shedding his lion's mane all over the driver's seat. Lots of hair but no Albert.

"So, to sum up," I said. "he leaves court, goes home, then jumps into his highly tinted Mercedes, drives straight to Leonwarra Airport, zero stops along the way, parks in the car park under a CCTV, fiddles with the gate, then drives the car out near the landing strip, and then he's gone for good, leaving the car at one end of the aerodrome."

"Exactly."

“Which end?”

“The northern end,” said Pete.

“Camera’s all the way on the freeway. Vision and fingerprints on the flares.”

“There you go,” said Pete. “You really can listen like a grown-up when I talk slow.”

“Any information on a pilot or a plane?” I asked.

“None whatsoever. It would’ve been a well-paid job, I imagine. Discretion required.”

“OK, thanks, mate.”

“You’re welcome, Closeau.”

We ended the call. Maybe not quite friends again, but talking friendly. Another triumph for Nan’s rules.

Saturday, September 17, 2022

St George's Road, Toorak, Melbourne.

"Oh my goodness," said Penelope Fenwick, "My diaries. Oh, Constable Taylor, thank you so much. Oh my. I never thought I'd live to see these again. Thank you."

Penny was holding the bag of diaries that Carole and Glenda, the Crime Services Team, had found under Kenny Carruthers' disgusting caravan.

Here she was, all gushy, beaming gratitude. Only ten minutes ago, I had to ask politely to be allowed in to see her. The invisible voice on the gate was not too keen on another copper dropping by for a chat. I had held up one of the diaries to the gate camera then I had held up the whole bag full of similar diaries. Then had to wait five minutes till Penny had a chance to check out the goods.

I could be patient. After I spoke to Detective Sergeant Peter Jordan about Albert Fenwick's disappearance, I forced myself to wait a week. Then I waited a few more days till the weekend.

Jarrajarra Police Station was closed on weekends. With luck, no one other than Wendy would know I had gone to Melbourne.

The Fenwick infamy had moved into a new phase. Albert was on the run, a fugitive with a fortune to spend on his freedom. Penny was being systematically forgotten by the media. I was too far down the food chain to know if that was by design.

She took one of her diaries out of the filthy bag to inspect. Left the bag on the table beside her.

"I presume these were discovered when you detained Mr Carruthers," she said. Looking at the bag full of diaries. Smiling. "Well done, Constable."

"Detained Ken Carruthers?" I said. "Good word, detained, covers a lot. Killed him at his body dump is what I remember, among all those dead people he'd buried on your brother's behalf. But, yeah, detained will do."

Penny was sitting up in an armchair in a magnificent sort of sunroom-greenhouse combo. Massive armchair, blanket over her legs. She looked very comfortable.

"Yes, indeed, a body dump," she said. "And you found your late friend Virginia."

"Wrapped in a tarp," I said, "head bashed in, and a few stray hairs from your brother in the mix."

"Indeed," she said. "I have no doubt you have all the evidence in the world, Constable, not that it will do you any good at all."

"No," I said.

"I warned you Albert was far too clever to ever face a trial, but you didn't listen. You stuck at it, the good honest chap you are, and now, I presume your dear friend, Mr Collins, is happy at last. His daughter returned. Congratulations to both of you."

What a cold merciless bitch, sitting there nursing her precious diaries in her lap.

She looked away. Probably read my mind. Everyone else does.

"I beg your pardon," she said. "That was totally uncalled for."

She took a moment to find better words.

"It's been quite traumatic the whole thing. The charges against me, then released from custody, all of that. Then Albert makes a hasty exit, as I always knew he would. Leaving me alone to face the courts. For his crimes, I should add."

Penny had decided that she was one of the victims here.

"My world has been tipped and turned around and then turned around again." She said. "I apologize for my rudeness. I hope you can forgive me."

I gave that a non-committal shrug. Don't think I'd be up for her forgiveness. Not in this lifetime.

"You don't seem too concerned," I said, "Albert has deserted, leaving you to face the music?"

"Face the music? How dramatic," She smiled. "But, yes, that would be your view, of course. Police are a necessary part of the justice system, Albert always said. Fortunately, for me, and Albert I suppose, you are just one small part."

"Rich old white lady," I said, "charity queen, best lawyers money can buy, not worried about what the police think, Too rich to be ashamed and not worried about your peers. They're all dead."

In for a penny, in for a pound. She didn't deserve to be so bloody self-satisfied. And comfortable, God Almighty, even her morning sit down was more luxurious than most people could imagine. Or was it just me, hating rich people from birth.

"Crudely put, Constable, but exactly right," she said. "I don't think I will be going to jail for anything I've done. Sorry to disappoint you."

"If you're so confident in your defence capability, why did Albert run away?"

"Well, he is lazy and self-indulgent for a start. Doesn't like being told what to do by judges and cannot abide being held to account by mere policemen," she said, looking at me.

"And, the other relevant item, my brother is a psychopathic killer. Hard to see a jury deciding otherwise."

"And you?"

"Me? I'm just another one of his victims." She was smiling that kind old charity queen smile. She could turn it on and off like a tap.

"You've rehearsed this already. With your lawyers?" I had to smile myself.

"Indeed, I have. I believe you know my new Barrister," she smiled. "Mr Oakley."

Bloody Jeremy Oakley QC. She was right. We didn't have a chance in hell of landing her behind bars. Time was a-wasting.

"Your diaries," I said. "I want a favour in return."

"Oh, here we go," she said. "The good Constable has a request. Do I need to write a cheque?"

"Save your money, Miss Fenwick, you're going to need it. I want to get inside your brother's house."

She laughed again.

"Oh my goodness," she was smirking. "You think you will find a clue and catch him. Oh, my dear Constable Taylor. You really are a hoot. By all means, search your earnest little heart out. Here was I thinking you were about to ask for money."

Penelope Fenwick, what did my Muay Thai buddy, Tina Harris, call her?

"A soul-shrivelled razor-lipped bitch-from-hell, Missus misery guts herself."

Hard to disagree.

She made a call to the mansion of her missing brother.

That's all I wanted from Penelope Fenwick.

Toorak Road, Toorak, Melbourne.

"Can I take a look at the garage, thanks?"

Dear old Penelope had put me in touch with Albert's 'man', Ralph, who was given the word to show me around Albert's mansion.

The place was not entirely deserted. There was Ralph and a couple of other staff and one bloke in a uniform I took to be security. He had a gun on his belt. That was my clue. It was a Glock G43X, not the biggest beast in the Glock range, but enough to deserve attention.

Ralph took me to the garage, I wasn't here to check gun permits.

There was a clean, mirror-polished steel ashtray at the side exit to the garage. The garage itself was a massive thing. You could fit six of the biggest if that's what you needed to do.

"Albert smoked his cigars outside?" I asked Ralph.

"Yes," he said. "Mr Albert liked to take a look around his cars, didn't want the cigar smell anywhere near them."

"Did he smoke inside the house?"

"No," said Ralph. There is another ashtray near the front exit."

"How many would he smoke a day?"

"Cigars, probably a dozen. Cigarettes a pack or more."

"Did he ever smoke in the car? On a trip or a slow drive through the city?"

"No, never. His office is only a few minutes from here. He didn't really take many long trips. Not till recently." Ralph just made a joke. He was a bit of a devil. A paid employee, but no love for the boss, maybe.

"All this care about where he smoked. It seems at odds with his usual behaviour."

"I believe Miss Penelope had words to him several times regarding the smell," said Ralph. "She was the only one he ever listened to, really."

So, Albert had allegedly driven from here to Leonwarra, two and a half hours with no known stops in transit. The first ninety minutes on the freeway were caught by CCTV. No two-minute ciggy breaks in all that way for a man with zero self-restraint and a thirty durrie-a-day habit.

So, maybe he smoked in the car, or maybe it wasn't Albert.

"Can I look inside the garage, please, Ralph?"

"Of course," he said and went to lead me in.

"I'd prefer to do it alone, thanks. You can check my bags on the way out if you like."

Ralph smiled. "I don't think that will be necessary, Constable. Go ahead," he said and waved me in. He was alright, Ralph.

It would have worked as a car museum. Not your average garage. The back wall was lined with closed-door cupboards. No cork pegboards here. Everything tucked away. Precise, ordered, organized, and nothing crammed in. No tool touching another. A shelf of unused tarps, neatly packed in their plastic wraps, all different sizes. Car cleaning shelves, rope shelves. Hemp ropes. A separate section of tall cupboards for longer items. No garden tools.

"Where are the garden tools," I shouted.

"Separate shed for gardening," Ralph shouted back through the closed side door of the garage.

Of course, there was a separate shed for gardening and one for the pool, no doubt.

"Thanks, Ralph."

One cupboard was different. The cupboard behind the only empty parking space. Presumably, the slot for the absent Mercedes. The shelf second from the bottom had various tinting products and polishing wax with a long manual carjack about 1.2 metres long, four feet. Crammed in at the back. Not bulldozed in by any means, but not where it belonged.

Why would a heavy carjack, on wheels, be anywhere but the bottom, floor-level shelf?

Why indeed.

The bottom shelf was six feet long, three feet deep, and totally empty.

Enough room for Rusty to make some space and sleep the night. Wait for Albert to get himself home on bail. Get in early before Albert arrives home with his personal security. That's how I would do it if I had to do it. If I had no choice but to do it.

I looked for footprints like my own. Steel capped Blundstones.

There was one print, just the one, not on the floor but against the end wall of the bottom empty shelf. Very faint, just the slightest touch, but it was there. Smaller than mine, about a size 10 US.

You had to get down, almost inside the cupboard and shine your torch to see it, even with daylight outside.

Carole and Glenda would never have missed this, but it was not their job. St Kilda Road and the St Kilda Police Station had CSUs of their own. Seems everyone had fallen for the idea of the rich man on the run, even the cops.

I took a tissue from my pocket and wiped away the footprint from the wall of the cupboard.

I'd seen enough, and time was a-wasting.

"Thanks, Ralph," I said. "I'm done."

"My pleasure, Constable," he answered. He held the door for me as I left the garage, then led me to the exit onto the street.

He was alright, Ralph.

Leonwarra Airport, South Gippsland, Victoria.

"There are a lot more sheds than I anticipated," I said, "and they are all so big."

"Yes," said the local airport expert. "Your bush hangars are big buggers, alright."

I had left home at 4:30 AM, and between Jarrajarra and Melbourne and then to Leonwarra I had spent seven hours on the road and over three hours faffing about being Sherlock Holmes and drinking coffee and shovelling down garage sandwiches.

I arrived at the Leonwarra airport just after 3:00 PM. I quickly found myself a local expert inside the building by the car park. Her name was Harriet Carew. "Call me Harry." Manager of the Leonwarra Air Academy. I found her in the main office of the flying school. She had her portable heater blowing hot and the fan on full. The first thing I learnt about Leonwarra, it was bloody cold.

Harry's building was at the end of the main road into the airport, one of several flying schools attached to the airport, the one right beside the Albert Fenwick gate. The very gate dear old Albert Master of Moneybags went through on his journey to somewhere far away.

Allegedly.

That's if it was Albert.

Whoever it was, he went through that gate, and he hadn't come back. My problem was this. There was way more to this airport than conveyed by the short CCTV movie Detective Pete had provided.

Leonwarra Airport was much larger than you could appreciate, even with a quick check on Google Maps. It was vast. Sparsely populated, but a lot of it. The two-kilometre landing strip was surrounded by a wire fence. Along the east side, the fence was lined by massive aircraft hangars. Many of them had their own gravel-based car parks and their own gated access to the landing area. Some of the buildings were big, shiny new kit structures. Others were as rough and ready as backyard chook sheds.

With all this access to the landing zone, why would an absconding murderer go through the one gate guaranteed to put him on TV?

Why indeed?

"Who do all these cars belong to?" I asked my local samaritan, Harry.

"Could be anyone, mate," she said. "Lot of people might leave their car here and go for a couple of days' holiday somewhere warmer. Might leave your car here and fly your plane to the races somewhere. Costs a small fortune to get here from Leonwarra by the taxi."

"The taxi?"

"Leonwarra, small town. We've only got the one."

"But, you wouldn't normally leave your Mercedes?" I said, stating the obvious.

"No," said Harry. "The locals are pretty honest, but yeah, you'd only leave a barn burner if you were doing an overnighter."

Most of the cars in the informal car parks were barn burners. Farm utes or old vans.

"Too many cars for you to keep track of?"

"Shit yeah," said Harry. "And it's not my job to keep track of who goes where. No one's job, really. None of my business. Takes all of my time running the flying school."

"So, the airport is all community property?" I asked

"Yeah," she said. "The place is owned by the shire and run by a volunteer committee, namely me. I collect the fees from all the users and pay most of that to the shire for the public dunnies, mowing the grass and looking after the strip. Pain in the bum, really."

"OK."

"To be honest, the shire do as little as they possibly can for as much money as they can gouge. Leave me and the bloke who runs the crop dusting to do the rest."

"Who owns the sheds?"

"The sheds and all that stuff have been built and paid for by the users. You rent your little strip of land along the edge here, and you whack up your own personal hangar if you've got the coin."

"Or you just park out in the open like there?" I asked, pointing at a bunch of the tied-down smaller planes.

"Exactly," said Harry. "Some of the better hangars are flying schools or the crop dusters. We're the ones here most of the time. The other users are just your in and outers. Some of them pool together and build themselves a nice comfy hangar with a bar in the back."

"Would there be like a log book or another camera somewhere recording the flights in and out?" I asked.

"No," she smiled, "Nothing like that. We are totally uncontrolled. No fancy control tower. It's not quite the Wild West here, but no one's looking over your shoulder."

"Flying in and out, how do you avoid crashing into each other?"

Her kind smile turned into a friendly laugh. I clearly didn't know much about private flying.

"Mostly, we use CTAF, which stands for Common Traffic Advisory Frequency, to announce our intentions. It's an audio channel, unrestricted. Open all the time. That works for us. Our traffic size is not exactly threatening."

"So you get on and declare, look out world, here I come?"

"Or words to the effect. Yeah," she said. Still amused by my aerial ignorance. Happy to explain.

"So, if you're sneaking in around 2:00 AM or later, maybe no one would notice?"

"If a tree falls in a deserted forest, does it make a sound?" she answered.

Bit cryptic, and I was thinking more along the lines of 'What if the tree didn't fall at all?'

The whole exit by private jet could be totally fake. There were so many ways in and out of this place, and late at night, no one was paying any attention at all.

Just a diversion, like Rusty Collins looking over your shoulder to convince you someone was creeping up behind you just before he clobbered you with his rubber sausage or his right glove if you were old enough to know better.

"I was starting to think you big city police weren't interested?" said Harry.

"Not interested?

"You're the first one I've seen since I sent the CCTV."

"You sent the CCTV? To where?"

"Well, I found the car first. No private cars on the strip is the rule, so the Mercedes at the end of the runway was a bit off. Then I found the flares, so then I checked my CCTV and found this Albert Fenwick fellow going through my gate. I guessed who he was from TV, that ridiculous hair, so I called the police here in town and sent them the video."

"Did anyone call you back?"

"Well the local guy came out for a looky-look, collected the flares, then the next day I get the call from a Detective in Melbourne."

"A Detective Jordan from Homicide?"

"Sounds about right. I told him about the car, the flares, same as I told you."

"So Detective Jordan already had a copy of the CCTV video? Didn't actually pay you a visit?"

"Yeah," she said, "He saw the video but never came for a visit. Long way to come, I suppose, when the bird has already flown."

"Anyone else interested?"

"Well, the local tow truck came and collected the Mercedes to take it to Melbourne Police, and the local newspaper came out to get photos of the process."

Harry had a laugh to herself.

"They wanted shots of the flares in place, but the flares had gone to the police already. So I cut a couple of lengths of plastic tubing and stuck them in the ground. Did the job. Someone from the local paper photoshopped some flame coming out of the empty tube. Very convincing"

"Fake news," I laughed with Harry.

"What's real anymore?" she said.

So, all Detective Pete had seen was the CCTV video, one gate, one bad guy in his Mercedes driving through, and he had fingerprints off the flares.

But there were gates everywhere, and parked cars by the dozen, in as many separate spaces not covered by CCTV.

There were a dozen ways the Albert disappearance script could have been written. Albert could have been dead or drugged already.

Moved by Rusty from the boot of the Mercedes to the back of an off-camera truck hidden behind one of the far sheds. Then Rusty, in a fat suit and crazy wig, does his little charade in front of the flying school camera.

Easy-bloody-peasy.

"Thanks, Harry," I said. "I appreciate your help."

Reached out and shook her hand.

"You're welcome, Constable. Hope you catch the mongrel. Murdering all those people and payin' his way out of prison. Disgusting. Just sorry he chose our little part of the world to fly away. Wish I could help you more."

"You've been terrific, Harry, thank you."

"I hope you find him and bring him to justice," Harry's last word.

"Thanks, mate," I said. "I'll do my best."

I was growing confident I'd find old Albert, and I was pretty sure where. My main worry was justice had found him already.

* * *

Back in the truck, I checked the Google. I could get a motel here in Leonwarra or make the five-hour drive home to Wendy. That was very tempting.

Or, I could finish this today, in what was left of it.

I checked Google Maps again. I had another destination in mind, and it would take me five hours to get there.

I recalled Rusty Collins' words after he'd seen the body of his daughter, Virginia.

> *"Albert Fenwick is going to know pain like he never imagined. He will feel exactly what my beautiful daughter felt, I promise you."*

'Exactly' was the key word.

I had one solid guess as to where Albert Fenwick was right now. If I was wrong, that would be the end of it. If I was right? I was not sure what I would do.

* * *

I made it to the Leonwarra Home Hardware right at 5:00 PM. They were set to lock the doors, but the lady who ran the place kindly let me in. Maybe my honest face, more likely my cop uniform.

Two shovels, one short, one long, both brand new and sharp. A mattock to break the earth, probably unnecessary, and four large torches and another two headlamps with a pack of batteries to keep them shining.

Back in the truck, fully equipped, I had a five-hour drive ahead of me. The town of Bairnsdale looked to be two-thirds of the way along the map, but the road was flat and straight. It would be most of the miles but only half the journey. The last third appeared to be a relentless, winding climb on narrow roads into the heart of the high country.

Strong coffee and sandwiches at Bairnsdale felt like a plan.

I set my truck radio to Gary Jubelin's Podcast, 'I Catch Killers', and set my map directions for the northern end of Deddick's Track, just past McKillop's Bridge, along the banks of the Snowy River.

The Clearing on Deddick's Track, Victoria.

The nighttime view of the body dump on Deddick's track hadn't changed much. It was still black as hell. So dark, with the car engine and lights all off, I could barely see my hand in front of my face.

I turned on the various torches and headlamps I'd purchased and set them all shining from the roof of my truck, pointing where I needed them. Lit it up like Christmas.

I put on the overalls I kept stashed behind my seat and then I used a thin canvas strap from the boot of my truck to make a shoulder strap for my digging tools. Dressed and ready to go, one headlamp in place, the other in my pocket, shovels and mattock slung over my shoulder, and my hands both free to carry torches, I headed off through the clearing, past the Parks Victoria shed with Carruthers' disgusting caravan and into the bush beyond.

I knew exactly where I was going. I had on my phone the GPS point of the former grave of Virginia Collins. Albert Fenwick was either battered and buried in a hole somewhere near and beneath that point, or he was living the good life in Thailand, perhaps or maybe even South America.

It was a relatively easy walk to where we had found Virginia. Three hundred metres along the ridge above and behind the clearing.

Due east from the shed, past the rocks where the metal tracks of the rusty old bulldozer had left their mark, past the spot where we'd found the abandoned shovel, to the mound where Virginia had remained buried and missing for twenty years.

Didn't take too much imagination to get angry at the worthless trash that had put her here. Albert Fenwick, Virginia's killer and Ken Carruthers, the cleaner.

You could terrify yourself being alone at night, deep in the high country under the canopy of trees and clouds. The sound of the wind shaking the branches above you. The snowgum branches they call the widow makers. Not hard to imagine terrors waiting for you behind the boundary of your lights.

Army training. Keep moving and get where you're going. Focus on that. I loved the bush and never felt nervous amongst it.

I had found my starting point, Virginia's former grave. Smoothed over dirt slightly higher than the surrounding earth, recently dug and refilled by the search team. The grass and weeds had barely started to grow back. It all looked almost the same as we had left it.

I could not imagine that Rusty would bury Fenwick where Virginia had lay. But nearby and downhill? That seemed possible. Probable.

Why was I here? Pretty simple. I just had to know.

It took a while. About an hour, walking through an imaginary grid of around two hundred square metres.

There was a spot of earth, just over the side of the ridge, twenty metres downhill and south-east from where Virginia had been buried. A small mound, mostly hidden in a tall clump of old, brown bracken, with shoots of bright green new growth bursting through.

Very easy to miss, especially in the dark. In another month, this would have been hidden under the aggressive growth of the spaghetti-like weed. If Albert was here, in the ground, it was an appropriate place. Bracken was poisonous, very fitting for a Thallium man like Albert.

The giveaway was the broken roots scattered around the mound. Bracken is like an iceberg. As pernicious as it is above the ground, it is even more prolific underneath. To dig through it you have to bust open the roots. In an old patch of thick bracken like this, there will be more roots than dirt.

This was either a grave we missed or Rusty had chosen well.

It was six weeks since the Virginia Collins' search team had decamped from this place. It was now two weeks since Albert went missing.

I started digging. In the relatively fresh grave, it was easy work. But re-digging a grave is still digging, and I'm no plumber, and I had no idea how to work the ancient backhoe sitting useless back in Ken Carruthers' shed.

All up, it took a few hours of hard work to find Albert.

Six feet down, a serious grave. The first sign of the man was his ridiculous hair. Even entombed, it beckoned like river weeds swaying in the current. The silver mane was most of what remained intact from his former, living self. The rest of him was not doing so well.

Finding the hair, I next exposed the head and then worked down the body. Like the other former occupants of the body dump, Albert was wrapped in a tarpaulin.

"He will feel exactly what my beautiful daughter felt, I promise you."

Under the tarp, it was not a pretty sight. I can't imagine Albert ever presented well, even in his expensive suits. In death, he was grotesque and damaged.

I knew enough from working around Carole and Glenda, our Crime Services Unit, to recognise the stages of decomposition.

Albert was toward the end of Stage Two, Bloat. Bacteria in the recently dead grow and reproduce until they generate gasses, which cause bloating. Albert's dead skin was red and blackening. Blood pooled in purplish patches where his skin touched the ground.

He was approaching Stage Three, Active Decay. The skin on his chest was beginning to liquefy, still intact but slipping away from the skeleton underneath.

He was broken as well.

He had a crushed eye socket, a broken arm and a broken leg. Snapped, swollen and ugly, twisted into horrific angles. Teeth dislodged. His chest cavity on the right side was crushed inwards, ribs broken.

His mouth was open, full of dirt. Gasping for one last breath.

Albert Fenwick, Master of Laws, heir to a fortune few could conceive, had been beaten nearly to death and then buried alive.

> *"Albert Fenwick will know pain like he never imagined."*

I threw my tools out of the grave that I had just re-opened and then climbed out.

I took a moment to consider my options. I had only one that worked for me. I filled in the grave and then restored the surrounding area to the form I'd found it. I did throw the evidence of cut bracken into the pit, but that was all I did to disguise Albert Fenwick's resting place.

September, early spring in the high country. I had little doubt the new bracken growth would enclose the site within a month.

I had no idea if the myth of Albert's fake escape would hold. It had taken me barely twenty-four hours to unravel Albert's murder and burial, but I had the advantage of knowing Rusty Collin's and his intentions.

Rick Martin, Rusty's lawyer and my old Muay Thai buddy, had told me, "It's not just the story, mate, but how you tell it and the bits you choose to push."

This story looked so flimsy. Detective Sergeant Peter Jordan might discover the truth. He may yet find Albert Fenwick's body, but he would get no help from me.

Rusty Collins had suffered twenty years of torture. I did not believe what happened here would make his life better, nor would criminal punishment make it worse.

Albert Fenwick had murdered as he pleased and lived a life of smug comfort. He had finally received justice in spades.

I wanted to know what happened to Virgina's murderer, and now I knew.

That was enough for me. Time to move on.

Sunday, September 18, 2022

Swimming hole, Murray River, Jarrajarra.

I made it home by lunchtime Sunday. It was a five-hour drive from Deddick's Track to Jarrajara, and I was running on fumes. I snatched an hour's sleep and a cup of coffee at the 24-hour garage in Bombala. The same garage Ken Carruthers and Jennifer McLain had stopped at on their bike ride to doom.

Lucky for me, I'd had a nap. When I got home, Wendy had the afternoon off work and was full of beans. We packed a lunch and jogged out to our secret swimming hole, past the caravan park and along the river, for our first swim of the new spring.

It was unbelievably cold. Wendy loved it, and I sooked through an epic aquatic marathon of nearly twenty seconds.

I told her everything, of course. No secrets in our house or river.

"So, how was old Albert looking?" asked Wendy.

"Not great," I said. "Battered, broken, ugly, dead,"

"And you're not going to report it?"

"No."

"You reckon Rusty's suffered enough?"

"Yep, I do."

"You're probably right," she said, then stopped to think.

"I assume you've broken a few serious laws here, Constable," she said.

"Well, I opened a grave, found a murder victim, then filled the grave in and forgot to report it. Yeah, I'd say I've pushed the legal envelope a bit. You're OK with that?"

"Well," said Wendy, "I guess you don't tell me how to deliver babies. I suppose I won't tell you how to be a policeman."

"But you're not," I paused to think about the word "bothered?"

"No, mate," she smiled. "As long as you're OK, I'm OK."

Sounded good to me.

Wendy was sitting there in the river, perfectly comfortable in the freezing water, talking to me, standing on the bank, wrapped in a towel and shivering. She was now about four months pregnant and had a tiny baby bump. So far, she had no complaints about being pregnant, and to my biased eye, she looked perfectly happy and totally beautiful.

“I am not going to waste my time worrying about people like the Fenwicks,” said Wendy, “they are just people I hear about on the news. People that rich live their lives like a TV soap opera. Hardly seems real.”

“They are real enough,” I said. “Or were real,” I added, thinking of dead Albert.

“No, mate,” she said, patting her pregnant belly. “This is what’s real, right here. This little one is who we need to focus on. Family first, job second.”

End of discussion as far as Wendy was concerned.

Friday, October 7, 2022

Jarrajarra Police Station.

For a bloke who'd been dead a month, Albert Fenwick was having a shit week.

First, early in the week, he'd been discovered again, or so it seemed. Not by me this time. Both of the major newspapers in the state of Victoria were reporting the appearance of an apparently alive and healthy Albert Fenwick.

It was one hell of a recovery from my own last glimpse of the dead Fenwick, but there he was or his facsimile. Both the Herald Sun and the Melbourne Age front-paged a telephoto shot of an obese man with a ridiculous, magnificent head of silver hair and a freshly grown beard limping around a luxurious swimming pool. This version of Albert was fully clothed in the tropical sun and leaning heavily on his familiar cane.

It was not a perfect picture, fuzzy and out of focus, but it told a story.

And the internet went wild. There were duplicate photos on all the major social media. From the Maldives, big men with big hair, any of whom could be, or maybe weren't, our Albert. Just as many net nuts supported his escape as condemned it.

I sensed the deft touch of Rusty's lawyer, Rick Martin, painting a picture and colouring in the bits that created a story. A story to suit his client.

The newspapers loved it.

Over the years, Australia had enjoyed a good supply of runaway bad guys. Robert Trimbole and Christopher Skase were just two who had shot through rather than face the accusations against them. Both of them had died overseas without ever facing justice in a local court. Not for lack of trying by Aussie Police.

So why not Albert Fenwick? It was always a great story, and Albert, the runaway rogue, felt like déjà vu all over again. The story would most likely run for years.

"Sorry," said Barney, "it still looks like a man in a fat suit and wig to me."

I was standing behind him when he spoke. I had not told Barney about finding Albert dead and didn't intend to. I was ready to test the limits of his telepathy. So far, I was holding.

Then, middle of the week, Albert Fenwick, Master of Laws, was sued, in absentia, for the wrongful death of Virginia Fenwick, nee Collins. The suit was lodged by Richard Martin, Solicitor, on behalf of Virginia's surviving relatives, her Dad, Rusty and her two adult children.

Albert had already lost millions in a previous action lodged by Richard Martin on behalf of Virginia's children, that time over a house.

That first legal claim was in 2010. This time, Albert would be on the hook for a lot more. Newspapers were suggesting one hundred million as a starting point. There was no cap on wrongful death lawsuits where the death was the result of deliberate action, and there wasn't much doubt surrounding the deliberate part.

Albert was in trouble every which way. I was almost sorry he was dead.

Then, this morning, I received a phone call from Detective Pete.

"Our very rich lady friend died this morning," said Pete.

"Penelope Fenwick?"

"The very same. Died of natural causes on her ninety-first birthday."

"Today was her birthday?" Bloody hell, bad day to die.

"Don't suppose any day is a good day for dying," said Pete.

We went quiet. We were both ready to make a bleak cop joke. Probably wasn't appropriate.

"I guess it's kind of sad," I said. "Dying on your birthday. Alone?"

"Sad is one word for it," said Pete, "I'd call her lucky. Lucky she didn't die in jail."

"She was right about one thing," I said. "We'll never get Albert into court."

"No," said Pete. "I don't think we ever will."

"Sounds like you've given up," I said.

"More like I don't see the point," said Pete.

I didn't answer that because I was worried I'd sound guilty.

"I've got a feeling in my water," he added, "old Albert has left the parade."

"You don't buy the silver wig in the tropics?"

“No. I believed the plane ride to freedom,” he said, “but no, I can’t cop the wig, and don’t insult me by pretending you believe it either.”

I said nothing.

“I’m sure Albert, the runaway, will play well in your mate, Richard Martin’s civil case,” he added. “Good luck to him. I hope they take Albert for the lot this time.”

“You’re not worried about your optics?” I asked. “Old Albert swanning around the tropics?”

He thought for a bit.

“I arrested him, the court let him out on bail. My optics are fine,” said Pete.

“You’re not flying out to make an arrest?”

“Well, I could probably get myself a trip to the Maldives out of it, but I don’t think I’d find him there, and that could make me look silly. Don’t you think?”

We both laughed. Maybe Pete hadn’t got lazy at all. He’d simply played soft in researching Albert’s disappearance.

“Shit week for the Fenwicks,” said Pete before he ended the call.

It really was, I thought, but I would keep that to myself.

If Detective Pete Jordan was willing to allow the myth of Albert on the run then that suited me. I was sick of the Fenwicks and their cohort. I had no guilt or sorrow for any of them.

Friday, November 4, 2022

Jarrajarra.

Main Street, 10:00 AM.

Time was rolling along. My life was back to Jarrajarra normal, whatever that was. Wendy, running, cold swimming, baby making, yellow post-it notes and coffee at the Jarrajarra cafe or Farrell's garage as often as possible. Plus, practice at the rifle range a couple of times a week. Serial killers and their body dumps were as far from my mind as I could place them.

Friday and the CFA BBQ was set on the main street, out front of the Fire Station. Greg Farrell was on the tongs. I had bought two perfect sausage sandwiches with onions and tomato sauce, one for Barney and one for me. Barney would grizzle about the fat content, but he wouldn't say no. He was skinny as a rake anyway.

* * *

I wandered back to the station. Friday morning, no hurry.

Barney was at the front desk playing Wordle when I came in. We had a daily game going, which he won, mostly. He saw the sausage and onions.

"Oh, Chris, what are you doing? My waist, my waist," he wailed.

"I can eat two," I said.

"Won't be necessary," said Barney.

The bell on the door rang as someone entered the Station. A courier, with a large size parcel addressed to me. Big but not very heavy.

I checked the sender. It was from R. Martin, Solicitor, Reservoir, Melbourne.

Rusty's lawyer. That caused a nervous flutter in my belly. Apart from Rusty, Wendy and me, Richard Martin was the only person likely to know that Rusty had murdered Albert Fenwick.

Given the effort going into convincing the media that Fenwick was still alive and currently enjoying the high life in the Maldives, I was sure Martin knew the truth.

But could anyone know I had found Fenwick's body?

It didn't seem possible.

"Would you like some privacy?" asked Barney.

"No, you're good, mate."

I opened the package and found another separate package inside. This one had been sent to Richard Martin, addressed to me. I recognized the rough block letter printing. Thick pencil, all capitals. I had seen my name printed just like that on a hundred or more junior Muay Thai tournament team sheets.

It had come from Rusty via Richard, no return address for Rusty.

I opened Rusty's pack, and it made me smile.

Two rubber exercise noodles. One pink, one blue, the same rubber sausages Rusty had belted all new students around the head with till they learnt to keep their guards up and watch the incoming whacks as if their life depended on it.

Firm rubber whacking sticks. Not hard enough to damage you, but they could sting. I had spent many hours as a kid ducking and diving and blocking these things.

They were wrapped in a circle, and inside the circle was a blue-covered paperback.

'Catch 22 by Joseph Heller.'

There was an envelope inside the cover and an inscription.

A hand-written inscription on the inside cover of the book. I read that first.

> *Dear Rusty,*
>
> *Happy Birthday, and thank you for teaching my boy to defend himself.*
>
> *I am not so sure about all his punching and kicking, but I am very grateful he has learned to duck. God bless you for all your good works and much love from me.*
>
> *Irene Roland*
>
> *Xxx*

Irene Rolands, my very own Nan. A birthday present for Rusty. One of her favourite books, no less. My goodness. Thirty years his senior, but the old girl wasn't too old for a flirty little note.

I had to take a breath to stop from having a cry. Oh dear.

Barney had made himself busy at the other end of the front desk, doing his best to leave me alone. I wiped a budding tear and opened the letter. It was from Rusty.

Hi Chrisso,

I'm sure you remember our rubber-whacking sticks. Hope you're going to teach your new bub the good stuff, a bit of Muay Thai, a bit of the Brazilian.

Didn't know if you're having a boy or a girl, so I got pink and blue, one for each. I'm sure they'll both get used eventually.

I found the book in the tin that was returned to me, under the photos. Your Nan, what a great woman she was. She would be proud of you, mate.

As for everything else, thank you for finding my girl. Nothing else matters, really. You found her like you said you would.

It makes me cry just to think about it.

How you did it is beyond me. Twenty years, I searched, and nothing came of it. But you were always a persistent little terror and smart as a shithouse rat. If you'd had an ounce more speed, who knows, we might have won a few more tournaments, hey.

I like thinking back on those days at the gym.

It was a great time and place for me, my girl, your lovely Nan and the whole gang, young and fit and having fun. My moment in the sun, I reckon.

Before the storm, hey.

Anyway, you will make a great Dad. So, have as many kids as you can, keep them close and love them to bits. Give my love to Wendy.

Love.

Rusty Collins xxx

PS: I am sure you have worked out what has happened since we spoke. Don't worry about me, Chrisso, you just do what you have to do. Don't compromise yourself on my behalf.

Do what you have to do. Goodness me, Rusty was giving me a licence to go after him for murder if I felt it right.

That wasn't going to happen.
Life is too short, and the good guys win so few.

THE END

About the Author

Geoff crossing the finishing line of the Great Ocean Road Marathon in Apollo Bay.

A colourful childhood amongst the Kensington housing commission flats in Melbourne, Australia, to writing software by the ski-slopes of Colorado, USA. Geoff Davis has lived an eventful life.

Ten grandchildren, an Australia sports medal, multiple wine-producing awards, and over fifty years of marriage to his high school sweetheart have given Geoff a unique perspective on life. Further informed by ravenous media consumption, with a particular focus on Australian history, conspiracy, and crime. Geoff's original style is equal parts historical fiction, thriller, and pitch-black comedy.

Reader's Group

Thank you for reading PROVOCATION.

If you'd like to read more of the Jarrajarra series, please join Geoff's free reading group. We will send advance chapters of the next book to group members. To join, head to:

www.geoffdavisbooks.com/readinggroup

Warm regards,

Wattlebird Books.

PS: One Last Thing

If you loved Geoff's book and would like to help spread the word to other potential readers, we would be immensely grateful if you could please leave a review on his Amazon page.

Your honest feedback will make a world of difference to an emerging independent author.

You can also contact Geoff directly at:
Geoff.davis.books@gmail.com

Thanks again.

Wattlebird Books.

Copyright

www.wattlebirdbooks.com

Wattlebird Books Publishing Company

Published by Wattlebird Books Publishing Company
Book design by Dune Assembly

ISBN: 978-0-6457513-2-1 (eBook)
ISBN: 978-0-6457513-3-8 (Paperback)

Index

Printed in Great Britain
by Amazon

49608079R00294